# MURDER IN PLANE SIGHT

# MURDER
# IN PLANE SIGHT

By Julie Holmes

CAMEL
PRESS

For more information go to: www.camelpress.com

julieholmesauthor.com

This is a work of fiction. Names, characters, places, brands, media, and incidents are either the product of the author's imagination or are used fictitiously.

Cover design by Aubrey White
Interior design by Jeanne Gustafson

Murder in Plane Sight

Copyright ©2019 by Julie Holmes

ISBN: 978–1–60381–754–7 (Trade Paper)

ISBN: 978–1–60381–753–0 (eBook)

Produced in the United States of America

*This book is dedicated to my mother,*
*who never got to see me accomplish this dream of mine.*
*I wish you were here.*

# MURDER IN PLANE SIGHT

# 1

Headlights glared in the rearview mirror. Sierra Bauer slowed, but not enough. Her car slid around the turn onto the service drive that ran past the Range Airlines maintenance hangar on the western side of the Minneapolis-St. Paul Airport. She steered into the skid, regained control. Cursed the timing of the snow.

The idiot stuck to her backside like duct tape, too damn close even for Minneapolis drivers in these two inches of fresh January snow. Sierra considered hitting the brakes.

A deep rumble, and her tailgater passed her.

A pickup truck.

In the glow of her headlights, she identified the color.

Black.

Her breath caught.

An outline of a pale rectangle peeked from the layer of snow on the rear bumper.

Her heart stuttered. Raced.

*It can't be his truck. How would he know where I am?*

The truck pulled ahead, sped toward the airport.

Her scar itched. She scratched at the rough line along her left ribs.

Wary now, she reached the gate for the Range Airlines employee lot, swiped her badge, and waited while a section of chain-link fencing rolled aside. It had been almost nine months since her brother died, but she could still hear him warning her to be cautious after what happened.

She swallowed the rise of grief. Kendrick had stood by her after the attack six years ago, stood strong for her. With her. In turn, she'd done everything she could for her brother, hadn't she? It hadn't been enough to keep him from being dragged back into the self-destructive habits he'd worked so hard to conquer.

Crisp sub-zero air carried flakes through the open window before she rolled it up and drove through the open gate to park in the glow of the building's perimeter lights. She hurried to the maintenance entrance, resisting the urge to look beyond the hangar toward the service road.

❖ ❖ ❖

SIERRA TAXIED THE DEHAVILLAND DASH-8 TURBOPROP onto the apron in front of the hangar, applied the right brake, and added power to the left engine. The plane spun until the tail pointed toward the hangar. She pulled the throttles to idle and shut off the fuel. The twin engines slowed, the dull whap of the propeller blades becoming a whoosh.

Lowell Hinckley sat beside her in the first officer's chair. "Thank God we made it back in one piece."

Hell, it would be pointless to remind him she was one of the first A&Ps—airframe and powerplant aircraft mechanics—at Range Air to become run-qualified on the Dash-8s when the company started bringing them into the system.

The plane jerked when the tug started pushing it tail-first into the hangar. Once the nose cleared the threshold of the tall doors, the back end of the plane swung sharply to the left. Sierra braced a hand on the console when the tug braked hard. The nose of the plane bobbed forward like a child's nodding toy. "You ever do this prop inspection?"

"No," he said, a note of distaste in his voice. Lowell, one of the mechanics visiting the main base at the Minneapolis-St. Paul airport—MSP for short—to learn the idiosyncrasies of the 37-passenger Dash-8s, worked at the commuter airline's Detroit maintenance facility. As more of the newly-leased Dash-8s were fed into the network, Range Air would retire Detroit's few remaining Fokker F27 dinosaurs.

Lowell made it well-known from his first day in MSP that women shouldn't do men's work. Tonight at the shift briefing he flapped his jaw about how he had avoided working with her so far and hoped his streak would continue. The third shift supervisor promptly assigned Lowell to assist Sierra with her propeller inspections.

It would be a waste of time to regale him with the number of car engines she had helped her grandfather rebuild. Grandpa Bauer had encouraged her penchant for taking things apart, much to her parents' chagrin. Putting things back together became the next challenge. Grandpa Bauer never stopped encouraging her and hadn't hesitated when she asked him to take her to her first airshow. That experience cemented her decision to go to aircraft maintenance school, where she excelled despite being one of only four women in the program. As the only female A&P—aircraft mechanic—at Range Air, she worked harder than her peers just to maintain their respect.

Tonight was her last for the week. Could she tolerate the misogynistic jerk for the ten-hour shift? It's 1993, for Pete's sake. She shouldn't take his Stone Age attitude personally. She had run into men like him before and had managed to convince them she knew what she was doing. Even the deHavilland representative chose to shadow her during his visit last month, and complimented her on her expertise.

She exited the plane with Lowell at her back. Built like a wrestler past his prime, he had six inches over her five-foot-four-inch frame. When he stepped on her heel, she turned and nailed him with a withering glare. "Lowell," she said in a low, calm voice, "we need an understanding here."

His eyebrows arched high. "Oh?"

She added a cold edge to her voice. "You will not hover so close I can smell the garlic in your sweat."

"And what is that supposed to mean?"

"Back the hell up."

He didn't respond. In the dense silence, Sierra suspected he ached to say something he'd probably regret later. Instead, he grimaced and strode toward the collection of rolling toolboxes in the opposite corner of the hangar, his movements stiff and jerky.

Warren Bates, the lead mechanic on third shift, appeared beside her. In his mid-thirties, with ten years of seniority more than her own four, Warren sported blood-shot eyes from new-baby-induced sleep deprivation. He handed her a small stack of pale green papers stapled together. "You okay with him? I can send Ted over."

"No, I'm fine." Tonight's schedule included an engine change, another plane in for an inspection, and a new Dash-8 halfway through its acceptance checks, not to mention the Fairchild Metro III in for a fuel leak repair.

"You sure?"

There was plenty of work to keep everyone busy. As long as Lowell stayed well beyond arm's reach, she could deal with him. "Yes, I'm sure."

He nodded. "You let me know if you have problems with him."

"Trust me, you'll know if I have problems with him." The other mechanics accepted her as one of their own, and some, like Warren, gave her the big brother treatment. Sierra, the only female A&P on Range Airline's payroll, earned their respect by working her ass off in a male-dominated field. She chose this path not because it was easy, but because she loved aircraft, and she enjoyed working with mechanical things. *You're better than them, Sis. Don't let anyone take that away from you.* Ken's words comforted her. She imagined him the way he used to be, the bright, confident brother who pushed her to follow her dream to work on airplanes the same way she had encouraged him to pursue flying.

"How was your drive in? My wife's supposed to be coming home from her sister's place tonight."

"It's a little slick." Sierra concentrated on sounding nonchalant. "Some idiot in a black pickup truck was on my ass from the ramp to the service road. Took the turn a little fast and almost lost it 'cause I didn't want him driving up my tailpipe."

Warren's brow rose. "We don't need any more idiots on the roads than there already are. You get a license plate number? We can call it in."

Tension tightened her throat. "No. Never mind." Her voice cracked, making her cringe. She fought an urge to look behind her.

"You okay?"

"Just peachy. I get to work with Lowell tonight."

Warren glanced past her, his expression that of someone who just swallowed a bug. "Everyone gets a turn working with him. I'll help you hide the body when he pisses you off." He headed across the hangar.

She chuckled. He would if it came to that.

Lowell rolled his toolbox into place in front of the left engine. With the Dash-8's high wings, the six-foot propeller blades cleared the ground by more than four feet. He looked up at the propeller hub, then at her, expectant. "What first, boss?" he asked, his voice thick with condescension.

He might be one of the most experienced mechanics on the Fokker turboprops, but the Dash-8 was about as similar to a Fokker as her Subaru wagon was to a Sherman tank. She was the expert here, not him, which ticked him off more than usual judging by his scowl and the red tips of his ears.

"Get the removal handles from the tool room," she pointed to the opposite wing, "and pull the right nose cone. Then start the inspection in the cockpit. I have to get the kit and the tools."

She made her way toward the tail and the parts room beyond, careful to avoid the puddles from the snow melting off the fuselage, until she reached the access for the aft maintenance compartment. Located on the underside of the fuselage where it started its upward slope, the maintenance panel itself was a foot and a half square held closed by two press-release latches. She inspected the piano hinge that ran along one side of the hatch for corrosion and damage, and then signed that entry off on her paperwork.

She opened the panel to access the maintenance bay, home to the auxiliary power unit, or APU, a turbine engine about the size of a five-gallon water cooler bottle. Like the larger engines that powered the plane, the APU had its own oil filter to change, oil level to inspect, and igniter plug to test. Sierra grabbed a three-step ladder to climb into the aft compartment.

Discomfort crept across her skin. She rubbed a hand over the sudden goosebumps on the back of her neck, but couldn't shake the unease.

Sierra slid her small Maglite from a back pocket and twisted it on before she ventured into the hell-hole. Working in the aft maintenance bay took flexibility to maneuver around the tangle of fluid lines and ducting. Her slender, petite frame gave her an advantage in that respect, and she didn't mind working in the confines of the space.

She swept her light over the APU. Fluorescent lavender-tinted fluid filled the oil level sight glass like the glowing eye of a B-movie creature. Next, she inspected the area below the mini-turbine engine that was the APU for signs of leaks. The surface was dry.

She turned left. Stopped.

Her light illuminated a navy-clad mass that reminded her of South American mummies frozen forever in the fetal position. "What the hell?" she breathed, and inched the light up.

Matted hair. Blood. Bone.

Her scream echoed in the metal cavern.

She dropped her flashlight and ducked out of the hell-hole, struggled to slow her breathing before she hyperventilated.

Warren reached her, took hold of her arm to steady her. "What happened? You sounded like someone was trying to kill you."

She squeezed her eyes shut, but couldn't erase the image. "Look. Hell-hole."

# 2

Airport police cordoned off the plane. The image of blood and bone smashed together stuck in Sierra's mind. No amount of shaking her head or rubbing her eyes could banish it.

Lowell had a bounce in his step as he rolled his toolbox toward the other Dash-8 scheduled for an inspection.

She paced from nose to wingtip and back, muscles like quivering strings of longbows pulled to their limit. Her jaw ached. She yawned to loosen the tension. She needed to think about something else.

The black pickup truck took over her mind. Six months ago she received the letter notifying her of Rune Thorsson's release from prison. Six months of dread followed. She scratched at the scar an inch below her left breast, the only remaining physical sign of his attack. While he spent six years behind bars, she struggled to overcome the psychological scars left by his attempt to control her. She had been a young, naive nineteen-year-old smitten by his focused interest in her. When she pushed back against his intentions, he put her in the hospital, fighting for her life.

"Miss Bauer?"

A man in a navy-blue parka approached, coat hanging open to reveal a maroon sweater over a white turtleneck, badge on a lanyard, black Dockers

6

tucked into snow-covered boots. She guessed him to be in his early to mid-thirties, maybe six feet tall, his square jaw and angular cheekbones covered in scruff that matched his short light-brown hair, his eyes the sharp blue of clear winter skies.

He shook snow from a gray watch cap, then stuffed it into a pocket of his coat along with a pair of leather gloves. He shifted his notepad to his left hand before he reached to her. "Miss Bauer, I'm Detective Quinn Moore from the MSP Airport Police Department. I understand you found the body."

She nodded. His warm, strong grip matched his rich voice, the combination loosening some of her nerves.

He made a note, then indicated a nearby platform stand. "Are you okay talking here, or do you want to use the office?" He leaned toward her as if afraid of being overheard. "Personally, I'd rather talk out here. I'll be sitting in an office doing paperwork all day tomorrow."

The four-foot-square platform stand offered plenty of room for them; they could sit on it without being in each other's personal space. "This is fine," she said and claimed her perch. She slid to the far edge to make room for the detective, but also to give herself some distance from him. The last time she had been interviewed by a cop—after the attack—it hadn't gone well.

Detective Moore sat beside her and leaned forward, elbows on his knees. "I know it's late—well, early for you—but the sooner we do this, the more you'll remember. Walk me through what happened."

She gave him a short version of her evening while Moore scratched notes on his pad. She tried not to think about the details, but cruel memories took the opportunity to return. She knew the slick feel of blood, the coppery smell, the chill that seeped in once the adrenaline faded. Her stomach roiled. She swallowed the fear she thought she'd conquered years ago.

Moore flipped to a fresh page in his notebook. "Did you see anyone or anything out of the ordinary when you went to the gate to pick up the plane?"

When Sierra and her ill-tempered ride-along arrived at the gate, the last ramp agents on the tarmac did little more than wave before leaving for the night. Even the fuel trucks abandoned their posts due to lack of activity. Or, most of them did.

"The only thing I noticed was a fuel truck hanging out at the end of our ramp, but that's not unusual. Sometimes they do that if they're waiting to fuel a plane that hasn't come in yet."

"Even when it's this late?"

"There are some red-eyes that fly out before midnight. As long as they aren't in the way, I don't pay much attention."

Should she mention the black truck?

*She was probably overreacting. Besides, a black truck has nothing to do with a dead body in an airplane.*

Behind Moore, a pair of men in navy coveralls with "BCA" on the back in big white letters, each with a large plastic toolbox in hand, crossed the yellow tape surrounding the plane and prepared to climb into the hell-hole. Sierra knew from reading crime novels by Tami Hoag and William Kent Krueger that "BCA" stood for Minnesota's Bureau of Criminal Apprehension, an FBI-like law enforcement entity that served the entire state.

Moore continued the interview. "When was the last time you looked in the aft maintenance bay of this plane?"

She glanced at the Dash-8's tail number. "Maybe a week ago."

"How often does someone look in the maintenance bay?"

"Depends on what maintenance is scheduled, or if there's a problem with the APU—the auxiliary power unit, or the mixing valve for the environmental system, or anything else that's exposed back there."

"Do you know where this plane has been the past few days? Or where it was earlier tonight?"

How long had Moore been part of the airport police? He should know the answer to that question. "No. You'll have to check the logbook, which should be in the office now." She pointed toward the back of the hangar. "The lead mechanic pulls the books when the planes come in."

"So, you don't know who else might have been working in that maintenance compartment?"

"Not unless I look at the flight log or the maintenance log."

"Would someone other than a mechanic have any reason to go into that compartment?"

Her temper prickled at the back of her throat. Patience escaped her when it came to people who couldn't connect dots like "maintenance" and "mechanics". "Can I ask you a question, Mr. Moore?"

He looked up from his notes. "Detective. And yes."

"How long have you been with the airport police? That's a *maintenance* compartment. By definition, only mechanics go in there."

He chuckled, a low, rolling sound that vibrated in Sierra's belly. "I know you're upset, and finding that," he gestured to the plane's tail, "doesn't help. I've been on the APD for a couple of years My routine includes unruly passengers, lost kids, and petty theft, so I'm still pretty green when it comes to airplanes. Humor me. Would someone other than a mechanic have any reason to go into that compartment? Pilots or anyone else?"

"No."

"Why did you open the maintenance bay door?"

That question cracked her restraint. She couldn't blunt the edge in her voice. "The plane is here for maintenance. I'm a mechanic. And you're asking me why I opened the maintenance bay access panel?"

"Hey, relax. I know it's a stupid question, but I have to ask it because lawyers need everything laid out so they don't have to think so hard."

His light-hearted comment defused her temper. She offered a small smile in response. "Sorry. Lack of common sense is one of my biggest pet peeves."

He flipped to a fresh page in his notepad. "I hear you, and I won't bore you with my extensive experience with people who don't have an ounce of it."

One of the men in navy coveralls tapped Moore on the shoulder. He excused himself, then huddled with the man out of earshot. Another man in dark gray coveralls with a patch in the shape of some sort of badge stood next to him, Polaroid camera in one hand and a few developing photographs in the other. The three of them spoke in hushed tones before Moore nodded. The two men returned to the knot of activity around the hell-hole access.

Moore reclaimed his seat on the platform, photos in hand. He examined each, then made a few notes before turning to her. "Miss Bauer, did you notice anything on the body? Maybe some jewelry?"

The sight of bone and blood she wanted to ignore didn't lend itself to noticing details. "I didn't stick around to look."

"I've got pictures of things we might be able to use to identify the body. I'd like you to look at them and tell me if you recognize anything." He handed her the small stack of photos.

She didn't want to see any of it again. *Just do it.* She took a deep breath and steeled her roiling gut.

The first picture showed a row of small metal pearls lining an ear, a dark red line like macabre paint tracing a path into the ear itself. In the second photo, a black watch band and partial analog face peeked from a navy cuff, the crystal webbed with fractures.

A gold ring like a ribbon-type spring wrapping a finger in the third photo made her hesitate. Had she seen something like this before? She didn't know for certain. It probably matched jewelry her sister had worn in her "every finger needs a ring" stage.

She handed the pictures back to Moore. "I'm sorry, Detective."

"Okay. One more question." He locked his gaze on her, the jovial air replaced by a hard, jaw-clenching edge.

"Did you know the victim?"

# 3

She shot to her feet, fists clenched, every muscle in her body snapped tight. She hit him with the most evil glare she could muster. "NO. Did you look? You can't see the face. How the hell would anyone recognize whomever that is? Are you fucking kidding me?"

Moore stood, tucked the photos into an inner pocket of his parka, and shoved his empty hand into the pocket of his Dockers. "I have to ask the question, Miss Bauer. You can stop being pissed."

She was fired up now; it would take her a while to come down. Her parents attributed her quick temper to her maternal grandmother and her full-blooded German stock. She paced in a tight circle to regain some composure. "Will I be on the short list of 'people of interest' since I was lucky enough to find the damn body? I should have let Lowell check the APU oil level."

"I knew you had nothing to do with it before we even started this interview. You discovered the body, that's all." She winced at the razor edge to his voice. She hadn't meant to rile him.

Moore scribbled some notes before checking his watch. "The medical examiner can't do anything with the body until it thaws, and the crime scene unit needs time to process the scene. When does your shift end?"

Her head felt like someone was twisting her brain. Her teeth ached. "What time is it?" she asked, too upset to check her own watch.

"Hey, Sierra, you okay?" Warren rounded the nose of the cordoned-off airplane, light brown hair an unkempt halo under his Range Air baseball cap. "You still talking to the cops?"

Before she could answer, Moore waved the question aside. "Miss Bauer, I'm done with you for tonight. Or this morning. Whatever. I need to talk to you," he indicated Warren, "and anyone else who saw the body or worked on the airplane."

"I'll go find Lowell." Warren let out a short whistle. "Sierra."

She managed to stop pacing. "Yeah?"

"I know it's your last night for the week, but if you need to take an extra day or two, for Christ's sake, take them. And you can head out. I'll sign you out at the end of the shift."

Warren was more big brother to her than she liked to admit. She also knew he wouldn't budge; if she tried to stick around, he'd probably make her sit in the corner until she complied. "Shit, Warren, I've got three and a half hours left of the shift." *Dammit.* "Sorry. I didn't mean to snap, it's just …"

He cut her off with a wave of a hand, then glanced at the crime scene technicians milling around the aft end of the aircraft. "We've got enough people on the other jobs. Put your tools away and get out of here." Before he disappeared around the far side of the plane, he pointed to his eyes, then to Sierra, his warning he'd be watching to make sure she followed instructions.

"Sonofabitch." She didn't like the idea of leaving early or taking time off. She wanted to work. Besides, by the end of her normal three- or four-day weekends, she always found herself wandering around her apartment with nothing to do. Her social life was about as exciting as watching snow fall. Which reminded her of the white fluffy stuff outside. If it was still snowing, driving home was going to suck.

"Miss Bauer, are you okay to drive home?" Moore's voice startled her. He'd been so quiet she'd forgotten he was still there, watching her.

She glanced over her shoulder, a habit she thought she'd conquered. *If that was his black pickup, was he watching her?* A shiver slithered through her. "Yeah, I guess."

"Give me your number in case I have more questions." Moore wrote as she recited her number for him, and then handed her a business card with his contact information on it after he wrote on the back. "My home number. If you think of anything else that might help me with this, don't hesitate to call. Anytime." His fingers brushed hers when he handed over the card. "And I mean any time."

His glancing touch caused a flush of heat through her middle.

She shuddered. Just because a guy made her swoon, it didn't mean she could trust him. *If only she'd realized what he was sooner.*

"Miss Bauer?"

She raised her gaze to Moore's face. She didn't anticipate the magnetic draw of those intense blue eyes. The rest of the world faded into the background.

He cupped her shoulder. "You sure you're good to drive home? It stopped snowing, but it's still pretty early. The plows probably haven't hit the residential streets yet. Be careful."

Heat leached from his hand and swelled through the rest of her. She blinked, breaking whatever spell she'd gone under. "Sure. Okay." She waved his card. "I'll call if I think of anything else."

# 4

Detective Quinn Moore followed Warren to the maintenance supervisor's office where Lowell Hinckley slouched on an aged metal chair like a high school rebel sans black leather jacket. Quinn passed by him to the place of authority behind the desk, shucked off his coat, and hung it on the back of the supervisor's chair before he introduced himself and sat.

"I don't know why you need to talk to me." Lowell straightened but managed to retain his defiant air. "I'm not the one who found the corpsicle."

"You were working on the inspection, right?"

Lowell shrugged. "Not much of an inspection. I barely got my toolbox out."

"Did you pick the plane up at the gate with Miss Bauer?"

"Huh," Lowell grunted, then folded his arms on the desk. "You got your suspect. Might as well let me get back to work."

Quinn leaned back. He'd run across people—men and women—like Hinckley before, all bravado and bluster until they realized they faced time behind bars. They were easier to find than a black bear in a snow-covered field. "Are you referring to Miss Bauer?"

"Duh."

"Why do you say that?"

Lowell tapped the desk. "She's the only one here who's been investigated by the FAA. I can't believe you haven't arrested her already."

Quinn hesitated, then made the note. "What did they investigate her for?"

"Killing her brother. They cleared her, though. Called it pilot error. They should've taken her license."

The fact Lowell pointed at Sierra because of a past investigation warned Quinn the man was unreliable. Besides, she'd been shaken up by the incident. Tension had radiated from her—he swore he felt it through the metal stand they had sat on.

He knew from experience that tension from shock was different than tension from fear of discovery. One settled in the extremities, evidenced by unsteady hands and fidgeting feet, while the other tended to stick to the main limbs as stiff movement. Sierra Bauer hadn't been able to sit still, and though she likely hadn't realized it, she'd opened and closed her fists like she exercised stress balls.

"How long have you worked with Miss Bauer?"

Lowell checked the clock on the wall above the door. "About two hours. That's counting the ride to the gate and the power runs at the run pad."

"How long have you worked for Range Airlines?"

"Twelve years. I work at the Detroit base."

"Why are you here in Minneapolis?"

"Training on the Dash-8s. We're starting to get them in Detroit." Lowell heaved a sigh. "I made it almost a week without working with her. Thinks she's hot shit because she can drive a Dash-8."

Quinn hated dealing with people like Hinckley. "Anything else?"

"She gets off telling me what to do. I know how to pull the fucking prop nose cone. I'd like to see her work on a Fokker prop. You need a six-foot torque wrench to tighten the nut on a Fokker prop. Takes three guys." He held up that number of fingers. "Guys. Probably take half a dozen women." He chuckled as if pleased as hell with himself. "And then they'd ask for help."

Give it up already, Quinn thought. "Did you see anything unusual at the gate when you went to pick up the airplane?"

Lowell hesitated. "No. Just planes, tugs, and fuel trucks. How the hell am I supposed to know what's unusual here? I work in Detroit."

"It's an airport. I imagine things are pretty much the same at any airport. So, you didn't see anything you thought was out of the ordinary at the gate?"

"No. Wait, I did see something. A woman driving a Dash-8. That's unusual. Good thing she didn't have to park it."

Quinn closed his eyes and pinched the bridge of his nose. He'd worked with female cops who were better officers than some of the men he'd worked with.

He accepted that people like Hinckley were the way they were. That didn't make it any easier to deal with them.

He stood and handed Lowell one of his business cards. "Thank you, Mr. Hinckley. If you think of anything else, call me." He led the way to the door, then went to find Warren, the only other person besides Sierra who'd seen the body before officers arrived on-scene. Once they settled in the office, Quinn asked for Warren's take on what happened.

His story followed Sierra's, at least the part about finding the body in the aft maintenance bay. Warren noticed a few things Sierra didn't, notably that the hands were tight against the face, a gold spiral ring on a finger, and a view of the brain through the hole in the skull.

"What makes you mention the hands?" Quinn asked.

Warren shrugged. "I don't know. They were close to the face, right? It's sick, but it made me think of how my son sleeps all curled up like that, with his hands next to his face." He squeezed his eyes shut and rubbed at them. "God, that's terrible. My son is a month old. How could I possibly think about him when I saw that body?"

"The brain does weird things when it's trying to figure something out," Quinn reassured him. "If it makes you feel any better, Miss Bauer thought it looked like a mummy."

A short chuckle burst from Warren. "That's much better."

Quinn checked his notes. "Do you know Miss Bauer was investigated by the FAA?"

Warren pulled his Range Air ball cap off, releasing a mop of light brown curly hair from the confines. He squeezed the bill between his hands. "Did she tell you that?"

"No, Mr. Hinckley did."

"Asshole," he grumbled. "Yes, I know."

"Do you know why?"

The silence in the office amplified the tick of the clock on the wall until the sound echoed like a disembodied heartbeat. "Look, I don't know any of the details," Warren said. "She didn't exactly advertise what happened. All I know is her brother died in a plane crash, and she signed the logbook. They determined the accident was pilot error, so what's that got to do with this?"

"I'm trying to figure out if that has anything to do with the body she found in the maintenance bay of an airplane."

Warren stood and dragged on his cap. "She found the body. That's it. If you think that FAA investigation relates to her finding a dead body in the hellhole, you don't know shit about aviation."

Quinn agreed; he still didn't know much about aviation even after two years on the APD. Anything involving aircraft fell into the FAA's jurisdiction. At MSP, anything having to do with crimes against a person belonged to the APD. Murder was murder, no matter where it occurred. "Sit down, Mr. Bates."

"I've got work to do." Warren leaned over the chair. "We've got an engine change that needs to be finished up by noon. I told you what I saw. What else is there?"

Quinn gauged the mechanic's mood. Impatient, frustrated, and probably spooked. Until he knew more about the victim, there wasn't much more to ask. He stood and handed his card to Warren. "Call me if you think of anything else."

Warren tucked the card into a pocket and left the office. Quinn followed him back into the hangar proper to check on the crime scene unit's progress.

Miss Sierra Bauer had neglected to mention the FAA investigation.

What else hadn't she told him?

# 5

Headlights followed her south on State Highway 77. Sierra watched, waited for the lights to peel off at every exit she passed. She tightened her grip on the steering wheel and tipped her head to loosen the muscles at the back of her neck.

Was someone watching her now?

She hoped she was overreacting. Maybe that person was heading home from a midnight movie. Maybe they worked some overtime hours from an afternoon shift. It wasn't like she was the only person on the road.

When she turned into the parking lot, she focused on the road that ran past her apartment building. A dark-colored pickup truck continued along the street, slowing as it drove out of sight beyond the bulk of the apartments.

She couldn't tell if the rear bumper had a sticker. She remembered the bold text, still legible on the sun-faded surface: My Truck, My Way. Would he still have that truck?

Anxiety propelled her to the building, its brick surface interspersed with rows of dark windows stacked six high, the ranks on the top three floors broken at regular intervals by narrow balconies with sliding glass doors. At this time of the morning, most people were asleep. The glow of leftover Christmas lights in a handful of windows touched the shadows with color.

Sierra pulled the glass security door shut and peered into the early morning dark, scanning the lot. No black pickup trucks creeping in the shadows. Whoever it was just happened to go the same way she did. Maybe the truck she'd seen on the service road had been late for a night shift.

She glanced behind her and winced at the painful protest of taut neck muscles. Paranoia tasted bitter on her tongue.

Fear paralyzed her for the first month after she received the notification letter until she chose to use that apprehension in more constructive ways. She contacted the prosecutor who had gotten Rune a stint in the Moose Lake Correctional Facility and made sure her restraining order was still valid. Lucky for her, the multiple violations before he had finally gotten locked away ensured the judge had granted her a fifty-year extension. She had gotten an unlisted phone number after the attack six years ago, and again four years ago when she moved back to the Twin Cities area, to this apartment, along with a post office box so her street address didn't appear on her mail. She retook self-defense classes to make sure her skills were fresh in her mind and body.

After weeks of waiting for him to show up somehow in spite of her efforts to remain hard to find, she thought it was over. She thought he'd given up.

Then she saw the truck. Like his.

To top off the evening, she found a dead body. Hair, blood, and bone stained her thoughts, all in stark detail. A freaking dead body in the hell-hole of her inspection plane. Who puts a dead body in an airplane maintenance bay?

Who was the dead body? Someone had cracked the skull, left a bloody window into gray matter. Positioned the body so the face couldn't be seen. No one would be able to recognize it.

She reached her apartment door. Caution returned. The hairs on the back of her neck electrified, ready to stand on end in an instant. She sucked in an unsteady breath before she unlocked her door. She knew she was alone in the apartment, but the unexpected appearance of the pickup truck tonight made her jumpy. She set the deadbolt, toed off her boots, and eased through the one-bedroom apartment, keys between her fingers like claws, turning on every light and checking behind every door and in every closet. The bedroom window remained locked behind the navy blackout curtains. In the living room she pushed the off-white vertical blinds aside, checked the latch on the sliding glass door to her tiny balcony, and made sure the length of old broom handle still occupied the sill track of the door, preventing it from being slid open more than a half inch.

Satisfied the apartment was empty and secure, she hung up her coat and unloaded her small flashlight, pen-sized screwdrivers, and the contents of her pockets with a clatter into the dish beside the sink. She slumped against the counter and rubbed her eyes with the heels of her hands until her vision went foggy.

The phone hanging on the wall beckoned to her. Part of her wanted to talk about tonight. What would she say? Hey, Mom, guess what? I found a dead body in an airplane today. She imagined Liza Bauer jumping into the car and heading to Sierra's apartment armed with chamomile tea and "trauma chocolate", the reserved Mozart chocolates supplied on a regular basis by her great-aunt, an international journalist. They weren't the red foil-wrapped ones found in every tourist trap in Bavaria, either. It was the good stuff, the blue foil-wrapped ones found only in Salzburg. She could almost taste the rich flavor and silky texture of milk chocolate surrounding a marzipan center.

Bad idea. Her mom was an environmental engineer, not a psychologist. She couldn't do anything to help. All she'd do is keep Sierra up until noon. Her therapist would tell her to write about it. She snorted. That never seemed to work for her; she filled sketchbooks with landscape drawings instead. Right now she was too tired to even think about drawing.

A glance at her watch confirmed she needed to get to bed sooner rather than later. A low whine from her stomach reminded her she missed her lunch break due to Detective Moore's interview. She fished his business card from the overloaded dish. Detective Quinn Moore. Could his name be more Irish? She tossed the card back.

Why was she even thinking about the cop who spent hours interviewing her about the body in the hell-hole?

Ohmygod. Blood and hair and bone twisted into a high-definition horror show in her mind. The biting odors of copper and iron materialized from her memory, even though she knew she hadn't smelled anything in the hell-hole except oil and jet exhaust. Cold invaded her until her teeth chattered like one of those stupid windup toys. It felt like the temperature in her apartment dropped forty degrees in an instant. The only thing missing was her breath in a white cloud.

She needed to get warm. She grabbed a change of clothes before she cranked on the hot water and stepped into the searing spray. Holy hot freaking springs, Batman. Once she adjusted the temperature to just below scalding, she huddled under the shower and willed the heat to chase away the chill that drew her shoulders tight.

Eyes closed, she imagined her quiet place to banish the nightmarish scenes. The more detail she envisioned, the less she shivered. Her quiet place tonight: a white sand beach in Hawaii, where the turquoise ocean lapped the shore with soothing whooshes and the sun bathed her in gentle warmth. Once that image came into focus, she added wind rustling the wide leaves of palm trees and seagulls laughing far offshore. That wind carried the salty scent of the Pacific, a perfume that embodied the vast water stretching to the horizon under a brilliant blue sky.

Her teeth stopped chattering, her shoulders loosened enough for her to straighten, and her skin smoothed. She sent silent thanks to her homeopathic nurse practitioner father for the lavender-scented shampoo and homemade soap she used to wash away everything but the calming energy from her quiet place. When she finished, warm fog filled the bathroom. She toweled off and pulled on long johns underneath her sweats, and thick woolen socks over her usual cotton ones.

She pulled a container of her dad's chicken stew from the freezer and tossed it into the microwave. Ten minutes later she had a bowl of comfort complete with home-grown potatoes, carrots, broccoli, kale, and chicken, with a jalapeno or two just to give it a kick. The scent of basil, garlic, and onion calmed her more. The stew tasted of sun and earth, green herbs and spicy pepper, buttery potatoes, and sweet carrots. Home.

The shower and the stew did their jobs, assisted by her quiet place. Muscles dulled at the edges. Her mind floated in a calm, quiet state. She crawled under the thick down comforter and turned out the lights.

In the darkness, she tried to ignore the rhythmic rush in her ears, imagining the echo of a seashell rather than breathing.

# 6

**D**etective Quinn Moore sat in his unmarked SUV outside the Range Air hangar and stared at a glob of snow sliding down the windshield. The crime scene techs were loading up their equipment, dragging cases like plows through the newly-fallen snow. Another clump of white stuff began its journey down the windshield. He adjusted the defrost temperature and unzipped his coat.

He had seen a great deal in his dozen years as a cop. During his tenure at the St. Paul Police Department, he saw victims of gun violence, of stabbings, of beatings. He'd taken a position on the Airport PD to get away from so much of the darker facets of human nature. They moved to Apple Valley, a quiet suburb east of Interstate 35 on the south side of the Minnesota River that cut through the southern reaches of the Twin Cities. Gretchen had insisted on the move, had begged him to work less and spend more time present in their ailing marriage. So he'd obliged. He thought they had been making progress.

Until he found the pregnancy test stick in the bathroom trash. He knew without a doubt the baby wasn't his; he told Gretchen about his vasectomy before they started discussing marriage. When he confronted her, she handed him the divorce papers, complete with her signature.

He left his job for her. He tried to work things out. And she'd played him.

He leaned back and stared at the headliner above him. Numb. That's what he'd been ever since. For the past year, every day, every hour he worked he escaped the fog that coated each waking moment. He figured he was running on about four hours of sleep, and even those were poisoned by memories of his love for her turned sour.

Eyes closed, an unbidden image of Miss Sierra Bauer vanquished thoughts of his ex-wife and her machinations. When the call came in, he hadn't expected to find a female aircraft mechanic at the center of the discovery. He certainly hadn't expected to see one so unlike his initial mental image of a female mechanic, who would have been named Bertha or Helga or something else suitable for a linebacker on a women's football team. Instead, she was petite with subtle curves, her oval face framed by shoulder-length hair a deep mahogany brown with a brilliant white lock that fell from the top of her scalp in a line past her temple. Her hazel eyes intrigued him, the left one a bit lighter and greener than the right, as if to carry the lack of color from that pale tress, suggesting the white streak was hereditary.

His parka became stifling. He shut the defroster off and rolled his window down a few inches. Judging by the bit of temper she'd displayed, he figured strong-willed might not be quite enough to describe her.

Sierra Bauer was striking, but not in a jaw-dropping kind of way. Quinn considered. With cheekbones just high enough to give contours to a face touched by a hint of pink and a dusting of freckles, she had a wholesome beauty, one that didn't need any make-up. She hadn't been wearing any, and his breath still vacated his lungs in a rush at the sight of her. He remembered the unexpected strength in her calloused hand when he shook it. Quinn looked at his palm and felt her grip again, the coolness of her fingers, the electric shock that struck him at that small contact.

If he asked her to dinner and a movie, would she accept? No, better yet, they could tour the ice sculpture garden at the St. Paul Winter Carnival.

He shook his head and willed her image away. *Focus on the case, not her.* She found the body, but that didn't make her a suspect.

It didn't rule her out, either.

Besides, he thought, it would be physically impossible for her to lift the dead weight of a body into the maintenance bay. She wasn't big enough and likely wasn't strong enough.

Unless she had help. The only person who fit that part was Warren, the lead mechanic. He couldn't imagine Lowell Hinckley spending any more time with her than necessary, but he could shove a body into that aft compartment.

According to the ME, the body, frozen solid in a fetal curl so tight the face almost touched the chest and the knees kissed the forehead, was that of a woman. The preliminary cause of death: a piece of bone lodged in her brain from the blow that cracked her skull open. The victim wore a navy blue uniform, but at MSP over half the airline and service personnel wore navy uniforms. Until the body thawed, they couldn't straighten it enough to view the face or identify any logo or name tag on the shirt. They couldn't hurry the defrosting process without damaging the body and tainting the evidence. Someone who died outside in the elements in a harsh Minnesota winter could be found frozen solid in a day or two. The sub-zero temperatures found at altitude would act on the body the same way.

It might be days before the forensics lab at the BCA could unfold the body and get a good image of the face. Maybe they'd be able to give him additional details, like her age, sooner. Quinn didn't hold much hope for progress unless someone reported a missing person who'd worked at the airport. He couldn't determine a motive or possible suspects until he knew the victim's name.

Then again, he had no way of knowing if the body was frozen before it was stashed in the maintenance bay—wait, yes he did. It'd taken the crime scene technicians almost an hour to wrestle the corpse through the maintenance bay hatch. The body must have been pliable when it was loaded.

Better yet, how did the perpetrator stuff a dead body through a foot and a half square hatch? How—why—did the perp climb into the maintenance bay far enough to shove the body up against the dome of the—what was it? Bulkhead? He pulled his notepad from his pocket and flipped through. Aft pressure bulkhead.

It boiled down to waiting. He needed to know Jane Doe's real name. This woman's loved ones were wondering where she was. Did she have a boyfriend? Husband? Kids?

A knock on the passenger window of the SUV startled him. Kevin Vierling, the crime scene team leader on duty, wore a blaze-orange stocking cap over his wild cornrow braids, and pressed his dark face against the glass until his nose, lips, and chin made an almost solid line of contact. He cupped his face with his hands, as if he needed the shade to see into the truck. Quinn groaned and hit the switch to open the window. "You owe me a clean window. Actually, this makes what, three?"

Kevin leaned back and peered along the side of the SUV. "Hey, you left my faceprint on the back window. I thought you'd clean that for sure."

Quinn grinned. He liked the ever-cheerful Kevin. "I was thinking about picking up some of those glass markers that auto salesmen use. I can add bunny ears to it for Easter."

The crime scene team leader folded his arms on the windowsill. "Just make sure the bow is purple. What are you still doing here? I thought you'd be back at the office by now working on paperwork." His eyes narrowed. "You had a dreamy look goin' on earlier. What's up with that? It can't be from the body we pulled out of that airplane."

Quinn's stomach twisted like he'd been caught stuffing lit firecrackers into his sister's Barbie hippie van. He had been grounded for a week after that, and he'd had to buy her a new one with his birthday money. "Just tired. Thinking about the case and who the victim might be." *Thinking about the woman who found the body.*

Kevin tsked. "Nope, that's not it. I saw something else in those baby blues." His mouth curved into a knowing grin. "She was cute. I wonder if she dyes that white stripe. Isn't there a rule against that?"

"Against what?"

"Dating the pretty little thing who found the body." Kevin shook a finger at him. "Don't lie to me, Quinn. You haven't gotten any since, shit, how many months before your divorce? That's been what, over a year now, hasn't it?" He shook his head, the free ends of his braids like bobble-head dolls bouncing around his face. "I told you that ain't healthy for a guy. That's how you get, what is it?" He snapped his fingers. "Blue balls."

Quinn opened his mouth to argue, but Kevin shut him down with another wave of his finger. "Hey, I keep telling you, just ask that blonde who's always manning one of the gates on Concourse B. You know she likes you. She never flirts with me like that."

"She knows you're married. And it's none of your business who I date."

Kevin made a rude raspberry noise. "As if you've started dating since Gretchen handed you the papers. Come on, how many women have I tried to fix you up with? My sister-in-law, her best friend, my wife's sorority sister," he ticked them off, "my cousin's sorority sister, the new teacher at Jeremy's school. Hell, I've even tried to get you to ask the intern at the morgue. You need to start sometime."

It started out as a friend trying to do a favor for another friend. *I don't need any help.* In Quinn's mind, it crossed the line from genuine help to tongue-biting annoyance weeks ago. *Besides, women are cruel, conniving bitches.* "I'm not ready yet."

"Well, you'd better get ready before those 'nads of yours match your eyes." Kevin leaned on the sill, suddenly somber. "Anyway, I just wanted to tell you I should be able to get the preliminary report on your desk by noon. Three at the latest."

Before he turned to leave, Kevin added, "Not all women are like your ex. You'll find a good one, but don't do anything stupid."

An image of a female mechanic with a white tress flashed in Quinn's mind. *I'll try not to.*

# 7

In his office at the Airport Police Operations Center an hour later, Quinn leaned back in his chair, the cheap bushings under the seat squeaking in protest. A glance at the time on his computer monitor told him it would be another four or five hours, minimum, until he got the reports from the medical examiner or the crime scene team. In the meantime, he had been working on his own reports, reviewing his notes. He stood, stretched, and headed toward the break room for another cup of the caffeinated version of rotgut they called coffee.

Maybe he should invest in his own coffee maker; he could drink his treasured Hawaiian Kona blend, the one luxury he indulged. Then again, the scent of fresh, palatable coffee might drive traffic to his office. Bad idea. A Dunn Bros coffee shop near Concourse A here in MSP's Lindbergh Terminal offered a fresh-brewed option, but that was too expensive to fuel him through a twenty-hour shift.

"Hey, Moore, how long you been here?" Officer Ward Stamford took up a position beside Quinn for his turn at the coffee maker. One of the two pots on the Bunn restaurant-style coffee machine had a coating of brown liquid on the bottom of the pot, with the burner light happily illuminated. Stamford rescued the pot and dumped the sludge into the nearby sink. "No wonder the coffee around here always tastes like tar. My grandma's chicory and dandelion root coffee tastes better than this stuff."

Quinn dumped the old filter packet from the basket and added a new one. One had to try pretty hard to screw up pre-measured coffee, so why did it always turn out like someone made it with Nescafé instant coffee left over from the seventies? He swapped the half-empty pot for Stamford's empty one and pressed the button to start a fresh pot. He looked at the dark liquid in his cup, complete with a rainbow sheen like an oil slick. He dumped the coffee into the sink and leaned against the lone table in the break room to wait for the fresh brew.

Stamford set his cup beside the coffee maker. "Well, how long? You look like you either forgot to shave or you didn't make it home to freshen up."

Quinn scratched at the stubble on his chin, itchy now that Stamford mentioned it. Yes, he did need to shave. "There was a call last night at Range Airlines. Got back about an hour ago."

Stamford, a twenty-five year veteran of the force, chose to stay on patrol despite being encouraged toward investigations by his superiors. When Quinn started at the Airport PD, Stamford had been his orientation officer. At six-foot-three with a build any aging running back would envy, Stamford was a gentle soul armed with a backbone of steel, a heart of gold, and an enviable way of calming people.

"Didn't hear about that one yet. What was it? Car break-in? Fence-jumper?"

"Dead body."

Stamford whistled low. "Range Air? A mechanic didn't walk into a prop, did they? Those guys should know better, especially after that ramp agent accident last year."

"No. Found a female frozen solid with a cracked skull stuffed into the aft maintenance bay of one of their planes."

"Homicide?" Stamford asked, bushy eyebrows arched high on his forehead. "Wow. Haven't had one of those here for years." He rubbed a hand across the tight black curls on his head, his temples frosted with gray. Quinn wondered how much longer the older man would stay on. As police work went, the airport was a model of Utopia compared to North Minneapolis or West Seventh in St. Paul, but that didn't make police work any less stressful on the front lines with the public.

Quinn waited for Stamford to pour a cup of fresh java before he filled his own. "Mechanic found her when she was starting her inspection."

"Wait, she? The mechanic?" At Quinn's nod, Stamford grinned. "I didn't know Range Air had a female mechanic. Good for her. I told you my middle daughter is an A&P for United, didn't I?"

"You did. And you've shown me pictures of every Airbus she ever worked on."

"She's on the 767 crew now. My wife and I are flying out to see her for spring break." He checked his watch. "Gotta go. Good luck with the homicide. Let me know if you need any help." With that, he left to start his rounds.

Back at his desk with fresh coffee that didn't smell like burnt dirt, Quinn paged through his notes. He had written up everything except the interview with Sierra Bauer. His mind conjured her image, waved it in front of him until all he could think about was her slightly-mismatched eyes, pale streak of hair, and slow smile. He scrunched his eyes shut and shook his head to reset his focus.

She was too interesting to stop wondering about. Why aircraft mechanic? Why the white lock of hair? Had she made it home this morning after the hours of questions? Was she sleeping now? What did she wear when she was sleeping?

*Okay, enough.* He stood and reviewed the whiteboard he was using to help him organize the information for the case. So far, he had a female victim frozen solid in a way that hid her face from view and prevented her hands from being accessible for fingerprints until she thawed out. Without an identity, he couldn't begin to pin down a motive, nor could he build a list of suspects. The jewelry the CSU team photographed was too generic to be useful.

Did Sierra Bauer recognize something in one of the pictures, or had he read her reaction wrong?

A frozen body meant the closest estimate to time of death the medical examiner could give him last night was twenty-four to thirty-six hours before discovery. He had looked at the plane's logbook and written down the flights prior to finding Jane Doe. That particular plane was parked overnight at the Minneapolis-St. Paul Airport two nights ago. Yesterday the plane flew a six a.m. route to Grand Forks, North Dakota, then back to MSP, and a final round-trip to Milwaukee, Wisconsin.

He drew a timeline and added the information.

The daytime temperatures on the ground yesterday in all three cities were well below freezing, with Milwaukee holding the record high temperature slot with a balmy fifteen degrees. Two nights ago, the thermometer sank into double digits below zero. The body could have been loaded at any of the three airports and had time and temperature to freeze.

Did it matter where the body was loaded? Not until he knew more, he decided.

How long would it take to shove a body into the compartment? Quinn attached his sketches of the maintenance bay panel to the board with magnets. One was of the fuselage including the cargo area aft to the tail, with measurements noted. Why would someone lift a body four feet through a foot-and-a-half square hole, shove it another four feet to rest against the bulkhead, and fold it into a fetal curl so tight an armadillo would be proud?

When he saw the crime scene up close, there hadn't been much room to maneuver around the tangle of lines and ducting without disturbing the body. Quinn needed photos of the crime scene. Kevin would send the entire collection to him with the crime scene report.

Who knew that opening was there? The maintenance bay panel was on the bottom of the fuselage as the tail section started its sloping rise. He'd walked around the other Dash-8 turboprops in the hangar. A casual observer would have a tough time seeing the panel even when standing at the aft end of the fuselage looking forward.

Someone who worked with the aircraft might know. In fact, anyone who had access to the aircraft within the time of departure could be a suspect, including ramp agents, fuel truck drivers, de-ice truck drivers, mechanics, pilots, and even passengers. So, he either had a very short list, or a very long one.

A cracked skull meant blood, hair, even pieces of bone left as evidence. This sort of injury often indicated a crime of passion, with either intention to kill or an accidental action that resulted in death. His victim might have been bludgeoned by her killer, or shoved so hard that whatever she hit her head against did the fatal damage. In a heat-of-the-moment scenario, either option seemed logical. Shoving a dead body with a traumatic head injury through a hole in an airplane would be messy, but there hadn't been as much of a mess as he expected. Someone killed her someplace else. Unless she was killed in close proximity to the plane, stuffing Jane Doe into it seemed like extra effort.

If the killer didn't want the body found, he wouldn't put it in an airplane. Mechanics would find a body anywhere on a plane.

Was the body meant as a message for a mechanic? A warning?

Quinn sighed. He could theorize all he wanted, but until he had more information, he wouldn't get very far.

He turned to the task of arranging the notes from his interview with Sierra Bauer into something report-worthy. She'd been straightforward in her answers the first time around. Asking the questions more than once ensured the interviewee's story stayed the same. When he asked the questions again, she answered them in the same way, but with a bit more uncertainty in her voice, as though she doubted her memory. When the third repetition came around, she'd gotten agitated, and he'd received, in his opinion, more than his share of eye rolls and sighs.

He'd long ago failed to improve his handwriting, and his abbreviations were non-standard, so he had to re-read a number of his notes. Sierra used industry jargon in her answers, and he wasn't sure what some of the terms meant.

Hell-hole? That was how she and Warren Bates referred to the aft maintenance bay. Power runs? PCU? He knew APU stood for the auxiliary power unit in the maintenance compartment. Pooky? What the hell was pooky? Or was it pookie? Pookee?

He finished going through his notes, and still had a list of jargon to define so he could fill out the report without an aviation dictionary. Wait, he knew what chocks were. The triangular blocks, like big rubber or wooden prisms, were placed on either side of the wheels to prevent airplanes from rolling. He scratched that off the list.

The sun had been up for over an hour by now, and it'd be at least another hour or two before he'd see any reports from the scene or whatever the medical examiner could determine from a frozen corpse. He was lucky the holidays were a few weeks past. Things slowed down in the medical examiner's office this time of year, at least until the St. Paul Winter Carnival got going next week, the last week in January. Even then, the weather determined just how many people would gather in St. Paul for the festivities.

A grumble in his belly reminded him he hadn't eaten breakfast yet. And he definitely wasn't in the market for Cinnabon, easily accessible in the airport mezzanine. The "need defined" list stared at him. According to the lead mechanic, Sierra was off for a few days. Would she be awake now to reset her internal clock? He'd worked his share of night shifts, and that first day off was always a choice between sleeping until noon or staying up all day so you could sleep through the night.

He could ask her to meet him for breakfast and kill three birds with one stone: define her jargon, find out more information about the plane and the maintenance bay, and ask her where the plane was parked when she picked it up at the gate. His subconscious nudged him. Okay, four things.

He could see her again.

*Can't get involved with a witness*, the little voice inside his head reminded him. *It's against the rules.*

She didn't witness anything, he reasoned, she just found the body. His ex-wife's infidelity soured his desire to seek out a relationship with anyone; he had not been interested in a woman since his divorce. That is, until he met Sierra Bauer. The touch-memory of her hand in his echoed in his palm. He felt the subtle roughness of her callouses and the surprising strength of her grip. And those eyes.

His stomach whined again. She was the subject matter expert when it came to the Dash-8. Besides, maybe she remembered something since last night. He flipped to the page in his notebook with her phone number and dialed. Each ring added a knotted twist to his empty stomach. When her answering machine got on the line, his cramped middle relaxed. He left a message, hung up, and settled in to wait for her call back.

*It's just breakfast. Nothing else.*

# 8

Sierra tossed and turned while the glowing red numbers on the clock advanced at the pace of molasses in a Minnesota winter. Images of bloody, shattered skulls stuck in her mind, stubbornly refusing to leave even in the wake of more detailed imagery of Hawaiian beaches. When she started hearing sounds of shuffling, of breathing not her own, dragging with them the fear she buried years ago, she struggled to remind herself it was all in her head.

Nightmare images hounded her until she gave up trying to sleep. No point in lying in bed and waiting for a reprieve. If she couldn't turn her brain off, she'd never get to sleep. She turned on the bedside table lamp and pulled out her worn copy of the Tao Te Ching. The ancient text's meditative verses often helped to quiet her restless mind.

Not this time. After half a dozen verses, she shut the book and tossed it aside. Frustration fueled a need to move. She shoved out of bed and peered out at the parking lot. Some cars were blanketed by the inches of snow that fell earlier, some were clear. None of the vehicles were black pickup trucks.

A tendril of acid wove through her and zeroed in on her scar, sending a sharp stab of pain through her side. She checked the clock. The YMCA was open now for lap swimming. At this point, she would have to wear herself out to get some sleep. After seeing the truck last night, the thought of driving ten miles to the Y made her second-guess the decision.

The old, familiar fear settled into her. *What if he follows me? What if no one else is there this early?*

She could use the fitness room in the apartment building. It might be empty.

Wait. Every time she went to the Y for an early morning lap swim, all the lanes were full. She wouldn't be alone.

*He cannot control me unless I allow it.* She hadn't recited the mantra for years. She had earned the right to do what she wanted when she wanted, and her imagination wasn't going to take that hard-earned freedom away from her. She gathered her things. A workout would give her something to think about besides violence.

❖  ❖  ❖

SHE SWAM MORE LAPS THAN USUAL to exhaust her body and mind enough for sleep, but after she hit double her regular routine, she gave up. Even her focus on laps and strokes morphed into imagined scenarios of the who, how, and why of the frozen body she found. Why was that person killed? Why the hell-hole? What if she knew the victim? The maze of questions drove her to give up trying to think of anything else.

As soon as she returned home, she checked behind each door in the apartment before shoving aside all the coats in her front closet and anything hanging in her bedroom closet. In defiance of those hard-to-break habits, she opened the blinds covering the sliding glass door, letting in the winter sun glistening off the snow on her personal balcony. Daylight meant safety. Maybe that's why she liked the night shift so much; it meant she wasn't home alone remembering the terror from her past. It didn't matter that she had worked so hard to get back to a normal life, where she could expect to feel secure. Some days the memories ambushed her anyway.

Being one of a handful of women in the aviation maintenance program at Thief River Falls Technical College in northern Minnesota was an advantage in the dating department, or so she thought at first. The few guys she dated back then never crossed that indeterminate line between "date" and "boyfriend", except one. As a tomboy who knew as much about car engines as they did, the guys in her classes saw her as one of their own more than as one of the girls.

No one had ever been interested in her as a woman before Rune.

He'd appealed to her by virtue of not only his good looks—he had the hair and eyes of John Stamos with the lean build and smile of Mark Harmon—and charm, but his politeness and humor. He was conscientious, liked to fish, knew how to fix cars, and didn't think football season superseded spending time with a girl on the weekends. After a couple dates, they started "going steady". He even seemed okay with her insistence that sex wasn't on the menu for a while.

The warning signs were tucked into the subtle nuances of his behavior. The novel experience of having a first boyfriend clouded the truth from her 19-year-old self. It started with his insistence on knowing when she went on errands, so he'd know when to call her. That progressed to accompanying her on those errands. From there the situation slipped into an ever-deepening pit of his demands to know where she was and whom she was with at every waking moment.

He suggested having sex with him would prove he could trust her. She refused. By that point, with him scrutinizing her every action, she felt trapped in the relationship. She survived her attempt to break up with him with a nice collection of bruises on her forearms. Her father had insisted both she and her sister learn and practice Tai Chi when they reached adolescence. It was the first time she used Tai Chi as a martial art and not just a way to meditate.

She thought that was finally the end of the relationship. Rune didn't. He tracked her, lurked around every corner and down every hall, at school and anywhere else she went. He was like a predator stalking prey. She couldn't get far enough away from him without dropping out of A&P school. She refused to surrender her dream. A restraining order escalated the control freak in him. Later, she discovered he had copied her apartment key.

One night she woke to the whisper of breathing. When she opened her eyes, a shadow leaned over her.

She shot out of bed, shoved past the figure, and scrambled to the bedroom door. She hit the light and got halfway across the threshold before he caught her arm. Yanked her to a stop.

"My uncle is one of the cops you begged to help you get that restraining order. He told you it wasn't necessary," he said, eyes crazy wild. He shook her. "How could you put a restraining order on me? I love you, Sierra."

His grip was like an iron cuff on her arm. Her pulse set a speed record as adrenaline crashed through her. "Let me go, Rune. You're not supposed to be here."

He grabbed her other arm. Lowered his face to hers. She smelled the sweet-sour liquor on his breath. "You want me." He leered at her in her thin sleeping tee like a lech who'd been stranded on a deserted island. "I thought good girls slept naked."

She rammed her head into his face. Missed his nose. Squirmed to break his hold.

He slapped her. Shoved her into the wall.

Her head thudded against the surface, sending pain shooting through her skull. She kicked at his knee.

He struck her again. Stars flashed in her head. "You ungrateful bitch."

She punched at him with her free hand. He released her, thrust a fist into her ribcage. She dropped to the ground, strained to breathe against the fire in her side. He kicked her. She heard a snap. Agony slammed like a hot knife slicing through every nerve.

He dragged her to her feet by her hair and threw her into the living room.

She landed on the sofa. It would take him only a few steps to reach her. She had to get out. Sierra sucked in a breath against the excruciating pain in her side and scrambled toward the kitchen, found the light switch.

He stalked toward her, a madness in his eyes like a rabid dog.

The phone hung on the wall at the other end of the narrow kitchen. A little farther. "How did you get in here?" She backed against the corner of the refrigerator, stumbled around it.

"You almost broke my nose last time. What did I do to deserve that?" He stopped, hands behind his back like a soldier at parade rest. Ogled her in her sleep T-shirt. He stepped closer, grabbed the front of his jeans. "Maybe if I'd fucked you, you wouldn't have told me to leave you alone." Another step.

She edged backward, pulse hammering like a machine gun. She had no roommate to wake or conveniently arrive home after a night out. The door was just on the other side of the passage wall holding the phone. *How much farther? A foot? Two feet?*

"Get out of here, Rune." Her voice trembled. She cleared her throat and tried again. "Get out of here."

"A restraining order—what the fuck" he sneered. "What makes you think you can do that and not be punished?"

"Get out of here before I call the cops." She reached behind her and felt the wall. The phone was at shoulder-height.

Screw the phone. How fast could she make it to the door?

He shook his head, eyes darting to the wall behind her. "I locked the door. You can't leave. You need to learn your lesson."

She'd never have time to open it before he reached her.

She turned. Grabbed at the phone.

"Bitch!" He snagged her shirt, jerked her back. Slammed her against the refrigerator door. She shoved him.

A metallic flash, then fire lanced through her.

Fear bolstered her strength. She thrust upward with the heel of her palm, connected with his nose. He howled like a wounded animal. She drilled her knee into his groin. He collapsed to the floor.

She grabbed a pan from the drying rack at the sink and pounded his head until he stopped groaning.

Blood. Everywhere. She could smell it, could taste the sharp tang. The floor was slick with it.

A handle stuck out from her red shirt—white. It was supposed to be white. Another agonizing breath.

Everything went numb. Her strength vanished. She snagged the phone off the wall before she slid to the floor. Cold. She shivered while she punched numbers with blood-slick fingers. Her teeth chattered when the 911 operator answered.

"Help," she croaked and managed to recite her address before the black closed in on her.

After the trial, Rune spent the next six years in prison. She spent them in therapy, working her way back to a state where she didn't jump at every noise in the dark. After the attack she found a different apartment, got an unlisted phone number, and spent time not studying or in therapy rebuilding her life. She graduated from A&P school and returned to the Twin Cities. A new apartment, new unlisted number, and new job with Range Airlines gave her the confidence to move past the trauma and toward a normal life. She'd done pretty well, too, until she got the letter notifying her of his release.

Dread returned like an icy fist that tried to crush her from the inside out. After a month of her fears going unfounded, she thought maybe he decided to move on, that it wasn't worth tracking her down.

Until she saw the pickup truck on the service road by the hangar—had she seen a bumper sticker, or had she imagined it?

Black pickup trucks were as common as snow drifts.

Would she ever be able to let her guard down again?

The blinking light on her answering machine caught her attention. She listened to the message and tried to ignore the spike in her pulse when she heard Detective Moore's voice. When he mentioned meeting at the Perkins restaurant in Burnsville, close to her neck of the woods, she checked the clock. According to the timestamp of the message, he'd called just before she got home.

She fished his card from the dish on the counter beside the door and dialed. When Moore answered, she thought she heard something like excitement in his voice. Or was it wishful thinking? She agreed to meet him in an hour, giving her enough time to shower and change.

After she hung up, she forced herself to slow down. *Relax.* It's his job. There's nothing there.

Something about Detective Quinn Moore sent a flush of heat through her.

That initial hit always faded, like the physical appeal of a hot guy before you find out he's a jackass.

She had firsthand experience. Hell, she had a scar to prove it.

# 9

Just off Interstate 35W at Highway 13, the restaurant boasted decor matching that of every other chain restaurant Sierra had ever visited, with some local flavor in the guise of black-and-gold high school team jerseys thrown in. Brilliant morning sun streamed through the windows, belying the frigid temperature outside. Scattered patrons hunched over cups of coffee and plates of breakfast. Bacon and maple syrup flavored the air along with the aromas of fresh coffee and fresh-baked cinnamon rolls.

Detective Moore sat in a small booth toward the back. He stood as she reached the booth, extending his hand in greeting. He wore the same maroon sweater over a white turtleneck and Dockers he had hours ago at the hangar. Stubble still coated his face, and he'd managed to acquire hat hair despite its short cut. She grasped his hand.

His solid grip sent a rush through her, like someone filled her with liquid heat. Did that mean she could try to trust him? Could she trust herself to make a good decision?

"Thank you for meeting with me here, Miss Bauer. Have you eaten yet?"

"No, I haven't." They sat, and Sierra noticed the bruise-colored circles under his eyes. "Have you been on duty since last night? You look tired."

He smiled and slid his menu toward her. "Gee, thanks. That's what I was going for." He leaned forward on the table. "You don't look terribly refreshed either. How did you sleep?"

She peeled off her coat and shoved it beside her. "Not well, thanks for asking." Awkward silence followed for a minute. He watched her, but it felt more casual than the way a cop would.

A waitress stopped by to top off Moore's coffee and take their orders. Sierra didn't bother looking at the menu. Whenever she got the opportunity, she always chose bacon with eggs over easy and hash browns. She grew up in a household where food was home-grown, home-raised, or locally-sourced, and more healthy than not. As a result, she'd had few opportunities to enjoy such "treats" as bacon, sausage, or processed food. She was lucky her mother loved BLTs, or Sierra may have gone through her first eighteen years without ever tasting the salty, smoky, meaty equivalent of chocolate.

Moore waited for her to order, then ordered the same, which her cynical side thought might be a ploy to throw her off-guard, though she wasn't sure why he would bother. The more common-sensible side thought he just liked the same thing she did and would've ordered it even if she had requested oatmeal. The waitress promised to return with glasses of water and one of orange juice for Sierra, then left them alone.

Moore flipped through pages of his notepad. "Have you thought of anything else about last night that might help the investigation?"

"No. I told you what I saw. You said you needed me to explain some things."

He nodded, set his pen down, and crossed his arms on the table. "Jargon, mostly. You kept calling the maintenance compartment a 'hell-hole.'"

"Did you climb in there?" At his nod, she continued. "Now, imagine that with a miniature jet engine running while sitting on the tarmac during a hot summer day. Oh, and keep in mind most of the guys are bigger than I am and have a tougher time moving around in there. Hence, hell-hole."

"Makes sense." He made a note. "Okay, power runs."

"We do power runs so we know if the engines and propellers are making the power they should. We park at the pad and run the engines to full power. There's a list of tests we put the engines through before and after the prop inspection."

"PCU?"

"Prop control unit. It controls the pitch of the propeller. It's a nut and screw setup. For the inspection, we run the nut to the bottom before we pull the transfer tube to change the o-rings."

He didn't write anything down this time, just stared at her. "What?" she asked.

A slow grin lightened his expression. "Do you realize only an airplane mechanic would understand all that? And you're reciting it like rote."

"Do you want me to break it down further?"

A chuckle escaped his lips and settled in her chest like a tiny bird come home to roost. "No. I know how to change spark plugs and oil filters, but I'm not enough of a mechanic to visualize that. How about pooky? Or is it pookee?"

"Have you heard of PRC? It's a composite sealant, like a two-part caulk, we use to seal panels to waterproof them. I don't know how we get 'pookie' out of PRC, but that's what we call it. And I don't know how to spell it. Does that help?"

He snickered. "I almost thought you were talking about Garfield's teddy bear."

His comment was so unexpected she stifled a guffaw. "You read Garfield?"

"Used to. It's been a while. It was one of my favorite comic strips when I was a kid."

It felt like she was having breakfast with a friend rather than a cop. There was a stereotype that went along with cops, and Garfield comic strips weren't part of it.

"My favorite is still Calvin and Hobbes."

"Man, I love Calvin and Hobbes. I've got almost all the collections," he said. "I read them when I've had a rough day, or week." He spun his coffee cup, his mood sobering a notch. "I almost wore them out after my ex-wife left. Calvin kept me sane."

There was a boundary between a conversation related to the case and one about his personal life. The fact he'd crossed it tightened Sierra's nerves. She'd dated enough men to know when something was off, but her intuition wasn't sounding the warning bell yet. "What happened?"

He stared at his cup for a moment, then shook his head. "I'm sorry, that was inappropriate. Forget I said anything."

She wanted to reach to him, touch his hand, reassure him somehow. She didn't get the sense he was speaking entirely as a cop, not that she'd spoken with many. Not all of them were this personable. The last time she'd talked to cops, back during the whole Rune nightmare, they'd all but accused her of being too sensitive, too paranoid, and too ungrateful. The experience tainted her view of cops from that point on.

Part of her wanted to think Moore let his guard down because they had some sort of connection.

That was selfish, she thought, and probably so far off the mark she'd need a map to find her way back.

He switched his focus from his coffee to her. Those brilliant blue eyes struck her again. "How difficult do you think it would be for someone to stuff a body into the, ah, hell-hole?"

"It wouldn't be easy. They'd have to lift or push the body into the plane first. The hatch panel is only about a foot and a half square. Even when we swap out the APU we have to jockey it a bit to get it to fit through the hole."

Moore scratched some notes. "So, if someone were to cram a body in there, they'd have to be strong enough to lift it into the plane, then tall enough to get inside, and strong enough again to slide the body forward while bent over or in an otherwise awkward position."

"Pretty much."

The waitress brought their breakfasts and left after topping off Moore's coffee. Sierra immediately positioned her eggs on top of her hash browns, speared the yolks, and let the thick yellow goo seep into the potatoes. Then she tasted the bacon. Salty, smoky, and perfectly meaty. It was an indulgence to savor.

"Man, this bacon is great." Moore bit off another piece. "Reminds me of the thick-sliced bacon my mom uses. The regular stuff just doesn't have the same crunch."

Sierra stared at his plate. He'd put his eggs on his hash browns but hadn't cut into them yet. Self-conscious, she set her bacon down and sipped her juice.

"Wow, did you feel the temperature drop just now?" he asked, his voice quiet.

She poked at her eggs with her fork. "What do you mean?"

He set his bacon down and folded his arms on the table. "You were comfortable. Now all of a sudden you're not. Why?"

"How can you possibly tell that?"

"I'm trained to read body language. So, why are you uncomfortable now?" He sounded concerned, more like a good friend than a happenstance acquaintance. She got along with most people just fine, but always held back enough to keep her distance. The few people she counted among her very good friends were the only ones she felt this comfortable with. It'd been like this with him last night when he interviewed her.

"Sierra?"

The way he said her name eased her discomfort. "Sorry. Just thinking how odd it is that we both put our eggs on our hash browns."

His eyebrows rose. "The temperature just returned to normal." He glanced at her plate. "I always put my eggs on my hash browns. Makes them less dry. Why the change just now?"

Everything she came up with in her mind sounded stupid. "Not sure."

"Liar," he said with a grin. "You're okay, now, though. Right?"

"Yes." And that seemed to satisfy him. She filled the next moment of awkward silence by sipping her orange juice. She peered across the table at his notes and decided she didn't want to work that hard to decipher the scribbles. "Can I ask about the case?"

He cut into his eggs, then mixed the runny yolks with his hash browns. "No."

"Are you kidding? I found the—" she stopped when he nailed her with a cold glare. She adjusted. "I'm already involved. Why can't I ask about it?"

"Because it's an ongoing investigation." He sounded like a recording. He shook pepper and salt onto his egg-potato mash. "Even if you are involved." Before she could ask another question, he pointed his fork at her. "I do, however, need your help."

"You need my help, but I can't ask about the case?"

He finished another forkful of eggy hash browns before he answered. "I don't make the rules, Miss Bauer. I just guess which ones to bend and how far in the interest of solving the case."

Oh, so it was "Miss Bauer" again. She liked it better when he called her by her given name. She pushed her potatoes around under the guise of sopping up more yolk while she decided how to react. Maybe if she helped him she could squeak some questions in. "What do you need my help with?"

He set his fork down and sipped his coffee. "I'd like you to come to the Range Air hangar with me. I want to take a closer look at the maintenance bay in that airplane."

"I thought you looked at it last night—er, this morning."

"I need a subject matter expert to answer my questions."

"There are other mechanics on duty. I'm off for a few days, and you heard Warren last night. I'm not supposed to be at the hangar."

"You are an expert, and you're already involved in the case." He leaned forward. "You saw how the body was positioned. Please? I'd also like you to show me where the plane was parked at the gate when you picked it up." He jerked back, then checked the display of a pager clipped to his belt. "Sorry. I've got to call in. Excuse me for a minute." He left the booth and headed to a hallway at the back of the restaurant that boasted a blue sign with a white phone icon.

Minutes later, he returned, a frown darkening his face more than the shadow of his beard.

"Bad news?" she asked.

He resumed his seat, planted his elbows on the table, then rubbed his face with his hands. "Depends on who you ask. Finish up. We need to go back to the crime scene."

# 10

Sierra pulled out of the parking lot and followed Detective Moore's unmarked Ford Explorer onto 35W heading north toward the airport. The man refused to explain what sparked this sudden urgency, instead assuring her he'd tell her once they arrived at the hangar. She grumbled. It wasn't enough she found a bloody corpse in her inspection airplane, she had to submit to scrutiny by a cute cop who wanted her help but refused to answer her questions.

She imagined what sort of bad news he'd received. Did they identify the body? Could they tell when the victim was killed? She tried to remember what she saw last night, but she'd vacated the hell-hole as fast as she could after she made her gruesome discovery.

Something niggled at her, something she should remember, but when she focused on it, it vanished.

Whatever it was, she didn't want to think about it. She hardly slept at all because of those images. Bringing them to mind again would sabotage her efforts to rest later, when all her awake ran out.

Interstate 494 was less congested than usual this time of day. One of the reasons she liked working third shift: the traffic, or lack of. She headed toward the heart of the Twin Cities on her way to work after most people headed home to the suburbs. The same was true of her drive home. She followed

Moore east on I-494 to the exit for the service road that ran past the Range Air hangar.

He stopped at the gated entrance, swiped his airport badge, and entered the lot. She followed before the gate closed and parked beside him, then waited in the crisp air while he slid an official-looking placard onto his dashboard.

"Okay, can you tell me what that call was about? I'm guessing you found out something about the case."

He didn't look at her, instead focused on the big blocky building in front of them. "The ME's office called to let me know the body thawed enough for them to loosen it a bit. They can't do the autopsy until it thaws completely, and they won't accelerate that. The tissue might get damaged if they warm it up too fast.

"The victim was wearing a Range Airlines ramp agent uniform." He zeroed in on her. "Do you know any ramp agents?"

*Holy shit.* Despite her heavy coat and hat, icy January air soaked into her as if to reinforce the implication. Sierra shivered, her breath a pattern of white plumes. "I work third shift. The most I ever see rampies is when I pick up planes from the gate, or when I drop them off at the gate in the morning."

"You didn't answer my question. Do you know any ramp agents?"

Ramp agents—rampies—were the worker ants of the commercial aviation world. Their jobs included guiding the planes to and from their parking spots, ensuring the planes were warm or cool for boarding passengers depending on the season, and giving the pilots the all-clear for starting engines. As a mechanic, she had only cursory interaction with them when their paths intersected at all.

It hit her like a jet blast. *The ring.* The last time she'd seen one like it, the manicured nails of the hand that wore it drew blood. Her blood.

Could it belong to the woman she blamed for her brother's return to his self-destructive ways? She skirted the question. "It's been almost two years since I worked the gate. I have no idea who any of the rampies are now."

His eyes narrowed. "Remember, you can't say anything to anyone. We have an open investigation and no identity for the victim. The news media doesn't know about it yet, otherwise this place would be crawling with those vultures."

"Mum's the word."

Moore headed toward the Range Airlines main office entrance. Sierra headed toward the maintenance entrance by habit until he called to her. "Hey, this way."

She trotted to Moore's side. "Why don't you use the maintenance entrance? I'm with you."

"Because," he said as he opened his coat and slipped a lanyard over his head, "I'm a cop, and the people in charge need to know I'm here." He clipped his badge onto the lanyard before opening the door for her.

The woman seated at the front desk smiled, a nice highlight to her shoulder-length silver curls and coral red pants suit. "May I help you?"

Moore showed his badge. "Detective Moore, Airport Police. I'm here to go over the crime scene. Miss Bauer is here to show me what she found."

The woman shook her head and tsked. "I heard about that. How awful!"

Sierra waited for Moore to sign in, then led him through the hallway and doors to the hangar. The Dash-8 subject to an engine change still occupied a corner of the hangar, but by the look of things, it wouldn't be long before the engine crew would pull the plane out for power runs. A tug pulled the Metro toward the opening hangar doors. Her plane sat tucked into the far corner of the hangar, yellow police tape still a barrier to unauthorized personnel.

"Hey, Sierra." She turned. A tall mechanic with a solid build waved her down. His beard matched his red hair right down to the faint streaks of gray.

"Kelly," she returned and introduced him to Detective Moore. Kelly Jaeger had years of experience on the Metros and an incredible skill with airframe maintenance. From the look of the clipboard in his hand, he was acting lead mechanic at the hangar today.

"I thought you were on your weekend. Heard about the dead body." Kelly nodded toward the cordoned-off plane. "When can we get that inspection finished?"

"No one touches that plane until I release it," Moore said.

"The suits are asking how long until they can send the plane out. Can we at least do the inspection?"

Moore shook his head. "I need this plane untouched until I have as much information as I can get from it."

Kelly frowned. "They aren't going to be happy about that."

He handed Kelly his business card. "Tell them they can call me if they have questions. I'll let them know when I don't need it anymore."

Moore nudged Sierra toward the plane. She resisted for a moment before continuing a path toward the yellow tape. She'd only worked with Kelly a few times, but she liked him. "Are you sure you can't give him any sort of estimate?"

"No. I might be able to let the plane go tomorrow or I might need it here until next week." He lifted the tape and let her duck under before he followed. "I haven't seen the crime scene photos yet, but I should have the file by the time I get back to the office. In the meantime, I have some questions I need your help with." He took off his coat and laid it on the platform stand they used during the interview.

Sierra followed suit. She felt out of place without her uniform, but comfortable despite the cold let in by the open hangar doors, now almost closed again. Box heaters mounted on the walls just below the high ceiling glowed orange and hummed as they strained to heat the hangar back to a reasonable sixtyish degrees. "What's first?"

Moore pulled the three-step ladder from its place under the aft bay access. "Can I get into here without a ladder?"

She hadn't had to get into the hell-hole without a ladder for ages. "Sure. Just hop up onto the edge of the hole."

He bent, then straightened, standing in the hatchway, everything north of his belt hidden inside the fuselage. "Now what?"

"Brace your hands behind you, then just hop up. Sit on the edge."

He tried, failed, tried again. His feet dangled half a foot above the floor. "I need some light in here."

Sierra retrieved a work light from a stand, plugged it into a nearby extension cord, and handed it up to Moore. She stood in the hatch after he pulled himself into the maintenance bay and chuckled at the sight of him crouched beside the APU, braced awkwardly against the shallow dome of the aft pressure bulkhead. "Comfy?"

"Not so much." He shuffled forward and grabbed at ducting to steady himself. "Can you do it? You're shorter than I am."

She turned until she faced aft, braced her hands on the forward edge, the lowest part, before hopping and lifting herself onto the former that outlined the hatch opening. The problem now: with Moore in the way, she couldn't maneuver around the lines and ducting. She scooted around the open hole until she faced forward, then got her feet under her, careful not to lean on any fluid lines. "Now what?"

Moore stared at her for a moment, then adjusted his position to a more comfortable spot. "This is where the body lay, right?" After she nodded, he shone the work light over the area at his feet and at the APU. "How many mechanics are needed to get the APU out of here?"

"Two. Someone disconnects all the lines and ducting, then removes the starter. Once it's stripped, one mechanic lowers it to another outside the hell-hole."

"What about that?" he asked, pointing to a burnished metal sphere about twice the size of a softball mounted on a flange.

"Fire bottle. If there's a fire in the APU, it'll blow. There's an explosive squib here," she pointed to a nodule on the bottle connected to a wire harness, "that releases high-pressure suppressant."

"It's so small."

"Small, but the contents are under pressure. The squib is sensitive, so we check the indicators on the outside of the fuselage to make sure it hasn't gone off when it isn't supposed to. When I was at A&P school, someone accidentally set one off in the hangar when it was sitting on a workbench. It got stuck in the insulation lining the ceiling about forty feet up, or it would've punched a hole right through it."

Moore whistled low. "Good to know. How heavy is the APU?"

"Somewhere between a hundred and a hundred and fifty pounds, I think, once it's stripped."

"How many mechanics to get the APU in?"

"I've never helped install one. There is at least one in here to pull the APU up, and at least one to lift from the bottom. There's a flange here," she pointed to a squarish projection, "which makes it harder to get it in and out. I think they usually have three guys to get it in and set it in position."

Moore said nothing for a minute, focused instead on the entry to the hell-hole. "Could you lift a hundred pounds through the hatch?"

"I can lift that much in front of me, like lifting the APU into position, but I don't think I can lift that much straight above my shoulders."

He made his way to the edge of the hatch and dropped to the floor. He crouched, disappeared from view, appeared again. "There's not much room in here."

"Hence the nickname. Finished?"

He nodded, and she handed him the work light before dropping out of the maintenance bay. She ducked to clear the fuselage. "Now what?"

He dug his notepad out of his coat pocket and added some scribbles to a fresh page. "I need to talk to the ramp agent supervisor. The office is at the terminal, right?"

"As far as I know."

He handed her coat to her before he donned his own. "You can ride with me. I'll bring you back here when we're finished."

A tingling began at the base of her neck, like someone hovered just out of eyesight, watching her. She glanced over her shoulder. "Whoa, hold on. What do you need me for?"

"Show me where the plane was parked before you brought it here." He turned and led the way out of the hangar.

"Fine, but I'm driving myself."

# 11

They reached the exit to the Lindbergh Terminal, named after the famous transcontinental aviator. She followed Moore's unmarked SUV to the Airport PD reserved parking area. Unsure of her chances to evade a parking ticket, she stayed in her car until he stood at her driver's side door. She rolled the window down. "You sure I can park here?"

He held up a piece of paper that looked like it should be left under a car wiper by a religious recruiter. "Park next to me and put this on your dashboard. You'll be fine."

She wasn't convinced, but took the paper from him, slid it onto the dash, and then parked beside Moore's vehicle. She fell into step beside him as they headed into the terminal. "If I get a ticket or towed, I'm blaming you."

"You won't." He held the door for her, then led her through the restricted access entrance into the terminal proper.

Passengers filled the corridors, the rolling thunder of hundreds of luggage wheels echoed with the din of conversation. Sierra checked the time. Almost noon. A push was starting, when almost all the flights loading were due to depart within twenty minutes of each other. A crowd of Japanese tourists gathered around the departure board, pointing and chattering. Sierra shook her head. As much as she loved aviation, she hated crowds. The press of people grated on nerves raw from fatigue.

Though Concourse G, where Range Airlines loaded and unloaded passengers, housed more than a dozen gates, there were only four ticket counters to go with the four doors leading from the concourse to the tarmac. She imagined loading passengers was like teachers loading kindergartners onto school buses, with boarding passes in place of colored cards.

When they reached Range Air's gates, Moore turned to her. "Where is the ramp agent office?"

"I have no idea. I know where the rampies go from the tarmac side, but I've never tried to navigate from inside the terminal."

"Fair enough." He slipped his airport badge into an armband holder, then onto his right arm. Sierra clipped her own badge onto her coat collar and followed him to the AOA, the Airport Operations Area, where the real action took place. Once outside, Sierra sucked in the crisp late-January air. Tainted with jet exhaust, the arctic cold caught in her throat. She pulled her hat down over her ears. Moore did the same. A Dash-8 headed toward the gate, one ramp agent marshaling it into its parking spot while another walked the wing to ensure it didn't hit the neighboring plane.

Moore leaned toward her and spoke over the noise. "Where was the plane parked before you brought it back to the hangar?"

She scanned the parking area, then wandered along the gate building. She didn't pay much attention to where the planes she picked up were parked, but she remembered the plane from last night sitting in the middle of the lineup. "About here." She reviewed the bold black-on-white numbers and letters mounted on the low gate building. "G18. I think."

Moore wandered around the tail of the Dash-8 currently parked in that spot. Though it snowed the night before, the asphalt shone black under an oily coating of deicing fluid, and any snow that escaped the process was now flattened into a slick dirty crust by boots, tugs, and planes. Sierra called to him when he crouched under the tail of the plane.

"I don't think you'll find anything. There's been at least three pushes this morning. Each one gets de-iced."

He touched the asphalt and rubbed his fingertips with his thumb. "Glycol, right?"

"It's a form of glycol, like super-charged antifreeze."

He rubbed a foot across the slick surface. "Not slippery."

"Try it with a coating of fresh snow on top, or an inch of slush. Plenty slippery then."

Moore straightened. "Lead on."

Sierra headed toward the door the ramp agents used farther along the building, about fifty feet closer to the body of the terminal than the Range

Air maintenance gate office. One of the exiting ramp agents stopped in the doorway, his bulk straining the zipper on his parka, dark shaggy hair and matching beard putting him in the running for a Grizzly Adams look-alike contest. "What's going on?"

Moore showed his badge. "Investigation. Who's the supervisor on duty?"

"I'm the lead on this shift."

Sierra read the man's name tag. "Curt, can you show us to the supervisor's office, please?" At his hesitation, she pointed to her airport badge and added, "I'm a Range Air mechanic. I don't know where the office is."

When he didn't react right away, she added, "We came from the hangar. Call them and talk to Kelly if you don't believe me."

"I believe you." Curt led them down a short corridor and into a room split in half by a partial wall that separated the far side from the main area. On that side of the room, lockers lined the walls, and a bench claimed the finishing touch. The near side of the room held a coffee vending machine and battered table with chairs. Cubicle walls topped with an assortment of tiny, wild-haired Troll dolls separated a desk from the rest of the room.

The man at the desk stood and peered over the cubicle wall before approaching. He wore business casual, his navy slacks and red sweater over a white turtleneck somehow out of place with a permed mullet and porn-star mustache. An embroidered Range Airlines logo graced the upper left side of his chest.

He shook hands with Moore while he eyed his badge, and barely glanced at Sierra. "I'm Bill Avery, ramp agent supervisor. How can I help you?"

Moore introduced himself, then pulled his notepad from a pocket and flipped to a fresh page. Sierra stayed silent, hanging back by the door; it was Moore's show. She turned her attention to the names, dates, and tail numbers covering a huge whiteboard mounted on a wall, absently noting which planes were Dash-8s and which were Metros by the tail numbers. Only one listed name was familiar to her; one of the first-shift mechanics was married to a ramp agent.

The name of the ramp agent Sierra used to know wasn't listed. A touch of guilt followed relief. No chance of running into her today.

"Does each ramp agent get assigned to a plane?" Moore asked.

"No. We keep track of which planes were cleaned and who did it." Bill crossed to the board and erased a time, replacing it with a later time. "My people work with whichever planes come in."

"Does anyone besides mechanics know about the aft maintenance bay on the Dash-8s?"

Bill shrugged. "Can't tell you. I haven't worked the ramp much since we brought the Dashes in. Curt?"

Furrows lined the lead ramp agent's forehead. Sierra thought he looked more constipated than confused. "The aft maintenance bay?" Curt asked.

Sierra jumped in before Moore continued. "The hell-hole. Under the tail behind the cargo bay there's a panel where the APU is. We use a three-step ladder to get into it."

The lines on Curt's forehead faded. "Oh, that. Only mechanics climb in there."

Bill peered at her. "I know you."

Sierra held back a groan. Most people didn't recognize her, they recognized the white streak in her otherwise dark brown hair, a trait inherited from her mother's side of the family. "I'm a mechanic."

"Sierra Bauer. She's a consultant on this case," Moore added.

Bill's eyes widened. "You're the girl mechanic. I remember you when you made us unload all the passengers."

Another reason she didn't miss working at the gate. "Pilots didn't write up the O2 until after you boarded the passengers. No one is supposed to be on the plane when we service the oxygen. You know, highly-flammable pressurized gas, in case something happens. Better safe and all that."

Moore steered the conversation back to business. "Check with the other ramp agents. Ask if they've seen pilots or anyone besides mechanics go into the maintenance bay. I also need copies of the roster for the past week, including anyone who called in sick or was on vacation. And contact information."

"Is this about the dead body they found in the airplane last night?" Curt asked. "Was it a rampie?"

"Dead body?" Bill's voice rose in pitch. "Today's my first day this week. I didn't hear about a body."

"I can't answer any questions right now." Moore handed each of the men a business card. "Ask your people who they saw go into the maintenance bay of any Dash-8 in the last few days, pilots or anyone besides mechanics, then call me."

Bill retrieved a copy of the roster that included contact information and handed it to him. "Is there anything else we can do to help, Detective?"

Moore scanned the list of names on the board, then the roster. He shot a sideways glance at Sierra, an eyebrow raised.

She answered what she expected was his unspoken question. "I only know Torgerson—well, not really. I know a first-shift mechanic who's married to a ramp agent. I don't even know her first name."

"Nell," said Curt. "Her name is Nell."

Furrows deepened on Moore's forehead. He started to say something, then shook his head just enough to notice. He scanned the roster again. "Are these contact numbers current?"

"They're current as far as I know." Bill let out a low whistle. "Oh my God. Is one of them dead? Is the body one of our people?"

"Mr. Avery. Curt." Moore spoke with authority. "This is a police investigation. I cannot confirm any assumptions you make. If you want to help the investigation, you will *not* mention any of this to anyone. Understood?"

# 12

An intensely silent Moore let the way back into the terminal. His dour mood, along with the chaotic din of the terminal kicked off an ache behind Sierra's eyes, accompanied by a slow dulling of her thought process and a rise of her own agitation, pretty typical for noon after she'd worked the night shift if she hadn't rested. After a few hours of sleep, maybe she'd feel civil again.

In the terminal's mezzanine, Moore veered toward the APD office. She didn't follow, instead aiming for the main entrance and, with any luck, no parking ticket.

"Where are you going?"

Don't turn around, she thought. She stopped and failed to suppress the urge to snap at him. "Home."

Silence. She jumped when he spoke again from a foot behind her. "I want to talk to you." The instant he laid a hand on her shoulder a sense of calm washed through her, cooling her irritation. "Just for a few minutes. Please." He sounded like he was trying to be patient.

She turned, avoided those incredible blue eyes. "Fine, but I have to get home. I need some sleep."

He nodded, then led the way to the APD offices. When he held the door for Sierra, she noted the creases tracing his forehead and the line of his jaw leading to a raised tendon in his neck. This Detective Moore seemed less friendly than the one who'd invited her to breakfast, or maybe he was just as tired as she was.

He stopped inside the main office in front of a desk with a high front and empty chair. On the wall behind the desk Sierra noticed an engraved plaque for the "World's Greatest Administrative Assistant". Someone had lined out the "Assistant" part with a black marker and replaced it with "Superhero". That same person must have added the hearts and stars around the name below, "Yvonne Maxwell". She had to smile at the sentiment.

Moore signed a clipboard tethered to the desk before he headed toward a hallway behind a small cluster of desks. Sierra stayed put.

He stopped and gestured down the hall. "My office is here. Please," he added, the courtesy sounding forced.

She winced at the edge to his voice, but couldn't keep the crabby out of hers. "No disrespect intended, but what is wrong with you?"

He unzipped his parka and planted hands on his hips. He lowered his head, eyes closed, and stilled for a minute. Sierra swore she could feel his angry vibes fade from the air. The tense atmosphere relaxed like a held breath released. "Better?" His voice sounded more pliant than before, and the furrows in his brow were now mere lines.

She nodded and followed him down the hall into a cramped office. Off-white walls gave the room an institutional feel enhanced by industrial brown carpeting and stark gray filing cabinets. A whiteboard covered most of one wall and displayed lists she recognized as information from the case. A huge metal desk that looked recycled from some WWII Army intake center filled the side of the office across from the door. A computer monitor sat atop a corner of the desk, with a stack of letter trays on the opposite corner. Framed certificates hung on the wall behind the desk.

Moore pulled the roster out of a pocket and tossed it onto his desk. He peeled off his coat and hung it on a coat tree before extending his hand to her. She gave him her coat, then waited until he indicated she should sit. The chair in front of the desk, a poppy red stackable unit left over from the seventies, was the only bright color in the room. He took his own seat in a leather office chair from the same era as hers. He leaned forward, arms crossed on the calendar blotter still showing last month: December, 1992. "Why didn't you tell me you knew a ramp agent?"

"What? Torgerson? I don't know her. Like I said, I just know one of the first-shift mechanics is married to a rampie, and his name is Torgerson. I told you, I haven't worked the ramp for two years. They have high turnover. Even if I did know any rampies from back then, they probably don't work here anymore."

"We need to keep the lid on this investigation. You can't tell anyone about the case."

She waited for him to continue, but he didn't. The fatigue-borne fog in her mind didn't help her confusion. He'd left the office door open, and voices from somewhere outside wafted in. She shook off the distraction. "I haven't said anything to anyone, not even my family."

"There are already rumors about someone finding a body in one of the planes."

Something lined up through the muddle in her head. "A rampie. That body is a rampie, isn't it?"

He didn't answer the question. "I appreciate your help, Miss Bauer, but this is serious. I don't know who did this, or why, or if he will repeat it."

"He?"

"Do you think a woman would be strong enough to lift a hundred and twenty pounds of dead weight into the hell-hole? Look, I'm not kidding. Your safety ..."

A voice from behind Sierra interrupted him. "Hey, CSU dropped this off for you." An older woman, straight black hair highlighted a vivid indigo, strode into view and handed Moore a thick manila envelope. Her purple paisley-print dress complemented her mahogany complexion. When she turned to leave, she smiled at Sierra. "He's a good kid. If I were twenty years younger, I'd set my sights on him now that he's available."

"Really, Yvonne?"

Yvonne turned back to a red-faced Moore. "You need to take some time off, kiddo. Don't you deny an old lady some good daydreams, now," she mock-scolded, waving a finger garnished with a large amethyst ring. "I don't want to see you here before seven tomorrow. You're young, you need your sleep, and for heaven's sake, shave." With that, and a wink at Sierra, she left.

Moore rubbed his stubble-roughened face with his hands before leaning back. "Sorry about that. Yvonne is like everyone's grandmother around here. Correction—she's like a grandmother channeling Cher. Are we clear? You are a witness, and I might need to ask you questions about the plane. Don't go digging around thinking you're going to help solve this. Got it?"

She stood. His suggestion she'd start poking around stoked her temper. God, she needed to get to bed before she said something really stupid. "Fine," she snapped. "Glad I could help." She headed to the door, snagged her coat from the rack, and shoved her arms into it.

"Sierra."

She glanced back at him, careful to avoid his gaze.

"Are you okay to drive home?"

She dug her keys out of a pocket. "I'm fine. Don't call me for a few hours. I need a nap."

"Don't leave town."

# 13

Quinn stared at the empty doorway for a full minute after she left. He could've kicked himself when he called her by her first name. That was unprofessional. He raked fingers through his hair and scratched at the stubble on his face. What captivated him about this woman? Sierra Bauer was almost the complete opposite of his ex-wife. She wore no makeup, and dressed casually in jeans and an emerald sweater that brought out the green highlights in her hazel eyes. She pulled her stocking cap off without a thought to how it affected her hair; she'd run her fingers through her hair once and hadn't fussed with it after. Sierra didn't carry a purse, and somehow it fit her. Quinn was willing to bet she didn't have a pair of shoes for every day of the month, either.

*Enough thinking about Sierra.* He pulled the report folders from the envelope and opened the top one. An initial scan of the medical examiner's report dimmed his mood. The body was still mostly-frozen, so the extent of the injuries wasn't immediately apparent except for the hole in the skull and broken bones that showed up on the x-ray. A handful of Polaroids accompanied the ME's report, including pictures of the body still folded into a tight fetal curl, face hidden from view. They'd managed to cut most of the uniform away, revealing additional bruising on the victim's back.

Whoever killed this woman didn't want her identity discovered right away. At least he had the victim's first name. While he couldn't positively identify the victim until he had fingerprint, dental, or family member confirmation, he did have a starting point.

He sifted through additional pictures of the jewelry, one of a tattoo of a pair of snowflakes on the left shoulder, and another of a fine gold chain with a pendant consisting of an emerald at the center of a pair of wings. A photo of the reverse side of the pendant showed letters engraved on each wing: R. T. and S. B.

Neither set of initials matched the victim's name. Maybe the pendant is an heirloom. Maybe the initials belong to someone the victim knew.

Kevin kept his promise to deliver the crime scene unit's report around noon. Photographs of the scene made up the bulk of the folder contents, including one of the fuselage with a tape measure near the maintenance bay access panel. A few inches shy of four feet high. Another picture showed the actual opening into the compartment, also with a tape measure for comparison. Twenty inches square.

He added the pictures to his board. The unknown subject made sure the victim couldn't be easily identified by tucking the face and hands into the body like an attempt at origami. Head wounds bled profusely, and the damage to the skull would be messy. There would be blood and hair evidence wherever she was attacked and killed. How far would the perpetrator move the body afterward?

According to the medical examiner, something like the corner of a desk or table matched the fatal head wound. Even if the suspect cleaned the area, with a head wound there was a chance something got left behind. Tiny flecks of paint were found in the brain tissue. Helpful, Quinn thought, until he remembered the sheer number of tugs, ground power units, and ground environmental units he'd seen at the gate, all with sharp corners. It could take days to test them, and that didn't count any tables, desks, or similar furniture that might match, or any evidence left by transporting a body with a head wound to the plane.

It might be futile to search for the instrument of his victim's demise, but he needed to try. He dialed Kevin, hoping he'd catch the tech before he clocked out for the day. He was about to hang up when Kevin answered.

"Kev, I need you to check the Range Air Dash-8 ramp for residue."

Dead air. Then, "Excuse me? I thought you said you wanted me to check an area three-quarters the size of a football field for residue. Do you see anything wrong with that?"

"I've narrowed it down for you. The plane was parked at gate G18. Oh, and the ME determined the vic hit her head on a sharp corner, so if you could check any tugs, ground power units, and—"

"You haven't slept, have you?" Kevin sounded exasperated. "I told you to go home and get a couple hours, didn't I?"

"No, as I recall, you told me to 'get some.'"

"You didn't do that either. When are you going to start listening to me? I'm looking out for you, you know." His sigh whooshed through the receiver. "I'll get a team out to that gate, but I can't guarantee we'll find anything. It snowed last night." With that, the connection ended.

Quinn hung up. Kevin was right, any evidence that might have been there would be gone for sure under the assault of snow, foot and plane traffic, and deicing fluid. He was taking a chance here at MSP. The Metropolitan Airports Commission was building a deice pad for the larger commercial jets, but the smaller turboprop aircraft were still deiced at their ramps. Last night's snow and two days' worth of deicing fluid might wipe out any evidence left behind.

He assumed the victim was killed at the airport; why kill her off-site and bring the body onto the AOA just to shove it into the maintenance bay of a Dash-8? It'd be easier and less risky to dispose of the body elsewhere.

If the victim was killed while on duty, he'd have a reason for the body to be stuffed into a plane rather than dumped somewhere off the airport grounds: convenience. He reviewed the ramp agent roster. Employees were listed by day and shift for the past two weeks. He highlighted the two names that matched the one on the victim's name tag.

He dialed the contact number for the first ramp agent on the list. The woman answered, and Quinn, careful not to alarm her, interviewed her about anything unusual she'd seen in the past few days at work. She couldn't offer any additional information and assured him she would call if she thought of anything.

He marked her off his list. He dialed the number for the other ramp agent whose name matched his victim. After three rings, a woman answered.

Quinn introduced himself. "Detective Quinn Moore with the Airport Police Department. May I speak with Tori Hjelle?"

A pause. "You're a cop?"

"Yes, ma'am. I can give you my badge number if you want to verify."

"No, I believe you. Tori's not here right now. Why do you want to talk to her?"

"She may have some information pertinent to an open case. When can I reach her here, or is there another number where I can reach her?"

"I haven't heard from her for a couple days, but I've been at my boyfriend's apartment. She might be staying at Pete's place."

"Who's Pete?"

Another pause. "Her boyfriend. Is Tori in trouble?"

Quinn made a note and tried to ignore the pinch at the back of his neck. "Not yet. Can I get your name, please?"

Another pause. "Cate—Catelyn Zahn." She spelled the name. "Tori's my cousin." Her voice pitched higher. "Is she okay?"

"When was the last time you spoke with her?"

"I think it was Sunday."

He glanced at the timeline on the board. Today was Wednesday. Sierra found the body late Tuesday night. Sunday night fit into the ME's time of death window. "Are you sure?"

"Yes, it must've been Sunday. I talked to her before I left for my shift—she asked me to watch Rascal because she had to work late. I'm sorry, I've been working on a big project for one of my classes. I'm having trouble remembering what day of the week it is."

The pinch extended to his gut. "Do you know if she had any tattoos?"

"Why would you ask that?" Cate's voice carried a note of distress. "She isn't in trouble, is she? She didn't get Pete in trouble, did she? Pete's too nice."

Quinn's cop sense latched onto her second question. He made a note to do a background check on Tori Hjelle. "I can't answer those questions until you answer mine. Did Tori have any tattoos?"

"She has a tattoo of two snowflakes in memory of her parents. They died in a winter plane crash when she was fifteen."

# 14

Catelyn Zahn and Tori Hjelle shared an apartment halfway between Highway 35W and Shakopee in Savage, a suburb on the southern border of the Twin Cities metropolitan area. Quinn parked at the apartment complex. He'd arranged to meet Cate before she headed to her job as an RN at nearby Fairview Hospital. Two squat buildings faced each other across a wide parking lot split by a row of small trees. He headed to the building on the left, found Hjelle and Zahn listed on the call panel, and buzzed the apartment.

The apartment was on the third of five floors and faced the parking lot. He knocked and held his badge in front of the peephole. Cate opened the door after the clunk of the deadbolt and the jingle of the chain. She gestured for him to enter, then closed the door and reset the deadbolt. She lowered her head as if embarrassed. "Sorry. Habit. I grew up in Northeast."

Northeast Minneapolis, Quinn mentally filled in. Not the best representation of the Twin Cities. Four wooden chairs surrounded a tiny kitchen table decorated with a vase of artificial daffodils. He accepted her offer of a chair at the table and a cup of fresh coffee. She handed him a mug emblazoned with Goldie the Gopher, the University of Minnesota mascot, before she sat across from him.

The coffee was better than he anticipated, or maybe he was just that tired. Cate, already dressed in cheery snowman-covered scrubs for work, sipped her own coffee. Quinn hadn't expected a young African-American woman. He must have stared a moment too long, because she smiled thinly. "I'm adopted, to answer your first question."

"I'm sorry, I didn't mean ..."

"No one does, but they all wonder, and the more insensitive ones ask outright. What did she do now?"

Her question threw Quinn for a moment. It was the same question he'd noted earlier. "Why do you ask?"

"You're a cop," Cate said, "and you're looking for her. It isn't the first time she's gotten into trouble with the law, but it's been a while."

He hadn't taken the time to look up any arrest record on Tori Hjelle. "Why do you think Tori's in trouble?"

"You're a cop asking questions. Tori has a history of ... being hard on people. She's been good for a while, but she's relapsed before."

It was the first time he'd heard that about anyone. "What do you mean?"

She tunneled fingers through her hair, allowing the black curls to stretch, then snap back like a phone cord. "After her folks died, she changed. She's always been a little spoiled as an only child, but after the accident, it was like she tried to share her anger with everyone else."

"Can you give me some examples?"

Cate blew out a breath. "She never met a good time she didn't like. She partied. After the accident, she started hitting the college parties. She used to brag about spiking the drinks of designated drivers with Everclear, and convincing people who were already drunk to take Ecstasy."

Quinn remembered his own college experience with Everclear, a potent grain alcohol, during a short-lived run of partying during his first year at St. Cloud State University. Those were the first and last Jell-O shots he'd ever had. He hadn't eaten Jell-O since.

"She got arrested one year when the cops raided a party. Her aunt and uncle put her in a program after that. She got better for a while, otherwise I wouldn't have let her move in." Cate stared at the coffee left in her mug. "She's been doing good since ..." she mumbled. "Did she get anyone hurt?"

"No, Miss Zahn. Tori's body was found late last night. I'm sorry for your loss."

He didn't expect her reaction. She nodded, lips pressed into a thin line. "Do her aunt and uncle know? They raised her—tried to—after her folks died." Cate shook her head. "Her mom's sister. Her dad was my uncle," she said, heading off Quinn's next question.

Quinn turned to a fresh page in his notepad. "Not yet. Can I get their contact information from you?"

Cate recited the information. "What happened to her? I mean, if the cops are asking questions."

"Did she have problems with anyone at the airport?"

Cate didn't answer. Quinn prodded. "She worked as a ramp agent for Range Airlines, right?"

"Part-time, yes."

"Did she ever mention any problems with other ramp agents?"

She toyed with her coffee cup. "What happened to her?"

"Someone killed her, I believe on airport grounds. Who did she have problems with?"

Cate checked her watch. "I've got to get going, or I'll be late for my shift." She stood and dumped her remaining coffee into the sink.

"Miss Zahn, someone killed your cousin. I need to find out who it might be. You mentioned her boyfriend."

"Peter Manelli. They've been together for about six months, I think. He's a vehicle mechanic for Castor Aviation Services, helped her get the internship there. He'd never hurt her."

*That's what they all think.* That belief often turned out to be wrong. "So, she worked part-time at Range Air as a ramp agent, and worked somewhere else besides going to school?"

"She was interning as a bookkeeper at Castor."

Quinn added a note. "How long did she work there?"

"Four, maybe five months, I think."

"What about school?"

"She is—was a grad student majoring in accounting at the University of Minnesota." She checked her watch. "I'm sorry, I have to get going."

He handed her his business card. "Is there a good time in the next day or so we can talk more about Tori?"

Cate slipped the card into her pocket. "Sure. Just call. I've got classes tomorrow all day at the U."

"You never answered my question. Who did she have problems with at the airport?"

She met his gaze with brown ones full of regret. "What does it matter? She's dead."

"I need a name, Miss Zahn. Please."

"Sierra Bauer."

# 15

Sierra claimed she hadn't worked at the gate for a couple years, and didn't know any ramp agents. Quinn sat in his SUV outside the apartment building and tried to recall her demeanor when he asked. She had hesitated before answering. Her reaction didn't set off his internal bullshit detector, nor did he get the sense she was hiding anything from him.

She couldn't have had anything to do with Tori's death. There was no way she could lift the body into the hell-hole.

Unless someone helped her.

Did he miss something because he was attracted to her? He shivered despite the hot air blasting from the vents. Cate refused to tell him the rest of the story before she left, insisting it would take too long and she couldn't afford to be late. He managed to set up another interview with her tomorrow at the University of Minnesota's Twin Cities campus.

Who else could tell him the story? Last night Lowell Hinckley mentioned a fatal plane crash that had resulted in an FAA investigation into Sierra Bauer. Hinckley seemed to have a major issue with women in general, and Sierra in particular. He needed to take anything Hinckley said with a healthy dose of salt, but something like an FAA investigation had to be considered no matter the outcome. She still worked as a mechanic, so whatever her involvement, she'd been cleared.

He had known Sierra for less than twenty-four hours. When he met her, she sparked an interest he hadn't felt in over a year. He welcomed those feelings; he'd been numb for too long. His marriage hadn't had that kind of intensity even in the beginning. What did he really know about her? She had worked as an aircraft mechanic for four years at Range Airlines. Had worked at the gate before going to the night shift. She was run-qualified on Dash-8s, specialized in propeller and associated systems, and had a temper. She liked Garfield and Calvin and Hobbes, put her eggs on her hash browns, and didn't worry about her hat messing up her hair.

Bottom line, he didn't know much. His experience with his ex-wife taught him to be wary about trusting another woman. Did he know Sierra enough to trust her?

❖ ❖ ❖

A GLANCE AT THE DASHBOARD CLOCK told him it was mid-afternoon, and over twelve hours since he'd been called to the scene of a dead body in an airplane. Quinn parked at the curb in front of the address Cate gave him for Tori's boyfriend, Peter Manelli. This house matched the others lining the street, dating from the end of WWII when the rapid influx of GIs returning home prompted a flurry of construction in all parts of the country. The tiny post-war bungalows with postage stamp lawns were designed to be afford-able and comfortable for a couple before family expansion required more space.

These days, the vintage homes were more suited to retirees downsizing after the kids left home and started families of their own. He walked past a construction dumpster on the front lawn to steps covered by an awning. He pressed the doorbell, but didn't hear any chimes. He pulled off a glove and knocked instead.

A loud bang from behind the door startled him. He put a hand on his gun and stepped to the side.

The door opened. A man about Quinn's age sucked on the side of a finger. Sawdust covered his beard. Quinn showed his badge and introduced himself. "I'm looking for Peter Manelli."

The man wiped his finger on his threadbare flannel shirt. "Why?"

"I need to ask him some questions about Tori Hjelle."

He narrowed his eyes. "Pete's not here. I'm his brother, Tom. What about Tori?"

"Do you know where Pete is or when he'll be back?"

"He in trouble? 'Cause Pete doesn't get into trouble. Neither does Tori."

"Do you mind if I come in for a few minutes?"

Tom Manelli peered at his badge before stepping back from the threshold. "Don't mind the mess. Watch that hole," he said, pointing toward a foot square void in the barren floor. A pair of sawhorses in the middle of the room held an old door as a makeshift table. Exposed studs and wiring formed walls to his left. Rolls of fiberglass insulation were stacked nearby.

Quinn decided standing would be a better idea than navigating through the obstacle course of sheetrock and assorted boards. "Do you know how I can get in touch with Pete?"

"He should be at work. Have you checked there?"

"Not yet. Is he working at Castor Aviation?"

At Tom's nod, Quinn made a note. "When was the last time you saw him?"

"What day is it? Wednesday? Saw him Monday. We finished the subfloor." He pointed at their feet.

"Did you talk to him yesterday?"

Tom crossed beefy arms on his chest. "Yeah, but just in the morning. Figured he stayed with Tori last night and headed to work from her place."

"Have you seen or spoken to your brother since yesterday morning?"

Silence. "Why?"

"What about his girlfriend?" Quinn asked. "When was the last time you spoke to her?"

"Tori? I answered the phone when she called on Sunday. We were watching the game. The Stars finished a penalty shot when she called."

"What time was that?"

"Shit, I don't know. Game started at seven. It was still the first period."

"Do you know why she called?"

Time ticked by. Quinn reminded himself to be quiet. Silence encouraged people to talk, if only to fill the air with noise.

"Pete said she called to tell him she was working late, and she wanted to talk to him at work the next day."

Something in his voice stirred Quinn's cop sense. "It sounds like either Pete or you weren't exactly excited to hear that."

Tom gathered up pieces of two-by-four boards littering the floor under the table. "She works second shift at Range Airlines. Sometimes it gets late."

Quinn waited, but Tom didn't continue. "Does your brother have problems working with Tori at Castor? Sometimes people in a relationship can't work together."

"No," Tom said, "that part is fine. He's a mechanic in the garage, she works in the business office in the hangar, so they don't see each other much during the days they're both working."

When he didn't add more, Quinn continued. "What bothered Pete about the call?"

"A couple months ago, Tori started talking about finding stuff in the books that would work great for her dissertation. Pete was worried she'd get fired if she put company information in her paper without permission. Every time he asked her if she was allowed to use it she shut him down."

*Interesting.* "Did he ever find out what she was talking about?"

"Not that I know of. A few weeks ago she started talking about setting the record straight and bringing them down. She was, like, joking, but one night Pete came home seriously pissed. He called her up and begged her to 'stop poking the bear.'"

"When was that?"

"I don't know, maybe last week." Tom paused. "Does this have something to do with Tori?"

Quinn knew better than to add fuel to Tom's suspicions. "How long has Pete been seeing Tori?"

"About six months, I suppose. Is my brother in trouble?"

"No." Not yet, Quinn thought. "Did you ever hear Pete or Tori mention the name Bauer?"

"Bauer? Nope. Why?"

"No reason." He gave Tom his card. "Tell your brother to call me."

❖  ❖  ❖

BACK AT THE APD OFFICE, Quinn added the information he'd learned to his makeshift "murder board". He added Cate Zahn and Peter Manelli to the "known associates" column, but refused to move Sierra's name to the list of suspects. Not yet, he thought. He wanted to talk to her first. He called Sierra, expecting her machine to answer since it was around four o'clock and she said she'd be sleeping for a few hours. When it did, he left a terse message to call him.

He had a few names, a minimal timeline, and far too many questions without answers.

He had a possible motive. If Tori told her boyfriend what she'd found, such as possible accounting errors, did she tell anyone else? Would that warrant killing her?

He needed to talk to the boyfriend and her boss at Castor Aviation. He needed to talk to Tori's adviser about her paper.

What was Sierra's part in all this?

"Are you still here?"

Quinn turned to find Kevin Vierling staring at the board, hands on hips, lips pursed. He glanced at the clock. Kevin's twelve-hour shift ended a few hours ago. "Me? You shoulda been out of here at noon."

"Yeah, well, someone asked about traces at the Range Air gate."

"There's more than one team around, Kev. What did Jaylynn say when you told her you were getting home late?"

"She said I'd better bring home her favorite wine and Godiva chocolate." Kevin's gaze tracked to him, and a frown took over his face. "Dammit, Quinn, when are you going to learn you have to sleep sometime? Those bags under your eyes look like eye black gone bad."

The mention of fatigue seemed to call it forth. The four hours of sleep he'd managed before the call to Range Air were long gone. Whatever energy had been fueling Quinn to this point abruptly vanished. He stuffed his hands into his pockets and dropped into his chair, which protested with a squeak. "When would you suggest I catch winks?"

The crime scene tech rested a hip on a corner of the desk. "Before you hurt yourself or someone else because you can't stay awake." He glanced at his watch. "You're going home tonight, right? To *sleep*," he added in a scolding tone.

Quinn leaned his head back and closed his eyes. For just a moment he began to drift, his mind carried aloft by fatigue. Then the image of a frozen body with a cracked skull in a maintenance bay interrupted the bliss. He leaned on the desk, chin in palms, elbows making indents on the blotter. He scrubbed at his face with his hands. "I can't sleep."

"Bullshit." Kevin leaned over him, cornrow braids dangling forward. "I'm going to let Chief Unger know you need to take a day."

"You know why I don't sleep very well."

"So you decide not to sleep at all? That just ain't healthy. You can't keep this up and you know it. It's been over a year since your divorce. I know your ex did a number on you. Get over it." He threw his hands up and sighed. "What good is being your friend if you aren't going to listen to me?"

"I was listening."

"To which part? The sleep part or your bitch ex-wife part?"

"Both. It was nice of you to stop by," Quinn said, hoping he didn't sound as irritated as he felt. "Did you want something?"

"Besides to chew your ass for not taking care of yourself? Yeah. Went to the gate where the plane was parked. The place is nothing but asphalt coated with de-ice fluid. There's nothing out there. Same with the two dozen pieces of equipment we tested. I'll send the report in tomorrow." He pointed at the board. "This your witness?" he asked, pointing to Sierra's name.

"She found the body."

"She knew the victim?" Kevin pointed to the notes Quinn had just added to the board. "Why isn't she in the list of suspects?"

Quinn rocked in his chair. Bushings squeaked. "She's not involved. There's no way she could lift a body into the maintenance bay."

Kevin turned to him, hands on hips. "She could've had help."

"Why are you so interested?"

Kevin held up his hands in surrender. "Just looking at the puzzle pieces. I wanted to check on you, then I'm going home."

"Gee, thanks, Mom." Quinn knew his friend meant well, and was actually glad Kevin stopped by to deliver the update. "I wasn't sure we'd find anything." He checked his watch, then gauged the length of the report he still needed to write. "And before you go off on another mothering binge, I will head home to get some sleep after I finish my report. Happy?"

Kevin leaned toward him, peering between narrowed lids. "I'm not sure I believe you. You're lucky Jaylynn isn't here." He straightened. "Don't make me send my wife to your house. She's a force of nature when it comes to mothering. Why do you think I always look so refreshed?" He flipped his braids over a shoulder and sashayed to the door. "Promise me you'll sleep."

Quinn couldn't help the smile that stretched across his face. "I promise."

# 16

When Sierra woke from her nap, the clock told her she had slept longer than she anticipated. Working third shift was tricky that way. On the first day of the work week, a late afternoon nap allowed her to stay alert through the shift. On the last day, an early morning nap kept her from wandering through the day like a zombie, but too much sleep meant a restless night.

Having gotten little to no sleep this morning after she'd been sent home from work meant she'd been tired and downright bitchy by the time she finished helping Moore. Maybe the enthusiastic swimming at the Y helped extend her nap, because she didn't remember tossing and turning. She'd been exhausted enough to fall asleep and escape the assault of nightmares that had no shortage of fuel.

After six hours of sleep, she still didn't feel rested. Grogginess dulled her mind, as if every thought had to shove its way through a viscous fog. She stared at the Mason jar filled with homemade cocoa mix on the kitchen counter and debated a mug of hot chocolate-flavored caffeine even though it was after seven. If she wanted to adjust her sleep schedule for the weekend, she needed to be able to sleep tonight. No cocoa, but mint tea would work just as well.

While she waited for her tea to steep, she noticed the message light on her answering machine blinking. She pressed the play button.

Her sister had left a message to call her back. About what, Sierra didn't know because the tape took that opportunity to snap. Again. Crap. Sierra pushed the stop button, opened the cover, and ejected the microcassette. The damn thing had ruined three cassettes in the past three months. She should have asked for a new machine for Christmas.

She swapped out the microcassette with her last good one before she called her parents. Her sister answered, and after a rushed five-minute conversation during which Sierra promised to play taxi driver early tomorrow, her mother got on the line.

For the next hour Sierra listened to family updates, from her Grandma Schumacher's trip through Scandinavia with her great-aunt, to Uncle Cam's frustration-filled house-building adventure, to the day-by-day itinerary for her parents' upcoming trip to Iceland. Sierra finally convinced her mom that any more information would have to wait until she'd gotten more sleep.

She hung up the phone and noticed Moore's card in the dish on the counter. Had he figured out who she found in the hell-hole yet? He had asked if she knew any ramp agents. She told him she hadn't worked at the gate for a couple years, so no, she didn't know any rampies.

Mostly true, she thought.

It wasn't until Moore said the body wore a Range Air ramp agent uniform that she realized where she had seen the ring in the picture. She was now almost certain the ring matched the one Sierra remembered on the woman's index finger. That night had been one of many she had picked her brother up from whatever club, bar, or party Tori coaxed him into. Sierra had dragged Ken by the arm toward the exit. Tori tried to stop her. She remembered shoving the woman back. She'd seen the ring when Tori accidentally scratched the back of her hand. Cate arrived just in time to steer her cousin away from Sierra.

Cate had tried. Sierra had tried. But they couldn't convince Tori and Ken to part ways. She tried to protect her big brother like he had protected her when they were kids, but nothing she did had been enough to save him.

After doctoring her tea, she lingered in the kitchen, taking in the crisp scent of mint. Part of her wanted to feel guilty for hoping the dead woman was Tori. The part of her that still mourned for her brother felt she deserved it for what she did to Ken.

Guilt rose to chastise her. No one deserved to die that way.

She headed into the living room and settled cross-legged onto the couch. Why bother to shove a body into a plane's maintenance bay? If the victim wore a rampie uniform, it stood to reason she was killed on the airport grounds. The airport must cover over three thousand acres of land. Lots of room to hide a body where no one would find it.

Whoever loaded that body onto her inspection plane must have AOA security clearance—permission to be in the Airport Operations Area with access to the aircraft. She had a red badge, the second highest clearance at the MSP airport, since working in the AOA was her job. Anyone who received a badge, especially a higher-clearance one, went through a background check, but that wouldn't prevent a psychopath who had never crossed the law from getting a badge.

When she thought about it, a lot of people were cleared to work in the AOA besides mechanics: pilots, ramp agents, and people like fuel truck drivers or emergency personnel like firefighters. Enough people that statistically at least a couple might have some sort of police record. That presented a wider field of possible culprits than she expected.

It all came down to the hell-hole. Who would know about it? Mechanics, and anyone who saw a mechanic climb into the hell-hole would know it's there. Pilots, probably. Maybe rampies.

Pilots wouldn't bother; it's not dirty in the hell-hole, but it isn't clean. Would a rampie bother? She thought for a moment. If a rampie killed someone and wanted to stash the body on a plane, they would likely go the easier route and leave the body in the cabin. Maybe even set it up in the back row like the person was sleeping, *Weekend at Bernie's* style.

A mechanic would be the most logical suspect. A mechanic would have time and opportunity. The last guy at the gate would be alone once his fellow mechanics taxied the inspection planes back to the hangar. He could use a company vehicle parked at the gate to go back to the hangar after he stuffed a body into one of the planes parked overnight at the gate. No one would find the body right away, either.

During the shift-rotation phase of her first year probation period at Range Air, she worked with almost every mechanic at one time or another. She couldn't think of a single one who would kill, but then again, people tended to be on better behavior at work.

Were any of the second-shift mechanics seeing any rampies? She had to believe there was at least one; most of the rampies were college students taking advantage of the flight benefits that came with working for an airline, and half were women. Working on third shift meant she didn't hear most of the gossip of who was seeing who. She could call Warren; he would know, and would tell her if she asked.

The ringing phone jolted her. She headed to the kitchen to answer it.

"Hello."

Silence.

"Hello," she repeated.

She heard the soft rasp of breathing. Hairs on the back of her neck stood straight.

"Hello?"

A low chuckle sent chills down her spine.

She slammed the receiver down. *It can't be him.* She had an unlisted number. Maybe it was some kids pranking random numbers. It'd been months since she'd gotten the letter. He hadn't appeared on her radar.

She checked the deadbolt on the door, turned off the light in the living room, then peered around the edge of the blinds covering the sliding door overlooking the parking lot. A scan of the lot, absent of any black pickup trucks, didn't reassure her.

She backed away from the window. Turned the lights back on. Checked the locks, the doors, the closets. She was alone.

The phone rang again. She swore, muscles rigid under the electric spell of adrenaline. Another ring. *Don't pick it up.* Another. She held her breath when the machine interrupted the next ring.

Silence. Then a low, harsh whisper.

"Did you miss me?"

# 17

Early the next morning, as the sun started to lighten the sky, she pulled into her parents' yard. Skeletal hedges and naked trees surrounded the remodeled farmhouse like a palisade. She grew up on the hobby farm, all five acres of it, south of Prior Lake and thirty miles outside the southern suburban border of the Twin Cities metro area. Sierra yawned again and tried not to grumble. Her offer to serve as her younger sister's chauffeur meant her parents didn't have to coordinate between their jobs and taking Kara to her University of Minnesota campus tour. It was less an issue of Kara getting there on her own, and more an issue of lack of transportation.

Instead of a restful night, Sierra had spent the time wondering where he was, how he found her phone number, and if he knew where she lived. Maybe she should have called Detective Moore, but she couldn't let her ex control her again. She had lived in fear six years ago and didn't want to go back. By morning she had talked herself into a sense of empowerment. Unfortunately, that process didn't foster anything like good sleep. Or memory, she realized with a yawn. She made a mental note to contact the phone company—during business hours, of course—to get a new unlisted number.

*I wish Ken was here.* After the attack, her brother spent almost a week at the hospital with her despite the reprimand he received from his superior officer.

His dog tag hung on her chest under her sweater, a talisman against the past, the first time she had worn it since the day she and her family spread his ashes on Kendrick Peak north of Flagstaff.

Before Sierra shut her car off, Kara bounded down the steps of the front deck, flaxen ponytail flying behind her. She skidded to the passenger door, wrenched it open, and leaped into the seat. She slammed the door closed, panting to catch her breath.

"Come on, let's go before Mom lectures me to death on campus safety."

Sierra grinned as she backed up and then headed down the drive. "You told her the tour was a group thing, right? And she knows I'll be there."

Her sister stared at her, eyes wide. "You are so not coming on the tour with me. Gawd, that's almost as embarrassing as having Mom or Dad there. Sheesh, I'm almost eighteen. I think I can go on a campus tour by myself."

Kara Bauer was light where Sierra was dark, her blond hair reaching past her shoulders. She had inherited their mother's green eyes along with the pale spot above her left ear, and was an inch taller than her older sister despite being eight years younger. She flipped the shade down to check her face in the mirror, then looked at Sierra. "Can you see my bruise?"

Sierra glanced over. Kara was wearing more makeup than usual, she noted, especially around her eye. "Right eye? From the basketball game the other night?"

"No, Elia's bony elbow from practice yesterday. I wish Coach would keep her on the outside for three-pointers. She's the best at those. Leave the layups to the rest of us."

"What's the plan?"

"We're all supposed to meet at Coffman Union, then we're heading to the engineering buildings. Through the tunnels, I think. I hope."

"How did you manage to get excused from your classes today?"

"Guidance counselor. There's a bunch of us doing campus tours today, but not all at the U of M." Kara pulled a sheet of paper from the folder she carried. "First the boring part, then the fun part. It should only be a few hours. You wanna stick around for lunch? We can eat in the food service area. Dad said they used to have really good Jell-O salad when he and Mom went there, with fresh strawberries and real whipped cream, not Cool Whip. Of course, that was a million years ago."

"Oh, gee, can we?" Sierra said with a healthy dose of sarcasm. She could drop her sister off, not pay for parking, and drive all the way back to the U when the tour was over, or she could use the wait to finish reading her current book and start another. She also brought her sketchpad in case she needed the distraction. Sketching landscapes had started as part of her therapy after she stopped journaling, and she continued the relaxing practice.

She navigated the never-ending road construction to the parking ramp near Coffman Union, the student union building. Kara headed to her tour group, leaving her older sister to find a seat to warm in a coffee shop at Coffman Union. Sierra found a booth in a corner and put her back to the wall, a good vantage from which she could watch everyone who walked past, a self-preservation habit she developed six years ago to keep her safe. And sane.

❖ ❖ ❖

QUINN FINISHED SORTING HIS NOTES and stifled a yawn. Last evening, after compiling the notes from his interview with Cate Zahn, reviewing the medical examiner's interim report of his victim, and finishing his own reports, he'd headed home. He managed to work in a shower and a quick meal of leftover takeout pizza before crashing. Sleep pulled him under as soon as his head hit the pillow.

He woke too soon; six hours of sleep wasn't much after a twenty-hour day, but his brain wouldn't settle enough to let him go back to sleep. Sierra Bauer occupied his mind all the way to the office this morning. He yearned to wrap her around him, wrap himself around her. He wondered what she smelled like. Tasted like. What did she do on her days off? Was she seeing anyone? Even knowing she might play a bigger part in this case didn't stifle the anticipation.

Ethics dictated he finish the case before he even consider asking her out. *If she's innocent.* Why hadn't Sierra mentioned she knew a ramp agent? What problems did Tori Hjelle have with her?

He rubbed his eyes before he reviewed his notes from yesterday's interviews, then added questions to his list for Cate Zahn before he contacted Tori's graduate adviser to set up an interview. He grabbed his travel mug, filled it with questionable coffee from the break room, and left for the U of M campus.

❖ ❖ ❖

DR. MOSKRIM BARUTHA LOOKED UP FROM HIS SEAT behind his desk when Quinn knocked on the door jamb. He badged the professor and sat in the visitor's chair. Barutha tapped a stack of papers into order and set them aside. "I've looked up Tori Hjelle's records. I'm not sure what you need, Detective. It's a shock when someone young dies, even more so when it seems that death was by violence."

"How do you know it was by violence?"

The professor raised his hands with palms up as if offering assurance. "Why else would a police officer want to ask about her?"

Quinn pulled out his notebook. "Her cousin said she was interning with a fixed-base operation at the airport. What do you know about that?"

Barutha leaned back in his chair, elbows on the armrests, fingers steepled. "When she mentioned interning at the airport, I wasn't sure it would help her with her paper. My fears were unfounded."

"What was her paper about?"

"Forensic accounting. She was researching the differences between a franchised FBO—fixed-base operation—and a small, family-owned operation. As I recall, she worked a few summers for her grandfather at a little airport near Duluth."

"Did you meet with her about her progress?"

"Of course." Barutha rested his arms on the desk and leaned forward. "I had to remind her to stay focused. She worked two jobs besides her graduate studies. She did extra research she didn't need to do. Mistakes are made when exhaustion dulls the senses."

I can relate, Quinn thought, and hid a yawn behind a hand. "When did you last meet with her?"

The professor tapped a few keys on his computer. "Two months ago, before Thanksgiving." He peered at the screen. "No, wait. She canceled that meeting. The last I spoke with her about her thesis was last October."

Quinn added to his notes. "How often do you meet with your grad students?"

"I try to meet with them about once a month."

"So, if she canceled the meeting in November, did you reschedule it for December before Christmas break?"

Barutha shook his head. "I never meet with grad students in December. There are too many other things going on, finals and such."

"What about this month?" Quinn asked.

More taps on the keyboard. "Nothing scheduled for this month. I was expecting her to contact me for another meeting by the end of the week, otherwise I would have reached out to her."

"Do you have a copy of her thesis? Maybe an early draft?"

"I'm sorry, Detective. I don't review drafts. My students are required to turn in a detailed outline that lays out the direction their research will take them. If you are looking for specifics about her research, the outline won't help you."

Quinn's final few questions didn't enlighten him any further. He thanked the professor for his time, then headed down Northrup Mall to Coffman

Union, where he would meet with Cate Zahn. The wide open space between the stately, columned buildings lining the Mall was buried under two feet of snow. Most of the metro area and part of Wisconsin was under a Winter Weather Warning in anticipation of another major storm rolling into the Twin Cities tonight. A glance at the steel-gray clouds didn't hint at how bad this storm would be. The forecast predicted everything from three inches to a foot or more.

It was January in Minnesota after all. He supposed he should be thankful they hadn't had a repeat of the '91 Halloween blizzard. It took a lot to shut down a northern city like Minneapolis in the winter, but two and a half feet of snow in less than twenty-four hours did a pretty good job of it. He checked his watch as he climbed the wide stairs to Coffman Union, the student services headquarters of the U's East Bank campus.

Inside the Union, he passed a table manned by a trio of students taking sign-ups for seats at President Clinton's upcoming inaugural address, courtesy of a student political club. He remembered those days of young fervor. He'd even done some fundraising for the Love Canal families President Carter hadn't relocated.

Quinn made his way to the coffee shop to meet Cate. He pulled off his hat and gloves while he scanned the tables and chairs arranged around the …

*What is* she *doing here?*

# 18

Sierra Bauer sat at a table with Cate, the two having an animated discussion that appeared more intense than cordial. Cate's voice held a note of pleading edged with regret. Sierra shook her head, her voice sounding stern with an apologetic tone.

Their obvious disagreement didn't prevent Sierra's mere presence from sending his pulse on a sprint.

When Sierra noticed him, her eyes locked with his, and she stilled, a faint smile tracing her lips until Cate nudged her, drawing her attention from him.

This is professional, he reminded himself. She knew the victim, and from the sound of it, the victim had issues with her. Or did Sierra have the issues? He focused on the case and the questions he needed to ask so by the time he reached their table he was back to being an impartial detective.

Sierra stood, extended a hand. "Detective Moore. Cate said she was meeting you here."

Quinn clasped her hand in his and felt his temperature rise until his coat became stifling. "Miss Bauer. Miss Zahn didn't mention she was meeting you here."

Her hand slipped from his after a moment's hesitation. "We didn't plan this. I'm here with my sister. My grandfather is replacing the heater core in Kara's car, she's on a campus tour, our parents are working, I've got the day off, and I have a vehicle. Hence, chauffeur."

Quinn shook Cate's hand in greeting. "Is this still a good time to talk?"

Cate gestured to an empty chair at their table. "Sure. I didn't know Sierra would be here either. We haven't seen each other since—" Her voice trailed off. She sent a sideways glance Sierra's way.

"I should have kept in touch, Cate. Give me a call sometime and we can catch up." Sierra tucked a sketchbook into a black backpack. "I'll leave you guys alone. Cate said you had more questions about the case, and she's only got an hour until her next class."

"No," Quinn said. He wanted to gauge her reaction when he asked Cate about Tori's problem with Sierra. "You're already involved in the case. Maybe you'll think of something else that will help."

Her expression soured. "I don't think that would be a good idea, Detective." She turned to Cate. "I don't blame you. I never have." She swung her backpack onto a shoulder and nodded to Quinn. "I suppose I'll be hearing from you after you're finished here."

"Cate told you the victim was her cousin, Tori," he said.

"Yes, she did. And she'll tell you the part of the story she knows." Her eyes started to glisten before she left.

Cate stared at her coffee. "Is she a suspect?" Her voice sounded listless and forlorn.

"Should she be?"

"I don't know," she said. "She hated Tori. Still does, even though she's dead."

Quinn readied his pen and pad. "Tell me why."

"She blames Tori for her brother's death."

He lowered his pen. Of all the reasons people killed for, love topped a list along with greed and power. If Sierra blamed Tori for her brother's death, she had a motive.

"What happened to her brother?"

"He died in a plane crash last year. When they investigated the crash, the FAA determined it was caused by pilot error. They found a blood alcohol level of point zero four."

"That's under the legal limit, even for aviation."

"And they found traces of Ecstasy in his blood."

He made a note to look up the FAA report on Ken Bauer's accident. "So, he might've been under the influence. Why would she blame Tori for that?"

Cate played with the cup of coffee in front of her. Silence tainted with regret swelled between them. "How much of the story do you want right now, Detective? It's a long one. I'm not sure an hour is enough."

It wasn't the answer he expected. "Give me the Cliff Notes version, enough to explain why Sierra blames Tori for her brother's death."

She sighed. "I told you yesterday about Tori, the types of things she used to do." After he nodded, she continued. "She met Ken at a holiday party Range Airlines held for the ramp agents, mechanics, and pilots. Sierra brought her brother as her guest. Since she had just moved in with me, Tori brought me as her guest."

"Did Tori know Sierra before the party?"

"I don't think so. She caught sight of Ken, though. They hit it off, and that's when Tori and Sierra met. It's the first time I met Sierra."

"Did they get along?"

Cate shrugged. "I guess. They were cordial, anyway. Sierra and I got along better than she did with Tori."

"Did Tori date Ken?"

"They started dating after the party. I suppose it was a few months later that things started getting weird. Ken didn't drink much, at least at first, but I think Tori encouraged him. After the first couple of months, he started calling Sierra to pick him up from wherever he and Tori were. Sometimes she'd drop Tori off at the apartment on her way home. If she's living in the same place, she's only about five miles away."

Quinn saw the bigger picture. "So, Sierra thought Tori was corrupting her brother?"

"She told me about the stuff Ken did in high school, how he went into the Air Force to get away from that scene, and why he was staying with her instead of with her folks. She tried to convince him to stop seeing Tori. I tried to get Tori to break things off. She'd gotten better for a while, otherwise I wouldn't have let her move in with me. Ken was a pilot, and maybe he reminded her of her dad and his plane crash, and maybe she went through all that anger again. I don't know. It seemed like she made it her mission to see how far down she could bring him.

"One night, Ken and Tori somehow made it back to our place. He could barely walk straight, and Tori wasn't much better. I called Sierra to take him home. God, it must've been two or three in the morning. Sierra showed up, took one look at Ken, and laid into Tori. She was furious. I couldn't calm her down. She shoved Tori. I know Sierra isn't a violent person, but her temper ..."

"Sierra physically threatened Tori?"

Cate nodded. "I think she would've thrown some punches if I hadn't been there. I got her to back off, and we managed to get Ken to her car. She warned Tori to stay away from her brother."

Quinn had been certain Sierra couldn't possibly be the person who cracked

Tori Hjelle's skull, but now? Doubt started creeping in. He knew she must be stronger than her petite frame suggested. As a mechanic, she'd be required to lift parts that weighed at least forty or fifty pounds on a regular basis. "What happened after that?"

"Ken left for his buddy's wedding in Colorado the next day. He never made it. Sierra blamed Tori."

"Did you talk to Sierra after that night?" Quinn asked.

"I tried to. At Ken's memorial service. No matter what I said, or how much I tried to apologize, she ignored me."

"Did Tori go to the memorial service?"

Silence. "No. I convinced her not to go because of what had happened that night." Cate looked up from her coffee, eyes moist. "After Ken died, Tori changed. It was like she finally realized what she'd been doing. Guilt, I suppose. She wanted to apologize to Sierra, to her family. Maybe I should have let her go." She shook her head. "Looking back, it was for the best."

"Why do you say that?"

Cate hesitated, as though weighing the consequences of her answer. "Before I left the memorial service, Sierra gave me a message for Tori.

"She said if she ever saw Tori again, she'd kill her."

# 19

Sierra Bauer had a strong motive to kill Tori. Hell, he probably would've wanted to kill her if she had done the same sort of thing to one of his brothers.

Sierra said Cate would tell him the part of the story she knew. He wondered what Cate didn't know. He checked his watch, then switched gears.

"What about her internship?"

"She worked part-time at Castor Aviation. She was using her experience there and from when she worked for Grandpa for her thesis. I remember a month ago or so—around Christmas, I think—when she mentioned she'd come across some weird stuff at work, and she needed to talk to Grandpa about it."

"Was she having problems with someone there?"

"None she ever talked about. We didn't see each other much. With school and work schedules, we probably only saw each other an hour or two a day except on weekends. Even then, she spent time with Pete and I spend time with Brent."

"Brent who?"

"Andrews. He's in med school, but thinking about going toward a nurse practitioner degree instead of an MD. It's cheaper and doesn't take as long."

"Do you know if anyone has notified Tori's boyfriend about her death? I haven't been able to reach him."

"I tried calling him after I found out. I left a message for him to call me, but I haven't heard from him yet." Cate checked her watch and got to her feet. "I'm sorry, Detective, but I've got class across campus."

He stood and handed her another business card. "Call me when you hear from Pete."

She nodded, gathered her backpack, and hustled out of the coffee shop.

Awkward silence filled in behind her. Quinn headed to the counter to order some coffee, relishing the opportunity to drink something not only palatable, but good. The implications of what Cate told him swirled in his head like papers caught in a gusty wind. He struggled to gather those bits and put them into an order that matched what he knew about Sierra so far.

A young woman approaching the entrance to the coffee shop caught his attention. She wore a University of Minnesota hooded sweatshirt, torn jeans, and combat boots that were the style these days. Her coat hung over one arm along with a folder sporting the university's maroon and gold "M". Her hair was gathered into a blond ponytail, but Quinn noticed a white spot above her left ear. Her facial structure matched Sierra's, with rounder features and a little more height. The skin around her right eye was a shade darker than the rest.

She stopped and scanned the coffee shop. He went up to her. "Excuse me, are you Sierra Bauer's sister?"

Her whole body stiffened. "Who are you?"

He showed his badge. "Detective Moore, Airport Police."

Suspicion filled her eyes. "Sure, you are."

"Sierra left when I arrived here to talk to Cate Zahn. Do you know her?"

Suspicion turned to recognition. "Cate Zahn? She was, like, my brother's girlfriend's cousin or something. I only met her once, at the memorial service."

"What about your brother's girlfriend? Did you know her very well?"

She shook her head. "He never brought her home. I've seen some pictures, and I remember some fights between Sierra and Ken about her, but I never met her. Why do you want to know?"

How much should he tell her? "It's for a case I'm working on. Why would Sierra and Ken fight about her?"

Sierra's sister crossed her arms on her chest, eyes narrowed. "Why don't you ask Sierra? Does she know you're asking about Ken's girlfriend?"

He avoided the question. "Why would she fight with your brother about his girlfriend?"

"Sierra didn't like her. Like, at all."

Before he could continue, he noticed Sierra heading toward them, her expression darkening as she approached. She nodded to Quinn in greeting, then focused on her sister. "Are you ready to head out?"

"So, are you going to introduce me to Detective Hottie?"

Sierra glanced at him. "He's too old for you, and I'm sure he's trying to figure out if I killed Tori because I hated her."

"Wait. What? Who got killed? You didn't say anything about—"

"I found Tori's body in an airplane at work."

Kara's eyes widened. "Tori? You mean Ken's girlfriend, Tori? Ohmygod. Are you serious? Did you tell Mom?"

"No, and I'm not going to." Sierra shook a finger at her sister. "And neither are you. Mom and Dad don't need to worry about this, okay? I can't tell them anything yet anyway because I don't know enough about what's going on. Promise me you won't tell them."

Her sister rolled her eyes. "But you will tell them, right?"

"Yes," Sierra said, "but not until he says I can because it's an open case. Detective Moore, this is my sister, Kara. K, this is Detective Moore, but I'm guessing he already introduced himself."

"He did, and he said he talked to Cate Zahn. Did you see her here?"

"Yes." Then, to Quinn, "Kara never met Tori, and doesn't know Cate, so leave her out of it."

"I'm trying to solve a case, Miss Bauer." He cringed inside; he didn't want to continue to address her formally.

He didn't want to investigate her as a possible murder suspect.

Sometimes his job sucked.

Her lips pressed into a thin line. "You got Cate's version of the story, which, I'm sure, included the night I shoved Tori and Cate had to break us up." She didn't wait for him to acknowledge her. "Let me know when you want the rest of the story."

"How about now?"

"Um," Kara interrupted, laying a hand on her sister's arm, "I've got to be at work in a couple hours, and we need to stop at Grandma and Grandpa's house to pick up my car."

"Sorry, Detective," Sierra's voice held an icy edge that made his shoulders tighten, "we'll have to wait to discuss it." She spun on her heel without another word and stormed toward the main entrance of the student union.

Kara sighed. "Sorry about that. I don't know much about what happened to Ken before he left for the Air Force. I was only four or five when he left. When he got out and came back home, he stayed with Sierra while he looked for a job. She was a lot closer to Ken than I was." She glanced in her sister's direction. "Gotta go." She smiled, gave him a small wave, then jogged off.

Quinn watched her long after she disappeared through the main entrance. Not the sister. Sierra.

He zipped his coat, pulled on his hat and gloves, and headed out into the January cold. He had learned enough to warrant putting Sierra Bauer at the top of the suspect column. He needed find out what happened to Ken Bauer, and what Sierra did to warrant the FAA's interest during the investigation. With any luck he would find something that would eliminate her from suspicion in Tori's death.

He knew that the ones closest to the victim often were the most likely to cause them harm. Neither Cate nor the brother had heard from Pete. In Quinn's experience, that meant one of two things: he'd fled, or something happened to him. According to Tom, Pete worked at Castor Aviation. Tori worked at the same fixed-base operation, or FBO.

Snowflakes floated down around him, a portent of the weather to come. Quinn checked his watch and gauged the time against the forecast for the storm. He should have time to stop at Castor Aviation before things got ugly.

# 20

Kara caught up with Sierra as she reached the bottom of the wide stone steps of Coffman Union. "You should ask him out."

Sierra stopped short. "Why?"

"Because he's cute." Kara said, amused. "And you like him."

She hated that her little sister was so observant. Kara put her hands on Sierra's shoulders and shook her. "Come on, he's perfect for you."

"How can you say that? You just met him. He's a cop, and the only reason I'm even talking to him is because I found a dead body in an airplane, and he's working the case." She tried to move forward, but Kara held her back.

"It's been six years since ... You aren't going to find anyone if you don't get back in the pool. Loosen up. Give him a chance." She bent close, green eyes inches from Sierra's. "You like him."

"How do you know I like him?"

"If you didn't like him, you wouldn't have blushed when I called him 'Detective Hottie'. I saw you try not to smile. Is he married? He wasn't wearing a ring."

"He's divorced." She stepped around her sister and continued toward the parking ramp.

Kara matched her stride beside her. "Well, that's good to know, right?"

Sierra knew Kara meant well. Just because the sweet, athletic Kara was dating on a regular basis didn't mean Sierra needed to. "Why do you think I need to date?"

"What are you going to do for the next two days if you're not working? Mope around your apartment? Wouldn't you rather go to dinner and a movie?"

After the phone call last night, staying in her apartment seemed like a safer option than going anywhere with someone she barely knew. "I'm pretty sure cops aren't allowed to get that personal with witnesses, even though I didn't actually see anything. After he talked to Cate, he probably put me on the suspect list. Besides, I just got a new two-thousand piece puzzle."

She couldn't see it, but Sierra knew her sister rolled her eyes. "When was the last time you were out on a date? I mean, more than a one-time dinner-and-a-movie date. C'mon, you're twenty-five. You're not supposed to be at home putting a puzzle together, you're supposed to be going on road trips with a cute guy who makes you feel good."

*Been there. It didn't turn out so well.* The back of her neck started to itch, and she scanned the area. "Why does it matter if I'm dating or not?"

Kara leaned toward her, demeanor sober and serious. "When was the last time you kissed a guy?"

"Why do you care?" she snapped.

Kara smiled, slow and smug. "Come on, after what, almost six years, you haven't kissed anyone. You can't tell me you haven't thought about kissing Mr. Hot Cop at least once."

Sierra's cheeks grew warm. Kara clapped. "Thought so." She looped an arm around Sierra's. "For Pete's sake, he's a *cop*, not some crazy stalker guy. Don't worry, Sis, I can help you out. Just give me Detective Cutie's number. I'll set everything up for you."

Sierra shoved her away. "Knock it off. I'm fine, and so is my love life."

"What love life?"

"Why are you concerned with my non-love life all of a sudden?"

"Because," Kara said as she slid into the passenger seat, "if you start seeing someone, Mom will stop bugging me about finding a steady boyfriend. You know how she gets."

Sierra chuckled as she opened the driver's door. "Yes, I do."

Something dark caught her attention. Anxiety sobered her. She gripped the keys in her hand until they radiated like claws from between her fingers. She scanned the parking ramp for trucks matching the one that passed her on the service road by the hangar.

Kara leaned over. "Hey, what's going on?"

After another look around the parking ramp, Sierra slid into her seat, shut the door, and hit the power locks. They clicked into place.

"Sierra? Are you okay?"

She didn't know how much her parents told her younger sister. Kara had just turned eleven when it happened. An echo of that sharp, excruciating pain flashed through her, dragging that old fear behind it like a plow baring those dark memories to a winter-chilled sky.

*Did you miss me?*

She jumped when Kara touched her hand, and almost failed to stop her reaction.

Kara leaned away from the sharp points of the keys mere inches from her face. She pressed Sierra's hand to the console between the bucket seats. "What the hell?" she hissed.

"Sorry." Her pulse raced. Sierra closed her eyes and tried to slow her breathing.

"What did you see?"

"Nothing," she managed.

Kara glanced around. "Bullshit." She tried to pry the keys from Sierra's hand. "You're freaking out. Let me drive." Her efforts were futile. Working as a mechanic gave Sierra grip strength that didn't falter. "Come on, give them to me."

She snatched her hand away, then shoved the ignition key home. "I'm fine." She started the engine and cranked the heater.

"Mom and Dad told me what happened. I know Ken got in trouble for coming home when he wasn't on leave. I've never seen you act like this, though." Kara stared out the windshield. "Sorry I pushed you about dating."

"That's not why. I thought I saw something. Someone."

"Who? Your ex-boyfriend? Isn't he in jail?"

Sierra hadn't told her parents about the letter; no point in them worrying about it. She knew she was being stubborn: she should tell them—and would, eventually. After the helplessness she felt during the FAA investigation, reinforced by the arrival of the letter, she had to prove to herself she could regain control of her life on her own. Part of conquering her past was being confident enough to handle life's wayward pitches. "There was a black pickup on the service road by the hangar the other night." She struggled to bury the fear that returned like a rabid ghost to haunt her. "Never mind. I'm probably just imagining things."

"You know there's about a hundred of those on the road all the time."

*She's right, and I'm overreacting.* Sierra pulled out of the ramp and headed east toward Interstate 94. She glanced into the rearview mirror.

A black pickup truck left the parking ramp and turned the opposite direction.

# 21

Quinn pulled into a parking spot on the "street side" of the business office, with a view through the fence to the apron where a small jet taxied past. Castor Aviation Services had a large hangar and a smaller garage for the fuel trucks, tugs, and vehicles the company used when providing services such as aircraft fueling, charters, and de-icing to both commercial and general aviation. The main desk boasted half a dozen green plants and a small model of a Learjet on a stand. Comfortable-looking couches provided seating along large windows overlooking the concrete expanse of the apron.

"May I help you?" The receptionist, a willowy red-haired woman with too-dark lipstick, smiled at him.

Quinn showed her his badge, then read her photo ID. "Cherie, I'm looking for Peter Manelli."

"I haven't seen Pete today. I'll call Marshall." She indicated the waiting area. "You can wait there."

Quinn thanked her, then wandered to the bank of windows. Three fuel trucks lined up along one side of the apron. A fourth truck slowed to a stop at the end of the line. The driver headed toward the office through the falling snow. Another man intercepted him, gesturing wildly. The fuel truck driver shook his head, shrugged, and continued toward the office, followed by the second man.

Lowell Hinckley.

Quinn hurried toward the hallway that led toward that side of the building until he reached a door marked "Authorized Access Only". He could claim authorization since he was airport police. Instead, he headed back to the front desk.

"Excuse me, Cherie, can you tell me why Lowell Hinckley is here?"

Before she could answer, the men came through the door, voices raised. Their disagreement ended when they noticed Quinn. Hinckley's eyes widened.

"Mr. Hinckley," Quinn said with distaste, "I didn't expect to find you here."

Lowell elbowed the fuel truck driver. "I wanted to make sure my buddy will be at Doolittle's tonight to watch the Gophers." He nodded at the driver, then touched a finger to his brow in a mock salute. "Gotta run." He left like a starving man late for dinner.

The fuel truck driver grimaced and handed a fistful of receipts to Cheri before turning to leave in silence.

"Excuse me," Quinn said. The man paused before he opened the door he'd come through a minute earlier. "How do you know Lowell Hinckley?"

He cocked his head until his neck cracked. "I know him."

Quinn assessed the man. Shorter than himself by an inch or so put the man at about five-foot eleven. The bulk of his coat hid his build, but from the look of his neck and the span of his shoulders, Quinn guessed he was in a league with fullbacks, with enough bulk to put up a good fight against a tackle. Late twenties, black hair, good-looking, with a newborn beard giving his skin a shadowy cast. "How long have you known him?"

The driver shoved his hands into his coat pockets. "None of your business. Cop." With that, he turned to leave.

"It is my business," Quinn said. "Hinckley is—"

Another man entered through the door for authorized personnel and stepped out of the way of the driver leaving. The newcomer approached Quinn. "I'm Marshall Kline. Can I help you?"

Marshall Kline stood no taller than Quinn's shoulder. His beard matched the silver-gray hat he wore and probably weighed more than the rest of his body. Not quite ZZ Top, Quinn thought, more Oak Ridge Boys.

Quinn introduced himself. "I'm looking for Peter Manelli."

"Pete? I'm looking for him, too." He scratched at his beard with fingers permanently stained by engine grease. "He in trouble?"

"No. I've been trying to get in touch with him. His brother said he might be here."

Marshall checked the clock on the wall above the windows overlooking the apron. "It's almost the end of shift. Follow me. We can talk on the way to the garage."

Quinn followed him through the door and down a hall lined with offices before exiting into a hangar about three-quarters the size of the Range Air hangar. Half a dozen planes were parked along the sides, with a helicopter and a small jet occupying the middle ground between the two rows. The sharp chink of a tool dropped on the concrete floor echoed in the metal cavern.

"How many mechanics work here?" Quinn asked.

"I think there are about ten A&Ps. I've got a dozen guys working in the garage, plus a couple part-timers." He adjusted his hat before pushing through a side door into the frigid January air.

They passed two fuel trucks, a tow tug, and a ground environmental unit before entering the garage. Inside, the scent of engines and gasoline permeated the air. Marshall pointed at a ground power unit with the engine exposed. "Pete's project."

"When did you see Pete last?"

"Day before yesterday. Tuesday." Marshall led the way into an office area at the back of the garage. "He stayed late trying to get that GPU running. Thought we needed it, but they found another one to use. No compression on cylinder number two. His notes say he pulled the head off and found pieces of the spark plug insert. Left some nice deep scratches on the cylinder walls. Cheap-ass Chinese crap. Told my parts guy to get Heli-Coils."

"Did Pete work yesterday?"

Marshall ushered him past a wall covered with ranks of clipboards and paperwork into a cramped office. "He was supposed to. I took yesterday off, wife had knee surgery. He didn't clock in."

Quinn pulled out his notepad. "Did he call in?"

"If he did, no one knows about it. The guys leave a message if they can't reach myself or Stan. No message, and Stan didn't talk to him. Pete's a great guy, hard worker, curious as hell. In the fifteen years I've been here, I've had a handful of guys as reliable as Pete." He leaned on the desk. "I was going to call him this morning, got caught up with a de-ice truck pump, then a fuel truck with a pressure problem."

"Did Stan try to call him yesterday?"

Marshall shook his head. "Stan's a great guy, don't get me wrong. He's more here-and-now. If you're here now, he's good. If you aren't, you're not even on his radar. I don't think Stan or any of the guys were in the garage much yesterday. The log lists three trucks and two tow tugs that crapped out by the terminals.

"Let me give Pete a call." He pulled a clipboard from under a pile of papers on the desk, then picked up the phone receiver and dialed. Quinn could hear rings from the receiver, then a voice answered followed by a tone. Marshall left a message for Pete to call, then hung up. "Is he in trouble?"

"Not at this point. Do you know Tori Hjelle?"

"Tori? Sure, she's Pete's girl. Works in the office a couple days a week. Bookkeeper or something."

"Have you seen her recently?"

"No, but I don't go to the office very often. She'll come to the garage once in a while."

"How was Pete's relationship with her?"

"If you're going to ask me if he hit her or anything, don't bother. He really likes that girl. That kid wouldn't hurt anyone."

"Did he ever mention any problems with Tori?" Quinn asked. "Did anyone else have problems with her?"

The door to the office opened, and a stocky man in a long wool coat entered, brushing snow from his dark thinning hair. Shorter than Quinn, he looked like he'd been wrongly relocated to the Midwest from either Wall Street or a comedy about nothing. He pulled off his leather gloves, then glanced at Quinn before addressing Marshall. "Why did I get another request for a portable compressor? I approved one last month." Then he turned to Quinn. "I heard a cop was on-site." He extended a hand. "Gil Randolph, financial administrator. What can I help you with?"

Gil Randolph was brusque, and though Quinn, as a matter of principle, tried to remain unbiased, this man drew his dislike out. He returned the greeting. "Detective Quinn Moore, Airport Police." He showed his badge. "I'm trying to find Peter Manelli. No one has heard from him since Tuesday."

Randolph pursed his lips and turned to Marshall, who answered the question before he could ask it.

"I already told Detective Moore Pete didn't show up for work yesterday or today."

"Well," Randolph said in a tone that indicated finality, "if you've already told him, why is he still here?"

"Mr. Randolph," Quinn said, "I understand Tori Hjelle worked for Castor Aviation."

The man frowned, something Quinn suspected he did often. "Tori? Yes, she works for me. What about her?"

"What sort of work did she do?"

"Bookkeeping." Randolph said. "Part-time intern through the U of M."

"When did you last talk to her?"

"Friday. Last week. Where is this going, Detective?"

Quinn added the information to his notes. "Who is her direct supervisor?"

"I am."

"Is there a place where we can talk about Tori?"

"Here's fine." Randolph glanced at Marshall in a way that barred any refusal.

Quinn noticed the interaction between the men. Randolph was in charge, no doubt about it, and Marshall didn't like him all that much. "Mr. Randolph, what type of employee was Tori? Was she good at her job? Dependable? Did she get along with her coworkers?"

"She always shows up on time and stays late if she needed to finish things. If she doesn't have to be at her other job."

"What's her other job?" Quinn asked.

"She works as a ramp agent for Range Airlines, I believe."

"Why would you hire an intern to work here?"

Randolph unbuttoned his coat and slid his hands into his trouser pockets. "Mr. Manelli referred her. She's quite good, has a real head for numbers."

"Has she mentioned any problems with other employees or anyone outside of work?"

An expression Quinn couldn't define flashed across Randolph's face. "No. She gets along with pretty much everyone, as far as I know."

"How long has Tori worked for you?"

"Since last summer. She took a few months off to help her grandfather at his FBO near Duluth. Why are you interested in my intern?"

Quinn made the note. Something, a hunch, warned him to be wary. "So, even though she was an intern, you rehired her after she took that much time off? She must be a stellar employee."

Randolph's eyes narrowed. "Like I said, she's got a head for numbers. She's attentive to details and a very good bookkeeper. And she knows aviation."

"Do you know about her thesis?"

"Her paper for school? Never talked much about it."

Quinn glanced at Marshall, who seemed busy at remaining quiet but listening. The mechanic shook his head just enough to notice. "Mr. Kline, did Pete ever mention Tori's paper?"

Marshall looked up as if startled. "All he ever mentions is how she's been spending a lot of time on it lately, and it bothers him when she talks about it, because he doesn't care about accounting. It's all numbers and Greek to him."

"Mr. Randolph, did Tori ever interview you for her thesis? Do you know what her paper is about?"

"She asked a few questions, but never said exactly what she was researching."

Something in his tone made Quinn wonder if the man was telling the whole story. "Mr. Randolph, do you know why Lowell Hinckley was here?"

"Hinckley? Is that name supposed to mean something to me?"

"Mr. Kline? Maybe you know. I saw Lowell Hinckley speaking with one of your fuel truck drivers."

"Oscar is in charge of the drivers," Marshall corrected. "We just make sure the trucks work. Who's Hinckley?"

Quinn decided neither man knew anything about Hinckley. He checked his watch. If the weather people were right, the snowstorm would hit full force in an hour or so, about the same time rush hour traffic would be clogging the roads. The sooner he finished his paperwork, the better. He wanted to get home before he got stuck at the office. Sleeping in the terminal was not on his list of fun things to do during a blizzard. "Thank you both for your help." He handed his card to each of them. "Call me if you hear from Pete or think of anything else."

"Wait," Randolph said, "what about Tori?"

"Tori Hjelle is dead."

# 22

Back in his office, Quinn shook a thick layer of snow off his hat. The roads weren't too bad yet, but at this rate, rush hour would be a nightmare. He hung up his coat, and then added the new information to his makeshift murder board. He didn't add Sierra's name to the suspect list yet. The hard evidence didn't support her involvement. At least that's what he told himself.

He did a background check on Miss Sierra Bauer. Six years ago, she took out a restraining order against a Mr. Rune Thorsson. She followed that with two complaints of being stalked by Thorsson, which the local authorities dismissed judging by the comments on the report from Deputy Chief Lawrence Eckert.

The police professionals who were supposed to serve and protect her let her down. He may not have any right to feel protective, or angry, or in any way invested in Sierra Bauer, but as he shuffled through the crime scene photos, he couldn't avoid it. Her apartment looked like a battle zone, with couch cushions tossed around, books and papers scattered, and damaged walls that bore the brunt of a fist or head or other blunt instrument.

The next images lured bile from his churning stomach. Blood stained the sand-colored linoleum floor. A scarlet handprint marked the wall. A phone receiver hung inches off the floor, dangling by a spiral cord. Another photo showed a close-up of an eight-inch hunting knife coated in blood. He sucked in a breath, let it out slowly before he paged to the next pictures. These were taken at the hospital, before the emergency surgery. A bloody two-inch slice, held together by butterfly bandages and surrounded by a halo of deep purple bruising on pale skin. Others showed contusions on her back and side.

The final picture fueled his anger. Clotted blood marred her lips and right cheek. A bandage wrapped her head. The report said she received more stitches along with a broken rib and a possible concussion. She went through hell and won. She fared far better than some of the other victims of violence he'd come across in his years on the force.

Quinn had seen victims of domestic abuse, interviewed them, and knew that a predisposition to being a victim, either through personal history or personality, often prevented them from fighting back. The interview after the attack, along with her testimony at the trial, painted a different portrait of Sierra Bauer. She was not a victim of domestic abuse, but of a stalker, a spurned ex-boyfriend who couldn't deal with rejection or her resistance to his control.

She's a fighter, he thought. Would she kill if cornered?

The next pictures showed the damage she inflicted on her attacker in return.

A low drone filled his ears. Everything outside the image in front of him vanished into a gray mental fog punctuated by his pulse echoing in the void.

The face of the fuel truck driver stared at him.

This Thorsson looked less like a fullback and more like a runner or swimmer. He displayed a bruised and broken nose, stitches on his scalp. She'd gotten some good hits in.

Did Sierra know he'd been released from the Moose Lake Correctional Facility six months ago?

She'd taken out a restraining order against him. Notifying her of his release was required by law.

He closed the file and took a moment to think. How had Thorsson managed to get a job where he had access to the AOA? And to Sierra?

*Did she know he worked at the airport?*

Next, he read the FAA report involving Sierra Bauer and the investigation of her brother's death. The FAA's rules were unforgiving. If a mechanic caused an aircraft to crash by something they did or didn't do, they could lose their A&P license. If that crash resulted in fatalities, there was no "could". The mechanic would lose his or her license, and never legally work on an aircraft in the United States again.

Sierra changed the oil on the Piper Cherokee the day before her brother took it to Colorado. The report's copy of the logbook page showed she signed off on the change and the subsequent engine run to check for leaks. The previous maintenance entry was the annual inspection signed off four months prior by an A&P mechanic holding an Inspection Authorization. According to the file, the FAA also investigated that mechanic. Like Sierra, he was cleared of any wrongdoing. After the investigation, the FAA determined pilot error caused the crash.

Lowell Hinckley's comments now made sense. She was working as a mechanic for Range Air when her brother died. Quinn flipped to the page in his own report. The man had a major stick up his ass about women in general, and about women working in a man's world in particular. He wondered how many other mechanics felt the same way.

He knew female cops who had earned the respect of their peers worked harder just to keep that respect. He suspected it was the same for Sierra. Being caught up in an FAA investigation would've put additional pressure on her to exceed expectations.

She took out a restraining order against an ex-boyfriend when she felt threatened by him, fought back against an attack by that same man, worked as an aircraft mechanic in a man's realm, and survived an FAA investigation while retaining that position. Sierra Bauer was no pushover. He looked at the image of the body pulled from the hell-hole. Would she do something like that to someone she believed threatened her brother?

Sierra had a beef with the victim, and what Cate told him about the confrontation opened up the possibility that she could have caused Tori harm if no one stopped her. He left a message on her machine yesterday, but he called again and left another; he needed the rest of the story, including whether she knew Rune Thorsson worked at the airport.

He went to the murder board and made the change.

Sierra Bauer topped the list of suspects.

Cate and Peter Manelli rounded out the list. Cate, because the people closest to the victim were always suspects until they were ruled out. Until he could get a more accurate window for the time of death, he couldn't ask for an alibi.

He examined the photo of the winged emerald.

R. T. and S. B.

Sierra's birthday was May first. Birthstone: emerald.

Something inside his chest grew dark and cold.

His gut said she was innocent. After the implosion of his marriage, could he trust it?

# 23

Sierra slowed to a crawl, leaving the manual transmission of her Subaru wagon in first gear. The lines of traffic crept along, tens of cars in nice rows all heading away from downtown Minneapolis. Dropping off her sister and a fifteen-minute conversation with her grandparents turned into a three-hour visit that included a generous sample of her grandmother's famous beef and barley soup. It also meant she managed to join the beginning of rush-hour traffic instead of avoiding it. To add to the joy, a constant shower of flakes heralded the predicted snowstorm.

Her sister's comments about dating still bothered her.

Why had she kept things going with Rune when the trouble started?

Now, as then, she chalked it up to her naivete and the novelty of it. She'd been nineteen, her first foray on her own, and one of a handful of women in a school of guys. She remembered the excitement: her first boyfriend, a hot guy and one who liked hiking and fishing as much as she did. She thought him charming and sweet for wanting to know where she was and what she was doing. When he got upset because she'd headed home one weekend without telling him, they'd had a shouting match. She started doubting the relationship, until he apologized with flowers and a wonderful night out.

She could see it now, as clear as the line of cars in front of her, the progression of his control. She had missed the red flag of his reaction to that first major "betrayal of his trust". Her instincts raised an uneasy feeling about him in the back of her mind, but she didn't listen. She'd been young, never popular in school, and too enamored by the whole idea of having a boyfriend for the first time.

After she returned from a day trip with some friends to the Royal Aviation Museum in Winnipeg, he lashed out at her for leaving, not to mention spending it with fellow aviation maintenance students, of whom only one other was female. That time he got physical, leaving hand-sized bruises on her arms.

Her scar started to itch. It started bothering her again after she got the letter. She scratched at it, conscious of the rough two-inch line even through her sweater. A black pickup truck eased up on her left. Her gut clenched when she recognized the make and model matched Rune's. A glance at the driver released some of the tension. The woman swayed to some unheard rhythm, and clothes in a laundry basket peeked above the rear windowsill.

Kara was right. There were a lot of black pickup trucks on the road. She scanned the traffic behind her in the rear view mirror, and counted five black trucks. She had to stop jumping at every shadow.

She needed a distraction. Her little sister was right, Detective Quinn Moore was cute. Did she want to start dating again? Her last date, months ago, entailed dinner and the newly-released movie, *The Bodyguard*. She almost enjoyed the movie. The company, not so much. Why was she even thinking ... It wasn't like she'd be going on any dates with him. Hell, there were probably three or four messages on her answering machine from him by now wanting to talk about the whole Tori mess.

She pressed her fingers to her chest where her brother's dog tag lay smooth against her skin under the thick knit of her sweater. A knot of grief swelled in her throat like a mouthful of stale toast too big to swallow. It had been nine months, but it felt like it happened last week. That single call had shattered her world. That call began a six-month FAA investigation and a suspension of her A&P license. Her days had been filled with anguish and worry that she'd lose the very things her brother encouraged her to strive for, until the FAA cleared her and reinstated her license.

If Ken hadn't been out with Tori that night, he wouldn't have had alcohol and drugs in his system. He wouldn't have crashed and died. He would be here now to convince Sierra not to worry, that he would stand with her and protect her as only a big brother could. She gripped the dog tag and blinked away tears.

When she reached her apartment complex, she scanned the parking lot for pickup trucks. She recognized a red one with a plow attached in front and a white one with a topper and a fist-sized rust hole in the rear fender.

She fitted her keys between her fingers in one smooth motion and hurried to the security door. She jammed the key into the lock, yanked the door open, and pulled the door shut behind her against the resistance of the closing cylinder. When she reached her apartment, she set the deadbolt and then checked behind every door, turning lights on as she went. She ran through each step of her safety procedures twice before she hung her coat in the closet. The answering machine's message light blinked. Three messages.

They could wait. The last thing she wanted to hear on the machine was a repeat of last night's haunting message. A glance at the clock elicited a groan. After business hours. Figures. After adding a reminder to the notepad by the phone, she turned on the evening news and settled onto the couch with a new library book. The futuristic cop mysteries were compelling enough to make J. D. Robb one of her favorite authors. She half-listened to the litany of winter weather advisories and up-to-date predictions of massive snow amounts in this wallop. The fact she wasn't working for the next couple days and didn't need to go anywhere reduced her interest in the looming winter blast.

Now that she'd had a chance to settle, she realized how much she hadn't slept. Eyelids heavy, she adjusted her position on the couch, pulled an afghan over her, and hoped she wouldn't dream about the body in the airplane, or black pickup trucks, or the detective working the case. Okay, maybe the detective was an acceptable subject. She tucked a bookmark into her book and laid it on her chest.

The ringing phone drew her back to the room. A check of the glowing digits on the VCR told her she'd been out for an hour. Mouth dry and cottony, she forced lingering fatigue away, got up, and answered the phone while filling a glass with water.

"Sierra? It's Cate. I'm sorry, I didn't know who to call. I ... oh God, I don't know what to do."

"Cate?" Sierra shook her head to clear the last cobwebs. "What's wrong?"

"Someone's been in the apartment. Oh my God."

"Cate, calm down. What happened?"

Her words fired in rapid succession, spaced with sharp wheezy breaths. "I just got home, the door was unlocked. The living room lights don't work. I turned on the kitchen light. Sierra, someone's been in here. Everything is everywhere. Even the couch cushions are a mess. There's stuffing everywhere."

Goosebumps roughened Sierra's skin. She scanned her apartment, the lights scant reassurance. Unease crept down her spine. She checked the deadbolt. "Who else did you call?"

"Just you. My folks are in Arizona visiting my brother, and Brent is working in the ER tonight." Her voice broke. "Oh, God, what do I do?"

"You have to report the break-in. Do you have Detective Moore's number?"

A sob, then, "Yes."

"Call him. Call 911. Do you have anyone there you can stay with?"

Another sob. "No. I'm scared." Cate's voice pitched high. "What should I do?"

That old fear clawed at her. She knew how it felt when someone invaded your sanctuary. Her dad stayed with her for a week after she got out of the hospital, and her mom stayed the following week. Having someone she trusted with her had made a huge difference. If Cate still lived in the same apartment, she was close.

"Are you still in the same place?"

"Yes."

"I'll come over, Cate, just stay there. I can wait with you until Detective Moore shows up. Lock the door and don't let anyone except the police in until I get there."

Cate thanked her amid more sobs and ended the call. Sierra locked her apartment, double-checked the doorknob, sprinted down the stairs to the building's security door. Snow pelted down, illuminated by the street lamps. Three inches of snow coated everything. She prayed she'd be home before the accumulation reached the predicted foot.

She cleared the snow from her vehicle and headed out of the lot.

# 24

Sierra pulled into the lot in front of Cate's building and parked in a cone of light lining the median. There were no police cars in sight. The local cops should have been here by now, even if Moore wasn't. Her drive had taken longer than she expected, but there was nothing wrong with slower when the weather turned. She found Cate's name on the call panel, pressed the buzzer, and waited.

No answer. She pressed it again. "Come on, Cate. I told you to stay put." A middle-aged woman in a knee-length wool coat appeared in the entry area of the building. Sierra knocked on the glass. The woman reached the door. "I'm here to see Cate Zahn, but I think the buzzer might be broken."

"It wouldn't surprise me. Mine was out last week." The woman brushed past Sierra as a car in the parking lot beeped.

Before she reached the stairs, a man hunkered into his pea coat shoved past her and out the door into the storm. "Jerk," she mumbled, and continued up the stairs. It'd been almost a year since she had been here. Nothing had changed, not even the tired vase of dried pampas grass in the corner of the landing. She headed down the hall to Cate's apartment.

She knocked. Called for Cate. No answer. She tried the doorknob. Locked. She pounded on the door. Tension cramped her middle. She raced back to the stairs and down to the first floor to find the manager's apartment.

Sierra pounded on the manager's door. Waited what felt like minutes. Pounded again. This time she heard a coarse voice from inside the apartment. "Hold your shorts." An older bald man opened the door as he pulled on a worn Carhartt hooded sweatshirt over an olive-gray button-down shirt. "Don't make a ruckus. I've got an old lady on two who I swear can hear a radio playing half a block away."

What the hell was taking Detective Moore so long?

"My friend, Cate Zahn, just called me, but now she isn't answering her door. She said someone broke into her apartment."

"No one called me. You sure she's in her apartment? Did she call the police?"

Sierra remembered the tremble in Cate's voice. "Yes, I'm sure. She called me twenty minutes ago. I told her to call 911 and stay put. Can you let me in so I can check on her?"

They headed up to Cate's floor. Sierra watched the hall in both directions, shoulders aching with tension, while the manager sorted the keys on his ring until he found the right one and unlocked the door.

She shoved past him into the apartment, dimly lit by one kitchen bulb. Drawers and their contents were strewn around the kitchen like a poltergeist gone mad. Ripped couch cushions were scattered across the room with stuffing pulled out. Videotapes were spread around the television.

The air grew heavy and unbreathable, like a thick band pressed against her ribs.

"Holy Moses. What the hell happened in here?"

The manager's voice reminded her she wasn't alone. The realization broke through the echoes from her past. She gulped air with lungs now free of constraint. Cate lay unmoving on the floor beside the coffee table, the pale beige carpeting around her head stained dark.

Sierra checked Cate's pulse the way her dad taught her when she was barely old enough for kindergarten. *There.* "Call an ambulance."

The manager whistled low when he saw Cate, or maybe it was the blood on the carpeting. He turned and swore. "Phone's gone."

*Shit.* She saw the phone laying across the room below a dent in the wall. She trembled as her past pressed in, threatening to bury her. She needed to focus on helping Cate, not the old fear. "Go call 911. She needs an ambulance."

He rushed out. The dark stain of blood appeared almost black in the dim light. A head wound could mean anything from a nasty gash to a concussion.

She couldn't do anything until the ambulance or Detective Moore arrived. *Where the hell is Detective Moore?* Whoever tore up the apartment must have still been here when Cate got home. Heard her call Sierra. When he heard her call Detective Moore, he attacked.

Which meant Moore probably didn't know about this yet.

Her gaze went to the phone on the floor. She didn't want to leave Cate alone. Would the manager return to the apartment after he called for help?

Maybe Cate had another phone in the apartment. She made her way around debris to a hallway. She hit the first light switch she found and blinked against the sudden brilliance. In the glow of the hall light she discovered two bedrooms, both of which looked like a cartoon Tasmanian Devil had spun its way through the rooms. Clothes, bedding, and furniture lay strewn everywhere. Careful to avoid touching anything, Sierra eased through each room, scanning for a phone.

She came up empty in the first bedroom, but in the second found a hot pink telephone on a bedside table. She checked for a dial tone. It worked. She pulled Moore's card from her pocket, dialed his number, and paced until he answered.

"Detective Moore."

"This is Sierra Bauer."

"Thanks for calling me back. I want the rest of the story."

"I'm at Cate's apartment. She's been attacked. The building manager is calling 911. How soon can you get here?"

His voice sounded tight, almost strained. "Is she okay?" She heard the jingle of keys in the background. "Are you okay?"

"I'm fine. Cate's alive, but it's bad."

❖  ❖  ❖

THE AMBULANCE AND A SAVAGE POLICE SQUAD arrived before Detective Moore did. The building manager led the EMTs and the officers to the apartment. Sierra answered their rapid-fire questions to the best of her ability and made sure they knew Detective Moore from the Airport PD was on his way. Once she convinced the officers she would answer the same damn questions for Moore, that this whole thing tied into a case he was working, and he would send them a copy of his report, they backed down. She sat at the kitchen table in the least disturbed area of the apartment to wait alone with the ghosts of her past.

Though she hadn't kept in touch with Cate, Sierra worried about what she'd been through. She knew the feeling of helplessness, the loss of security, the lack of control. Something cold and tight settled in her, caused her to shiver until she couldn't stop her teeth from chattering. Sierra huddled into her coat, zipped it to the very top, pulled her hat down over her ears, and shoved mittened hands into the pockets. It felt like the very core of winter set up shop inside her.

The apartment, the blood, the telephone ripped from the wall and tossed into a corner, everything brought it back. It felt like her efforts to return to her confident, empowered self vanished. She wanted someone to hold her and tell her she was safe, like her dad used to do when she was little.

She heard Moore enter the apartment. It had only been ten minutes after the other cops and the EMTs arrived, but it felt like hours. Snow coated him like a mantle. He displayed his badge to the uniformed officers, shot off instructions, then made his way to the living room.

Sierra waited, closed her eyes to concentrate on a mountain forest vista. Her efforts were futile; she sensed the movement around her, heard terse voices that raised memories of the cops who tried to persuade the doctors to let them question her before trying to save her life.

One of the EMTs completed her assessment of Cate's injuries. Her partner returned with the gurney, and they prepared to move Cate onto it. Moore approached them. "How is she?"

"Her wrist is fractured, she has a pretty good gash on her head, lots of bruises, and a probable concussion."

Moore nodded and handed his card to one of the techs. "Have the attending physician call me when she's stable. She's part of a case I'm working on. Wait here." He left the apartment, and returned a minute later with one of the Savage officers. "Officer Hanson will ride along to take her statement in case she wakes up on the way. Thank you, Officer."

While the medical techs took the unconscious Cate away, Moore gestured to the building manager lurking in the hallway outside the apartment, eyes glued to the activity. Sierra waited while Moore questioned the man.

She fidgeted, finally stood to wander the apartment and work off some of the nervous energy, avoiding the debris scattered on the floor. At the main window, she eased a curtain aside and peeked out. The lights glowed a dull orange through the thick curtain of flakes. Mounds of snow filled the lot, the shapes of the vehicles lost under the white blanket. An SUV pulled into a space, its red color quickly masked by white. Two people ran to the building in the long-step lope used to hit as little of the snow as possible.

Another vehicle, a black pickup truck, crept through the lot between parked cars and stopped in front of her vehicle. The storm hampered her view, but she thought she saw a form lean out the driver's window and wave at her. Fear launched her pulse into overdrive.

A hand on her shoulder startled her. "Sierra? Are you okay?"

"Define okay," she said. "I'm not hurt if that's what you're asking."

"Look at me," Moore said. The dim lighting in the room made it hard to see his eyes, but after a moment, they registered. She wondered how they could be so incredibly blue and still emote a warmth that chased the rest of the chill from her.

He blinked as if he suddenly remembered something. "Good," he said, relief evident in his voice. He pushed the curtains farther aside and peered into the night. The truck drove forward again, rounded the far side of the lot, and exited into the street. "No one should be out driving in this. It's bad out there." He turned to her. "I need to ask you some questions." Whatever he saw on her face made him frown. "What's wrong?"

Shadows cloaked the chaos of the apartment, hiding the reality of it from immediate notice. "Everything," she whispered, a shudder rolling through her. Someone had killed a woman Sierra despised and crammed her into the maintenance bay of an inspection plane.

Sierra found her.

Now someone had broken into the dead woman's apartment, trashed it, and knocked her roommate around until she lost consciousness.

Sierra found her.

*Shit.*

# 25

Moore gestured back toward the dining area where she'd sat earlier. She returned to her seat. He followed suit. "The crime scene unit should be here soon." His voice was low and quiet. "Tell me what happened."

She told him everything, from Cate's frantic phone call to her arrival here, the broken buzzer—now that she thought about it, the buzzer probably worked just fine. To Cate's locked apartment and no answer to her pounding on the door. To the building manager letting her into the apartment and finding Cate unconscious on the floor. To the search for a phone and the call she made to him. He didn't interrupt, instead taking notes as she spoke.

The crime scene unit showed up about the time Sierra finished. Moore excused himself to give the team lead instructions, leaving her to wonder what it took to catalog a scene like this. The crime scene tech was about Moore's height, but more solid. She heard Moore call him Kevin before the tech started directing his team, the white "BCA" on his coat glowing in the dim light. It made sense, she thought, that the Bureau of Criminal Apprehension would supply the crime scene unit since the APD probably didn't have their own, and the BCA could work anywhere in the entire state.

The crime scene team set up work lights, turning the twilight in the apartment into noon brilliance. Moore returned to his chair. "It'll be a few hours before they finish." He leaned back and studied her. "Why did Cate call you? I thought you didn't get along."

Guilt surfaced, as it always did when she thought about Ken's memorial service and how she treated Cate. She'd had a chance to apologize today at the U, but she had allowed her disdain for Tori to color her interaction with Cate yet again.

"We saw each other today at the U. I suppose she called me because no one else is around, and I live close by. She said her boyfriend is working and her parents are in Arizona." Another pang of guilt washed through her. "If it wasn't snowing, I would've been here sooner."

He nodded and paged back in his notes. "Sooner may not have been better. Why didn't she call me or 911 first?"

"I don't know. I asked if she called you, then told her to call you right after we were done talking. Maybe she was in the middle of dialing your number when …" When someone came out of the darkness and attacked her. She squeezed her eyes shut. She knew. She knew the shock, the jolt of fear, the desperate search for escape.

Moore laid a hand on her knee. His tone testified to his concern. "I know this is hard for you. We can take a break if you need to."

"I'm fine," she said, her anxiety hovering, held at bay by the weight of his hand. She should be uncomfortable with a man touching her like this, but it felt reassuring.

He pulled his hand back. "I read your files. The police reports, the restraining order, the report of the attack. I saw the pictures from the scene."

Her temper surged, a hot flare she snagged and shoved back before it escaped. She had no right to accuse him of invading her privacy. It was his job, and after he talked with Cate earlier, he would have looked into her background. That's what cops did. She paused while she lined up her next words in her head. "That has nothing to do with this."

The words triggered the little voice that reminded her of the black pickup truck she'd just seen in the parking lot. *God, he actually waved.*

His voice took on an edge. "Yes, it does." He glanced at the CSU team working less than twenty feet away, then stood. "Let's go into the hallway." He headed toward the door without checking to see if she followed.

She made her way to the hall, where she found him pacing, hands on hips, his parka open and spread like the wings of a bird trying to settle itself. He stopped about ten feet away and turned toward her as soon as she entered the hallway. He tipped his head, indicating she should follow. "They don't need to hear this."

She glanced back into the daylight-bright room, then continued in his direction.

"Who was in the truck? The one in the parking lot, the black one that stopped in front of your car."

She hesitated. Her skin crawled, like eyes watched her from the shadows. She glanced over her shoulder. Her sister's words came back to her. "Do you have any idea how many black pickup trucks there are?"

Moore approached, stopped within arm's reach. "Rune Thorsson drove a black truck. His sentence was up six months ago." Before she could argue, he continued. "You took out a restraining order on him. You testified against him. They sent you a registered letter to let you know he was being released." His voice, his eyes hardened. "How long has he been here?"

She swallowed hard, her mouth suddenly dry. For weeks after she received the letter, every black pickup she saw lit her fight-or-flight instinct. She had gone back to a therapist, and on her recommendation spent the next month in an intense self-defense refresher course. She fought like hell to keep fear from controlling her life again. "He was up in Moose Lake. Why would he bother to come down here after six years? He's probably in Duluth."

"I saw him at Castor Aviation earlier today. He works there."

Her heart, her lungs stopped working. Her fingers were ice-cold sticks. A rush of sound in her ears echoed in her head: *nonononono.*

"Sierra."

His voice broke into her consciousness.

*Did you miss me?*

"Sierra."

Shivers filled her, settled in her bones, jump-started her heart. Her pulse hammered. Before her knees gave out, her back pressed against a flat surface. She slid down. Something hot wrapped around her fingers. That heat seeped into her, drawing calm with it. The drone in her head quieted.

Moore knelt beside her. He released her hands, backed out of reach, and pulled a pair of Polaroids from a pocket. "Sierra, can you hear me?"

She didn't trust her voice. She nodded.

He toyed with the pictures. "I thought ... I'm sorry, I didn't ... I have to ask you. Do you recognize this?" He turned the photos to face her.

The pendant brought her back to the day she thought it was over. The day she told Rune she wouldn't see him anymore. His grudging acquiescence after she rejected him—and his gift—a second time. Sincere, or so she thought. She had anticipated a long-overdue return to freedom.

She hadn't anticipated the weeks of stalking that followed.

"Where did you find that?"

"They found it with Tori's body. Why are your and Rune Thorsson's initials on it?"

Warm. Too warm. She trembled, making her efforts to take off her coat harder since she was on the floor leaning against a wall, but she managed with a little help from Moore. Sweat rolled down her chest, and she shoved her sleeves to her elbows.

"Why did the ME find this on the body?" he asked.

"I don't know. He tried to give it to me, a peace offering or something, after I told him I never wanted to see him again." She had called him on purpose to break up so she wouldn't have to see his tantrum. He approached her in person an hour later while she was studying at the riverside park.

"You never took it."

"No. God, I just wanted it to be over. Believe me. When I didn't accept his gift, he … lost it. He just freaked out."

"Look, I've dealt with enough victims of abuse to know—"

"It was not abuse." The words erupted from her, a sudden burst of red-hot temper that echoed in the empty hallway. "I was young and naive, but I broke it off before it turned into abuse. I pushed back."

"Yes, you did, but stalking is a form of emotional and mental abuse." He pocketed the pictures. "He stalked you after you thought you were safe with the restraining order. You survived a traumatic attack after he invaded your apartment, your sanctuary. Then you come over here to help a friend, and you see another invasion, another attack, and it brings it all back."

Her scar itched like a hundred ants were trying to dig their way out.

# 26

"Have you seen him? Not just the truck, but have you actually seen him?" Moore asked. "He works at the airport."

"No."

"When did you first see the truck?"

"On the service road the night ..." She faltered, anxiety jumbling her thoughts like a knot of loose cables. "The night I found the body."

"Are you sure that was his truck tonight? Did you see him?"

"No, but who the hell else would stop in front of my car, wave at me, then drive off?"

"How would he know you were here?" His eyes darkened. Flat cop eyes. "Are you sure you haven't seen or talked to him?"

She met Moore's stare. "I have not seen him." That tiny fact had fueled her equally small hope that it was all in her imagination, and her nightmare hadn't returned in person to haunt her.

Moore shot that hope to Hell and back.

"All I saw was that damn truck. There are black trucks all over the place. I can't be sure it was even his."

"Have you talked to him?"

Ice traced her spine. "He called. And before you ask, I don't know how he got my number. It's unlisted." Under Moore's unrelenting gaze, she added the pieces together, the pendant, Tori's body, Rune at Castor Aviation. "You can't possibly think I had anything to do with any of this. Did you miss the whole 'stalker' part of the reports?"

"Would he kill for you?"

She remembered Rune's eyes full of crazy devotion the day she refused his gift. "I don't know. I didn't even meet Tori until after he went to prison. How would he know about her?"

Moore stood and offered her a hand up. She pushed to her feet without assistance and scooped up her coat.

"I get that this whole deal is going to be tough for you."

"Which deal? The one where I see my stalker around every corner now that I know he's here for sure, or the one where you suspect I had something to do with Tori's death?" Temper simmered through her. "How could you think I would be involved with the man who tried to kill me? That makes no sense."

He tunneled fingers through his hair, agitation coloring his movements. "I'm trying to figure out who killed Tori Hjelle. You have history with her. Is it a coincidence you found her? Is it coincidence your stalker ex-boyfriend works at the same company she did? Is Cate a coincidence? You found her, too."

Frustration radiating from him. "I can't believe in coincidences in my job. I need to listen to my gut, and dammit …" He breathed an exasperated sigh.

"Promise you will call me anytime you see his truck. Or him. Understood?"

He steered her toward the apartment with a hand on her back. She blinked in the sudden brightness of the room, then reclaimed her seat at the table. The crime scene techs milled about in near-silence broken by the sound of camera shutters and low murmurs.

Moore pulled out his notepad before he took off his coat and settled in a chair. "Let's go over this again. You said Cate called you. When you got here, you thought the buzzer didn't work. If Cate didn't let you in, how did you get into the building through the security door?"

"A woman leaving the building let me in."

"Did you see anyone else?"

"Just some guy. He shoved me on his way out." Her voice trailed off as realization hit her. "He was hunched into his coat. I didn't think anything of it, except he didn't even say 'excuse me' when he bumped into me." She didn't think her shoulders could tighten any further.

"Do you think it might've been whomever did this?" she asked.

"It's possible. From what you said, it's likely he was still in the apartment when Cate got home and called you. We won't be able to get more details until she wakes up. It can't be an accident that someone killed Tori, and a day after her body was found someone broke into her apartment and tossed it. They were looking for something.

"Was Rune the man who shoved you on the stairs?"

The ramifications of his question injected adrenaline into her cramped muscles, ratcheting them until her neck ached. She understood his logic, but it had been six years since she'd been that close to her ex-boyfriend. The Rune she remembered had the lean build of a runner. "I don't think so. He was too big, like athletic too big."

"Did he look at you? Do you think he knew you were heading to Cate's apartment?"

"No. He had a dark hat—maybe black—and his collar was up like he was protecting his face."

Creases at the corners of Moore's eyes echoed the furrows on his forehead. "Are you sure it wasn't Thorsson? Think. Do you remember anything else about him?"

"I wasn't paying attention. I was worried about Cate. She sounded hysterical on the phone." She squeezed her eyes closed, as if that would help clarify the image. "He was hunched over, like walking against a strong wind. He wore a black or navy pea coat, and a black or navy watch cap. I don't remember seeing his hands." She searched her memory for more, but found only frustration. "I don't remember anything else. I wish I could."

"Maybe you'll think of something later." Moore scratched at the stubble on his face. He looked weary, more so than he had earlier at Coffman Union. "I don't like the thought of Thorsson seeing you here."

*Neither do I.* If it had been Rune … She swallowed hard, gripped her brother's dog tag through her sweater like a security blanket.

"I still haven't heard from Tori's boyfriend, and neither has Cate or his boss at Castor Aviation. The person who did this and put Cate in the hospital is dangerous. If it's the same person who killed Tori, he's even more dangerous. If he was here in the apartment, he heard Cate talking to you on the phone. Do you remember what she said? Did she say your name?"

"I don't know."

Moore pressed his lips into a thin line. "He probably heard her say she was going to call me, or saw her look at my card. When she hung up with you, he attacked her."

She had come to the same conclusion. *What if he'd still been here when she got here?* The ache in her neck and shoulders crept down her back and into the muscles lining her ribs. "You're not making me feel any better."

His intensity darkened. "I'm not trying to make you feel better. This isn't *Murder, She Wrote* or *Columbo*, this is real. And dangerous. I don't want anyone else getting hurt." With the last, he hit her with those brilliant blue eyes. "You live what, four or five miles from here?"

"About that."

"Do you have a roommate?" A pause. "Boyfriend? Someone to stay with you at your apartment?"

"No. Neither." She hadn't needed to worry about being alone for a long time.

"How far away do your parents live?"

"They're south of Prior Lake, about twenty minutes from here depending on traffic and weather."

He stood and crossed the room to speak with Kevin, who raised an eyebrow, then shook his head. She couldn't hear what he said, but Moore pulled away and headed toward the window. When he shoved the curtain aside, all Sierra could see was the room reflected on the window like a mirror. He cupped hands around his eyes and leaned against the glass for a minute before settling the curtain back into place. He gestured at Kevin, then took the walkie-talkie the tech pulled from his belt. After a few minutes of distorted conversation with someone on the other end, he handed the walkie-talkie back to Kevin and took one last look out the window.

Moore stepped around the technician taking pictures and notes at each of the plastic tent markers scattered around the room and reclaimed his seat at the kitchen table. "It's bad out there. We've gotten at least seven inches of snow, the wind's kicked up, and they are pulling the plows off the roads. It isn't going to get any better for a few more hours.

"I won't let you drive to Prior Lake in this weather. I don't want you staying alone at your apartment as long as I think the person who did this might have seen you. He was looking for something and didn't find it, or he wouldn't have still been here when Cate got home. The perpetrator might be watching this building. If he saw you ..."

She already hit that logic marker. "He might think I know about whatever he's looking for." A shiver trembled through her. She didn't want to lead anyone to her apartment.

"I could stay at a hotel tonight." Would she feel safe somewhere unfamiliar? She would still be alone. After this, she wouldn't sleep no matter where she stayed.

Moore paced, hands on hips, looking like he was in the middle of a mental tug-of-war by the indecision playing across his face. He reminded Sierra of Columbo, but Moore was younger, taller, and far better looking than Peter Falk. He stopped in mid-step, and she suspected that one side of the rope war was face down in the mud.

Kevin made his way to Moore and started whispering harshly, but not intelligibly enough for her to make out the words. From where she sat, it looked like the technician was either warning the detective or scolding him. Moore responded in kind, the sharp edge in his voice carrying to her even if his words didn't.

Kevin shook his head. Moore turned away and headed back toward Sierra. She stood, arms crossed tight on her chest. "Well, what did he tell you not to do that you're going to do anyway?"

For the first time, he looked genuinely surprised. "You didn't hear any of that, did you?"

"No, but it reminded me of some quote unquote 'discussions' my parents had. I always found out later one ended up doing whatever the other one warned against."

His eyes narrowed. "If that really was Thorsson's truck, or if he did this," he gestured to the mess, "he may violate the restraining order, which he's done before. Do you have any friends or other family closer, where you can stay until the storm's over and the roads are cleared?"

"Most of my family lives farther south, like Rochester south. I've got some relatives up in Andover and Cambridge, but that's completely on the other side of the Cities."

He scratched his head and frowned. Sierra caught his quick look toward the crime scene team leader, who was watching from the other side of the room. Kevin shook his head just enough to send his cornrow braids bobbing.

"Kevin and his team will be here for a while. I need to check on Cate. They should be at Fairview Ridges on the other side of 35W. There are hotels on Burnsville Parkway over by 35W."

She placed the location on her mental map. A couple miles farther east, Interstate 35W ran north and south as the boundary between Savage and Burnsville. "I think I know where they are. I'll find them."

He tramped in a tight circle, one hand on a hip, the other at the back of his neck. He stopped. "I'd have a unit stick around to keep an eye on you, but with this weather, I can't justify asking.

"If Thorsson's out there, you are in danger. If it is Tori's boyfriend, and he thinks you know something, he's going to go after you," Moore said. "You'll ride with me. No sense having us both on the road. I have to come back here in the morning to take a closer look at the scene. I'll bring you back then."

His words didn't register at first.

The image of Tori Hjelle's remains invaded her mind, followed by the image of Cate Zahn unconscious on a floor stained with blood.

Moore targeted her with those intense blue eyes. "I will be your security at the hotel."

*Rune works at the airport. He knows my phone number. He might be outside the building right now, waiting until I'm alone.*

He was a cop. It was a hotel. She would be safe with him nearby, right? She wouldn't be alone.

Part of her insisted it was a very bad idea, hotel or not. The part of her that was normally quiet and content to let the other part take center stage squeezed the warning into submission.

*Rune won't know where I am.*

# 27

Quinn's insides squirmed like a nest of eels as uncertainty showed in the set of her jaw and the crease in her brow. He didn't dare glance at Kevin. This was against protocol, and he was very well aware of what might happen if the chief found out. He wouldn't let her stay alone, not after what happened to Cate, not after seeing the destruction of the apartment, and not after learning the man who tried to kill her might have been outside waving at her. After spending years in jail, he may consider finishing the job out of revenge.

If she couldn't go to her parents' house, no other scenarios made Quinn confident she'd be safe. Would she listen to reason? He hoped knowing how close she came to getting hurt would tone down any protests she might have.

And under it all, he ignored the real reason he worried about her.

"Okay," she said, voice barely audible.

The breath he'd been holding whooshed out. "I will tell Kevin where we're going in case something happens. I'll let the building manager know your vehicle is in the lot so he doesn't have it towed. Wait for me in the hall, please."

He expected her to protest after the bits of her temper he'd seen. Instead she gathered her coat and headed out the door in silence.

Quinn turned. Kevin was right behind him, tsking and shaking his head. He bent close to discourage eavesdroppers. "I know you like this woman.

Don't do anything stupid before you close the case. After the case is finished and filed, have at it."

"It's a hotel, for cripe's sake."

"Exactly."

Quinn pointed to the dark spot beside the coffee table, the only piece of furniture that escaped the cyclone that had gone through the apartment. "You didn't see what happened to Cate. Our unknown subject beat her up, broke her wrist, and topped it off with a head wound that made a lovely stain on the nice carpeting." He suppressed a shudder twisted with an unreasonable worry. "Sierra survived an attack by a stalker who was released from Moose Lake Correctional six months ago. I saw him at the airport today, and she thinks she saw him in the lot out here. He called her unlisted phone number. I'm not leaving her alone."

"Be careful. If they aren't plowing, it'll be bad out there, especially the side roads. If I find anything too interesting to wait until I get the report put together, I'll call."

"I'll let you know where we are and the number where you can reach me after we check in." Quinn left the crime scene team to do their work. Judging by the amount of damage done, he suspected it would be the wee hours of the morning before they finished documenting everything.

Sierra waited in the hallway in stoic silence. He notified the manager that CSU would be in the apartment for a while, the scene would be off-limits until he cleared it, and Sierra's vehicle, a blue Subaru Legacy wagon, would be in the lot until she returned in the morning to pick it up. Sierra led the way to the security door and pulled her hat down over her ears before venturing into the blizzard.

Snow pelted his face, icy needles pricking his bare skin. The sheer volume of falling snow dimmed the light from the parking lot lamps. Wind drove fat flakes almost horizontal. Sierra trudged in the direction of the CSU van through a half foot of snow, then stopped and turned back to him, a mittened hand shielding her face. "Where is your car?"

He tipped his head toward the snow-covered SUV parked beside her vehicle. "That one." He pressed the unlock button on the key fob, and the Explorer beeped. *Breach of protocol.* Extraordinary circumstances, he reasoned as he brushed the thick blanket of snow from the vehicle.

What other choice did he have? He made the decision he thought was best for her safety. His personal feelings had nothing to do with this.

*Right.*

With the weather, he couldn't justify asking a unit to babysit her. It made more sense to take the duty himself.

*At a hotel.*

They'll have adjoining rooms, so he would be right there if she needed him. He's a professional. It's his job to protect.

*Remember that.*

He climbed into the driver's seat and started the truck while she retrieved a bag from the back of her car before she beeped it locked. She settled into the passenger seat, kicked snow off her boots, and slammed the door. She set her bag on the floor. "In case you're wondering about the extra clothes, I learned my lesson after one of the guys forgot to drain a fuel line before changing a valve. You aren't going to the hospital in this, are you?" she asked. "You can hardly see the apartment building across the lot. Besides, Fairview is farther than the hotels, if I remember right."

The snow reflected the blinding glare of the headlights back into his eyes. This was not going to be easy. He couldn't imagine what it was like for his on-duty compatriots. On his side were snow tires and four-wheel drive. And, if people heeded the no-travel advisory, deserted roads. "I have to check on Cate. If she's awake, I need to talk to her."

"So call the hospital when we get to the hotel. There's no point in the extra trip if she's still unconscious."

In the dim light of the truck he couldn't see her face well enough to read her expression. "I agree. You don't like driving in this, do you?"

She gripped the handle above the door like it might fly away. "Do you?" she countered.

He didn't bother answering. No one with any common sense would go out in this weather. He turned up the police radio and listened to the chatter. No travel recommended. The advantages of being in the city versus outstate Minnesota: plenty of buildings to break the wind, and roads were lined with streetlights. In outstate Minnesota, if the visibility didn't make driving impossible, the snow camouflaging the road would.

"I don't have a choice. Point for you."

She grumbled. "You're not one of those guys who keep track of how many times they were right, are you? Because that's just juvenile."

The disgust in her voice and the matter-of-fact statement made him smile. "No, I'm not one of those guys, as long as you're not one of those women who do the same, then rub it in for months afterward."

"Like I said, that's just juvenile. Can't change the past, only learn from it. Or not, and repeat it."

Her words soothed the emotional scars left by his ex-wife's betrayal. "Who said that?"

"My dad. If someone famous said it, I don't know who it was. Probably Sun Tzu, or Confucius, or Batman."

Quinn grinned at her humor, then quickly sobered. An SUV navigated the road in front of them. He slowed from an almost crawl to a full crawl, and debated passing the vehicle. There was no one else on this four-lane stretch of road. He decided it was safer to pass, if only to put more distance between them and the SUV. He edged into the left lane and trusted the snow tires to keep the Explorer on course. The other vehicle slowed, and Quinn eased back into the right lane once he cleared the other truck by a couple car lengths.

Sierra sat beside him, one hand tucked under her leg, the other with a death grip on the overhead handle, eyes closed. He didn't need to worry that she was alone.

He reviewed the case again in his mind. Why would Thorsson break into Tori's apartment? The lock might have been picked; there had been no signs of damage to the door or jamb. Peter Manelli was still in the wind. He also worked at Castor. He likely had a key. He could have tossed the apartment.

What was he looking for?

Someone left the pendant on Tori's body, or did Tori find it? She wasn't wearing it; it was in her uniform pocket. Thorsson fueled planes where Tori worked part-time. It could have fallen out of his pocket. She could have found it on the ramp.

Could it have fallen out of Sierra's pocket?

No, he thought, not after her reaction to the news that Thorsson worked at the airport. He felt certain she had told him the truth about the pendant.

Did Sierra hate Tori enough to kill her?

He didn't get the sense she would kill anyone, but he had seen enough in his years as a cop to know that sometimes the perpetrator was the last person anyone suspected.

# 28

Creeping from stoplight to stoplight for what seemed like hours, they managed to reach the first hotel west of the interstate along Burnsville Parkway. Moore instructed Sierra to stay in the truck while he went in to check for rooms despite the neon "No Vacancy" sign. The worst part about driving in a blizzard during the day was no visibility. At night, that was aggravated by the headlights reflected back into the driver's eyes by the snow. It was almost easier to drive through a blizzard at night with no lights. At least she wasn't driving, Moore was.

It was snowing so hard the windshield was almost completely covered by the time he returned to the truck.

"No vacancy, huh?" she asked.

He brushed snow from his hat. "No."

Sarcasm seeped into her voice. "So, that's what the red 'No Vacancy' sign means."

She didn't look at him, yet felt the heat of his glare. "Sometimes they do that because the rooms are reserved. It doesn't mean they're all occupied."

"Except in this case."

"There are a few more hotels up the road. One of them should have some rooms available."

"That's what everyone's saying about now."

"I tried to get the desk attendant to call ahead, but the jerk gave me the 'funneling customers to the competition' line, and it didn't matter that I'm a cop. Look, I'm sorry about this whole business, but I'm not leaving you alone without some sort of protection."

She ventured a glance at him. He stared at the windshield as if contemplating the wisdom of continuing on. Deep down, she appreciated his effort at looking out for her. "Hey, I'm sorry. I really hate driving in this kind of weather, in case you haven't already guessed."

He cleared the snow off the windshield, then shifted the SUV into gear and headed back to the main road. "So do I, but it could be worse."

The characteristic Minnesota saying cracked some of her tension. "Sure. We could be driving a Yugo with bald tires through a foot of snow. Of course, we wouldn't get very far."

His quiet chuckle settled like a soft warm glow in her belly. "True." He maneuvered through the turn for the next hotel. This one had "Vacancy" lit in orange neon. Once he parked the Explorer, he grabbed something Sierra couldn't identify from behind her seat before they trotted across the lot to the main entrance. They stomped snow from their boots before heading to the desk.

Moore asked for two rooms, either adjoining or next to each other across or down the hall. The desk attendant, a stern-looking woman with creased, leathery skin tilted her head up to look through the half-moon lenses of her glasses. Her voice, low and gravelly, confirmed decades of smoking. "I've got three rooms left. None are adjoining, next to each other, or on the same floor." She tipped her head forward and looked over the lenses at them. "I've got three with single king beds."

"Are you sure there aren't any rooms with two beds available?" Moore asked.

The desk attendant, whose name tag said "Wendy", pressed her lips into a thin line. "I've got three rooms open, each with one bed." She turned just enough to include Sierra in her visual range. "I can give you a cot if you need it."

"How many other hotels are on this stretch?" Sierra asked.

Wendy heaved a sigh and pulled off her reading glasses. "Two more down the road, but I'll tell you right now, the last six people to check in said we were the only one with rooms left."

Sierra wondered if the woman's claim was true, or just a sales pitch. Then again, did they want to continue trudging down the road to find out she was right?

Moore must have come to the same conclusion. "Fine. Give me one of the rooms and a cot."

Wendy nodded. Sierra wandered the small lobby while Moore finished the details. The place smelled like old fabric, musty and dry. Arrangements of artificial flowers supported thick coatings of dust.

She jumped when he tugged on her sleeve. "Sorry." He handed her a key card and led the way to the elevator.

❖ ❖ ❖

THE ROOM WAS AT THE END OF THE HALLWAY on the third floor, close to the vestibule that held the ice machine and a vending machine. Moore indicated for her to wait in the hall, then drew his gun before opening the door.

The weight of the situation hit her, wrapped a cold, dark fist around her, trapping her lungs. Rune might be following her. Some lunatic attacked Cate, trashed her apartment. That same lunatic might have seen Sierra.

Moore's voice floated somewhere outside her head, but she couldn't understand the words. He gripped her shoulder, and the vise around her chest dissipated like vapor. "Sierra, are you listening? The room is clear. You okay?"

"I'm not sure." She closed her eyes and took a deep breath, then let it out slowly before she headed into the room. "This whole thing doesn't seem real. I mean, stuff like this happens on television and in movies."

"To tell you the truth, this is new territory for me, too." He shed his coat and hung it in the barely-a-closet just inside the door.

A knock at the door had Moore drawing his gun and peering through the peephole. "Yes?" he called through the door.

"Someone asked for a cot."

Moore held his gun behind him and answered the door. An older man rolled a folded cot into the room. Atop the cot was a stack of bedding and a pillow. "There should be extra blankets." He pointed to the shelf above the rod of the almost-closet. "If you need any more pillows or blankets, just call the desk. G'night, folks."

"Thank you," said Moore as he tipped the man, then closed the door and locked it after he left. He holstered his gun as he crossed to the small table in a corner of the room, its surface covered with the requisite fliers from local eateries and other offerings. "You hungry? I missed dinner, and my stomach is not happy about it."

"Do you really think anyone's going to deliver in this weather?" She felt like a kindergartner on the first day of class, lost but not. She dropped her duffel and explored the confines of the room all the way to the bathroom and back. With the cot laid out, she thought, they would be staying in even closer quarters.

He lifted a flyer, then peered out the curtains. "Pizza?" he asked. "They should be right across the highway, but I can't see that far in the storm. They've got chicken if you'd rather have that."

Nothing sounded good after the day she had. "Whatever you want is fine. I'm not hungry right now."

He dialed the number on the flyer and placed an order for pizza. Next, he pulled a card from his wallet and dialed a number. He left a message with their room and contact number before he hung up and turned his attention to her. "Aren't you warm?"

She realized she still wore her coat. And now that he mentioned it, she was warm. She hung her coat next to his. A small duffel bag lay below his coat. "Is this yours?"

He rested a hip on the table. "Just like you, I learned my lesson. I always have a change of clothes, just in case. There's nothing worse than jumping into a pond to rescue someone and not being able to change into something dry that doesn't smell like swamp. You can relax. The pizza won't be here for a bit."

She paced the room for the five seconds it took to do a complete circuit. She wished for the familiar comfort of her apartment. She was in this awkward situation because someone broke into Cate's apartment, tore it up, and put Cate in the hospital. Because that someone might know Sierra went to help Cate, and she didn't want that person to know where she lived. Because it might have been Rune waving at her in the parking lot.

She wouldn't be here at all if she hadn't found Tori's body. Even in death the woman screwed up her life.

"Sierra, why don't you sit down? You look like you're ready to fall down."

She'd almost forgotten about Moore. "I'm fine. I can't sit, I have to move around." She continued to pace, but in the confines of the hotel room, it didn't help. She wanted to walk, run, something to bleed off the anxiety. How could she stay in a one-bed hotel room with a cop, a man she barely knew?

She turned, and he was there, hands cupping her shoulders. A layer of tension melted away. "I know this is weird, and I know you are not comfortable, but you need to relax." Moore gave her a gentle shove toward the bed. "Sit down. Let's talk."

# 29

She complied, uncertain why she did so without resisting. She should protest, if only for the principle of it.

He dragged the chair from the table and arranged it so he sat directly in front of her, his notepad on his lap. "I know this may not be the best time, after what happened with Cate, but let's do this now. You promised to tell me the rest of the story."

She fingered her brother's dog tag through her sweater, the memento still lying against her skin. She would rather talk about her stalking ex than the woman who stole her only brother from her. "Do we really have to do this now?"

"What else are we going to do? I forgot my deck of cards at home." His levity made her smile. "How did you know Tori?"

A deep breath. *I can do this.* "She dated my brother."

"When did they start dating?"

"After the company party, about a year ago now. I brought Ken to the party, Tori brought Cate. Ken noticed Tori right away, but that wasn't hard—she had long hair then, with a hot pink streak in it." It started so innocently, she thought. "I think they went on a date the next night or something."

"Did your brother and Tori get along? Did they fight? How often did they go out?"

The Ken who had returned from the military, the competent, clean-cut, respectable Ken contrasted with the partying, risk-taking high schooler he had been before he left. Everyone in the family had worried about him, about not whether they would get a call in the middle of the night, but when. Once he signed up for the military, they hoped his self-destructive activities were over. The Air Force had been good for him; he had found discipline, responsibility, and a passion for flying. It hadn't taken long after he met Tori for Ken to return to the unmotivated, unconcerned, party-hearty version of himself. Tori resurrected that part of him. Sierra shook her head, but failed to dispel the memories. "I'm sorry, Detective."

"Quinn. Call me Quinn." He started again, then hesitated before continuing. "It's less formal, but I think it'll help." He cleared his throat. "Let's try again. How long did they date?"

She held onto the anger even after Kendrick's ashes were spread over the mountains by the wind. Why didn't her brother see what was happening? Why hadn't he listened to her? What more could she have done? She couldn't reach him those last weeks before ... She shoved off the bed and headed toward the door.

He intercepted her. "Okay, I get it. You're still upset about whatever happened."

"How does this help find out who ... dammit, I didn't kill her. There was a time I wanted to, and I think if I met her again it wouldn't be pleasant, but I didn't kill her."

"Then help me find out who did." He gestured toward the bed. "Sit down. Tell me about Ken."

The pizza arrived before she started. She still wasn't hungry, but after the first bite of tangy sauce and gooey cheese, she figured the least she could do was help him eat it. She waited until Quinn—odd that he wanted her to call him by name—finished off a couple pieces before she told him about her older brother, how he encouraged her to follow her own path before and after he left home to join the Air Force.

"Was he a pilot?"

She nodded. "He flew E-3s—the AWACS planes—and transports." The time he invited her along on a short transport haul between MSP and Duluth cinched her decision to work in aviation. The combination of general mechanics she learned from her grandfather and the awe of flying machines sent her down the road of aviation maintenance.

"Was Ken still in the Air Force when you brought him to the company party?" Quinn asked.

"No. He finished his obligation and was staying with me while he looked for a job." Ken had been adamant about not living at home. It was a matter of pride, he'd said. He could fly multi-million dollar aircraft, protect the country, and he could damn well get his civilian life on track without moving back in with Mom and Dad. No one ever mentioned the real reason he didn't want to stay at home.

Too many of his old friends still lived in the area.

He had helped her after the attack, and she helped him in return. She offered what little room she had until he found a job and his own place.

He had left home a wandering spirit without concrete goals, and returned after his stint in the military a focused, disciplined man who still enjoyed an afternoon of fishing with his sister.

Quinn wiped his hands on a washcloth from the bathroom, then handed it to her. "Why didn't he stay with your folks? They aren't that far out of the Cities if they're just south of Prior Lake."

"He didn't want to slide back into old habits."

"Such as?"

"During high school he worked part-time after school, but he also took every opportunity to party with his buddies. By staying with me, Ken avoided the temptation to return to those old, self-destructive patterns."

"You and your brother were close."

"Yes."

"What happened after he met Tori?" he asked. "Why are you still so angry about Tori and your brother?"

Sierra didn't want to remember her brother slipping away from the considerate, outgoing, confident man he'd become in the Air Force. She scooted onto the bed against the pillows and headboard, and drew her knees to her chin, anchored them with her arms around her legs, and closed her eyes. She couldn't tell him. What would he think of her?

The bed jostled. She opened her eyes. He sat at the foot of the bed, legs crossed. "No notebook," he said with a show of empty hands. "Talk it through."

After a deep, calming breath, she launched into the story of how Tori Hjelle enticed Ken back into bars, drinking, and partying. Quinn listened in silence, his attention focused on her.

"After the first couple months he started staying out until dawn. Sometimes I came home from work before he got in. God, he couldn't see it, didn't see it, or didn't want to see it, I don't know. He'd still be crashed when I left for work. He missed interviews and didn't return calls from potential employers. I tried to help him. I couldn't stand to see … It hurt to see him like that."

Her hands ached from clenching them. Her knees started to burn from being stuck in the same position too long. A thick knot of tension settled at the back of her throat. "I told him he was ruining his opportunities to find a job and transition into civilian life. I even asked Cate to talk to Tori, to get her to stop seeing Ken, or at least stop the partying. Cate told me about the things Tori did after her parents died. I knew then that she was reason he went back to his old habits from high school. I begged him to stop seeing her. He didn't—wouldn't listen to me, and Cate said Tori ignored her."

"What happened?"

Tears welled. The frustration, the anger, the pain of losing him, the helpless feelings rolled through her. "One night Cate called me at three in the morning to come pick Ken up at her apartment. I wasn't sleeping well even on days I didn't work, so I was up, but tired. When I got there, I found Ken passed out on the couch. He was so pale, almost gray. Tori was on her feet, but she could hardly stand." When Sierra lost her temper, Tori just laughed at her.

Cate talked her down. Sierra had never felt that much raw rage. She couldn't bear to see her beloved brother like that. Would she have beaten Tori up? How far would she have gone?

"Cate said you shoved Tori. She kept you separated," Quinn said.

"Yes. I think if Cate hadn't been there, I—" She stopped. Tori's laugh echoed in her head. She fished a tissue out of a pocket, dabbed at her eyes. "Cate helped me drag Ken to my car, then rode home with me to help get him to my apartment. I took her back home, apologized for all the awful things I had said earlier. I didn't talk to her again until the memorial service."

Silence closed in around her, a smothering blanket woven of loss, anger, regret, and guilt. That night was the last time she saw her brother. Tears rolled down her cheeks. She hadn't gotten a chance to talk to him before he took off, even though she left a note for him to call her; she worked the morning shift that day for another mechanic. She should have called to check on him, to tell him to wait a day before leaving, to wait until she got home from work so they could talk.

Did she do enough? Could she have done more? She tried to let go of the guilt, tried to convince herself it wasn't her fault. Ken chose to go back to his old habits. He chose to ignore her pleas. She buried her face against her knees, swallowed the sobs that squeezed through a throat tight with grief.

"Sierra." Quinn settled beside her on the bed, wrapped his arms around her, and pulled her to him.

She burrowed into the comfort he offered and mourned for her brother.

# 30

Quinn held her until she ran out of tears. She wept until her breath hitched. He couldn't remember when he'd held someone like this. Had he held his brother when his nephew died? Had he held his mother when his grandfather—her father—died? Or when they learned of the hereditary condition that stole his nephew's life?

If so, that would have been the last time.

He learned not to hold on too tightly. They always left when he did. His beloved grandfather left him after succumbing to pancreatic cancer. His best friend, lost to the actions of a drunk driver. His nephew, the one who thought the world of Quinn, fell victim to the unknown time bomb in his family's genes.

They both had suffered from loss. He understood her in a way that surprised him after knowing her for such a short time.

He rested a cheek on Sierra's head and combed his fingers through her fine hair. He risked his case, his career, tonight by assigning himself to her security and bringing her here.

He risked his heart by sitting here, holding her.

Hell, who was he kidding? He could no longer consider her just a civilian involved in a case. They were, for all intents and purposes, strangers, yet Quinn felt like she belonged here, in his arms. She just ... belonged.

He released her when she pulled away, the sudden cool sending a shiver through him. "Oh man, I'm so sorry." She sidled a few inches, putting space between them. "This is awkward. I didn't mean to break down like that."

"No worries." Discomfort mixed with concern spawned an urge to move. He got up and retrieved a hand towel and box of tissues from the bathroom.

She accepted both. "Thank you."

He didn't want to continue the interview, but he had to reestablish the boundary. *Professional, not personal.*

He wished he could close the case now.

"Did you see Tori after that night? Maybe at work?"

She didn't answer for a moment, staring at the tissue in her hands instead. "After the accident, while the investigation was active, I worked at the hangar. I didn't switch shifts or sub for anyone on first or second shift. The higher-ups wanted to keep me off the line. I definitely wanted no opportunity to run across her."

"So, no?" When she didn't answer for more than a minute, he prodded. "Sierra? Did you ever see Tori after that night you picked Ken up?"

"Once," she said, her voice low and tight. "After the investigation finished, I headed to the gate to pick up an inspection plane. I saw her overnighting another plane, and ... I was still pissed at her."

"What did you do?" He'd seen her temper, heard Cate's testimony of her potential for physical confrontation. *Please, don't say you assaulted her.*

"I knew if I confronted her I might do something I'd regret. I'd just survived an FAA investigation, and if things got ugly, I might lose my job anyway. If there are ramp agents available, we're supposed to ask them to give us a start. I did it myself, with the mechanic riding along, like we do when there aren't any ramp agents around."

Quinn let out a breath he didn't realize he held. "Was that the only time?"

She nodded, then raised her eyes to his. "Can we be done for tonight?"

He checked the time. Almost midnight. His energy washed out of him, ushering fatigue in its wake. "I think so. It's late."

She took her bag to the bathroom and closed the door while he set up the cot. Damn awkward, he thought.

By the time Quinn finished his turn in the bathroom, Sierra had turned out the lights by the bed and curled into a tight ball facing away from him and the cot. Disappointment sank through him. He wanted to say goodnight and hear her say it back. Sentimental, he knew, and another gesture that made this exercise less official, more personal. He crept to the bed and listened. She breathed slow and steady, already asleep.

He reached to her, then stopped. He wanted to touch her, just a brush on her shoulder, a tiny gesture. To do what? Reassure himself, he realized. "Good night, Sierra," he whispered. He turned off the final light, climbed into the cot, checked for his gun within reach, then gave in to the exhaustion dragging him into sleep.

❖ ❖ ❖

SOFA CUSHIONS, THEIR INNARDS SHREDDED, surrounded the couch. Shadows huddled in every corner, hiding movement that taunted, dared her to investigate. Silence permeated the apartment, a viscous unseen fog that swallowed every sound. Tendrils of fear wrapped around Sierra's throat, trapping her voice. Her racing pulse thudded through her, the rhythm of terror echoing in her head.

Her brother Ken appeared, unconscious, on the barren couch. She stepped toward him and Tori appeared, pink hair glowing like a will-o'-the-wisp fastened to her scalp. Her mouth gaped, baring fangs dripping blood.

She couldn't move, couldn't run, couldn't scream. Her muscles burned with her effort to escape her invisible bonds.

Another shadow oozed into view, loomed over her, became Rune. His eyes were too big, too wild, too evil. He opened his mouth, but the silence filled her ears like wax. Then he turned, lifted a sledgehammer over his head, and brought it down on Tori over and over, until she was nothing but a body curled into a ball.

He turned toward her, weapon raised. Acid etched through muscles straining to break free. She struggled, choked on her fear. The hammer began its arc.

Black. She blinked against the darkness, straining to see something, anything. She held her breath and listened. Something. She turned, now able to move. No, stay still. *Listen.*

Breathing. She swallowed the fear this time. *Not again.* She raised fists and focused on the sound. *Over there.*

Something grabbed her wrist.

# 31

She lashed out.

Something caught her other wrist. She screamed.

"Stop!" Hands clamped hers to her sides. She bounced face-first into something soft. Weight on her back pressed her into that something.

"Sierra, wake the hell up." The voice spoke close, breath against her cheek. "You're dreaming. Wake up."

The dark shattered. Reality seeped in. She listened to the rush of blood in her ears. Inhaled the scent of clean but worn linens. Felt the bed beneath her.

"Are you awake?"

His voice dissipated the lingering fear. Her pulse slowed, and her breathing followed suit.

"Sierra?" He didn't release her or let up on the pressure forcing her onto the bed. "Can you hear me?"

"Yes," she croaked, her throat complaining at the effort.

"Who am I?" he asked.

"Quinn."

The weight pressing on her lifted, and he let go of her wrists. Trembling, she got her hands under her and pushed to a sitting position. The T-shirt she wore stuck to her sweaty skin. She pulled the quilted bedspread to her, wrapped it around her shoulders, and tried to banish the echoes of the nightmare.

Quinn sat on the edge of the bed beside her. Worry lines creased his brow, and concern filled his eyes. "Do you have nightmares like that often?"

"Not like that." Her voice sounded as rough and raw as her throat felt. "Can you get me some water, please?"

He rose and went to the bathroom. A moment later he returned and handed her a cup of water before reclaiming his seat on the bed. "Can you tell me about it?"

She shivered again, this time from the memory of terror more than cold. She shook her head. "I don't want to remember it."

He didn't respond for a moment. "Maybe start easy. Was anyone you know in the dream?"

"Ken. Tori. Rune. In my apartment."

Quinn pressed his lips into a thin line. "Ken and Tori? That makes sense, since we talked about them earlier. Your ex? You thought you saw him at Cate's place. Tell me the rest of it."

She took a deep breath, then told him everything, from the vivid silence, to her paralysis, to Rune's deconstruction of Tori into the frozen body she found in the hell-hole, to the darkness and the hand on her wrist.

"I'm sorry about that," he said. "I woke up when you started thrashing around. When you got out of bed, I thought you were awake, but you didn't respond. I know you aren't supposed to wake someone who's sleepwalking, but I didn't want you to trip over the cot or anything else." He chuckled, a rich sound from deep within. "You just about nailed me with a wicked right hook. You're stronger than you look."

"Thanks, I think." She had managed only a couple hours of sleep judging by the time on the clock. She quieted her churning mind, blocking images from her nightmare with a detailed vision of a log cabin nestled in thick woods near a mountain lake. Her muscles, weakened by adrenaline withdrawal and fatigue, dragged her back toward sleep.

❖   ❖   ❖

LIGHT EASED IN AROUND THE EDGES OF THE CURTAIN, illuminating the room enough for Quinn to see. A glance at his watch confirmed it was past rush hour. He sat up, rubbed his eyes, and stretched. Who knew a hotel cot would be so comfortable? He crept to the bed, where Sierra lay curled into the blankets, facing away from the window and toward the cot. Slow and smooth, the rhythm of her breathing assured him she still slept.

Good, he thought. After her nightmare last night, on top of the whole apartment invasion and assault on Cate, she needed to rest. Her nightmare-induced sleepwalking earlier still rattled him. It wasn't the sleepwalking, but the speed and strength of her response when he took hold of her. He barely managed to block her fist. She reacted, whether consciously or not, fast and with fury, and stronger than he expected for her size.

Until he finished the case, he needed to keep his interaction with her professional. Last night, however, put another nail in the coffin of his impartiality. When she broke down while telling him about her brother and the victim, he had offered a shoulder to cry on. He might have given a quick hug to any other witness, but he wouldn't have comforted someone he met in the course of his job like he held Sierra last night.

Guilt grew within him. Hell, when had his impartiality where she was concerned vacated the premises?

The night he was called to a body in an airplane.

If the case affected him personally, protocol dictated he turn the case over to someone who could be impartial. The problem? No one else in the APD was qualified to work this case. They would have to turn it over to the BCA.

He didn't want to do that.

He showered and completed his morning routine as quietly as he could, then turned on the desk lamp. The glare lit the room more than he wanted, but the sooner Sierra woke, the sooner they could leave the hotel. He peered out the window. Patches of asphalt revealed by the action of snowplows and the salt-sand mixture they used peeked through packed snow. The main roads were clear.

Quinn called the hospital to check on Cate's status, then called the office and listened to his voice mail. Kevin hadn't left a message, leading him to wonder if the CS team was finished cataloging the scene. There had been a lot to record, but they should be finished by now. He tried again to contact Peter Manelli, Tori's elusive boyfriend. He left a message for Pete, then tried Castor Aviation. Marshall Kline assured him he'd call as soon as Pete showed up.

"Shit." The hissed curse came from the bed. Sierra sat up and rubbed her eyes, then stretched like a cat, arms reaching toward the ceiling. For a moment, he wondered what that lean torso would feel like under his hands. When she noticed him, he banished the thought like a kid hiding a wrapper from a forbidden treat. "It's after nine. How long have you been up?"

"Long enough. Why don't you do whatever it is you do in the morning, then we'll head over to the hospital. The nurse said Cate regained consciousness a few hours ago. She's sleeping now. Hopefully she can give us something to help identify the man who tore up her apartment and assaulted her."

She nodded, gathered her bag, and headed to the bathroom.

When she emerged twenty minutes later in a navy Range Airlines sweat-shirt and jeans, hair towel-dried from her shower, Quinn tried not to notice his pulse bumping into a higher orbit. He hooked his badge to his belt and pulled on his shoulder harness. He needed to be Detective Moore now, all business and professional detachment.

"After we stop at the hospital, we'll go to the apartment. You can pick up your car."

"Detective Moore," she started, and his detachment faltered at the edge in her voice, "are you going to get into trouble because of this whole thing?"

He wanted her to call him by his given name, but that would torpedo his effort to remain professional. "I made the decision, and I'm going to deal with whatever falls out. I broke rules by bringing you here, even if it was for your protection. The fewer people who know, the better."

She stared at him. "Are you serious? You could get fired over this?"

He hesitated. "I did this to keep you safe from whomever tossed Cate's apartment and put her in the hospital. There were extenuating circumstances with the blizzard. I won't get fired."

"But you could get into trouble? Desk duty for a week or something?"

"Or something," he conceded.

She shook her head, mouth agape. "All I did was find a dead body. Why risk your job over me?"

He avoided answering. "You ready to go?"

"No, wait." She held out a hand, palm toward him as though holding him back. "Look, I know you—cops—do a lot of things to protect the rest of us, and I can't for a minute guess how stressful some of those things are, but," she paused, "you guys probably don't hear it enough. Thank you."

# 32

Quinn wrinkled his nose at the odor of disinfectant and the underlying stink of sickness. He had never liked hospitals, the smell, the sterility of the machines and rooms. It reminded him too much of the heartbreaking weeks his nephew spent in the hospital before he died.

Sierra didn't appear bothered by the atmosphere. She had spent a week in the hospital recovering after the attack. Maybe she associated the place with better memories than his.

The bed closest to the door was empty. Cate Zahn occupied the far bed, accompanied by a man in his late twenties sitting beside her, holding her hand. They were talking in hushed tones until Quinn knocked. He showed his badge to the young man he presumed was Cate's boyfriend. "Detective Moore, Airport PD. I'm here to talk to Cate about last night."

The man reached to him in greeting. "Brent Andrews. The doctor said you were coming by."

Sierra stepped around Quinn. "Hi, Cate. How are you doing?"

"Lousy."

Brent checked his watch. "I've got to go. I've got a practical to study for." He leaned over Cate to kiss her. "I can't keep Rascal any longer. Amir is threatening to skin her. What should I do?"

Cate sighed. "Sierra, I hate to ask you this, but I don't have any other ideas right now. Can you take Rascal for a few days, just until I get out of here or Pete calls me back?"

"Who's Rascal?"

"Tori's pet ferret," Cate said. "She's okay, just upset that Tori hasn't given her any attention for a while. Brent took her because I had to work extra hours so I wasn't at home, but he can't keep her any longer."

Brent added, "I've got her in my car. It's only been about a half hour, and I wrapped her pretty good."

Sierra tucked her stocking cap into a coat pocket. "We had a lot of animals when I was growing up, but I've never taken care of a ferret before. I know they're not like cats or dogs."

"She's kinda like a cat mixed with a little gremlin," Brent said. "She's mischievous, but right now she just wants attention, and I'm not going to be around much for the next few days to watch her."

"Please?" Cate pleaded. "Just until we can get a hold of Pete. My only other option is to take her to an animal shelter."

After another moment, Sierra surrendered. "Okay, but I'm only off for two more days."

"She's in her carrier right now," Brent said. "I've got some of her things, food and stuff. I'll give you the instructions Cate gave me. You'll need more food, her bigger cage, and more toys. It's all at Cate's place." He looked at Quinn. "I'm guessing I won't be allowed in there because it's some sort of crime scene."

He nodded. He hadn't talked to Kevin, but the scene needed to be closed for another day or two, until he was certain he'd gotten all the information he could. "I'll make sure Sierra can get what she needs."

Sierra turned to Quinn and lowered her voice. "Can I move her into your vehicle, or do I have to wait until you're done here?"

Wary of eyes on them, he gestured for her to follow him into the hall. Once out of earshot, he handed her his keys. He wasn't supposed to give his keys to a civilian, even if that civilian did power runs on multi-million dollar aircraft. Yet another rule broken. "I don't know how long this is going to take."

"If Brent has her in a blanket, I'm sure another half an hour won't hurt her. Any longer than that and I'll have to run the heater. Thank you," she added.

"Just do it quietly, please."

Once Sierra left with Brent, Quinn sat on the chair beside Cate's bed, notebook ready. "What happened yesterday after we met at the U?"

Cate brushed a crease from her sheet. "After my classes, I stopped at Southdale Mall to pick up a few things on my way home. Oh, wait, my last class got out early because the professor was sick and the TA had another class. So maybe I got home earlier than usual." She closed her eyes, and Quinn was afraid for a moment that she'd fallen asleep. "As soon as I opened the door to the apartment, I knew something was wrong. I suppose I called Sierra because I'd just talked to her, and she isn't that far away. I guess I should have called 911 first."

"Sierra told you to call me," Quinn said.

Cate nodded. "After I hung up with her, I started to dial 911. Then someone ripped the phone out of my hand and tore it off the wall."

"Did you get a look at him?"

"No." She touched the brace on her wrist. "He wore a ski mask." Her breath hitched. "He kept asking me where they were. He insisted I knew what he was looking for, that I knew what he wanted and where Tori hid them. I told him I didn't know. He hit me." She shuddered. "Then he pushed me, or maybe I fell. That's all I remember until I woke up here."

"Is there anything you can tell me about him? How tall was he? What was he wearing? Did you recognize his voice?"

"No. He was taller than me, maybe your height. He wore black. I think he wore gloves."

When he heard the soft rustle of her coat, Quinn glanced up. Sierra slipped into the room and sat in a chair beside the door.

"What about his shoes or his coat?" Quinn asked. "Do you remember anything about them?"

"No," Cate said. "I was so scared. I don't remember much. I'm sorry, I wish I could help, I really do. It all happened so fast."

This went back to Tori. "I know I asked you before, but I'm going to ask you again. Did Tori have problems with anyone? Did she ever tell you if someone was bothering her? Not just at the airport, but maybe at school."

Cate shook her head. "We didn't see each other that often, with school and our jobs. Or we were out with our boyfriends. But ... I don't know. It's probably nothing."

"Anything, even if it turns out to be nothing, is helpful," Quinn reassured her.

"There were a few times when she would get a phone call. I thought it was weird, because after she answered, she didn't say anything, and then she hung up and went straight to her room."

"Did she stay in her room?"

"No. She came back after, I don't know, less than five minutes. I asked her one time who it was, or if she even knew who it was. She always told me it wasn't my business." Cate frowned. "I started to wonder if she was cheating on Pete."

Quinn looked up from his notes. "Do you know if you ever answered the phone when this person called? Did he or she ask for Tori? Would you recognize the voice?"

"I don't know. Last week, maybe the week before, I answered the phone a couple times, but the person just hung up."

Sierra drew in a sharp breath. He turned. "Sierra?" he prompted.

"Sorry." She drew a finger across her lips promising silence.

He made a mental note to ask what triggered her reaction after he finished with Cate. He returned his attention to Cate. "Okay. Do you have any idea what he was looking for? Did Tori have valuables?"

Cate shook her head. "I've been trying to figure out what he'd be looking for. I can't think of anything."

Quinn remembered something Tom Manelli said about Tori and her research. "What about her grad paper? What do you know about that?"

"Not much."

"Did she ever talk to you about it?"

Cate squeezed her eyes closed for a moment. "Not exactly. After Ken died, Tori changed. She wanted to fix things, kept saying stuff like finding out what really happened." She waved at Sierra to stop her interruption. "Just listen. One night, a couple weeks ago, I overheard her on the phone when I got home from work. She was talking to Grandpa about planes and what sounded like an inspection. She finished and hung up before I took my coat off."

Quinn leaned back, juggling pieces of the case in his head. "Do you know anything about that?"

"Not much. I asked Tori what she was talking to Grandpa about. All she said was she thought she found something big, but she needed more information."

"Did it have to do with her paper?"

Cate shrugged. "Maybe. I'm sorry, Detective, but I really don't know more than that."

"If you can remember anything at all, call me." He handed her another business card.

Sierra took the opportunity to approach Cate's bed. "I've got Rascal. Call me when you get home or you hear from Pete, okay?"

"Sure. Thanks."

She lingered. "Cate, I'm sorry. I should have told you a long time ago, but the stuff Tori did ... I shouldn't have treated you like that. It wasn't your fault."

Cate smiled. "Thank you. I know how hard Tori could be on people. I'm sorry she didn't change before your brother died." She spread her arms.

Sierra bent to hug her. "I promise I'll keep in touch this time," she said, voice quiet with a meek quality that surprised Quinn, especially after she nearly clocked him while sleepwalking.

Once they got to the parking ramp, Sierra returned Quinn's keys. "Did she remember anything?"

"Nothing useful. He was looking for something Tori had, and he apparently didn't find it in the apartment." He pulled her to a stop. "When she was talking about the weird phone calls, what did you realize?"

"What do you mean?"

"You interrupted when Cate talked about answering the phone and the person hung up." When she didn't respond, he continued. "Sierra, if you have something to contribute, now would be a good time."

"When someone calls and the wrong person answers, don't they ask for the person they want to talk to?"

"Yes, usually."

"So why wouldn't the person ask for Tori instead of hanging up on Cate?"

"Good question." If Tori was seeing someone other than Pete, would that someone hang up on Cate? Why would Tori answer phone calls from a love interest and not say anything before hanging up? "Anything else?"

"Not right now."

He scanned her face for any sign she was holding something back, but saw none. Once they reached the Explorer, he beeped it open and peered into the back seat. "Where's the ferret?"

Sierra went to the rear of the SUV and opened the lift gate. "I put her back here." One side of the cargo area held a cardboard box containing a bag labeled "ferret litter", another bag labeled "food", and a folder labeled "Instructions". A covered litter box sat on the other side of a small animal carrier wrapped in a faded quilt. "I am so not cut out to babysit a ferret. A cat or dog, yes. A member of the weasel family, not so much."

She closed the lift gate. "I didn't realize you could litter-train ferrets. Sure beats changing the paper in the bottom of the cage." She slid into the passenger seat and fastened her seat belt as he started the vehicle and left the parking ramp. "Am I the only one who thinks it's strange no one has heard from Tori's boyfriend since she died?"

That was Quinn's next focus. "No. He's got a reputation for returning calls and calling in if he'll be a little late. His supervisor hasn't seen or heard from him since Tuesday."

"Wouldn't Tori's boyfriend call Cate if he hadn't heard from Tori for a couple days?"

"One would think." Which, in his experience, meant one of two things. Either Pete was the killer and he's gone to ground, or something happened to him. He suspected the latter. If Pete was the one who attacked Cate, she would have recognized his voice, if nothing else.

"Do you think something happened to him?"

Quinn marveled at how their thoughts seemed to be in sync. "That's what I need to find out. The boyfriend is the next person who might know if someone wanted to hurt Tori."

"What do you think the guy who attacked Cate was looking for? I mean, Tori was going to school, working as a rampie at the airport part-time, and was interning as a bookkeeper at an FBO, right? What on earth would she have that would be worth killing her for?"

Quinn remembered what Pete's brother said. *She started talking about setting the record straight and bringing them down.*

"Once I know that, I've got a motive."

❖ ❖ ❖

WHEN THEY ARRIVED AT THE APARTMENT COMPLEX, Quinn was lucky enough to find a parking spot next to Sierra's car. He brushed off the thick coating of snow while she started the vehicle. They transferred Rascal and her assorted gear into the wagon. She barked and squeaked her annoyance, but her protests gained nothing but a scoff from Sierra. She peeled the quilt from the door of the carrier and peered in. "Be nice." She covered the carrier back up before shutting the lift gate.

In Cate's apartment, Sierra stopped in the living room and stared at the spot on the carpet. "You okay?" he asked.

"It could've been worse. He could have killed her. Maybe he would have if he hadn't known I was coming over."

"She'll be fine." Quinn set a hand on the small of her back and nudged her toward the hallway and the bedrooms. If Tori kept a pet ferret, he reasoned the cage and anything else should be in her room.

The bed was separated, sheets torn off and sliced. The box spring, still in place on the frame, bore two long slashes in an "X". The mattress leaned against the far wall, with a matching "X" cut into it. Stuffing from the mattress covered the room like it had self-destructed. Drawers were pulled out, clothes discarded all over the floor. The contents of the closet were in a loose pile in a corner. A student desk in another corner of the room was upended, papers scattered. A computer monitor lay beneath a hole in the wall where it had struck, but the main part of the computer was nowhere in sight.

"Looks like a troll had a tantrum in here." After her light-hearted comment, Sierra stood in solemn silence at the threshold to the room, arms wrapped around herself, as though trying to contain memories triggered by the destruction.

Quinn suppressed a sudden desire to comfort her. *Keep it professional.* After last night, holding her against him while she mourned for her brother, the mantra was losing its effectiveness.

"Any idea where the ferret stuff is?" Sierra picked her way around the mess, then noticed him staring at her.

Guilt heated his cheeks.

"What?" she asked.

"Nothing." Whatever it was, it wasn't "nothing". "Nothing" didn't kick his pulse into high gear.

She did.

Under the desk she found a metal ferret cage on its side with an assortment of small dog toys inside. "See any food or litter around?" She lifted a sheet that had been tossed into a pile nearby. "Never mind." She pulled a bag of litter the size of a five-gallon bucket from under the sheet, then rummaged around before pulling a huge black canvas bag from the mess and peering inside. "Food." She added the bale of litter to the bag and set it atop the cage. "I'd better go."

"I'll call you when I find Tori's boyfriend so you can unload the ferret."

She gathered the bag and the cage. "Be careful, Quinn," she said before she left.

It was too late for that. He'd already fallen too far to recover.

# 33

Quinn sipped a fresh cup of barely-palatable coffee and stared at the whiteboard. What did he know about Tori Hjelle? She liked to play with people, and not in a nice way. Cate told him at her worst, Tori liked to spike the drinks of designated drivers. According to Sierra, Tori dragged Kendrick Bauer back into a partying lifestyle he escaped via the Air Force.

After Sierra tried and failed to stop her brother from seeing Tori, did she try to do more to break Tori's hold on her brother? He remembered how she wept in his arms last night. Would Sierra try vigilante justice for her brother by killing Tori?

Did she tell him the whole story? What about the pendant? He wanted to believe her, but so far the evidence didn't rule her out. He had to leave her name in the suspect column.

Cate said Tori changed after Ken died, tried to make up for the bad things she'd done. Tori, a grad student in forensic accounting, used the FBO as a case study for her thesis, but he didn't have access to a current draft of her paper or the supporting evidence for anything she might claim in it. Was that the key to her death?

Tom Manelli said she talked about setting the record straight, something that could bring them down. Pete insisted she get permission to use company information in her thesis. Did she find something that made Castor Aviation vulnerable to an investigation?

If the wrong person discovered what she knew, or if she told the wrong person, she may have caused her own death. Someone killed her to silence her. If that person knew Tori hid incriminating evidence, the break-in and search at Cate's apartment made sense.

If he was right, and if he could find whatever Tori discovered on the company, he'd have a solid motive. As it stood now, he only had circumstantial evidence, and precious little of that.

Officer Ward Stamford popped his head in. "Moore, I need some help. You available?"

Used to the sudden emergencies typical of police work, Quinn grabbed his coat from the rack and followed Stamford through the terminal to an access door that led to the AOA. "What's up?" he asked.

Stamford climbed into the driver's seat of a marked APD Explorer as Quinn settled into the passenger seat. "Twin-engine plane landed without incident, but the pilot lost control on the taxiway and collided with a de-ice truck. Four passengers and one pilot in the plane, a driver and passenger in the truck. No injuries, and minor damage to the truck." With lights on but no sirens, Stamford called ground control in the tower, standard procedure any time a vehicle might wander into the path of taxiing aircraft.

Odd, Quinn thought, but not unheard of. Anything having to do with a plane was the FAA's domain, but the APD had jurisdiction when ground vehicles were involved.

"The FAA doesn't have anyone available right now, so they asked us to process the scene. Camera's in the glove box."

Quinn pulled the Polaroid camera used to document scenes from the glove compartment, along with additional film. When they arrived, the fire department was working to separate the wing from the cab of the de-ice truck, where it managed to slice into the windshield. The truck belonged to Castor Aviation Services according to the distinctive green and white livery and the logo painted on the doors.

He photographed the plane, the truck, and the damage. The nose wheel of the twin-engine Beechcraft canted ninety degrees from the centerline of the plane. From the way the plane now sat in relation to the taxiway, it appeared that it veered in a sharp arc that sent it into the path of the de-ice truck. Quinn took some close-up pictures of the point of contact between the wingtip and the windshield, and of the nose wheel.

After he finished with the camera and stowed it, he took out his notepad to interview the driver and passenger from the de-ice truck. "Tell me what happened," he said after he introduced himself.

The driver adjusted his sunglasses. "I was heading to Concourse G, minding my own business, when this yahoo comes racing down the taxiway, then spins the plane around and nails me with the wing."

"Did it look like he had control of the plane when it spun around?"

"It looked like he was in a goddamn hurry. And he wasn't paying attention, neither. He drifted, then got his head out of his ass and saw where the hell he was going."

"So, the plane spun around when he tried to steer it back to the taxiway?"

"Yah, I guess. Come on, I don't pay no attention to those planes."

Quinn gauged the distance between the painted lines of the taxiway bordering the AOA and the painted lines of the vehicle "road". Almost fifty yards separated the two, but he also knew the vehicle lines were a suggestion rather than the rule. Because so many support vehicles drove back and forth across the AOA, the indicated road helped keep them out of the aircraft right-of-way. With the number of planes coming and going, sometimes service vehicles got in the way. That didn't explain why the truck was yards from the painted roadway.

"Why are you all the way over here when the road is over there?" he asked, pointing with his pen.

"Dumb-ass rampies think they can go where-the-fuck-ever they want. There were three baggage trains in the way. Looked like they were trying to figure out where the hell they were going. I had to go around them."

Still, Quinn suspected the plane had been taxiing too fast to its destination. Common sense suggested a pilot shouldn't taxi any faster than he could react.

"Look, I gotta get back to the garage," said the driver. "We've got a list of planes to de-ice, and I gotta swap this truck out for a different one. We done here?"

Quinn finished the interview. By now, two men wearing green parkas with Castor Aviation's logo were hooking a tow bar up to the plane's nose wheel. He intercepted them before they moved the plane. "Who's in charge here?"

The man on the tug hopped off, shouted some instructions over the roar of a Boeing 737 on its takeoff roll, then approached Quinn. "Bill Carlson, lead mechanic on the shift. We have to get this bird out of the way."

"Where are you putting this plane?"

"Why?" Carlson asked, his attitude borderline belligerent. "You're not FAA or NTSB."

"Because I need to tell the FAA where to send their agent when one is available."

Another man approached, his cheeks, ears, and nose bright red from the January cold and lack of a stocking cap. He answered Quinn's unasked question like he was being imposed upon. "Kent Wiseman. This is my plane." He addressed Carlson. "Do you have room for it?"

Carlson nodded. "We have room in Hangar 3 on the north side. Don't worry, Mr. Wiseman, we'll get it there."

Wiseman shrugged his shoulders to his ears. Quinn knew from experience that didn't do much for warmth. "Let me know. I've got to call the insurance company before you guys fix it."

"Excuse me, Mr. Wiseman, have you spoken with Officer Stamford?" asked Quinn.

"Yes. I need to get these people someplace warm." He proceeded to discuss logistics with Carlson.

Quinn reached Stamford as he finished interviewing the last passenger. Once the passengers were in a van headed to the general aviation terminal, he joined Stamford in the police SUV. The Castor Aviation mechanics started towing the plane in the direction of the FBO. "Do you know where Wiseman's hangar is?"

Stamford followed the plane. "He keeps his plane at the Crystal Airport, but he does a lot of business with Castor Aviation."

Quinn watched the progress of the tow tug along the taxiway. "Is it just me, or does it seem odd that the nose wheel turned like that?"

"He said everything was fine until he tried to recover after drifting off the taxiway."

Planes stuck to the taxiways for a reason, and pilots paid attention to what they were doing whether they were on the ground or in the air, because the machines were too expensive for carelessness. "Did he say why he drifted?"

"He was in a hurry. Wanted to get the passengers unloaded in time for them to get from here to downtown St. Paul for a meeting in," Stamford checked his watch, "a half-hour. If he'd taken his time, they'd be across the river by now."

The airport lay between the Twin Cities of Minneapolis and St. Paul, far enough south to allow planes to give the cityscape straddling the Mississippi River a wide berth. "So, he drifted, then over-corrected?"

"According to Mr. Wiseman, he lost steering when he tried to get back to the taxiway. The plane spun before he managed to hit the brakes." He looked over at Quinn. "The part that won't be going in the report is the part where he was in a heated discussion with one of the passengers about whether a taxi or a shuttle would be faster to get downtown."

Quinn skimmed Stamford's notes. The passengers all stated the same series of events: a hard landing, fast taxi, and a sudden jerk before the plane spun and hit the truck. It didn't sound right. "I'm going to call someone to take a look at the plane."

# 34

Sierra reviewed the ferret care instructions. She had grown up with a variety of animals, from rabbits to ducks to goats, but none with the wily reputation of the weasel family, unless she counted the orphaned mink kit her sister cared for until the Minnesota DNR took it to a wildlife rehabilitation center. She positioned the food and water as indicated in the diagram, and thought ferrets were way too picky about where their stuff was. There was supposed to be a soft pillow in the bottom of the cage, but since she had the cage and no pillow, she made do with an old towel.

Rascal still complained, growling and scratching at the carrier prison.

There were detailed instructions on taking Rascal out of the carrier and putting her in the cage without getting bitten; she'd seen the needle-like canines of the little carnivore. She dug out a pair of leather work gloves, made sure the cage door was open, then sat beside it with the carrier in her lap. Rascal seemed to know she was about to be freed, and got ready to make a run for it.

"Be good and I'll give you a treat, okay?" Beady eyes stared through the carrier door. Somehow she didn't think the animal believed her. She took a deep breath, then opened the carrier door.

Rascal scooted through the opening as soon as it was wide enough for her to squeeze through. Sierra caught her by the scruff of her neck, but just barely.

Rascal wore a harness that prevented Sierra from getting a good grip on her scruff, but allowed her another way to hang onto the slender creature. She guided the ferret into the cage and closed the door before Rascal could escape. "Ha!" she said, triumphant.

True to her word, she held a ferret treat next to the cage. Rascal reached out with her paws and grabbed it, devouring it like it was the first food she'd seen in days. Once it was gone, she sat and stared at Sierra, white facial markings stark against her cinnamon coat. The tip of her tail matched her mask. She was pretty, Sierra thought, but she wasn't a cat or dog. Then again, Sierra would be in trouble no matter what animal it was. Pets weren't allowed where she lived.

Sierra moved the cage and the litter box to the bathroom. She needed to run some errands, and suspected Rascal would appreciate room to stretch a bit. She set the litter box in the bathtub, the cage on the floor beside the tub, and coaxed Rascal into letting Sierra pick her up without gloves.

She set the ferret in the litter box to make sure Rascal knew where it was. She settled on the bathroom floor with the door closed. Rascal inspected the litter box, used it, then investigated the tub before she scurried over the edge and along the corner of the room until she reached Sierra.

Rascal's nose twitched. Sierra remained still. The ferret climbed onto her lap and sniffed at her hands before scaling her chest to bring her face to Sierra's.

"Don't you dare bite me," she warned in a whisper. "I'm a lot bigger than you are."

Rascal didn't seem phased by the threat. She worked her nose under Sierra's fingers, begging to be petted.

Wow, Sierra thought. She didn't expect a ferret to be so tame, especially with a stranger. She ran her fingers through the soft, short fur on Rascal's head. Not quite like a cat, she thought as she scratched at Rascal's ears. The ferret curled into her lap and closed her eyes, relishing the attention.

When the phone rang, Rascal zipped off Sierra's lap and into her cage, burrowing under the towel. Sierra slipped out of the bathroom and closed the door to prevent the little beast's escape, then answered the phone just as the machine picked up.

"Sierra? It's Quinn. Are you busy?"

❖  ❖  ❖

BEFORE SHE LEFT, SIERRA OPENED HER APARTMENT BLINDS and squinted against the brilliance, using a hand to shield her eyes until they adjusted.

Sunlight glared off the vast white expanses of new-fallen snow. The placid landscape bore no evidence of the nasty blizzard the night before, outside of the additional snow pile off the far side of the building's parking lot and the few vehicles still disguised as snow mounds. It never ceased to amaze her how brutal a winter storm could be one night, and how innocuous a cloudless blue sky and blazing sun could be the next day.

Movement from the street caught her attention. A black pickup truck rolled to a stop on the shoulder of the main road across from the entrance to the lot. A shadowed figure moved inside the cab, but it was too far away for her to see the driver. She waited, eyes glued to the truck. The figure stopped moving. No one exited the truck. It sat at the curb as if it had no intention of moving anytime soon.

She retreated from the window and hoped the driver hadn't noticed her. Quinn asked for her help at the airport, and she had errands to run, not the least of which was picking up groceries. A person could live off canned goods during a Minnesota winter only so long. She needed fresh vegetables and fruit and a host of other items on her list.

It could be someone waiting for a friend, or passing time before an appointment, or waiting for the bus that stopped across the street. Letting the mere presence of a black truck dictate her movements made her feel vulnerable all over again.

Quinn said he saw Rune at Castor Aviation. Fear slithered through her. If that was true, it meant her ex-boyfriend had breached one of the places she felt most secure. She had never seen him, but that didn't mean he hadn't been watching her. How long had he been working there? How could they hire him? How did he get through the background check?

She still had a restraining order against him. She shouldn't be scared. Pissed, yes. Afraid, no. Hell, she had taken a year's worth of Krav Maga self-defense classes in case something happened again. Steeled by determination, she double-checked her list and grabbed her airport badge. She paused for a moment at the phone, the old safety advice playing through her head. She should call someone to let them know where she was going, when she expected to get there, and when she expected to return. Who? Her parents were too far away. Cate lived close, but she was in the hospital. Quinn. He had called her and knew she was on her way to the airport. She left her apartment, locking the door behind her.

The truck appeared empty when she drove past it.

Maybe she was wrong about the truck at Cate's apartment last night. She shuddered at the memory of the destruction in the apartment. How would Rune know about Cate? Sierra met her long after the trial that won him a five-year stint at the Moose Lake Correctional Facility.

Quinn had suggested whoever trashed Cate's place and put her in the hospital knew Tori. Maybe even killed her. She recalled the odd phone calls Cate mentioned, when Tori would answer, say nothing, and then hang up. If they were annoying fundraising calls, it made sense that she wouldn't bother to say anything, but why would she go to her room after the call?

Cate said she answered the phone a couple times, and the person hung up. A wrong number, or the person who had been calling Tori? A normal caller would ask if Tori was available. If the caller hung up on Cate instead …

Sierra knew the pattern. Six years ago, she wouldn't answer the phone until after the answering machine picked it up and the person on the other end started to leave a message. It allowed her to mitigate the invasion of her privacy; if Rune always got the answering machine when he called, he wouldn't know if she was really home. It didn't prevent him from sitting outside her apartment building, or following her to school, or to the grocery store, or anywhere else.

Did someone harass Tori? That would explain why she went to her room; she would be recording the date and time of the call, and maybe what, if anything, the caller said. Why wouldn't she tell Cate? That had been Sierra's lesson; always tell someone. It could make the difference in survival.

# 35

Quinn paced the waiting area. Cherie, Castor Aviation's receptionist, kept one eye on Quinn and one on Stamford, her stink-eye glare clear evidence she wasn't pleased with their presence.

Sierra pushed through the front door of the FBO office, AOA badge on display in a holder on her left arm. She approached Quinn, stopped outside of arm's reach, and pulled off her mittens. "Hey," she said by way of greeting. "What's up?"

Quinn introduced her to Officer Stamford before Cherie interrupted. "Excuse me, Officer, but who is she?"

"A consultant," Quinn said before he gestured to Stamford to lead the way to the apron.

"Wait, you need an escort," Cherie said, her voice sharp enough to make him cringe.

Stamford, one hand on the exit door, turned to face her. "Ma'am, we appreciate your concern, but that won't be necessary. We're here because the FAA asked us to look at a plane. We need to verify some things before they scare up an agent to check the plane out. I think we're okay without an escort."

"I don't think Roger would—"

The closing door cut off the rest of the protest. They drove to Hangar 3 and parked on the north side. The five-foot gap of the partially-closed hangar door allowed them easy access. Quinn followed Stamford and Sierra inside.

Two single-engine airplanes were parked in the rear of the hangar, with the twin-engine plane in front. Sierra wandered toward the twin. "What did you want me to look at?"

Quinn answered. "Can you see anything wrong with the nose wheel? When we got to the scene, it was almost ninety degrees off center."

She slid a small Maglite from her pocket and twisted it on before crouching in front of the nose wheel. Her head disappeared into the wheel well, where the gear retracted during flight. A minute later, she ducked out from under the plane and straightened. "I've never seen the nose gear on a Queen Air," she pointed a thumb at the plane, "but it looks to me like the steering link seized."

"Can you translate that into something other than airplane-speak?" Stamford asked.

"You can look for yourself, but basically, there's a mounting bracket," she made a narrow "C" with a finger and thumb, "that the steering linkage connects to." She slipped the end of her flashlight between her fingers. "If the linkage can't pivot, the weakest point breaks. The steering linkage jammed up and got stuck off-center."

"Would a hard landing cause it to seize?"

"It shouldn't." She crouched under the plane's nose. "I'd invite you to look, but there's not enough room in here." Her voice sounded like she was in a cave on the other side of the hangar.

Stamford leaned toward Quinn. "I'm going to get the camera. Never know what the FAA will ask for." He headed out of the hangar.

She backed away from the plane. "Where'd Stamford go?"

"To get the camera." Her cool demeanor unsettled him. He resisted the urge to close the distance between them. "You okay?"

"Not really."

Before he could ask her to explain, Stamford returned, the snap of the camera popping open echoing in the metal cave. "Can you take some pictures of the damage you think made the pilot lose control?" He looked between her and Quinn, lingering on Quinn before handing the camera to Sierra. "Make sure to get as much of the damage as you can."

She took the camera and returned to the wheel well. Stamford glanced at him. "You just happen to know an aircraft mechanic? She's the one from your frozen corpse case, isn't she." It wasn't exactly a question. "She found the body."

Quinn nodded, but didn't say anything. The less said, the better.

One dark eyebrow arched. "Isn't she a suspect?"

"Yes, but there's no way she could physically lift a dead body into the aft maintenance bay."

Clicks from the wheel well echoed quietly in the silence. "You sure about that? She's a mechanic. Probably stronger than she looks."

A memory of Sierra lashing out during her nightmare flashed through his mind. He knew from personal experience she was strong. "Maybe, but have you ever tried to lift something about your own body weight straight up through a foot-and-a-half square hole?"

"What if she had help?"

Sierra ducked out of the wheel well, a stack of photos in one hand, camera in the other. She handed them to Stamford. "Those bushings aren't under a lot of stress, but debris gets in the wheel well, and if they aren't greased, there's nothing to prevent dust and moisture from getting in. The steering linkage is bent, and the bushing looks corroded, but unless I take it apart, it's hard to see."

"Is that sort of thing a common problem?" Stamford asked.

"I don't know if it is on this plane or in general aviation as a rule. The Dash-8 steering is different. I do know those bushings corrode, and sometimes there are service bulletins that require replacing them because of problems. I've never worked on a Queen Air, even though we had one at A&P school. I'm going by what I know about airplanes."

"Excuse me, what are you doing here?"

All three of them turned. A well-dressed middle-aged man in a parka approached them, clipboard in hand. "Officers. Andrew Jindahl. I'm the FAA agent assigned to Castor Aviation. I didn't realize you would be here."

"Just making sure we have everything you might need," Stamford said in his I'm-here-to-help voice. "This is my colleague, Detective Quinn Moore, and Sierra Bauer, an A&P from Range Airlines. She's acting as our civilian consultant."

Jindahl nodded in greeting, flashing a politician's smile. "I appreciate you taking care of the mess, though I'm curious as to why a Castor Aviation mechanic isn't here instead."

"I'm working with her on another case," Quinn said. "I thought Castor's mechanics were busy since no one was here."

Jindahl's smile lost a bit of cordiality. "I see."

Stamford responded to his change of attitude. "We wanted to cover the bases for you. I'll write up a report as soon as we get back to the APD office. I'll send the photos along with it."

"Photos? Of the accident?"

Stamford nodded. "That, and the damage to the de-ice truck and the plane.

I'd like to reference them in my report. Miss Bauer said it looks like the steering link bushing failed."

Quinn waited for Sierra to say something. He didn't expect her to stand by in silence. "I'm sure Miss Bauer could—"

"I'm sorry to interrupt, but I have to be going," she said in a no-nonsense tone that made Quinn wince. "I've got a few things to do this afternoon before it gets dark." She headed toward the open hangar door without another word.

"Thank you for your help, Miss Bauer," Stamford said, nodding and touching the brim of his hat as she passed by.

"No problem."

Quinn waited until she crossed the threshold of the hangar door before he excused himself and followed her. Once outside the hangar, he trotted to catch up to her before she reached the Castor Aviation office. "Sierra, wait."

She stopped, one hand on the door handle, but didn't turn to him.

"Why didn't you offer more information about the damage?"

Now she faced him, hazel eyes guarded. "It's the FAA." She spoke in a quiet, resolute voice. "You don't offer information. You wait until they ask a question, then you answer it. He didn't ask, so I didn't tell. He'll figure it out."

"You didn't like him, did you?"

"The FAA spent months threatening my career. I don't like any of them."

# 36

Her errands took longer than she expected. Typical, Sierra thought. The combination of spontaneous detours and getting caught in rush hour traffic meant she didn't get back to her apartment until long after the sun went down.

She shouldn't have gone into Barnes and Noble. Once she stepped into a bookstore, she couldn't tear herself away for at least an hour. Even though she could've checked them out from the library, she succumbed to the temptation to pick up a few new additions to her collection. Besides, it was an opportunity to indulge her love of being surrounded by books.

She parked and unloaded two bags of groceries, then considered the one remaining bag. She'd have to make more than one trip. Her habit was to use the stairs to her fourth floor apartment, but she considered using the elevator when she had to juggle her bags to unlock the security door.

After three flights of stairs with her load, she second-guessed her decision, but by then there was no point in taking the elevator. She could handle one more flight of stairs. Once she reached her apartment she let her bags slide to the ground, then tested the knob before she slid her key into the lock.

The knob turned easily.

She never forgot to lock the door. Except for that one time she ran down the street to the laundromat to swap her clothes into the dryer.

Cate's words came back to her. *The door was unlocked.*

She picked up her bags and headed back the way she came. Once at her vehicle, she ran through her options. She had to call Quinn, but she didn't know any of her neighbors well enough to ask if she could make a call, a disadvantage of having a schedule opposite that of most people. The laundromat was open; she could use the pay phone there. After locking her car, she ran the block and a half to the laundromat.

The place was busy. Three women occupied chairs, one reading from a thick textbook, another deep in a novel, and a third watching a pair of preschoolers play hide and seek. Sierra checked the pay phone, heard the dial tone, and released a breath she didn't realize she was holding.

She retrieved Quinn's card from her pocket and dialed, praying he would answer. Felt a hot jolt at the sound of his voice on the other end. "Quinn, it's—"

"Sierra," he finished. A tight edge of alarm laced his voice. "Are you okay?"

"Yes. No." She explained her concern, assured him she didn't open the door to the apartment, and was now a safe distance away at the laundromat.

"Stay put. It'll take me about a half hour to get there. Do not go into your apartment."

"Don't worry, I won't," she promised. She hung up and surveyed the ranks of machines and a row of empty chairs and tables. A half hour of twiddling her thumbs would drive her crazy. She hurried back to her car in the lot at the apartment complex to grab one of her new books. When she reached her vehicle, she glanced up at her living room window.

The blinds were closed.

She had opened them before she left because it'd been sunny. Safety over wasted gas, she decided, and drove the block and a half back to the laundromat to wait for Quinn. Once there, she settled into an uncomfortable resin chair with a clear view of the door, as far from the chaos of chasing preschoolers as she could manage. She glanced at the clock and noted the time. Thirty minutes until Quinn should get there.

She had a safe place to stay until Quinn arrived.

She cracked open her new Tami Hoag mystery and tried to focus on the book. Who would be in her apartment? Was it the same person who attacked Cate? How much damage would she find? Was the invader still there?

A glance at the clock. Five minutes. She tried the book again.

Another glance. Two more minutes. She closed her eyes. *Quinn will get here as soon as he can. I'm not alone.*

Giggles and pounding of shoes followed by a gruff command to settle down punctuated the drone of a dryer. She imagined her quiet place on the beach, then tried the book again. Managed to sink into it.

A dryer buzzed the end of its cycle.

The hairs on the back of her neck rose. Unease crept down her spine.

"Did you miss me?"

Her blood froze. *Too close.* She swore, dropped the book, shot to her feet, fists ready.

Rune Thorsson leaned against a washing machine less than six feet away, hands in the pockets of a fleece-lined flannel coat. Once lean and lanky, he now looked like he'd been spending all his spare time in the gym.

*Don't show fear.* "What the hell are you doing here?" she demanded, her voice steady while the rest of her trembled like a magnitude-seven quake.

"Hey, language. There's kids around." He still looked respectable, like a neighborhood insurance salesman on his day off. His voice, smooth as greased lightning, grated on her nerves like a metal file. "You look good, Sierra."

She wanted to run, but didn't dare take her eyes off him. "You're too close. The restraining order is still valid."

He smiled, a slow grin that made her stomach turn. "I just wanted to say 'hi'. I won't even take my hands out." He gestured to make a point, hands buried in his coat pockets.

Her pulse hammered. She swallowed through the tightness in her throat. "The cops are on their way."

"Oh, did you call them with your secret phone?" he said, condescension dripping from his words.

"Hey, you, leave her alone." The mother of the two preschoolers, a formidable woman who looked like she could take him down a couple notches, approached Rune. "I know guys like you. She said she has a restraining order. Get out of here before I call the cops."

He winked at her. "Good to see you again, Sierra." He sidled past the mother, who refused to step aside, and left the laundromat.

Sierra couldn't move, couldn't breathe until she saw his black pickup truck back out of the laundromat parking spot beside her car and drive away.

"Are you okay, sweetie?" The mother laid a hand on Sierra's shoulder. "My sister made some bad decisions a few years back," she said. "Men like that are bullies and cowards. Don't go back to him. And for Christ's sake, don't drop the restraining order." She offered a smile and a reassuring squeeze. "You okay? Can I call someone for you?"

"Thank you, I'm fine. I appreciate your help. Someone is on the way," she said.

Her nightmare had returned. It *was* his truck following her.

He knew where she lived.

"Sierra?"

The sound of Quinn's voice released the tension in her shoulders. She scooped her book from the floor as she rubbed at the ache at the back of her neck. "Thank you again. My friend is here," she said to the woman.

"The cop?" the woman asked after a glance at Quinn heading their way. Sierra nodded. "Good. Now, where did those two go?" She headed off to track down her wayward children.

Quinn looked at Sierra in a way she suspected he did when he was trying to figure out what he missed. "What happened? And I don't mean the apartment."

She stared out the window at the now-vacant parking spot. *How did he find me?*

Quinn steered her toward the door. "Let's go outside."

Once they stood in the frigid January evening, he repeated his request more firmly. "Talk to me."

"Rune showed up."

His expression darkened. "Rune Thorsson? When?"

"A few minutes before you did. He didn't do anything." With other people there, she had been safe, or so she thought. "I was reading. I can't believe I didn't notice him until he was right there." The admission made her feel like an idiot. Who sits in a laundromat reading a book and not notice someone standing five feet away?

"He didn't need to do anything except let you know he's watching you. How long has he been following you?"

"I don't know."

His stoic expression made him look more like a cop than she'd ever seen. "How long do you think he's been following you, Sierra?"

Her breath clouded the air between them. "I already told you the first time I thought I saw his truck was the night I found the body. I didn't even know if it was really him or just a black pickup. It's not like those are rare around here."

"You thought it was him in the lot at Cate's apartment."

"He got out of prison six months ago. I expected him to show up then. When that first month went by and nothing happened, I thought it was over, that he had moved on."

Quinn dug his notebook from a pocket, made a few notes, then tucked the pad away. "I'm not done with that, but we need to check your apartment."

She hoped things wouldn't be as bad as she feared.

# 37

Quinn followed her from the laundromat and parked beside her in the lot. He rounded his vehicle, checked his weapon, and leaned close. "Are you sure you locked the door?"

"Absolutely." She pointed at the sliding doors of her apartment balcony on the fourth floor. "I opened the blinds before I left. I remember because I thought about the sun and the calm and how nasty the storm was last night. Now they're closed."

"I won't bother telling you to wait out here because I know you won't listen, so stay behind me."

She followed him up four flights of stairs to her floor. Stopped at the door to her apartment. Quinn drew his gun, motioned for her to stay put. He turned the knob. "It's locked."

"What?" Sierra tried. "I know it was unlocked earlier." Why would someone break into her apartment, then lock the door when they left?

Quinn inspected the lock. "It doesn't look damaged." He held out a hand. "Key?"

She gave him her key ring. "Stay here," he said. "I need to clear the apartment." He unlocked the door, then nudged it open before slipping past.

Time slowed to a slug's pace while she waited, giving her ample opportunity to imagine the state of her apartment. She cringed at the thought of someone invading her sanctuary. Six years ago, it'd taken weeks after a move to a new apartment, and nights accompanied by a family member, before she felt comfortable living alone again.

The door swung open the rest of the way, but the look on Quinn's face told her she wouldn't like what he found. She shoved past him. He closed the door and grabbed her arm. "You're okay. That's the most important part."

She pulled away. This tiny one-bedroom apartment had been her home for the four years she had been working for Range Air. A familiar dread sent chills through her when she stepped into the main living area.

Couch cushions were scattered across the living room, each shredded like a wild animal tried to find a treat inside. Her television lay face down on the floor. Puzzle pieces from boxes formerly stacked beside the entertainment center peppered the floor.

"Your bedroom is the same. The only place that was spared is the bathroom."

"Rascal. I put Rascal in the bathroom before I left."

"The cage and litter box are still in the tub, but I have no idea where she is. The door was open when I came in."

Though she believed him, she checked for herself. It gave her a sense of control when her world spun into chaos. The bathroom was ferret-free. "Shit. We can't let a ferret loose in the building. We need to find her. Where would a ferret hide?"

Quinn blocked her from entering her bedroom. "The bedroom is bad. Some of the pictures are … damaged."

It didn't register right away.

Of the few pictures she had, there were two she prized above the rest. One was of her grandfather doing what he loved most—fishing. He stood on a dock with the sunset behind him, line in the water.

The other was of her and Ken, a photo snapped in front of the Queen Air in the school's hangar the day she finished her orals and practicals for her A&P license. He'd come to see her before he returned to his Air Force base in Colorado.

She looked past him. Her chest constricted until she thought her heart would explode. Both frames were shattered. Both photographs were torn to pieces and scattered like forgotten debris carried by the wind.

"It was the last time I got to fish with Grandpa. He died of a heart attack a week later." She tried to push around Quinn, reached toward the torn pieces.

He held her back. "Sierra, you can't touch anything."

She caught sight of a ragged piece of photo. Her brother, wearing a goofy grin and his Air Force uniform, a torn edge where he wrapped an arm around her. Her eyes burned. She swallowed the thick grief swelling in her throat. "I couldn't get home to see Ken because I was taking my finals and my A&P exams. He came up on his last day home to see me." Her vision blurred with tears. She wiped them with a sleeve. "He encouraged me. Reminded me I needed to be able to fix the airplane he planned to buy once he got discharged."

"I'm sorry, Sierra."

They were only pictures, but the images helped keep treasured memories fresh in her mind. The raw violence of it hurt the most.

Quinn rubbed her arms. "You okay?"

She nodded. He let her pass and stood in silence while she took a good look around the room.

Bedsheets were tossed into a pile. The mattress leaned against the wall, innards exposed by an "X" cut into it. A matching cut on the box spring. Dresser drawers emptied and tossed across the room. A pile of clothes from the closet discarded in a corner topped by one of her uniform shirts, navy blue with her name embroidered on a white patch opposite the Range Air logo. The pile moved. "Quinn, close the door. Rascal's in here."

She waited until he did so before dismantling the pile. Halfway through, a long lump started to work its way out of the pile. She pounced on the lump, using the clothes to trap the ferret. She eased up on one side, and Rascal headed toward freedom. As soon as her nose appeared, Sierra snagged Rascal's harness and pulled her tight against her body to prevent the ferret from squirming away. That didn't stop Rascal from scratching and trying to bite. Quinn disappeared from the room and returned moments later with the cage. Sierra shoved Rascal through the cage door, then latched it shut before the ferret could turn and sink her needle-like teeth into her hand. "Thanks," she said.

Rascal trembled, but didn't look too worse for wear. Scared, Sierra thought. The scratches on her hands weeped blood. Those teeth and claws were great weapons; if the bad guy managed by some miracle to catch and hold onto the ferret, he wouldn't have escaped unscathed. She brought the cage back into the bathroom as Rascal buried herself deeper into the comforting folds of the towel.

Burrowing into a warm, quiet space sounded good about now. The sanctity of her home, the safety it promised, had been destroyed. Sierra felt like the bit of land under her feet had been washed away by a sudden squall. *It's just stuff. I didn't get hurt like Cate did.*

Quinn hung up the phone. "I called this in. It looks like Cate's apartment. Whomever did this was probably looking for the same thing he was looking for at Cate's and didn't find."

"Why would he think I have it?"

Quinn pinched the bridge of his nose. "The only reason I can think of is that he saw you at Cate's apartment today with that big bag and the cage. Maybe he thought since you were taking the ferret stuff, you and Tori were friends, and maybe she gave whatever it is he's looking for to you. That means he must have followed you here and was watching the apartment. Where did you go after you left the airport?"

"I ran errands. Picked up groceries. I stopped at Barnes and Noble because I haven't been there in forever."

"Barnes and Noble?" His lips curved into a slow smile. "Let me guess. You were there for a while." At her answering nod, he continued. "When did you get home?"

"I don't know. I called you when I got back."

"So, about four hours." He pulled out his notebook and added to a fresh page. "Long enough for him to toss the apartment."

"Do you think he was actually here when I got home?"

"If the door was unlocked when you got here, and it was locked when we came back, I'd say it's highly probable." He gestured to the kitchen table and chairs, an island that had escaped the chaos. She sat as he followed suit. "Did you notice anything else odd or unusual when you got home from Cate's apartment?"

"No. I saw a black pickup truck park at the curb before I left for the airport. When I drove by it, it looked empty."

Quinn leaned back in his chair, eyes narrowed. "Thorsson's truck?"

"I don't know. I thought so, but when I didn't see anyone in it, I wasn't sure. He used to have a bumper sticker on his truck. There was snow on the bumper, so I couldn't see any stickers or anything."

"You thought he was at Cate's apartment, too." He left the implication unsaid. She hit the same conclusion.

"Why would Rune toss Cate's apartment? I didn't even know her until a year ago, while he was in jail. I can understand if he tossed mine for some sick game of his." The realization sank home. Rune Thorsson, the man who'd tried to kill her, knew where she worked. Knew where she lived. Somehow knew her unlisted phone number.

She couldn't stay here tonight. Not after seeing Rune far closer than the 200-foot distance he was supposed to keep according to the restraining order.

"Do you think Thorsson would kill Tori?" Quinn asked.

"Why? I didn't know Tori back then. Why would he just pick random people?"

"Not random. You believe Tori corrupted your brother. What if Thorsson killed her for you? What if he did it to persuade you to let him back into your life? What if he did it to frame you, as payback?"

*Oh God.* It sounded logical in a sick, psychopathic kind of way. She swallowed bile at the thought of Rune digging through her past. She had thought he decided she wasn't worth the effort when he didn't pop onto her radar after his release.

"I'm putting him on my list of suspects. And I'm going to request an arrest warrant for him—he violated the restraining order. Any problem with that?" His tone carried something akin to anger.

"Why are you so pissy?"

He stopped writing and lifted his eyes to hers. Something in them drilled through to her chest, where a low burn settled. "I don't like that your apartment was torn apart by someone apparently looking for something he didn't find at Cate's place. I don't like that the man who tried to kill you six years ago stopped by the laundromat after you called me about a home invasion." He straightened, never breaking eye contact. "Why aren't you more upset about Thorsson showing up at the laundromat?"

Her temper drove her to her feet. "What am I supposed to do? Do you know I spent a year learning Krav Maga so the next time he got too close I could do more than hope Tai Chi really is a martial art? I fucking fought for my life. I'm not going to fall apart because that asshole decided to violate the restraining order."

He stood, lips pressed into a thin line. "Bring it down, Sierra."

She tightened her fists, then shoved around him to pace the length of the small kitchen. She almost reached the far end of the room when he grabbed her shoulder from behind. She fought to keep her mad going, but his touch made it fall apart.

"The team should be here soon to process the apartment. Does Thorsson know where your parents live?"

She nodded. The one time she had brought Rune home he'd charmed her parents. She didn't remember why she thought that was a good idea back then. First boyfriend emotional high, she supposed.

Quinn turned her toward him. She suppressed an urge to squirm under his intense gaze. "You're staying with me until I get this guy and arrest Thorsson for harassing you."

It was the way he said it that relit her temper. She welcomed the anger; it was better than feeling like she had no control. "Are you freaking kidding me? I am not helpless. I can stay—"

"You will stay with me because that way I'll know you're safe. I've got an extra bedroom." He squeezed her shoulders until she flinched. "Listen to me.

The person who went through Cate's apartment tailed you here. Assuming whoever he was didn't find whatever he was looking for, he could be out there"—he stabbed a finger toward the living room windows—"waiting for you to leave. What makes you think he won't follow you to your parents' place? Then there's Thorsson, who just violated the restraining order and knows where your family lives. Hell, he could be the person that did this for all we know. That's two very dangerous men who could follow you. I don't want to risk putting you and your family in danger."

"What makes you think either one won't follow me to your place?" she fired back, and wrenched out of his grip. He had a huge point about bringing this mess home to her parents. "How is my staying with you going to stop him from doing this," she swept an arm, "to your place? A hotel would be a better—"

"It's too hard to control access in a hotel. It worked last night because of the blizzard. I can ask someone to watch the house when I'm not there."

"Not the best thing to tell someone who has a stalker."

"Sonofabitch," he breathed. "I didn't mean it like that and you know it. You are a strong woman, both physically and mentally, but it'd be better to have some backup in case something does happen."

Dammit, he was right. "How are you going to explain why the person who found the dead body in your homicide case is staying at your house?"

He answered with silence. He paced the length of the apartment, one hand on a hip, the other pinching the bridge of his nose. "You know, this would be a lot easier if I didn't like you so much." He met her gaze, hit her with those intense eyes of his.

The retort she'd been ready to launch faded on her tongue. Her heart chased the thoughts careening in her mind. His words echoed in her head. *Easier if I didn't like you so much.*

They'd only known each other for a few days. She cried on his shoulder last night. Told him what happened to her brother. He rescued her from one of the worst dreams she'd had in years.

His touch soothed her. No one, not even her parents, could do that.

*He likes me.*

# 38

She stared at him, jaw dropped. Quinn didn't dare say anything more. Hell, he could've kicked himself for saying as much as he did. Everything would be so much easier if he didn't harbor these feelings for her.

The image of Tori Hjelle's battered remains stained his mind, followed closely by the image of Cate Zahn unconscious after the assault. He was supposed to be solving the case, not putting his career at risk by getting tangled up with a woman he hardly knew.

The bad guys wouldn't try to hurt her while she was with him. She'd be safe.

When she called earlier to tell him of the break-in, he couldn't describe the worry—he shouldn't feel like his world might jump its axis if something bad happened to her. He shouldn't feel like his life finally saw the dawn after an endless night, not after knowing her for a mere three days.

Too many people he cared about had left him, each time cutting into his soul. After the divorce, he promised himself he would stop caring so much. Maybe then the pain wouldn't be so unbearable. It was a great theory.

Then he met Sierra Bauer.

She ran a hand through her chestnut hair and that fascinating white tress, and wrapped her arms around her middle. "I'll stay at a hotel. I'll even pick a good one that has security cameras in the lobby."

She was a suspect. He still didn't know how the pendant with her and her stalker's initials came to be found on his murder victim's body.

Anything beyond protocol could—would—jeopardize the case.

He'd already broken protocol by staying with her in the hotel room last night, even if it was his only choice to keep her safe. "I can't control access in a hotel. You have a stalker who tried to kill you, and an unknown subject who killed Tori, assaulted Cate, and tore up her apartment and yours.

"My place is the one place where I know you'll be safe."

She looked away, rubbed hands over her face. Stared at the disaster area around her. "Okay," she said, voice quiet.

He was surprised at her acquiescence. Shocked, even. Glad, though, that he didn't have to run through the list of pros and cons.

"I have to bring Rascal. Do you have a place to keep her so I can let her out of the cage?"

He'd forgotten about the ferret. "I've got a basement."

"Too big. She's a ferret. Think curious kitten mixed with rambunctious puppy and some raccoon wiles tossed in. Wherever we put her needs to be small without a lot of opportunity for her to get hurt or into trouble."

That ruled out the laundry room, his home office, and the garage. Not many options left. "We can keep her in the guest bathroom. That arrangement seemed to work here."

A knock interrupted them. Though he expected the crime scene team, Quinn drew his gun and peered through the peephole. Kevin's dark face filled the fish-eye field of view. He put up his gun and opened the door. Kevin stepped aside to allow his team more room to bring in the equipment.

"You seem to be having a run on home invasions, buddy." Kevin peered behind Quinn in Sierra's direction. "Is this her apartment?" he asked, voice low to avoid eavesdropping. "I thought you weren't going to move on her until after you solved this thing."

"It's not like that."

"It's not like that … yet." Kevin's stern tone eroded Quinn's patience. "This doesn't look good for you or your case."

"She's in real danger. Her stalker ex-boyfriend tried to kill her six years ago. He finished his stay at Moose Lake Correctional and violated the restraining order tonight. And if it wasn't him, the unknown subject from last night," he swept an arm toward the living room, "is a close second." He struggled to keep from shouting. "I'm trying to keep her safe."

Kevin narrowed his eyes. "Just keep it at 'safe' until the case is closed. Don't go getting your ass canned because you screwed up."

"I won't. She knew the victim, she found the victim, she has a stalker who doesn't believe in restraining orders. She needs to be protected." I shouldn't have to defend my actions, Quinn thought.

"Excuse me," Sierra interrupted, "but how many days is this going to take?"

Quinn turned toward her. "We don't have any good suspects, and it'll take the team at least a day to process the whole apartment. I say plan a couple days."

Kevin nodded confirmation.

"I'm not sure if anything is missing, but I'll let you know if I think of something." She addressed Kevin. "Is it okay for me to gather some things? I'll try not to move stuff around much."

"Have you moved anything?" Kevin asked.

"Just enough to find Rascal—a ferret. She got loose and hid in my room under some clothes."

"We'll make some notes. I'll send one of my team in there with you. Tell them what you moved and where."

She nodded. Kevin instructed a woman on the team to follow her, then joined the crime scene techs setting up in the main living area.

Quinn canvassed the other residents on Sierra's floor. Few of the apartments were occupied, and the people who were home during the past few hours hadn't seen or heard anything notable. After a conversation with the building manager about phone calls and possible disturbances—another dead end—he returned to Sierra's apartment.

Kevin had a point about his plan to bring her to his place. He counted the threats against her: a known person who had stalked and attacked her in the past, and an unknown person who searched for something and would not hesitate to hurt her to find it.

He couldn't control outside threats. That was one of the hardest things for cops to come to terms with. He had to be satisfied with what he could control, and that meant making sure Sierra was someplace he knew well.

She waited at the kitchen table, rolling travel bag beside her. Rascal's cage and other supplies occupied the table. The ferret peeked from the folds of a towel in the cage.

"Do you need help putting Rascal in the carrier?"

"She's pretty scared. I don't want to aggravate things by moving her again. I've got the quilt from Cate's boyfriend I can wrap around her cage and just leave her in that." Her tone was resigned, as though she expected to suffer some undeserved fate. She didn't look at him, focused instead on the ferret burrowing into the towel.

Dammit, he didn't want her to feel like a prisoner. *She really doesn't have a choice, not if I have any say in it.* He returned his attention to her apartment, where Kevin and his crew already started the grid documentation. Numbered plastic markers littered the debris like super-sized confetti.

He pulled Kevin aside. "Let me know if you find anything to help me get this guy."

Kevin looked up from his notes. "She wasn't home when this happen, right?"

"No. She was running errands and found the door unlocked when she got back. She went to the laundromat a block and a half away and called me."

"Probably a good thing. The guy might've still been here like he was at the other scene. You sure about this little plan of yours?"

Quinn didn't answer. Kevin shook his head, noted where his team members were, and tugged Quinn toward the bathroom. He spoke in a harsh whisper. "This is dangerous territory, my friend. You're walking a fine line. I don't want to see you get suspended over something like this."

"I won't get suspended unless someone says something. Once the case is closed—"

"But the case isn't closed yet. Quinn, you can't let her stay—"

"It's not your problem."

Kevin leaned against the vanity, arms crossed. "So it's like that? That whole 'love at first sight' thing you scoff at when I talk about Jaylynn? You know there's no such thing."

"I suppose I deserve that."

"Yes, you do. And if it's real, then you deserve her, but you didn't hear me say that until you close the case. Just be careful. Your ex did a number on you. I'd hate to see you go through that again. She's still a suspect. Remember that."

"She's not involved," Quinn insisted.

"I hope you're right." Kevin returned to the task of processing the scene.

Sierra still sat quietly staring at the ferret. Quinn zipped his coat and pulled on his gloves. "Ready?"

She stood and adjusted her stocking cap without a glance at him. "Yes." She wrapped a faded quilt around the cage before lifting it, careful not to tip it.

"Let me help you." Quinn grabbed the ferret supplies and followed her to the parking lot. He scanned the area, searching first for a black pickup truck, then for any other vehicles that appeared occupied. He opened the back of her car for her and shoved the bags of groceries aside to make room for the cage and associated supplies, then loaded the rest of her things while she started the engine.

He stood at the driver's door. She rolled the window down, breath a white cloud in the icy air. "Am I following you or what?"

"Sierra, I'm sorry if … I don't mean to make you feel like … I'm just—"

She looked up at him, but he couldn't read her eyes in the shadows. "I get it, but I don't like it. I'm trying to remember you're the cop, and you're trying to protect me."

"Sierra, I don't want you feeling like … I wish I wasn't the reason." He leaned into the window. "I'll follow you to make sure no one else does." He gave her verbal directions to his house, and then handed her a written copy.

"Don't worry, I'll be right behind you, but just in case I have to discourage a follower." He pulled two keys from his keychain and handed them to her. "House. Garage. Park in the garage. There's a button beside the door from the garage into the house that opens and closes the door. And don't forget to lock the garage door and the house door."

She tucked the keys into her pocket. "How are you going to get in?"

"I can go through the garage. I've got the remote in the Explorer. I'll knock on that door. Make sure it's me. Don't just open the door."

"Yes, Dad," she said, a snide tone to her voice. "You heard the part where I learned Krav Maga, right? They teach that to soldiers."

"Self-defense doesn't work very well if the bad guy has a gun."

# 39

The overhead garage door of the ranch-style house opened as she turned into Quinn's driveway, confirming she'd managed to follow his directions through the residential streets of the southern suburb of Apple Valley even at night. She admired a bay window overlooking a line of barren bushes half-buried in the snow before she pulled into the garage and shut off her vehicle. Quinn parked the Explorer in the driveway behind the other stall of the garage.

A push lawn mower and snowblower occupied the space between her spot and the stall occupied by a green Ford Bronco II a few years older than the unmarked SUV Quinn drove. A workbench lined the back wall, complete with tool- and fastener-laden pegboard above.

Quinn ducked under the garage door as it lowered and checked the smaller walk-in door before scooping Rascal's cage out of the back of her vehicle. Sierra handed his keys back to him before she grabbed the rest of the ferret supplies and followed. He unlocked the house door, found the light switch, wiped his boots on the rugs in the narrow entryway, then headed through the house.

In front of her as she entered the house stood a gun cabinet large enough to hold rifles, with a smaller metal lockbox on top. She followed Quinn's path. A closet on her left and a wooden bench on her right below a row of coat hooks offered a multitude of places to stash winter gear. The kitchen lay beyond the entryway. She passed a small dining area beyond a peninsula counter on her way into the hall after him. A faint scent of coffee and hint of pine cleaner hung in the air.

"I put Rascal in the guest bathroom, but I didn't take the quilt off her cage." Quinn stepped back from the threshold of the bathroom. "You might want to move her when you take a shower. There's not a lot of room."

Sierra set the litter box behind the cage. He wasn't exaggerating. The three-quarter bath, done in pale blue accented with royal blue towels and rugs, had four inches to spare on either side of the cage. She unwrapped the cage and loaded the ferret's food dish, adding a couple treats on the top.

She handed the black bag of supplies to Quinn, then opened the cage and slipped out of the bathroom, closing the door behind her.

He dropped the bag in the next room down the hall. "This is the guest room. It's not much."

A blue denim patchwork quilt covered a double bed opposite a window with heavy curtains. A vintage three-drawer dresser below the window held a tabletop water fountain, power cord wrapped around its base. A small collection of books like those she'd seen on her father's shelves occupied the opposite corner of the dresser, including *The Prophet* and *Siddhartha*. The carpet and walls were shades of neutral, with a print of Van Gogh's *Irises* on the wall above the bed. Basic, she thought. Less *Better Homes and Gardens*, more a bachelor's version of *Midwest Living*.

"There's a small closet here, and if you need more blankets or towels there's a linen closet in the hall opposite the bathroom."

This was his house. Her only reason for being here: someone looking for an unknown something they thought she might have destroyed her apartment.

Her home, her sanctuary, taken from her again.

She hated it, the fear, the worry, the constant urge to look over her shoulder. Anger helped. Anger shoved the fear aside and channeled the anxiety into a sort of barrier, a shield to protect her from the helplessness.

She must've been quiet too long, because Quinn rested a hand on her shoulder.

His touch doused her anger. She wanted to keep her mad going; the anger gave her the illusion she was doing something to allay the feelings of violation.

"Sierra?"

Tears threatened before she tamped down the burning in her eyes and swallowed the thickness trying to choke her. "I'll go get my stuff."

He followed her as far as the gun cabinet, where he unloaded his service weapon and put it into the small gun locker before he hung up his coat. She brought her travel bag back to the bedroom, then peeked into the bathroom to check on Rascal. The ferret tracked along the wall, stopping only to wriggle her nose at the intrusion.

Sierra closed the door and returned to the kitchen. A wood floor—pine, she thought—accented cabinets stained a honey oak, giving the room a cozy feel enhanced by a deep-green marble countertop. A peninsula complete with upper cupboards and bar-type seating separated the kitchen from the small dining area.

Quinn pulled a handful of flyers from a drawer. "Hungry? What do you feel like? There's a great Chinese place ..."

"Seriously?" Without a second thought, she opened the refrigerator. Four bottles of beer, an almost-empty half-gallon of milk, a carton of six eggs, and a package of tofu populated the shelves.

She closed the fridge. "Help me bring in the groceries. I'll make something."

"You can leave them out in your car. They shouldn't freeze, the garage is insulated."

"Not the point. I have to do something. I may as well cook." She headed to the garage without waiting for him. By the time she had opened the lift gate of her Subaru wagon and pulled out a grocery bag, Quinn stood beside her.

He gestured for her to put it back in her car. "These are your groceries."

"I'm donating them to the cause, because a partial carton of eggs and a package of tofu isn't going to cut it." She pushed the bag at him until he took it from her, and handed him another bag for his other arm. She grabbed the last bag and closed the door. "Let me guess. It's been a while since you went shopping."

"It's on my list," he groused.

"It's the least I can do."

"Sierra," his tone softened. He set the bags on the kitchen counter, then took hers. "I wish there was a better way to keep you safe without endangering your family."

If she had a task to do, she wouldn't dwell on it. "Give me the short tour of the kitchen."

He stared at her. "Why?"

"Please," she said, keeping her voice even and her frustration under control. "I need to do *some*thing. If you want to put the groceries away since you know where they go, I'll start cooking."

"You don't need to."

"Quinn, let me do this. I have to keep myself occupied or I'm going to go nuts."

Those brilliant blue eyes of his met hers. Her agitation quieted. "Okay," he said. "It's been a long time since anyone I wasn't related to cooked for me."

It'd been a long time since she had cooked for someone besides herself. Even when she visited her parents, her dad insisted on doing the cooking. Not that her mom couldn't cook, but her dad did a better job of it. After a quick orientation, she started putting together one of her favorites, a recipe she didn't make for herself, and one she never seemed to be able to finish on her own at her parents' house; her dad always managed to elbow in.

After the home invasion, after the incident with Rune at the laundromat, she felt like her normal life had gone into an uncontrolled spin. Tonight, cooking would help her regain some sense of control.

❖ ❖ ❖

QUINN COULDN'T TAKE HIS EYES OFF HER working in his kitchen. Most kitchens were the same basic setup: stove, refrigerator, and sink all within a few steps of each other. Everything she did had confidence written on it, like a sous chef making the special of the night. He offered to help, but she declined.

Despite her apparent comfort in an unfamiliar house, a stiffness laced her movements, like her muscles held tightly-wound springs. She came close to breaking down earlier in the guest bedroom, something he anticipated happening sooner rather than later. Not many people could go through the things she had the past couple of days without cracking.

He recognized her anger as a coping mechanism. He'd been there, had used it like a life raft after his marriage dissolved. Anger sustained him through the divorce proceedings, through the months after. The problem with using anger as a shield: it took a lot of energy to sustain.

Muscle and joint aches, ulcers, even hair loss convinced him he needed to put the anger and guilt away before it scarred him for the rest of his life. His sister steered him to a path that included learning how to forgive and let go of the things he could not control.

It had taken time, and his sister's prodding, but when he finally gave himself permission to release the anger, his ailments faded. He still felt the pain of betrayal, regret for what he lost, but he gave up the damaging emotions.

Sierra adjusted the flame of the gas burner for a low simmer, set a large sieve flat-side down over the pot to prevent spatters, and checked the time before washing her hands in the sink.

"That's it?"

"For an hour. Then we can boil the pasta and toast the garlic bread."

Quinn pulled two bottles of Schell's Firebrick lager from the fridge and opened them before handing one to her. "Do you cook a lot?"

"Not really. It's just me, so I don't usually do much beyond cooking a chicken breast and steaming some vegetables. I'll make more on my weekends so I have leftovers to bring to work."

He used to do that, too. "I should probably give you the rest of the tour. You've met the kitchen and entry way." He gestured to the dining area with its small oak table and four matching oak chairs. "Here's the dining room." He led the way into the opposite room, turning on the light in the ceiling fan. "And the living room."

Sierra ignored the pair of deep brown, brushed leather recliners flanking a matching couch arranged in front of the console television at the center of a built-in entertainment center, instead wandering across the thick forest green carpeting to the other half of the room. The stereo system shared space with a built-in bookcase that formed the entire wall. She perused his music collection, his books, and lingered in front of his guitar on a stand in a corner. "Do you play?"

"Not much." He had started playing the guitar after his best friend died. Music could keep his mind off the loss of yet another person he loved.

"Have you read these books? The *Tao Te Ching*? Or the *Art of War*?" She slid *The Zen of Motorcycle Maintenance* out an inch. "I never made it through this one. I started reading mysteries instead."

A small cloud of dust chased her finger as she ran it across the spines of the books. "Kinda off-genre for you, aren't they? I mean, you've got a bunch of Executioner books," she brushed along another shelf, "and Robert Ludlum and Stephen Coonts aren't exactly light reading." She turned, her white lock draping the side of her face like spun ice.

He leaned back, resting a hip on the back of the couch. "I started reading them so my sister would stop bugging me about letting go of my anger."

"You don't seem the angry type. Not much, anyway."

Those days were behind him, and he worked at keeping them there. "I used to be. It was bad enough that I got ulcers and my hair started to fall out."

"Anger? Or stress?"

"Both I suppose, but mostly anger."

She continued to trace his music collection. Her movements still displayed the stiffness he'd notice in the kitchen. "Sierra, you can't keep the anger going. It isn't healthy."

"I'm not angry," she said too quickly.

He'd given his sister the same answer more than once. Colleen hadn't relented. "You still feel guilty about your brother. Sierra, he chose to do what he did. You didn't make him."

She spun, a dark rage flashing in her eyes. "What the hell, Quinn? I didn't think I was going to get psychoanalyzed by a cop."

His analytical side ordered him to back off. The other side of him, the one that had encouraged him to bring her here in the first place, didn't agree. "Just hear me out. You're angry at yourself because you couldn't do more to save him. Why aren't you angry at him for refusing to listen to you?"

Her voice held an edge that could cut stone. "What gives you the right? Why do you care?" She closed her eyes and inhaled deeply. A whoosh of breath, then she continued. "Sorry. God, this sucks." Her voice cracked.

"Look, I know what it's like. I used anger to keep the rest at bay, so I wouldn't feel like my life was a mess. At least forgive your brother for not listening to you."

"Did you forgive your ex-wife for whatever she did that ended your marriage?"

The old pain returned, as raw as it had been that awful day. Did Sierra know how much that question hurt? "Eventually." Forgiveness, however, didn't soften the wounds; he learned to live with them.

"Did you feel better after?"

"It helped. It allowed me to let go of the anger. My hair stopped falling out and my ulcers healed."

Silence settled around them, thick and heavy as wet snow. Quinn waited, expectant.

She brushed past him. "I'm going to change, then start the noodles."

Had he gone too far?

# 40

Quinn filled a pot with water and set it on the stove, added some salt, then lit the burner and adjusted the flame. The spicy aroma of garlic and basil, backed by the heady perfume of rich tomato with a touch of oregano, filled the kitchen with whispers of Italy. His stomach still churned despite the distraction. He lifted the sieve Sierra had put on top of the sauce to prevent spatters. His mouth watered.

"You can taste it, see if it needs anything."

He replaced the sieve before turning toward her. She now wore black sweat-pants with a thick cable-knit sweater in a moss color that complemented her brown hair and hazel eyes. She looked like quiet comfort. He imagined lazy Sunday afternoons with her, curled up together on the couch watching old movies.

"It should be ready."

Her voice knocked him out of his reverie. "I put water on for the noodles. I'll change." He passed by her on the way to his bedroom, almost reached to her as he used to with his wife years ago.

*Can't,* he thought. She was here so he could protect her. Until he closed the case, he couldn't get close to her. Until he knew, without a doubt, she had nothing to do with Tori's murder, he needed to keep his distance.

❖   ❖   ❖

HE CHANGED INTO SWEATPANTS and a blue quarter-zip sweater with a snow-flake design around the neck. On his way back to the kitchen, he stopped to peek into the guest bathroom, wary. He didn't need a ferret loose in the house. The towel bunched in one corner of the cage moved, and Rascal poked her head out just enough to sniff the air before retreating into her hiding spot. Quinn closed the door.

When he returned to the kitchen, Sierra indicated the dinnerware stacked on top of the peninsula counter. She checked something in the oven. "The garlic toast is almost ready. If you want to bring the plates over here, we can leave the stuff on the stove to stay warm."

This should feel awkward, he thought. As his guest, she shouldn't be cooking for him. Like any good Minnesotan, he felt *he* imposed on *her* since she cooked and he hadn't brought any wine.

Quinn set his pager on the counter, then scooped up the plates and slid past Sierra to set them beside the stove. They were, for all intents and purposes, strangers, yet she … belonged.

Eager for a distraction, he crossed behind her to the refrigerator. "I don't have any wine. Beer okay? Or water?"

"Beer's fine. After the past few days, I think I need to start stocking wine or something."

He pulled the last two bottles of lager from the fridge, grabbed the magnetic bottle opener from its place on the freezer door, and popped the tops. Once they settled at the table with plates full of pasta, Quinn tasted her creation. Tangy tomato sauce danced on his tongue, a flavor sensation that made him think of gondolas and a leaning tower. "Oh my … wow," he breathed.

She grinned. "Grandma's secret recipe. She says she learned it from an Italian woman she worked for while she was in college."

"And she taught your grandmother?"

"No, more like she guarded a family secret, so Grandma watched her make the sauce, then spent months figuring out the recipe."

"This is incredible. Thank you."

Her cheeks flushed deep pink. "You're welcome. This is the first time it actually tastes like Grandma's." She looped the white lock of hair behind her ear, a simple movement that sent heat rolling through him.

*God, could she look any more beautiful?* He finished another forkful. "If it's any consolation, my grandma can't make sauce like this even if it's out of a jar, but her shepherd's pie is a work of art."

She leaned back in her chair. "I don't get it. I get the Dash-8, since Tori worked for Range Air, but why the hell-hole? It'd be a pain in the ass to shove a dead body through that hatch. Did the crime scene team find anything?"

Normally he'd breathe, eat, sleep a case until he figured it out. He wanted to savor her company instead, this "now". His house felt like a home for the first time in over a year. "Nothing we can't discuss later," he said.

"Sorry. It's been bugging me. Wouldn't it be easier to just dump the body somewhere else? Why go through the trouble of putting it in an airplane?"

He had wondered the same thing. "It reminds me of how sometimes killers will pose bodies. Gangs do it, serial killers do it, and even people whose reasons are more spur-of-the-moment passion or anger do it. They pose the body to send a message."

She sipped her beer. "Okay, so who would they be sending a message to? The only people who go into the hell-hole are mechanics. Which means a Range Air mechanic would be involved. But involved in what?"

He debated telling her about seeing Lowell at Castor Aviation. That fact didn't fit into the case any way he could see.

"The other thing that's been bugging me are those weird phone calls Cate mentioned." Her mood darkened perceptibly. "You know who calls and doesn't leave a message or ask for another person." It wasn't a question, and she didn't wait for him to respond. "What if someone was harassing Tori, maybe stalking her?"

He understood why she went that direction. "I don't think she had that problem."

"What makes you so sure?"

"Cate didn't mention that Tori was scared." He watched her, judged his next words and her possible response. "You didn't have a roommate. If you would have had one, would you have confided in her? What if she was family?"

She toyed with her pasta. "I suppose I would have. Especially family." Another moment. "Then why would she answer the phone and not say anything? Cate said after a call, Tori would go to her bedroom for a few minutes. Doesn't that sound like recording the time of the call to you? Maybe she waited to hear what the person said so she could write that down, too. They want that stuff before they issue any sort of stop-it-or-get-in-trouble paperwork."

"Cease and desist," he supplied. A restraining order would be one of the next steps. He knew Sierra had gone through the process herself, not that it had done any good. "I didn't find anything like that for her."

"Maybe she asked about it, but was told not to come back until she had some solid evidence to *prove* she wasn't imagining things." Frustration laced her voice. "And it would explain why when Cate answered, the caller hung up."

Quinn laid a hand on her forearm and felt the tautness in her muscles. "Sierra, you're safe. I don't think—"

She didn't look at him. "I get that you can't chase down every creep, because some people really do imagine things, or see something that isn't what it seems." She pulled away. "They don't give up. And they let you know they are watching."

A mental image of a winged emerald appeared. *That has to be a coincidence. Rune Thorsson is a stalker. He probably dropped it on the tarmac for her to see, and Tori found it first.*

Sierra closed her eyes, took in a deep breath, and let it out slowly. When she opened her eyes, he noticed a fresh determination in the hazel depths. "You said it could be a message. If shoving her body into the hell-hole is a message to some Range Air mechanic, which mechanic? What is the message?" She used her fork for emphasis. "Someone felt it necessary to go through Tori's apartment and mine. Tori must have had something someone wants pretty badly. What did she have and where did she put it?"

She took a bite of spaghetti. "She worked at Range Air and Castor Aviation. What could she get her hands on at either place that someone would kill for? Drugs?" She shook her head. "Too obvious. And stupid. Tori was a bitch, but she wasn't stupid, according to Cate."

"Cate said Tori changed after your brother died," Quinn said.

Sierra looked at him with a mix of grief and anger. "And you believe her?"

"What if Cate's right? Maybe Tori did change. Cate said Tori wanted to find out what really happened. Her boyfriend's brother said Tori talked about setting the record straight. Her parents died in a plane crash. Maybe after Ken died in the plane crash it shocked her into changing her ways."

"You mean, like scaring her straight? I don't know. I have a hard time believing that."

Quinn pushed his plate forward and rested his arms on the table. There had to be more to Tori's story. "Cate said Tori got into a lot of trouble after her folks died, but cleaned up her act. That was the only reason she let Tori move in with her. Would Ken have dated her if she was doing stuff he was trying to stay away from? That's why he didn't want to stay at your folks' place, right?"

Sierra stared at her plate. "In the beginning, Ken thought she was cute and vibrant and fun. They always went to plays or movies, not to clubs or places like that."

"Then what happened? They started going to clubs at some point, right?"

She nodded. "Wait a minute. Ken planned to buy a plane when he got out of the Air Force. He saved up for it for years. It was maybe a month or two after they started dating when he found a Cherokee in his price range. When I went with him to look at it, he mentioned Tori didn't want him to buy it. She had flown with her dad many times when she was a kid, but she refused to go on a test flight with Ken. He couldn't convince her to fly with him."

"Why not?"

"If her parents died in a plane crash, maybe she associated the plane with tragedy. It's like people who are scared to fly not because they've never flown, but because someone they knew died in a plane crash."

Something clicked. "Let me guess. After Ken bought the plane, he and Tori started going to clubs." Quinn pondered. According to Cate, Tori turned to the dark side after her parents died. Why hadn't she kept her partying ways after Ken died?

"You said Tori wanted to find out what really happened. Maybe she found something," Sierra said. "Whatever it was must have something to do with the airport, otherwise why would someone kill her on airport grounds and jam her body into an airplane?"

Quinn leaned back in his chair. She had just narrated his thoughts on the case almost verbatim.

Her eyebrows arched high. "What?" She wiped at her mouth. "Did I miss something? My face?"

"You didn't tell me you were telepathic."

"Huh?" She blinked, then gave him a crooked smile that kicked his pulse into a higher gear. "So, you're saying I could be a detective?"

"And give up working on airplanes? Somehow I don't think you'd go for that."

Her grin faded. "Why do you say that?"

"You went through an FAA investigation and stuck with aviation. I think you want to be around aircraft, and maybe that's something your brother encouraged you to do. You admired him, and if he thought you were on the right path for you, his approval wiped out any of your doubts."

She blinked, eyes glistening before she dabbed at them with her napkin. "You've already gone through everything I just said." At his nod, she continued. "What pieces are missing?"

He wanted to let it go tonight and get back to the comfortable atmosphere they started with. She was too close to his professional territory, and the case involved her. "Let's change the subject. What else do you like to cook?"

The distraction carried the conversation through another round of spaghetti. When Quinn checked his watch, he did a double-take. It didn't feel like they'd been talking that long. "Crap. It's almost midnight."

"Seriously?" She rose and started to gather the dishes.

He snagged his own before she took them. "You're the guest, and you cooked," he said by way of explanation, "which means I wash." He followed her to the sink, where she rinsed her plate. As if it were second nature, he came up close behind her, reached around her to set his plate in the sink, and then took hers from her hand and set it atop his.

She stilled for a moment. Whether it was the heady aroma of garlic and oregano or simple fatigue, he didn't think about what he did next. With a hand on her hip, he nudged her to turn around. It felt natural, like they went through the same ritual as part of everyday life.

She faced him, her back to the sink, and made no move to push him away. His pulse thundered like a stampede of wild horses, drowning out the little voice trying to warn him he couldn't uncross this line. He brushed her cheek with the back of a finger. Her breath shuddered. He bent to her lips.

Soft. Sweet. She tasted like raindrops in spring. The need he abandoned over a year ago surged through him. He had to feel her, the texture of her skin, the fine silk of her hair, the strength hidden out of sight. She didn't resist, leaning into him when he wrapped his arms around her, answering his deepening kiss by parting her lips, giving him permission.

He pulled her close, slid a hand under her sweater. Her smooth skin burned under his touch. He worked the hooks of her bra loose, and released the soft mounds of her breasts. She moaned into his mouth, driving his desire beyond intense into the realm of supernova.

The shrill staccato of his beeper shattered the frenzy. He broke from her, shivered at the sudden loss of her body against him. "Shit." He struggled to slow his breathing as he checked his pager. He recognized the number. Dispatch.

"Work?" she asked, face flushed.

"Yeah." He wanted to ignore the call. God, he wanted her. Instead, he lifted the receiver of the kitchen phone and dialed the number on the pager display. "Moore here," he said when the voice on the other end answered. He listened, then hung up.

"You have to leave," she said, her voice soft with the barest hint of husky.

He nodded. She trembled just enough for him to notice. Her cheeks still showed rosy color that had nothing to do with makeup. "The state patrol got a call about a pickup truck that went through the ice on the river."

"If the state patrol is already out there, why did they call you?"

"The truck belongs to Peter Manelli, Tori's boyfriend."

# 41

Red and blue lights flashed a crazy tempo, like strobe lights in a dance club. Spotlights on tripods illuminated the path from the road up ahead to the river down a steep bank. Quinn parked at the end of a line made up of a Minnesota State Patrol car, a State Patrol SUV, an ambulance, and a BCA van. A tow truck beyond the head of the line pulled ahead to bring the pickup truck at the end of its hoist onto the pavement. Two divers in dry suits followed the ice-coated truck into the circle of activity. He found the officer securing the scene and introduced himself, hanging his badge on a lanyard around his neck. "Who found it?"

The State Patrol officer scanned the area. His name tag said "Chen". "Ice fisherman. Line got caught up on it."

Ice fishing at this hour? Must be a die-hard. "How did he know it was a vehicle?"

"Fish finder. When the divers went in, they confirmed it. Truck is registered to Peter Manelli, who appears to be at the wheel." Chen shook his head. "If it hadn't been for that fisher, we wouldn't have found it until spring. Manelli's brother reported him missing yesterday."

It had been three days since anyone heard from Pete. "Has anyone notified the next of kin?"

"We are waiting to confirm the identity of the victim. What's your part in all this? This is outside your jurisdiction."

"He's connected to a homicide I'm working."

Chen whistled, a plume of breath like smoke from his lips. "Homicide at the airport? That's a new one."

"First for me at the airport. Used to work Homicide in St. Paul. Where's the fisherman?"

Chen motioned to the ambulance. "Should be there staying warm along with the divers and a BCA agent. They're doing the scene analysis, and they'll do the forensics on the truck."

Quinn handed Chen a card. "Will you make sure I get a copy of the report and the crime scene forensics?" At the officer's nod, Quinn thanked him and headed to the ambulance. Two EMTs attended to the divers and a civilian cradling a thermos cup of hot coffee between his hands. The man, in his late seventies or early eighties judging by the generous number of deep lines on his face and a perpetual windburn, wore tan Carhartt insulated overalls and completed the ensemble with an ear-flap hat. An image of Walter Matthau as a grumpy old man flashed through his mind.

He introduced himself to the fisherman and asked what happened. The fisher couldn't tell him much about the truck, but started on a litany of night fishing on the Minnesota River. Best time to fish, he insisted, was the wee hours of the morning, long before dawn. Quinn nodded, smiled, and extricated himself from the conversation as quickly and graciously as he could. Questions to the divers yielded nothing more.

Despite inter-department cooperation, this wasn't his investigation, and with both the state patrol and the BCA on site, he suspected he would be the last to know the important stuff, like who sat in the driver's seat.

He headed toward the truck pulled from the river. One BCA agent was taking pictures of the truck from every angle while another tried to open the driver's door. It didn't budge. Judging by the speed at which the truck went from wet to coated in ice, Quinn suspected the doors were frozen shut. He managed to get close enough to see a driver behind the wheel, but the icy glaze on the windows made it impossible to see any details.

A BCA agent stepped between him and the truck, parka zipped to the base of her red-tipped nose. "You can't be here."

Quinn showed his badge. "When will you know the identity of the driver?"

"Not until we get the truck back to the lab and thawed out. Everything's frozen solid."

He handed her his card. "I'm working a homicide case that may involve Manelli. I need a copy of the reports as soon as possible."

She countered with a request for a formal requisition for the reports.

Paperwork slowed everything down, especially when it involved departments in multiple jurisdictions. Careful not to grumble too much, he got the case number from her, as well as the state patrol's reference number.

He headed back to his vehicle. Why the Minnesota River? The last time anyone saw Manelli was at the airport. Pete had to cross the river to get to the house he shared with his brother. Did he have an unfortunate accident on the way home, or did someone intercept him? Whatever his girlfriend stashed was important enough for someone to kill her, ransack her apartment and assault her cousin, and follow Sierra home and toss her apartment as well, because someone saw her leave with ferret supplies, and who else but a good friend would babysit a pet ferret?

What did he know about Tori? Graduate student at the U trying to finish an advanced degree in forensic accounting.

Forensic accounting. She was doing more research than her adviser expected. Tom Manelli said Pete told him Tori found something interesting for her paper. Tori interned at a fixed-base operation as a bookkeeper reconciling job expenses every week, according to her supervisor, Gil Randolph. That by itself didn't mean much, but put together with her thesis and the bit of information from Manelli's brother, it meant she might have found something someone wanted to keep quiet.

According to Tom Manelli, Tori talked about setting the record straight and bringing them down.

Them who?

A flatbed truck lumbered past him toward the scene. Once the flatbed jockeyed around enough to load the pickup, Quinn turned his SUV around and left the scene. They didn't have a positive ID, but his gut told him Peter Manelli sat behind the wheel, and Tori's missing boyfriend hadn't drowned in the river.

He couldn't get the reports as soon as he wanted, but he'd run the case with what his instincts told him. When Tori didn't give up the prize, whatever it might be, the next logical person was her boyfriend. Tori's apartment would be the next target. He suspected Cate was in the wrong place at the wrong time.

He checked his watch and groaned. Fatigue numbed his mind as he turned into the residential area and followed the familiar route to his house. He'd grab a few hours of sleep, then move Manelli from the suspect column to victim and start digging into Castor Aviation.

He turned into his driveway and secured the Explorer. Light glowed around the edges of the living room curtains. Was Sierra still awake? He went through the garage and into the house, locking the doors behind him. After he stowed his service weapon and hung up his winter gear, he headed into the kitchen. The dishes were put away, and a peek into the refrigerator showed a container of spaghetti perfect for him to bring to work for lunch.

"Sierra?" He checked the living room. Empty. He switched the light off and headed down the hallway. A quick check of the bathroom showed Rascal's cage closed, the ferret burrowed into the towel.

He continued to the guest bedroom, the hall light reaching into the room through the wide opening of the door left ajar. Curled in a ball outside the glow of the hall light, Sierra huddled under the patchwork quilt. Her quiet breathing matched the serene look on her face, her white lock of hair bright against the dark of the rest.

He shouldn't feel like she belonged in his life. Not yet. Still, he couldn't imagine it any other way. Maybe the question should be whether she felt the same way. She let him hold her while she mourned for her brother. She hadn't protested when he kissed her. She hadn't put up the struggle he expected when he insisted she stay at his house while he searched for whomever tore up her apartment. Not that she'd had a lot of options, especially when her ex-boyfriend seemed unconcerned about violating the restraining order. He made a mental note to submit the arrest warrant paperwork for Rune Thorsson first thing in the morning when he returned to the office.

He stood for a moment and watched her sleep. Part of him wanted to snuggle with her under the quilt. The other part reminded him how precarious his position already was if anyone found out she was staying in his guest room. He closed her door until only a narrow opening remained before he finished his nightly routine and turned in.

Quinn lay awake. The time on the clock seemed to change once an hour. Hell, he'd been up plenty the past few days working on the case. He should be able to sleep. At first he thought it was typical case-solving energy, the type that kept his brain churning so much he couldn't quiet it enough to sleep. But his thoughts weren't consumed by shifting puzzle pieces.

He'd been sleeping alone for over a year. Tonight, the bed seemed bigger and more empty than usual. He lay in the middle, arms outstretched to either side, and listened to the wind outside, picked out the sound of tiny crystalline grains of snow blowing against the window. He wondered how large the drifts would be once the wind finally stopped building them.

His thoughts circled around the woman sleeping in his spare bedroom.

He knew how hard it could be to sleep in an unfamiliar bed in an unfamiliar place. Was she warm enough? He liked to keep the house temperature cooler, especially at night. Was sixty-five too cool?

He shouldn't be thinking about her. She certainly shouldn't have a part in his imagined daily routine. Another glance at the glowing red numbers told him the past hour had only lasted ten minutes. He sighed, and tried to quiet his mind enough to get some sleep.

A loud thud followed by a curse jolted him out of bed.

# 42

Pain radiated through her forehead, competing with the sharp burning from the cramp in her calf. Who the hell was stupid enough to open a door and get their head in the way? Someone who was half-asleep hobbling with a Charley horse trying to navigate in the dark in a strange house.

"Sierra?" Light glared. She shielded her eyes until the brilliance dimmed. "You okay?"

"Yes, just …" She tried to straighten her leg to ease out of the cramp. "Ack! No." Quinn caught her before she lost her balance and steered her back to the bed.

"Cramp?"

She gritted her teeth and tried again to straighten her leg and rub the cramp out of the muscle. "I hate these." She sucked in air as the arch of her foot joined in. "Shit. Now my foot."

Quinn settled beside her on the bed. "Relax your leg."

"If I could relax it, I wouldn't have any cramps."

He laid warm hands on her bare leg, one under her knee, the other at the bottom of her foot, cupping her arch. He helped her straighten it, stretching the knotted muscle.

"Ow! Wait."

"Relax. Here." He pulled her leg into his lap and started massaging her calf with gentle but steady pressure. Heat flushed through her. His ministrations loosened her cramp, but tightened other things. "Better?" he asked.

"Yeah, thanks." Did she sound as breathless as she felt? She pulled her leg away. "I don't get them very often, but when I do, they hurt like hell." She checked the clock on the table beside the bed. Three in the morning. "Did you just get home?"

"About a half-hour ago."

"I tried to wait up, but I fell asleep." She shivered in the cool of the room; the heat that had flooded her when Quinn worked on her cramp had vanished.

"Are you warm enough in here? I keep the house cool at night." He wrapped an arm around her. "Why would you wait up?"

"I want to know what happened. You said they found Tori's boyfriend's truck."

He brushed her hair from her face and pulled her against him. The room was getting warmer again. "They found Manelli's truck in the Minnesota River."

"He's dead?" Goosebumps rose despite Quinn's body heat. Tori was dead. If her boyfriend was dead, too, Cate was lucky, she thought.

Quinn rubbed her arm. "You're cold. Here," he said, coaxing her to stand so he could gather the quilt off the bed. He drew her back to the bed before pulling the quilt around them both, trapping his heat under the blanket with her. "Better?"

She leaned into him, relishing the strength of his arms. She nodded against him. "Much. Thank you." At that moment, she wanted nothing more than to be as close to him as she could.

He rested a cheek on her head. Ran a hand along her arm. "Good. Hey, it's late. You should go back to sleep."

His touch tingled through her. The memory of their kiss in the kitchen tightened things low in her belly. It had been so long since she had kissed someone. She'd forgotten the rush.

He'd made the rest of the world vanish with his kiss, his hands against her skin. She longed for that contact again, even if it meant giving herself to him. *What if it didn't work between them?*

Quinn lifted her chin. Met her lips with his. She opened to him. He delved into her, hand cupping her cheek. She reveled in the sensation of his tongue against hers, sparking an electric surge that danced along her nerves until her entire body hummed.

Doubt rose. *You're not even dating him.*

*You haven't done this before.*

He traced the length of her body, the lines of muscle along her side. Slid his hand under her sleeping tee. Followed the gentle sweep of her ribs.

Stopped.

"It's just a scar," she whispered into his mouth. "Don't stop."

His fingertips feathered across the rough skin. She gasped when he cupped her breast, ran a thumb across her sensitive nipple. Her body clenched, arched toward him. She gripped his bicep to steady herself as the sensations rolled through her. Something began to build inside. She needed more, wanted more.

He tasted her bit by bit, kissed down her neck, her skin alive with every touch. He rose on his knees to remove his shirt before pulling hers over her head. He caught her mouth in another kiss.

Her nerves sizzled. She ran hands across his shoulders, down his arms, over his back, his skin smooth under her fingers, his muscles moving under the surface like waves. He broke from her just long enough to finish undressing them both, allowing him to explore even farther without hindrance. He slid an arm under her, pulled her tighter against him until she couldn't tell where she left off and he began.

He kissed his way to her breasts while his hand traced a line from her belly to her center, brushed the barest of touches across her most sensitive parts.

Pleasure exploded through her. Wave after wave surged until she didn't think she could contain it. She cried out.

He captured her mouth once more, set a knee between her legs. Eased his way into her.

*Oh. God. Yes.*

She broke the kiss, sucked in a breath when a sharp pain bit through her reverie when he was halfway home. Before she could register it, her body arched into him. Took him in. Reveled in the hot, the thick, the rhythm.

Pressure built. Surged. Flared time and again.

Her velvet heat pulsed as fire erupted through him.

Quinn collapsed atop her, muscles trembling. God, it'd never been like this, not with his ex, not with anyone before. He brushed Sierra's hair from her forehead before he pressed his lips to it, continued to the tip of her nose, to her mouth. Her eyes were bleary, lids half-closed. He planted light kisses on her eyelids, then traced her cheek with a finger. "Sierra," he whispered, enjoying the cadence of her name on his tongue.

"Wow," she breathed. "I never imagined ..."

He rolled to his back and pulled her with him, held her tight against his side, her head on his shoulder, hand on his chest.

Reality seeped through the afterglow of sex. He'd offered her hospitality, safety, and what had he done? He didn't sleep with anyone he just met.

But it felt *right*. It felt right from the first moment he saw her sitting on a metal work stand to the moment he held her while she struggled with a nightmare. He couldn't ignore that.

*What if it hadn't been right for her?*

Shit, he'd never thought about her perspective. He chose not to listen to reason, followed his emotions instead.

That didn't account for her emotions.

Her body stiffened. "Shit." She pushed up, braced on an elbow. "No condom."

"While I was in college, my nephew was diagnosed with a rare, more deadly version of PKD—a kidney disease. He died before his fifth birthday. Neil and his wife were devastated. After two of my brothers and I found out we're carriers, I had a vasectomy." Her concern, though, opened the floor for his own. "Are you okay with this? I'm so sorry, I didn't mean to, it just ..."

"Happened," she finished. She settled back on him. "Hell, I never make it past the second date with guys, not since ... My sister says I'm too critical."

It was the way she said it. His insides added a knot to the twisted mass in his gut. He asked, even though he thought he knew the answer. "Was this your first time?"

Silence. "Yes."

A huge crash echoed inside his head. He pushed to a sitting position, dislodging her.

"Quinn, what is it?" she asked, sitting upright beside him. She wrapped the quilt around her shoulders. "It wasn't your fault," she said, as if she could read his mind.

He looked into her eyes, one slightly lighter than the other. "Yes, it was. I shouldn't have taken advantage of you." He started to stand, but she held him back.

"You think you took advantage of me? You don't get to feel all guilty because this happened." She touched a finger to his lips when he started to speak. "Shut up and lay down."

Something in her tone weakened his protest. She pushed him back, then snuggled in beside him, leg over his, hand on his chest, head on his shoulder. She pulled the quilt over them both and wriggled until she was comfortable. "For crying out loud, I'm twenty-five years old."

"It doesn't matter how old—"

"Hush." She propped up on an elbow, raised up enough to look into his eyes. "I didn't want to come here tonight, but not because I was afraid of being in a strange place with someone I just met, but because I was afraid of how I felt about someone I just met. It wasn't all you.

"I blame my dad, who's a nurse practitioner specializing in homeopathic and holistic medicine. I grew up in a home where nature and the universe rules, and intuition is the universe's way of communicating with us. I've never had this kind of connection with anyone." She wiggled her fingers and drew them away. "Okay, I'm finished with the spooky New Age stuff now." She rolled away, turned to her side, her back to him, and curled under the quilt. "I don't blame you for anything, Quinn. I'm glad it was you, for what it's worth."

Anything he had wanted to say vanished in the mild shock generating the white noise inside his head. His thoughts kept circling around her confession. He wasn't one to scoff at the idea of intuition. Cops called it a gut feeling. It was everything, from that first handshake, to the unexpected meeting at Coffman Union, to her call from Cate's apartment, to the decision to bring her here. The irresistible need she awakened in him after so long without.

Everything about her stirred emotions in him.

He slid to her, pulled her tight against him because he needed to feel her, her skin, her heat. He breathed against her neck. "You won't be afraid of what I have to say now, will you? Since we're coming clean here. By the way, I like how you just come right out and say it. Sure beats having to guess." He held her in place when she started to turn toward him.

"I was planning to ask you out as soon as I closed the case. I've even planned our first date." She relaxed, but tension still lined slack muscles. "I shouldn't have met you for breakfast. I should have made you come to the APD office in the terminal. It was an excuse to see you."

He let her roll to her back now, so he could see her face. He kept his arm around her as he propped an elbow and rested his head in his hand, eyes on her. "You have no idea how scared I was when you said you might have seen the man who attacked Cate and tossed her apartment. After I saw the crime scene photos from your attack," he traced the line of her scar, "and realized I'd seen Thorsson at Castor, I …"

He what? Thought she knew?

Her reaction to that bit of news had told him otherwise. "When you said Thorsson found you at the laundromat, I had to keep you safe. Bringing you here is against the rules."

"That's what you were discussing with Kevin."

He nodded. "Protocol is to send you home with a patrol to watch your place. Or, if that might be dangerous, put you in a hotel with a patrol or a guard, either hotel security or an officer." He caressed her cheek, soft under his fingertips.

"Tonight the meal, the conversation," he hesitated, "the kiss. I've never felt anything like this for anyone, not even my former wife." He touched her lips with his, a kiss of reassurance. "That doesn't mean what I did was right."

"What did I say about the guilt trip thing?"

"Even with the break-in and Thorsson, I could get suspended for bringing you here."

"Suspended?" Eyes wide, she sat up. "You brought me here knowing you could get suspended? What the hell were you thinking? You could lose your job if they find out."

He wanted her again, wanted to taste her, needed to feel her against him, around him. He cut her off with a kiss, long and deep. "You heard the part about how I feel, right?"

"It's your job, Quinn."

He'd made the mistake of putting his job first too many times. He sat at the edge of the bed. "My job ruined my marriage. I was a rookie when we got married. She wasn't going in blind. I wanted my detective shield and I worked for it, at the expense of time with my wife. She begged me to take time off, but I didn't. I made detective, and she thought—hoped, I suppose—that I would be able to spend more time at home instead of on the streets.

"It didn't work out that way. She insisted I find another job that wasn't St. Paul or Minneapolis, somewhere the cases wouldn't be a round-the-clock focus, so I could spare some time for her." Acid churned in his stomach at the memory of those fights. "I got the job at the airport, and we moved here. I had more time for her, but by then it seemed she lost hope that we could fix whatever was wrong. I tried. I thought she was trying.

"Things got better for a while. Then I found the pregnancy test." The sinking feeling from that day echoed through him, the dread, the cold certainty that his marriage was beyond saving.

Sierra, wrapped in the quilt, sat next to him. "She knew you had a vasectomy, right?"

"Of course. I told her when we were dating and things started getting serious between us." He stood, crossed to the curtained window.

"So she left a positive pregnancy test somewhere her detective husband, who's had a vasectomy, will find it. Sounds like a coward's way of telling you she's seeing someone else and wants out." Arms wrapped around him from behind. The soft mounds of her breasts pressed into his back. "I'm sorry, Quinn. I could say I'm sorry things turned out like that for you, but I'm not."

He turned in her arms until he could see her face. "You're not?"

"No." A slow smile stretched across her lips. "Because if things hadn't happened the way they did, we wouldn't be here right now."

# 43

A hissed curse and a sudden chill woke Sierra. Goosebumps rose. The bed shifted. She shivered before the quilt, tucked in again, restored the warmth. The sensation of him cuddled against her back faded. Another whispered expletive and a thud finished the process of chasing fatigue from her. Pale light seeped around the edges of the curtain.

The door to the guest room opened, and his silhouette filled the gap. "Quinn."

He turned back. "Shh. You sleep. You were up late."

A glance at the clock's glowing display answered her next question. "So were you."

He turned on the light, still dimmed from earlier, and sat on the bed. At some point before he reached the door, he'd tossed on the old t-shirt and fitted boxers he wore last night. This morning, she corrected. Sleeping attire, she suspected. "Go back to sleep," he said as he brushed her hair from her eyes.

She tried to sit up, but the quilt was trapped under him. She propped up on an elbow, quilt to her chin. "You haven't slept more than four hours. You can't—"

He found her mouth with his. The kiss fired her pulse and took her breath away. She exhaled hard when he pulled back, a hunger low in her belly.

"I have to. It's late already."

"You got a call at midnight and didn't get home until three. Even cops need to sleep." She noted the bags under his eyes, and remembered the same look the first night they met. She knew what it was like to work when tired, and her job didn't need the same mental acumen his did. "You don't sleep much, do you?"

He gave her a quick kiss on her forehead before he stood. "I sleep enough. I've got to go in." He headed toward the door.

"You don't." When he looked back, eyebrow raised, she explained. "Sleep enough. You don't sleep enough, and you know it." She slipped out of bed, fully aware she was both naked and cold, and pressed against him, face upturned, arms around his neck. Her hips twitched into his, the emptiness in her core unfamiliar. "Come back to bed. You need another hour or two."

He held her hips steady and kissed her long and deep. "I wish I could. I really have to go to the office."

She saw the conflict in his eyes, recognized it. Duty versus want. She wanted to feel his weight on her, his heat.

She *wanted* him.

She had only known him for a few days. The rest of her ignored it. This wasn't the fresh-faced new-boyfriend awe that blinded her so many years ago. This felt certain. Comfortable. "Tell me you've slept more than a dozen hours in the past three days."

He looked past her, avoiding her eyes. She pulled his chin down, encouraging him to meet her gaze. "You can't work effectively, Detective, unless you get enough sleep."

He frowned. "Don't call me that. Not after last night."

"I got your attention. And technically it was this morning."

He shook his head. "I'm so sorry. I didn't know you were … I shouldn't have done that."

She saw the guilt in his eyes, in the lines of his forehead and tight press of his lips. "Quinn." She grabbed his shoulders, spun them around and pushed him toward the bed. "I did hear you say you were already planning our first date, right? And probably a second one. And a third, unless things went horribly wrong. And you know what," she placed a hand on his chest to stop him from escaping, "I would've agreed. And at some point we would've done this."

"That's no excuse for taking advantage—"

She shoved him back until he fell onto the bed, then climbed beside him, leaned over him, sank into those intense blue eyes. "Really? 'Taking advantage of' sounds like I resisted." She kissed him, a soft chaste touch.

He pulled her close, deepened the kiss, maneuvered them both until they were under the quilt. "I haven't felt like this with anyone, Sierra. I don't want to screw it up."

Her heart swelled at his words. She wanted him to take her again, make her feel like there was nothing else in the world except the two of them. She rolled atop him. "Show me," she whispered.

❖ ❖ ❖

AN HOUR LATER, Sierra eased out from under Quinn's arm. He didn't wake. She tucked the quilt around him and made a mental note to wake him in another hour. He needed sleep, and though she could've crashed for another few hours, she wanted to be awake when he left.

A memory of his touch, of his body entwined with hers sent a shudder through her. She felt warm and fuzzy, alive in a way she'd never imagined. She grabbed her sweats and crept out of the bedroom, closing the door behind her.

He had a point, she thought. Two people were supposed to date, get to know each other a bit before sleeping together. A lot of things weren't supposed to happen the way they did. Ken wasn't supposed to die in a plane crash. Rune wasn't supposed to come back.

She wasn't supposed to sleep with a guy when she couldn't go on more than two dates with anyone after her ex-boyfriend tried to kill her. She wasn't supposed to feel like she had known a man for years when they only just met. Hell, they should at least know how many brothers and sisters the other has before one stays the night. She knew he had at least two brothers and one sister. How many more? What did his parents do for a living?

Who cares? Quinn is all that matters.

Rascal ventured out from the towel when she entered the bathroom. She dug a ferret treat from the bag and gave it to the little beast, who took it back to the towel to eat. After her morning routine, she checked the clock in the kitchen. It was mid-morning, though the clouds outside made it hard to tell the difference. She had a little time before she needed to wake him, so she searched for coffee. What she found made her smile. Her journalist great-aunt had brought Kona coffee back from a jaunt to the Big Island. Its mellow, rich aroma and matching taste made her think of morning mists on the slope of an active volcano. Maybe she could take Quinn on a Hawaiian vacation, since she got the associated employee discount for the flight.

The thought made her pause. Taking him on a vacation when they weren't even dating? That, of course, dismissed the fact they'd slept together. No second thoughts, no resistance, no question.

God, she could spend all her time pondering the situation. Instead, she started a pot of coffee, then hunted for ingredients. If Quinn wasn't going to get enough sleep, he damn well would get a decent breakfast.

Twenty minutes later, she checked the hash browns, then turned off the burner.

"You didn't have to cook." His voice startled her. She turned. He entered the kitchen, wearing what she considered his work clothes: navy slacks with a navy sweater vest over a white turtleneck. He tugged on his shoulder holster, then pulled her to him and greeted her with a kiss that quickened her pulse. "How long have you been up?"

"Long enough." She retrieved another frying pan from the cabinet beside the stove and pulled the carton of eggs from the refrigerator. "Eggs will be ready in a few minutes. You might as well have something more substantial than coffee or a donut to get you through lunch at the very least. Besides, I'm up."

Blue eyes locked to hers, sent a shock wave through her. "Please don't take this the wrong way, but it feels like we've been doing this for a long time. Tell me I'm not crazy."

She loaded a plate with hash browns and added two over-easy eggs before handing it to him, then leaned against the counter. "I've thought about that. And if I told my mother how this happened, she'd freak."

"What about your dad?"

"My dad is a New Age mindful thinker. I think he would be okay with it." She fixed her own plate of hash browns and an egg before joining him at the table. "So, can you tell me what else happened last night? You said they found Tori's boyfriend's truck, but you never said if he's dead or not."

He pushed his potatoes around on his plate before he answered. "The state patrol and BCA were both on-scene, so I won't know anything until I get copies of the reports, but someone was behind the wheel, and I'd lay money down that it was Manelli."

She shivered at the thought. "First Tori, then Cate and her apartment, then my apartment, now Manelli."

"No one's heard from Manelli since Tuesday. I suspect whomever killed Tori went to Manelli before he went to Cate's apartment." He sipped his coffee. "I didn't know I had hash browns."

"You had potatoes, and I know the secret to crispy hash browns." she said with a grin. "If Manelli's dead, whoever killed him didn't get whatever he's looking for. He didn't find it at Cate's, or at my place. Where does the bad guy go from here? We don't even know what 'it' is."

Quinn finished his breakfast. "It's my job to figure that out. You stay here today. Please. I don't want to worry about you and your stalker ex-boyfriend, or the guy who broke into your apartment."

She had expected as much. Deep down, she knew he didn't intend it to sound controlling, but after the close encounter at the laundromat and her apartment break-in, she couldn't avoid hearing the subtle demand in his words. Maybe the aftereffects of their lovemaking helped tone down her response. "You're lucky I brought groceries."

He bussed his dishes to the sink. She did the same, adding her plate and silverware to his, and followed him to the entryway. He checked his gun, then tucked it into his shoulder holster before donning his coat and boots. She crossed her arms and leaned against the wall, wondering again at the whole everyday feel of it.

He cupped her cheek before he kissed her. "I'm not sure when I'll be home, but I'll call if it gets too late."

She waited until the heat from his kiss dissipated. "I work tonight. My shift starts at nine-thirty."

He froze. "No."

As she expected. Her temper rumbled. "I am going to work tonight," she repeated, adding steel to her voice.

He closed his eyes for a moment, like he was trying to calm himself. "Sierra, you cannot go back until I catch this guy. When you are here, I know you are safe. Our unknown subject and Thorsson don't know you're here. Warren even said you could take some time. Hell, he practically ordered you to take a few days off."

Part of her melted at his concern. "I think you know why I will go to work tonight and not stay here like some—" She choked on the word. "Besides, he already searched my apartment. He knows I don't have whatever it is he's looking for."

"Just until I have someone in custody. Please?"

"Quinn, I'm not going to let fear control me. Been there, fought back, and still went through therapy and years of self-condemnation before I accepted that I made some bad choices and still came out better than a lot of people do. I won't avoid things because of fear."

"I'm the one who's scared, Sierra. Someone killed Tori. Killed her boyfriend. Put her roommate in the hospital. If you had surprised him at your apartment, you'd probably be there, too.

"Thorsson works at the airport. His little stunt at the laundromat proves he knows more about your life here than you thought. You have to assume he knows you work there, too. Once the warrant is issued, it'll take time to bring him in."

"I get it. If I cave in to what you want, it's like the situation he created is controlling me all over again. You get that, right?"

"I'm not him."

"I know, Quinn. You're so far from him it's like you're in a whole different dimension. I get that you're worried about me, and I appreciate it, but don't argue with me on this."

He sighed, a pleading look on his face, before he opened the door to the garage. "Will you at least call me before you leave and when you get to the hangar?"

"I'll call you when I get to work."

# 44

Quinn submitted the warrant paperwork for Rune Thorsson, then continued compiling the report for the break-in at Sierra's apartment. Anything to distract him from the fact she was going to work tonight. Not only was his suspect still at large, but her stalker ex-boyfriend drove a fuel truck at the airport. It was a small miracle she hadn't known Thorsson worked so close to her.

Yvonne entered his office, manila envelope in hand. She took one look at him and cocked her head to one side. "You look a helluva lot better than you did yesterday. What happened?" Before he answered, she added with a conspiratorial whisper, "No, don't tell me, but I like it. As long as it's legal." She handed him the envelope. "From the ME's office."

Quinn slid the medical examiner's preliminary report for Peter Manelli out of the envelope. Impressive. He had expected to wait at least a week before seeing any paperwork. He thanked Yvonne, but before he could review it, Kevin appeared in the doorway, paper evidence bag in hand and a frown on his face.

"It's about time. Thought you were going to take a day off when you weren't here by seven."

"I got a call at midnight. A fisherman found the vic's boyfriend's truck in the river. State patrol called me in since I put out an alert for him. Got home late."

Kevin dropped the evidence bag in front of Quinn with a thud. He planted his hands on the edge of the desk and leaned over. "You did it, didn't you?"

Guilt settled beside worry at Kevin's demeanor. "Did what?"

Kevin straightened, crossed the room to close the office door. "Exactly what I warned you about doing." He shook his head. "The case is still open and she's still a suspect."

"I know that, but you're wrong about her being a suspect. If she was involved, why would someone trash her apartment like they did Cate's?"

"How do you know someone else trashed it?"

The accusation hung in the air like a noxious cloud. Quinn the cop shoved the worried boyfriend mentality aside. Sierra was the first on scene at Cate's apartment, but Cate said a man assaulted her. He took Sierra's word about her own apartment break-in because he hadn't found any evidence to the contrary.

Why would she toss her own apartment like that? The photo of the winged emerald on the board stirred up more suspicion. It didn't make sense.

"Before you tell me your new girlfriend is innocent," Kevin handed him a pair of latex gloves, "open the bag."

Quinn pulled on the gloves and removed the contents of the bag.

About the size of a large fist, the bronze-hued unit had a plastic plug on either side. Two mounting holes indicated the part didn't function on its own. A white tie wrap attached a plastic resealable bag containing folded pages to the metal object. Quinn read the document through the plastic.

The main logo was unfamiliar, but he recognized some of the information. Beechcraft. Hydraulic pump. PSI. Authorized signature.

"Where did you find this?"

"Now, that's an interesting question. My team found it in a backpack in her bedroom closet."

There must be some explanation for this. The Sierra he knew wouldn't ...
*Just how well did he know her?*

"Did you find her fingerprints on it?" Quinn asked.

"No. It's clean, no fingerprints. Same with the paper. Someone was very careful."

"We don't know it's hers."

Kevin slammed an open hand on the desk. "Really, Quinn? We found it in her closet. Who else would it belong to? She's a suspect, and you're sleeping with her."

Quinn shoved to his feet, fury and betrayal twisting inside like some evil vortex. "Don't accuse her of—"

"I told you to wait until the case is closed. The Quinn I know wouldn't jeopardize his job over a woman."

He would over this woman, Quinn thought as he remembered the morning's "bonding" activities. "I'm sure there's an explanation."

"Of course you are." Kevin threw his hands up. "You're so deep into her you can't see the facts. Did you find anyone else who could corroborate her story?" At Quinn's lack of response, Kevin picked up the phone receiver. "Call her. Tell her what we found. Better yet, have her come in and show it to her."

*What if she did stage the break-in?*

Why would she do that?

*No one would toss their own apartment. He'd never suspect her for that or any of the rest.*

He took the receiver from Kevin and dialed home. After two rings, she answered. His heart stuttered at the sound of her voice.

"Sierra, it's me. You need to come to the office." He glanced at Kevin, who seemed far too interested in the murder board. "CSU found something in your apartment."

"Like what?"

"Park beside my SUV like before. I'll put the parking authorization under my windshield wiper."

Silence. When she spoke again, he heard the strain in her voice. "What did they find, Quinn?"

"Just come in."

❖   ❖   ❖

A HALF-HOUR LATER, AND AFTER KEVIN LEFT, Quinn tried to review the medical examiner's report through the chaos in his mind. He stood when he noticed Yvonne escorting Sierra to his office.

Yvonne looked between them, then shook her head and tsked. "You behave, kiddo," she said, emphasizing with a finger pointing at him. To Sierra, she added a sigh. "Don't you break his heart, now. I'm too old to be picking up those pieces." She left, closing the door behind her.

Sierra crossed the office, stiffness lacing her movements. "What did they find?"

No greeting, no small talk, straight to the subject. He wanted to reassure her, hold her. *Professional, not personal.* "Thank you for ..."

"Quinn." Hands on her hips, with that bold white streak against her dark hair, she looked ready to kick some serious ass. "I'm here because you asked me to come, even though I'm supposed to be on 'house arrest.'" She made air quotes. "And don't try to talk me out of going to work tonight."

He sank to his chair, planted elbows on his desk, and rubbed his face. "Bring it down, Sierra. Kevin came by when I got in."

She crossed her arms on her chest, closing herself off from him. She scanned the whiteboard. "You still think I might have something to do with Tori's death, don't you?"

He'd forgotten to cover the board. Too late now. He slid the evidence bag over and handed her a pair of latex gloves. "This is what CSU found. Put these on before you touch it."

She tugged on the gloves, then removed the contents of the paper evidence bag. Quinn watched her, waited for her reaction while his insides tumbled as if kneaded by an invisible hand.

After examining the part, she read the documentation in the plastic bag. Color drained from her face. "You found a hydraulic pump for an airplane?"

"Do you work at another airport? Is it a part you picked up for someone else?"

"No. Why the hell would I ..." Her voice cracked. "You don't think I'd actually keep an airplane part in my apartment, do you? That's just asking for trouble. Shit, Quinn, I had the FAA on my ass for six months after my brother's plane went down. Why would I keep a part like this? I could lose my job and my license."

"Where did it come from?"

"I don't know. The only person who's been in my apartment besides you and me and your people is the person who trashed my place."

"You think that person planted the part in your apartment?"

"I sure as hell didn't put it there." She stared at him, incredulity in her eyes. "You don't believe me."

He fought to keep his face neutral. "Why would someone leave an airplane part in your apartment?"

"I don't know." Shock lost ground to a fierce anger. "I get it, it's your job to be suspicious. I can tell you right now there is no way I'd keep a part like that. Do you have any idea what it takes to get aircraft parts? It's not like you can just go down to the local auto parts store and pick one up. You can't even legally use screws or bolts from a hardware store."

She pointed to the documentation. "This says it's for a Beechcraft. I've never worked on any Beeches. Did CSU find my fingerprints on it?"

"No."

"Then why would you think ... If the person who went through my apartment is the same one who tossed Cate's place, it would be tied to the case, wouldn't it?" She examined the part. "I've never seen a hydraulic pump for a Beechcraft." She pulled a plastic cap off what looked like a connector. Inside were three spindle-prongs. She replaced the cap, then set the unit on the desk.

"Can I pull the paperwork out of the bag?"

Quinn nodded. She slid the documentation out of the bag and unfolded it. Paged through it. Compared values on it to the part.

Realization struck him. He wasn't equipped to analyze this sort of evidence. She was the expert. He couldn't tell by looking at the part what it was. He, and CSU, based their conclusions solely on the paperwork attached to it. She could tell him anything to take suspicion off her.

He needed to find someone else to verify the part they found matched the paperwork.

"This is wrong," she said.

"What do you mean, wrong?"

She turned the documentation so he could see it. "Here is the part number." She pointed to a flat area on the unit with numbers etched on it. "It matches the data. Same with the serial number. The date of manufacture is hard to tell, see how the year is mangled just enough? And the manufacturer's name isn't there at all."

She pointed to the Authorized Signature on the documentation. "The paperwork doesn't look like it was signed off by a QA—quality assurance— inspector. They have a stamp they use along with their signature to prevent forgeries. It doesn't say anywhere whether the part is overhauled or new, either. It should say on the paperwork.

"You missed all that because you don't know to look for it. I'm not blaming you for that, but I can't believe you would think I would keep an airplane part in my apartment. Even auto mechanics don't do that."

"What does it mean if the paperwork is wrong?"

"It means the part should not be put on an airplane until the paperwork is straightened out."

Quinn didn't know much about aviation, but he did know, like law enforcement, paperwork was a huge part of the process. "So, bad paperwork means what?"

"Either someone wasn't paying attention, or this is a counterfeit part."

"Counterfeit? You mean like counterfeit money counterfeit?"

"Yes. Airplane parts are expensive. It's just like anything else. Counterfeit is cheaper than legitimate." She sat in one of the chairs in front of his desk. "Do you really think I had something to do with Tori's murder?"

He hesitated. She blamed Tori for her brother's death. The pendant found on Tori's body might have been planted to make it look like she was involved. Did the same theory apply to the aircraft part found in her apartment?

"I take that as a 'yes.'" The accusation in her eyes pierced his heart, opening a cold, dark hole in his chest.

"Sierra," he said, intent on reassurance, "I know you didn't have anything to do with—"

"If that's true, then why didn't you answer me?"

He rubbed his temples with a hand, thumb and forefinger pinching his head. "I have to work with the evidence, Sierra."

"Evidence? What evidence do you have that lands me on the 'could be guilty' list? You haven't asked me if I have an alibi for the time of death. As I figure it, the only time the plane could've been accessed without anyone seeing anything is when it was parked overnight at the gate. Guess what? I was working. I have a time card to prove it. I haven't been anything but honest with you."

The cop took over. "You didn't tell me you recognized Tori's ring. You didn't tell me you knew a ramp agent."

She wiped at her eyes. "The ring—they're in style. It seems like everyone is wearing those rings. And I had no idea if Tori was still a ramp agent. I didn't keep tabs on her after my brother died. Get someone else to look at that part, because I know you can't take just my word for it."

"The pendant with your initials—"

"If you think I lied about refusing it when Rune tried to give it to me, then I might as well leave."

He knew she meant more than his office. "Sierra ..."

Tears filled her eyes. "I may have hated Tori for what she did to my brother, but I would never kill her or anyone else. Not unless I had no other choice." Her voice faded into a faraway shadow of itself. She swiped at her cheeks and stood.

He leaned forward and grabbed her arm. "Don't ..."

She tried to wrench her arm from him. He held on. "Let me go."

He rounded his desk, wrapped his arms around her, and held on. She struggled, but he tightened his embrace, desperate to feel her against him. He pressed his cheek to the top of her head as she quieted. "Sierra, I'm so sorry."

"You can't have it both ways, Quinn. Either you think I'm guilty or you don't."

He loosened his grip, and she shoved him back, breaking free. Tears traced her cheeks.

"Someone planted that part in my apartment. I'd say it was the person who trashed my place. I'm a good mechanic, and I'll be damned if I'm going to hand the FAA another reason to suspend my license. There's no way in hell I would keep a part like that. I'd better get back to the house." She pulled a crumpled tissue from a pocket and wiped her face dry. "I have to get some sleep before I go to work." She exited the office without looking back.

He broke something between them by doing his job. Just like he broke what he had with Gretchen by doing his job.

That didn't compare to what he and Sierra had.

# 45

After ten minutes reading the same sentence in the report, Quinn tossed it aside. He couldn't concentrate. His mind kept chewing on Sierra.

He shouldn't be falling for her so damn fast. Hell, their "relationship" didn't even include a first date. He shouldn't be thinking about her smile, or the way that white tress highlights her eyes. He had lost people he cared about. It hurt every time. Logical or not, if something happened to her, he knew it would hurt worse than anything he'd gone through before.

He needed to solve this case. Then he could think about her. Them.

Manelli didn't die in the river. According to the medical examiner, the preliminary cause of death was blunt force trauma. Quinn shuffled through photos of the body, paying extra attention to the bruising and cuts the ME noted were defensive in nature. Manelli fought with someone before he was killed. By the look of the gashes on the back of his head, someone clubbed him good. Manelli was five-foot-ten and built like a kid who'd grown up doing manual labor on a farm before going into automotive maintenance. He put up a fight.

Quinn paged through his notes and called the state patrol district office armed with the reference number for the report. After navigating the phone transfer maze, he managed to talk to a real live officer. He knew they wouldn't have much information yet, especially since the BCA was doing the forensics analysis, but he thought they might have something he could use. According to the state patrol, the truck was in neutral when it went over the steep bank and into the Minnesota River. Marks on the rear bumper suggested another vehicle contacted the chromed surface. He finished with a repeated request for a copy of the report before he hung up.

He leaned back in his chair and stared at the board. Tori knew something. Did she tell anyone before she was killed? Was she killed by accident before she revealed her secret, or on purpose to keep her quiet?

Quinn went to the board and made a list of everyone the unknown subject had contact with.

Tori, now dead. He added the mysterious phone calls she received. Was she being harassed by the UNSUB?

Peter, also now dead.

Cate, assaulted, and apartment searched.

He tried to put himself in the perpetrator's position. He's looking for something Tori has, but she won't give it to him. He kills her, maybe in a rage since she won't cooperate, then shoves her into the hell-hole, makes sure she can't be readily identified. Is it a warning? A message? Then he checks with the boyfriend. Same thing. If Peter knows what or where the prize is, he doesn't say. The UNSUB kills him, hides the body in the river in the victim's own truck.

Quinn made a note. *Why the hell-hole? Why the river?* Who's next on the list? The roommate. Search for the prize in Tori's apartment. He can't find it. He grills Cate, but not for long because she called a friend over. He has to leave before Sierra arrives, because that complicates the apartment search already compromised by the roommate.

Who's left? The friend. Quinn felt certain the culprit was the man who shoved past Sierra on her way up to Cate's apartment. He wished she had gotten a better look at him. What's his next move? He has no more leads, except Sierra. She goes into Tori's apartment building and later leaves with an empty cage and a big black bag. She must be a good friend if she's taking pet stuff. Does she know where the prize is hidden?

He follows Sierra home. Quinn's insides churned at the thought she might have suffered the same fate as Cate or worse if she hadn't noticed her apartment door unlocked and called him. The perpetrator didn't find the prize in Sierra's apartment, either.

If Cate knew what Tori hid, she might tell Sierra. Sierra didn't know Tori that well, and it had been almost a year since Tori dated Ken Bauer, but the perp didn't know that.

Everything still came back to something valuable enough to kill for. The airplane part in its evidence bag occupied a corner of his desk. Why plant it in Sierra's apartment?

He started a fresh scenario in his head. Tori found something odd with the books, something that fed her research for her thesis. Creative accounting by Castor? Wouldn't she mention it to her supervisor?

Love. Hate. Greed. Anger. The main reasons one person killed another. He crossed the first two off. Nothing in the evidence so far indicated this to be a crime of passion. This felt more like a cover up. What if Tori used what she found to blackmail Castor Aviation?

Greed.

He circled it. He made a note to check Tori's financials, but that didn't fit with the version of Tori that Cate talked about, the one who wanted to find out what really happened.

What really happened when?

"Moore, what's the status on the homicide case with the body in the airplane?" APD Chief Ansel Unger filled the doorway of Quinn's office like a brick with legs.

It took a second for Quinn to return his thoughts to the outside world. He realized he forgot to send his report to the chief yesterday. "I received the ME's report on Manelli. The preliminary cause of death is blunt force trauma. He had a number of defensive wounds and some nasty gashes on his head. I called the state patrol, got some information from them, but I'll have to wait for a copy of the report. Haven't seen the forensics report from the BCA yet. I think Castor Aviation Services has some creative accounting problems they want to keep under wraps. At any cost."

Unger entered the office and studied the board, sipping from a travel mug that smelled like butterscotch, advertising his penchant for caramel cappuccino. "You have suspects."

Quinn hadn't gotten around to updating that. He lined out Peter Manelli's name, writing "Victim #2" behind it. He did the same to Sierra's name, and wrote "Physically impossible" behind it.

"That's it?" Unger asked. "You worked in St. Paul. I'm sure you discovered more than one person who did something you thought they couldn't do, like the four-foot nothing grandma who takes down a six-foot tall twenty-year-old with a knife. You need a better reason than that." The chief pursed his lips. "You need evidence. That won't fly in court and you know it." He pointed to the timeline where Sierra's and Tori's names were written, along with the police shorthand for assault. "They knew each other, your vic and Bauer. A prosecutor will latch onto that like a leech."

The chief was right. Quinn rewrote her name, searched his brain for any reason to cross her off the list that didn't involve his feelings for her. "She didn't do it."

"Maybe not, but you need proof. You're off your game." Unger peered at him. "I haven't approved any time off for you since when? Last January? That's a year ago."

Quinn shrugged. When he worked, he didn't brood over the past. His relationship—okay, maybe he was being a bit presumptuous, but it felt right—with Sierra would change that. Had already changed that. *If he hadn't damaged what they had beyond repair.* "That sounds about right."

"After this case, you will take some time. You work like that, and you'll burn out sooner." Unger headed toward the door. "Ask for help. That's what the BCA is for. If this is too big, ask for help. I know you're used to handling stuff like this in St. Paul, but we're not St. Paul."

"I know, sir. Thank you."

As the chief left, Stamford entered, followed by the FAA agent from the incident with the plane and the de-ice truck. "Thought I'd catch you here. This is Agent Andrew Jindahl, from the Queen Air incident."

Quinn extended a hand to Jindahl, still impeccably dressed more like a CEO than a government agent. "I remember. What can I help you with?"

"He wants to know if we have any other information about that plane-truck collision. I told him I didn't have anything more than what I put in the report. He asked to see you." Stamford's radio squawked. "Sorry, but I'd better go." To Jindahl, "Detective Moore will help if he can." He touched a finger to his brow and left the office.

"I'm sorry, Agent Jindahl, but I'm not sure how much I can help," Quinn said. "Officer Stamford wrote up the report."

"Did that report include what your civilian consultant found?"

"I'm sure it did. Officer Stamford is very thorough."

The whiteboard drew Jindahl's attention. "So the rumors are true. I don't know that I've ever heard of a dead body in an airplane. Any luck?"

Quinn chastised himself again for neglecting to cover the board. He hadn't worked a homicide at the APD until now, and St. Paul had a different setup for working homicide cases where wandering civilian eyes couldn't see. "I'm sorry, but I can't discuss an ongoing case."

"Well, if I can be of any assistance, let me know." He handed Quinn a business card.

The evidence bag caught Quinn's eye. "Actually, maybe you can help me." He pulled a pair of latex gloves from a drawer and handed them to Jindahl. "I'd like your opinion on something, if you don't mind."

"Not at all."

Quinn pulled on another pair of gloves, then carefully removed the hydraulic pump from the bag. "Can you tell me what this is?"

Jindahl turned the part in his hands. He examined the documentation in the plastic bag, then the part. "It's a hydraulic pump."

Quinn took the pump, then eased the documentation out of the bag and handed it to Jindahl. "What about the paperwork? Is there anything wrong with it?"

After comparing the paperwork with the part, Jindahl frowned. "Where did you get this?"

"I can't discuss that. Why?"

"This part is counterfeit."

Relief eased the knots in his shoulders. "How can you tell it's counterfeit?"

"The paperwork isn't complete, and the part is missing a required piece of information on the data plate." Jindahl glanced at the board before he continued. "I'm going to have to confiscate this."

Quinn took the part and paperwork and shoved them into the evidence bag. "I can't let you take it. It's evidence in an open case."

Jindahl pulled off the gloves and graced him with a politician's smile. "May I remind you, Detective, that aviation is my domain, and federal government trumps locals. I need to take that part."

"I will send the part to the FAA after I close my investigation. Until then, it stays in Evidence," said Quinn as he led the agent to the door. "I appreciate your help with this, Agent Jindahl. I'll let you know when I can release the part to the FAA."

"Before I go," Jindahl said, "where did you find the part? I'll have to start an investigation. Possession of counterfeit aircraft parts is a major offense."

"Again, I can't discuss an open case."

"I hope your open case doesn't jeopardize passengers." With that, Jindahl left.

Quinn took the part to the APD evidence locker and checked it in. Sierra had been right about the part. If someone planted the part in her apartment, they must know the ramifications and how they could affect her.

Sierra had a target on her back.

# 46

Quinn followed the timeline on the board. The case started with Tori's death and the discovery of her body in an airplane.

Tori worked at Range Air and Castor Aviation. Peter Manelli worked at Castor. Rune Thorsson worked there.

Too many coincidences.

Thorsson worked at the airport. Sierra insisted on working tonight.

She said she had no idea Thorsson had been working at Castor Aviation for the past few months. The airport was big enough that the chances of her running into her ex-boyfriend might be remote, especially since she worked nights.

Castor Aviation Services started as a single FBO at Chicago's O'Hare Airport, and expanded from a general aviation operation into providing services from fueling commercial aircraft to charter flights. Throughout the company's almost forty years of existence, it developed into a sort of franchise recognized at airports across the country. Castor Aviation Services stretched from Montana to Michigan, Minnesota to Missouri. The business reports he requested showed sizable profits for a privately-held company, but Quinn couldn't tell how the company's profits compared to others in the industry, or how each individual franchise fared in the whole.

Tori used her experience at Castor Aviation for her paper. Tori's adviser never saw a draft. Quinn called the hospital to talk to Cate. They transferred him to her room. He introduced himself when she picked up.

"Detective Moore, did you find Pete? I called him again this morning and left a message."

"I'm sorry, Cate. An ice fisherman found Pete's truck in the river early this morning. He was inside."

"Oh my God. Are you sure?"

"Yes. I got the report from the medical examiner. It's him."

Silence. "Do you think he committed suicide?"

That was not what he expected. "No. Why would he commit suicide?"

"He loved her. If Tori died, maybe he was sad enough to do it."

"How do you know he loved her?"

He heard muffled speech in the background before Cate answered. "We went on couples dates, Tori and Pete and Brent and I. You could tell. Tori loved him, too. I had to listen to her gush about him. Not that I have anything against gushing, but after the first month, it got old."

"Do you know anything about Tori's thesis? Did she ever talk about it, or the research she was doing? Did she ever ask you to read it?"

"No. Why?"

Quinn thought. "Do you know where she kept it? Did she have anything on paper?"

"I think it was only on her computer. Maybe she had a printed copy somewhere, but I'm not sure. I never saw her working on it. Did you find her computer in the apartment?"

He'd looked for it on the CSU report. "No." His discussion with Sierra last night about Tori and Ken surfaced in his memory. "You said Tori's parents died in a plane crash. Do you know what happened?"

Silence. "Uncle Dan—I mean, Tori's dad did a lot of ferrying planes from the Cities to Grandpa's FBO and back. I remember that night. Tori stayed at our house because her parents were going to stay in Duluth over the weekend. It started snowing on the way. I think they crashed somewhere near Pine City."

Quinn made a note. "Do you know which airport they left from?"

"I think it was MSP."

More than one fixed-base operation called MSP home, but one stood out in Quinn's mind. "Do you remember anything else? The type of airplane? The time of day they left?"

"I'm sorry, Detective, I don't remember. I wish I did."

"That's fine. Has your doctor told you when you can go home?"

"They said I could go home tonight. Brent is getting off at four, so he'll pick me up. Do you know how Rascal's doing? I tried calling Sierra, but her answering machine doesn't pick up. Is she okay?"

"Rascal's doing fine," said Quinn.

"Can I go back to my apartment yet?"

"It's not a crime scene any more, but it's still a disaster. Do you have somewhere to stay?"

"I'll stay with Brent. Can you tell Sierra I can't take Rascal back yet? If Pete's gone—I can't believe he's dead—I'll have to keep her, but not until I get my apartment put back together." She sighed. "It's going to take forever."

He got Brent's contact information from her before he finished the call, and then went to the board to add the information about Tori's parents. Tori's dad and Ken Bauer were both pilots. Both died in plane crashes. There shouldn't be a connection between them other than coincidence a decade apart.

On a hunch, Quinn called Sierra at his place. When his machine picked up, he checked the time. She's probably taking a nap before her shift, he thought. He left a message with his question and asked her to call him as soon as she listened to it.

Tori worked as a part-time bookkeeper. Aviation involved a lot of money, the reason few people other than doctors, lawyers, or C-level executives even owned small aircraft. Tori might have found something in the books that could hurt the FBO. Quinn dug into Castor Aviation Services' financial audit history. There'd been an audit finding about five years ago with the records of their Milwaukee base, but nothing other than that. He leaned back in his chair and stretched, then checked the time. Groaned. The thing about research: it sucked the day away.

He rubbed sore neck muscles. His empty stomach growled. It had been a long time since breakfast, and he had forgotten the spaghetti lunch Sierra made up for him. He didn't want to fall into a routine, not yet. He didn't know her favorite color, or her favorite ice cream flavor, or if she even liked ice cream. Maybe she was lactose-intolerant. He didn't know her favorite song, or band, or much of anything.

He left the quiet of the office and entered the chaos of the terminal. Travelers filled the corridors, rushing to the gates, sauntering from the gates, the rolling wheels of their suitcases echoing like the drone of rocks tumbling down a hillside. He picked up a sandwich from one of the chain outlets, then headed back to the APD offices. He needed evidence tying Castor Aviation to Tori's murder. He just didn't know where to find it.

If Tori's body was put in the hell-hole to be a message or a warning, who was it meant for? Sierra? A cold dread settled heavy in him at the sight of the winged emerald. If Sierra was right, Thorsson had the necklace. If he planted it on the body, it meant he killed Tori.

Or had he dropped it on the tarmac, intending Sierra to find it, and Tori found it instead?

Either way, that line of thinking made him worry more about Sierra and her plan to return to work.

Quinn saw Lowell Hinckley at Castor Aviation the day he spoke with Pete Manelli's boss and Tori's boss. Hinckley worked with Sierra the night she found the body. The man seemed to be a world-class jerk with no love for women in aviation maintenance.

Lowell Hinckley had been talking to Rune Thorsson.

# 47

After she returned from her unexpected trip to the airport, Sierra occupied her time with a workout in Quinn's home gym in the basement, reading—or rather, trying to read, and playing with Rascal. Staying in someone else's house put her in the position of not wanting to impose. Oddly, she felt more at home here than she thought she should. It was his home, his territory.

What would it be like to discover the person you loved was sleeping with someone else? She tried to imagine being on the receiving end of that knowledge, but since she'd never been in love, it was a hard thing to conjure. It must have cut deep, she thought, deep enough that he would have a tough time trusting another woman in his life, which didn't excuse his behavior earlier at the office, but might explain it.

She napped for a few hours, then got ready for her night shift at the airport. The nice thing about working as a mechanic: she didn't have to decide what to wear. She donned her navy uniform over thermal underwear; the hangar never got much warmer than fifty or sixty degrees. She tucked her small Maglite into a back pocket, and a pen along with a pair of pocket screwdrivers into her front shirt pocket. Besides the flashlight, the screwdrivers—one for straight-slotted screws, the second for Phillips head screws—were suitable for most minor tasks. Her badge, displayed in a clear holder, attached with a magnetic clasp to the front of the opposite pocket.

She made sure Rascal had food and water before she closed the door to the guest bathroom. On her way through the kitchen to grab the spaghetti Quinn forgot, she noticed the message light blinking on the answering machine.

His house, his machine, she thought. Still, if he wanted to contact her while she napped, he'd leave a message. She pressed the button. Quinn's voice warmed her.

"Sierra, you're probably sleeping, but call me when you get this, please. Did Ken keep his plane at MSP? Which FBO did he use? Hey, I'm sorry about earlier. I didn't mean … Let's talk. Call me."

His question caught her off-guard. How would knowing where Ken kept his plane help the case? Ken had rented a hangar at Flying Cloud Airport in Eden Prairie, a western suburb. She thought back to her conversation with Quinn about Ken and Tori. The Cherokee's previous owner hangared the plane at MSP. She reviewed the maintenance logs before Ken bought it. Much of the work was done by mechanics at Castor Aviation.

Coincidence, she thought as she donned her navy parka to head out. Castor probably did a lot of general aviation work; they were the most-recognized FBO on the field. She would let Quinn know when she called him from the hangar.

❖  ❖  ❖

THE THING SHE LIKED ABOUT WORKING THIRD SHIFT, besides the dollar and a half extra per hour shift differential, was the work she did on the planes. Sierra had spent a few months her first year at Range Air rotating through first and second shifts at the gate. She didn't mind it, but the work was usually limited to tire changes, an occasional brake change, oxygen charge, and oil sample pulls. Even the light inspections done at the gate to check lights, brakes, tires, and selected cockpit items took less than an hour if they found no discrepancies.

The more involved inspections and maintenance took place on third shift, without the departure deadlines that gate work ran against. She did everything from changing starter/generators to rigging engine control units to troubleshooting electrical problems. Even the occasional riveting job and fuel valve change added variety that kept things interesting.

When she arrived at the hangar, a black pickup parked at the side of the service road beyond the hangar sent chills through her. As an extra precaution, she waited for the gate to close behind her before she found a parking space. *He can't get in here.* The thought gave her little comfort after the close call at the laundromat. Quinn promised to submit a warrant. Maybe Rune had been arrested and put back in jail by now.

In the hangar the familiar scents of planes and turbine exhaust greeted her like a welcome mat. A hum reverberated in the metal cavern while the heaters struggled to heat the cold air. The low rumble and thwap of a turboprop engine started up outside.

Her crime scene aircraft and associated yellow tape were absent. Quinn must have called and released the plane. Which reminded her she promised to call him once she got to work. Despite her frustration that he thought she might be involved in Tori's death, she hoped he would solve the case sooner rather than later, so they could start working on their relationship.

She looked forward to it.

When she reached the break room to use the phone, she found Rick Sellman, the night shift supervisor, involved in a pretty intense phone conversation. She'd call Quinn later.

After she stashed her lunch in the break room, she headed to the maintenance office to receive her assignments for the night. Third shift started with the run-qualified mechanics heading to the gate to taxi the night's inspection airplanes back to the hangar. Warren Bates, third shift lead, was in the office with a stack of paperwork and three other mechanics, one of whom was the second shift hangar lead filling Warren in for the shift turnover.

The center of the tabletop island that provided desk and work space in the maintenance office held two maintenance manuals, a cardboard box about the size of three stacked card decks, and a burnished gold-colored sphere two-thirds the size of a volleyball. Fire bottle, Sierra thought, and checked immediately for the protective plastic plug that covered the electrodes for the explosive squib. She had never changed one, but she respected the danger they could present. The fire bottle that stuck forty feet up in the ceiling insulation of the hangar at A&P school left no doubt as to how much pressure that small metal globe contained.

Warren made a show of checking his watch. "Are you sure you're supposed to be here tonight, Bauer?"

"I'm going to go ape-shit if I take any more time off. Please tell me we have a full hangar tonight."

"Looks like. And you and Seth are the only run-qualified guys on tonight. Seth already headed to the gate to help second shift bring 841 and 842 back." He said the tail numbers as if each digit stood alone. "You and Charlie go to the gate." He shoved the small cardboard box toward her. "Eight-two-one is staying at the gate, but we need to pull oil samples. It's due in," he checked his watch, "at about ten, so you've got time to get out there."

Oil samples had to be pulled from the Dash-8's Pratt & Whitney engines within ten minutes of engine shutdown, otherwise the engines had to be run for another ten minutes to get the oil hot again. She grabbed the box and made sure both bottles were present and empty. Charlie wandered into the maintenance office, all six foot three of him. He was younger than Sierra with two years less seniority, but he was a good airframe guy.

She grimaced at the appearance of the mechanic who followed him. Unfortunately, Lowell Hinckley was still here. She groaned and hoped she didn't get stuck with him again. Who knew what she'd find in the hell-hole this time.

"Pull the samples, then put it to bed. Bring 802 back," Warren said. "It's got a PCU inspection tonight, so you'll be working on it anyway." He slid a packet of papers toward her. "Here's the paperwork. Take the truck. Second shift will bring it back."

Sierra saluted with a finger to her brow. "Aye, aye."

"Wait," Lowell said, "I'd like to pull the oil sample."

What? she thought. Lowell *wanted* to go to the gate with her after bitching about having to do so a mere four days ago?

Warren looked at her. "Well?"

*When Hell freezes over.* "Charlie's working toward getting run-qualified." She added a look she hoped Warren would interpret as her definitive refusal.

He gave her an almost-perceptible nod. "Lowell. I've got you working on 841's APU replacement."

"I could start on that when we get back. I'd like to work on getting run-qual-ified. In Detroit we only have one guy right now for the Dash-8s besides the shift supervisors and a couple leads."

*To hell with being subtle.* "Lowell, I do *not* want to find another dead body. You ride with someone else."

"Hey, that's enough." Warren reached toward her with a hand, indicating she needed to back off. "Charlie's going to the gate with you."

Rick Sellman joined the group in the maintenance office. Sierra liked Rick as a supervisor, but he could be moody, in which case he liked to mix things up. His phone conversation must have gone poorly judging by the scowl he managed to wipe off his face once he entered the office. "Who's going to the gate?"

Lowell interrupted Warren's reply. "I'd like to ride along. I need more time in the Dash-8 to get run-qualified."

*Shit.* She knew if she said anything Rick would stick her with Lowell for sure.

"I've got Charlie going to the gate with Sierra," Warren said. "Charlie's closer to getting qualified." He glanced at Sierra, who tried not to react. Warren was in her corner. Rick, not so much.

"Tonight your last night, Lowell?" Rick asked.

"Yes. I'm heading back to Detroit right after the shift."

Thank God, Sierra thought.

Rick looked at her with an intensity that dashed any hope of changing his mind. "Lowell, you ride with Sierra."

# 48

"Sierra, have him ride left seat," Rick added. "You do the engine runs on the way back."

Warren gave a small shrug and mouthed, "Sorry."

"By the way, the only truck here is the Beast," Rick said. "I promise it's due to be taken out back and shot next month."

*Crap.* The Beast should've been retired two decades ago. The oldest of the three trucks they used to go back and forth from the hangar to the gate, it was the only one with a manual transmission. "I'll believe that when I see its cold dead husk wheels up." She addressed Lowell, swallowing her distaste. "I'll grab my wrench and pliers, then meet you at the truck."

"Um, I can't drive a stick," he said.

Someone his age probably learned to drive in a stick. If he was looking for ammunition to start off the night, he was going to be disappointed. "You're in luck, I can." She tossed Rick a glare before leaving the office.

The Beast, a vintage one-ton utility truck, had a long, angled shifter combined with a worn clutch that made shifting gears tricky. Her grandfather's insistence she learn how to work a manual transmission made her one of the few mechanics who could drive the damn thing. Kudos to her for being a woman and able to drive a stick when most of the guys couldn't.

She drove across the airport along the road marked for vehicles, safely out of the way of aircraft. She slowed to a stop to wait for an Airbus to cross, then coaxed the Beast into first.

It complained with a solid grinding of gears.

"You call that driving a stick?" Lowell stared out the passenger window. "Shit, I could drive a fucking stick when I was in sixth grade."

"Is that so?" She knew it. "Didn't think I could drive a stick, did you? Let's agree to not speak unless it has to do with maintenance, okay?"

"Bitch."

"Not even close." When they reached the gate, Sierra shifted the Beast into first and turned it off. It dieseled, sputtering into silence.

"Where's 802?" Lowell asked.

Only one Dash-8 was visible. The rest would be behind the gate building that extended onto the tarmac like a tentacle from the main body of the terminal. "Probably on the other side of the gate."

Sierra wondered for a moment if Quinn was in the APD office in the terminal or at home. She had planned to call him before she left the hangar; she made a mental note to call him when she got back.

Brad Grady, the second shift lead, met her at the door to the gate office, his beard glistening with ice crystals where his breath had frozen in it. Sierra had worked with him during her stint on second shift back when she started with Range Air. "When's 821 due in?"

"It's running about ten minutes late. We'll take this one," he indicated the visible Dash-8, "back to the hangar."

"What about the truck?"

Grady scowled at the Beast. "Leave it here. Maybe someone will steal it." His radio crackled, and the maintenance dispatcher announced 821 was five minutes out. "Need to pull oil samples on it."

Sierra nodded and waved the cardboard box she pulled from a pocket. "I've got the kit. We'll pull samples, put it to bed, and bring eight-oh-two back. Is she on the other side?"

Grady nodded. "Some rampie pulled the ground power plug out again. The APU works."

As long as the auxiliary power unit worked, she could start the engines off the power generated by the mini-turbine engine.

"Do you have safety wire?" Grady asked. "If so, I'll lock the office."

Sierra noticed Lowell pull a small round canister with a pigtail of silvery wire from a pocket. "Got the wire. You can lock up."

Grady closed up the maintenance office and found a ramp agent to give him a start on the Dash-8 he would taxi to the hangar. Two Range Air rampies still manned the gate, enough to marshal the incoming plane to a parking spot, unload the cargo, and shepherd the passengers to the terminal.

Sierra motioned the other agent over and asked him to park 821 in front of the maintenance office. Lowell grabbed a stepladder. Sierra muscled the rolling maintenance stand into position before she held out her hand for the safety wire canister. She pulled her safety wire pliers from her back pocket and snipped off a foot-long length of flexible stainless steel wire used to prevent bolts, plugs, and connectors from vibrating loose.

Safety wire pliers were unique. The short, angled jaws were flat with a wire cutter at their base, and locked in the closed position to hold the wire while the twisting knob was pulled. She tucked her pliers into her back pocket and handed Lowell one of the oil sample bottles. "Try not to spill much."

"I know how to take an oil sample," he spat.

Be professional, she reminded herself. "Just wipe it good so you can do the leak check."

Soon the T-tail of a Dash-8 appeared behind a Boeing 737 unloading at another gate of the terminal. Once the plane parked and the pilots shut the engines down, Sierra and Lowell headed to the engine nacelles. Sierra performed the task by rote: open the outboard cowl panel, cut and pull the old wire off the plug, stash it in her pocket. Unscrew the plug, fill the bottle, reseat the plug.

She'd gotten good enough that she made little mess. After she tucked the bottle into a pocket and tightened the plug, she added the safety wire, wiped any remaining oil from around the plug, closed the panel, and pushed the stand back to its home against the side of the gate building.

She filled out the label on the bottle while Lowell finished the other engine. By the time he and his ladder were clear of the plane, the passengers and pilots had all vacated the premises. Procedure required a five-minute engine run to make sure the plugs didn't leak. She headed to the cockpit, pulled the airstair closed behind her, and then fired up the APU. The mini-turbine spooled up and lit with a low rumble.

She settled into the left seat, powered the engine bus, and waited for Lowell to turn his attention to her. He stood in front of the plane to give her a start, but seemed distracted by a fuel truck stopping beyond the Range Air gate area. "C'mon, Lowell," she grumbled. When he finally turned back to the plane, she held up two fingers for engine number two, always the right engine, and the first engine started.

Once he gave the signal, she started the engine. The blades whapped through the air, a smooth beat made by the feathered props, blades angled so the flats faced the direction of rotation like long narrow paddles on a waterwheel.

She repeated the process with the left engine, then brought the power up to just above idle and timed the run. After five minutes she shut the engines and the APU down, made sure the power was off, and deplaned, closing the airstair behind her. Lowell rounded the nose of the plane, ladder in hand. She searched for two additional sets of chocks while he checked the left engine for leaks.

The fuel truck crept toward the left front side of the airplane. Odd, she thought. Range Air didn't have any more flights tonight. There were a couple larger planes still being loaded at one of the main gates across the tarmac. The driver of the truck, stocking cap pulled low, parked, then pulled out a clipboard. Catching up on paperwork, she thought.

She shoved a set of chocks around each main gear. Lowell caught up with her when she opened the cargo bay to gather the overnight equipment stored there. He bumped into her, attention behind him. She shoved him. "Back off, Lowell. What the hell is your problem? Watch what you're doing." She handed her bottle of oil and the box to him. "Start prepping 802. Might as well fire up the APU and get some heat going." He nodded and helped her grab the overnight equipment from the cargo compartment.

Sierra snagged the brace attached to the cargo door and pulled. The door rolled to a stop at the bottom sill. She turned the handle to lock it before she bent to pick up an engine plug and blade sheath.

Unease twisted in her gut.

Pain flashed through her skull.

The world went black.

# 49

Quinn checked the clock again. Third shift at Range Air started an hour ago, and still no call from Sierra. She said she'd call when she got to work. Even if she couldn't call right away, she would call within the first hour, wouldn't she? If she taxied a plane from the gate, she should be back at the hangar by now, right? A sudden odd, itchy feeling ran up his spine and settled in his chest.

He had felt like this only once, just before Sierra called from the laundromat. Habit had him lifting the receiver of his desk phone. If he called the number for Range Air, would it ring in the hangar or in the closed business office?

He called anyway. His knotted stomach cinched tighter with each ring until someone answered.

"Range Airlines, Maintenance Office."

"This is Detective Moore from the Airport PD. I want to speak to the shift supervisor."

A pause. "Detective Moore, this is Warren Bates. I'm the lead mechanic tonight. The night shift supervisor is on another call right now. Can I help you, or do you want to talk to Rick?"

Warren Bates had stood up for Sierra during his interview the night she found the body. "I need to speak with Sierra."

"She went to the gate to bring back an inspection plane."

"How long ago?"

"She's doing engine runs with another mechanic who's trying to get run-qualified. Might take a little longer than usual."

Quinn stood, worry electrifying his nerves. "Which mechanic?"

"Why are you asking about Sierra?" Warren asked. "She didn't find another body, did she?"

He didn't have patience for this tonight. "Mr. Bates, Sierra is in danger. Who's riding with her?"

"Lowell Hinckley."

❖ ❖ ❖

WHEN SIERRA WOKE, the pain in her head glowed behind her eyes like lightning with each throbbing pulse. Black. She could see nothing, hear nothing, smelled metal, concrete, paper, and her own sweat. She still wore her parka and was sweltering in it. Her arms were tied behind her back, her ankles anchored to chair legs, and either the room was too dark to let in any outside light, or there was some sort of bag over her head preventing her from seeing. She tried to open her mouth, but it felt like duct tape was fastened around her head.

Fear shot through her. Where was she? Why was she still alive? Not that she didn't appreciate being able to breathe, but that just allowed her to imagine what came next. Did she have torture to look forward to? A beating? Fingers cut off joint by joint? Her head pounded like someone was nailing spikes into it. Breathe, she thought. Breathe. In. Out. She could wait, or she could figure out a way to get free and fight. Fighting sounded good right now. It sounded way better than waiting.

She closed her eyes despite the darkness; it was easier to use her other senses when she did. She listened hard. No rustling of cloth. No breathing. The chair was metal, rigid, with a single upright holding the backrest. Her wrists were bound behind the upright by a narrow plastic strip. Zip tie, she thought. There was no way she could break the tie, and she couldn't stand up, not with her legs fastened to the chair. She tried to stand anyway, and nearly tipped over.

No one said anything, confirming she was alone. With a little wiggling and some twisting she managed to reach her back pockets. She hoped whoever did this hadn't taken her tools. If she could reach her safety wire pliers, maybe she could use them to cut through the zip tie.

More twisting, and she felt the long narrow pliers under the cover of her coat. She walked the coat up with her fingers until she exposed the hard metal. She inched the pliers out of her pocket, focused on not dropping them.

Getting the pliers was one thing, using them was something else. Safety wire pliers had a locking tab used to keep the jaws tight when twisting the wire. She slid the lock open. That was the easy part.

Her problem: even though the handles were long, the spread of the jaws was relatively small. The wire-cutter was at the base of the narrow spread; she might not be able to open the jaws wide enough. Even if she could, she'd have no leverage to close the handles.

Her fingers started to cramp. She focused on the feel of the pliers she used so often, manipulating them until the jaws were pointed at her wrists. She opened the handles as much as she could manage, then slid the pliers up along her arm, thrusting blindly until she hit the tie. Her wrists ached from the movement. She worked the handle, tried to squeeze it closed.

It slipped. She hung onto the knurled knob of the twisting spindle as the rest of the pliers dropped toward the floor. She stopped, listened hard. No sound of anyone approaching. She pulled the pliers back, a slow chore made harder when her numbing fingers began rejecting her instructions. She stopped to flex them, listened again. Still silence except for her own breathing. She maneuvered the pliers back into place and worked them against the plastic trapping her wrists.

The low rumble of a truck broke the silence. Doors slammed. Masculine voices argued, but they weren't close enough for her to understand the words. She worked faster. If she could get loose, she had a chance.

"What the hell were you thinking? She found the body."

"She knows Tori. She took pet stuff from her apartment."

Sierra froze.

*Rune.*

"Did you find anything at her place?"

"No. I didn't find anything at Tori's apartment either. I can't get to the roommate. She's staying with her boyfriend."

Tori's apartment? Sierra thought back to the night Cate called. To the man who shoved past her on the stairs.

To the bigger-than-she-remembered Rune who approached her in the laundromat.

A slam that sounded like a fist on a table. "This has gotten too messy. We need those files."

"Then let me get it out of her."

"And what if she doesn't know either? Why did you have to go and kill Tori?

She was the only one who knew where those files are. Now we got the cops looking for them and you."

Sierra focused on the pliers. Squeeze. Release. Squeeze. Release. She couldn't tell if she was making any progress at all. Squeeze, release. Squeeze. Resistance. Squeeze. Over and over, until her fingers cramped. She tested the tie. Pulled. Twisted. It felt like the tie was cutting into her bones. She continued to work the handles of the pliers until the zip tie popped apart.

Heavy footsteps approached.

❖ ❖ ❖

QUINN DIALED THE NUMBER FOR CASTOR AVIATION. An automated female voice gave him numbered options. Who would even be around this time of night? He mashed the "0" on the keypad to bypass the automated attendant.

When the call was picked up, Quinn introduced himself and dove right into his questions. "Are all of your fuel trucks accounted for?"

"Why do you want to know?"

"I'm working on a homicide case. If you don't tell me, I'm going to charge you with obstruction of justice."

"Well, shit. Hey, Morrie, are all the fuel trucks in line?"

Quinn waited, stomach tightening into a lead weight. In the background, he heard the answer. One truck was missing.

"Okay, thanks," the Castor representative said to someone away from the phone, then into the phone. "Nope, we got 'em all. One was parked in the wrong spot."

"Are there any fuel truck drivers hanging around?"

A long pause. "Who did you say you were?"

"*Detective* Quinn Moore, Airport *Police*," he repeated. "Are there any fuel truck drivers hanging around?"

Again, the Castor representative called to someone away from the phone, then into the phone. "We got three drivers here right now. You wanna talk to them, Officer?" he asked with a sneer in his voice.

"No, I want their names."

"Well, fuck." Then, away from the phone, Quinn heard him call Morrie over, tell him a cop was on the other end, then a different voice spoke.

"Sorry, I don't know what's going on here."

Quinn introduced himself yet again. "I want the names of all the fuel truck drivers who've parked their trucks in the past hour."

The rustle of paper heralded the requested list. "Got a pen?" He didn't wait, instead rattled off the names of the drivers. Quinn scribbled the names, but the one he expected wasn't on the list. He asked for the name of the fuel truck driver supervisor.

"Oscar Clement. He ain't here right now. He comes in at five."

"Is Rune Thorsson still there?"

"He ain't working tonight."

"Humor me."

Morrie yelled at someone in the background. After he got a response, he spoke to Quinn. "He's here."

# 50

"Thorsson, phone," a voice bellowed. A curse, then the footsteps headed away from the room she was in.

A door slammed.

Sierra let out the breath she was holding.

Freed her legs.

Pulled off the hood and ripped the tape from her mouth. She listened. Faint thuds, like doors closing far away, reached her through the silence.

She didn't know how long she'd been unconscious, and she didn't know how long it'd taken to work her way free.

Lowell Hinckley. He had to be involved somehow. Why else would he have wanted to ride with her?

If Hinckley was involved, would he go back to the hangar? What would he say when someone asked about her? What if he didn't go back to the hangar? How long would it take before someone realized they weren't there? Would her supervisor call Quinn? Would Warren?

The fuel truck that stopped by the plane. Quinn said Rune worked for Castor Aviation as a fuel truck driver.

Her scar twinged. She couldn't let Rune corner her again.

She couldn't dwell on the past if she wanted to get through the now. A hand to her back pocket confirmed her suspicion. Besides neglecting to take her safety wire pliers, the kidnapper forgot to take her flashlight. He also left her screwdrivers in her shirt pocket.

Why hadn't they taken her tools?

They didn't think she was much of a threat.

Then she would become a threat. She turned on her flashlight and adjusted the lens until the beam was as wide as possible. The chair occupied the largest available space in the room, which wasn't saying much. Ranks of steel shelving units loaded with plastic-wrapped parts, assorted cardboard boxes, and bare metal assemblies filled the long, narrow room and lined the walls. Small colored bins held screws, bolts, washers, and rivets.

Parts room. Familiar territory. If she could fend off whomever snatched her, she could hold out until Quinn found her. If he even knew where to start looking. She played the light around the rest of the room. The remaining wall of her prison was similar to chain-link fencing, with a single door to access the parts behind the cage.

Beyond the parts cage a battered metal desk set ninety degrees to the wall faced the entry path from a wooden door. Behind the desk a vintage office chair complete with duct-taped cushion held a sealed cardboard box. Atop the desk sat a phone along with three piles of green-tagged parts and paperwork.

Once she got out of the parts cage, she could call Quinn. One-inch-square steel tubing made up the frame of the cage door, which fit into a matching cutout in the cage wall, again reinforced by one-inch-square steel tubing. The hinges were on the outside of the cage, and an index card-sized metal plate backed whatever lock opened from the other side.

Even if she had a crowbar she wouldn't be able to bend the door jamb away from the latch. The steel tubing wouldn't yield unless she used a ten-foot cheater bar. She tested the door and managed about an eighth of an inch of movement. "Sonofabitch," she breathed.

She took inventory of the parts available. A landing gear assembly for a smaller airplane. Good hammer, better weapon. Magnetos for reciprocating engines. Oil filters. Hoses. Fluid lines. A landing gear bracket for something bigger than a Piper Cherokee looked promising. Each replacement part had a yellow tag listing the part number, serial number, manufacturer, the signature of the inspector who authorized the part for use, and date the part was inspected. She picked up a few, trying to piece together something she could use to breach the cage door.

The landing gear bracket caught her eye again. She examined the part more closely, skimmed the paperwork. Something about it didn't seem right. She picked up another part, this one a hydraulic pump. She couldn't see anything wrong with that part, then took a closer look at a flap actuator. There, she thought.

"Where the hell have you been?" The voice carried through the wooden door. "Why haven't you started?"

She couldn't hear the answer. She would break out or break whoever put her in here. She hunted for something more suitable as a weapon, and found a control rod about two feet long. Light enough to swing yet heavy enough to cause some damage.

They kidnapped her.

They underestimated her.

# 51

As Sierra crept closer to the cage door, a small metal sphere caught her eye. About three times the size of a softball with a narrow mounting flange around the middle, a fitting on one end protruded from the orb near a connector socket with two small electrodes covered by a plastic red cap.

Fire bottle.

She listened hard, but couldn't hear the voices from earlier. Either the men were speaking in normal tones somewhere away from the room, or they weren't talking at all. She could wait until someone opened the parts cage from the outside and ambush them, or she could try to bust through. She knew the fire bottle would have enough force to punch through the metal grid of the cage, but if she could hit the door latch, she wouldn't have to spend extra time trying to pry the cage breach big enough to squeeze through.

She found a section of aluminum skin in a shallow trough shape, propped it on the chair, and peered along the length. The bottle needed enough room to accelerate as much as it could before it hit the latch. She set the fire bottle so the "north pole" pointed at the cage door, adjusted the back end of her makeshift channel, and gauged the angle of the fire bottle one last time. She had only one shot at this.

The red plastic cap guarded the electrodes from stray charges that might set the bottle off. She removed the cap, cut the extra safety wire she'd pocketed earlier into two pieces, then wrapped each tightly around an electrode, careful not to let the wires touch each other. Even something as small as a static charge could set off the explosive squib that released the high-pressure extinguisher in the bottle.

Another check of the angle and the bottle's position, then she pulled the two AA batteries from her flashlight, dousing it. The pair in series should give her enough juice to blow the bottle. If she needed more than that, she'd have to rethink her plan. She held the batteries positive to negative, then pressed a wire against one end. Draped her coat over her just in case. Took a deep breath. Closed her eyes. Lowered her head out of the exhaust area. Touched the second wire to the other end.

BOOM!

Pressure slammed into her chest as the concussive sound echoed in the room. Her heart thudded as pain joined the ringing in her ears. Nothing like advertising she was awake and free from her chair.

She loaded the batteries back into her flashlight, and then checked her handiwork. The metal sphere was embedded in the cage door where it tore the backing plate for the lock from the grating, the mounting flange caught like a square pin crammed into a circular hole. Square steel tubing bowed outward, exposing the catch.

She grabbed the control rod and wedged one end between the frame of the door and the jamb, then pried the catch free. The parts cage door popped open.

The sound of a key in the lock made it through the lingering din in her ears. "What the hell? Thorsson, get your fucking ass over here. I thought you tied her up."

*Shit.* She dashed to the space behind the wooden door, control rod in one hand, one of her screwdrivers in the other, and imagined herself fighting her way into the hangar.

Past a bigger, broader Rune.

The door shoved inward.

He stepped across the threshold. She threw her weight against the door, pinning him against the frame. She slammed the control rod down on his wrist and jabbed the point of the screwdriver into his knee.

"Fuck!" He drew back, then someone else wrestled the door open.

*Hinckley.*

"What the hell?" he exclaimed.

She swung the control rod up toward his face. Missed, hit his shoulder instead. Stabbed a screwdriver into his hand.

He swore and lunged toward her.

She danced out of reach and past him into the hangar. Rune stood in her path.

A man's voice came from somewhere on her right. "Don't kill her. We need those files."

"Oh, I won't kill her." Rune sneered. "I'll just soften her up a little."

She wasn't going down without a fight, and her fight-or-flight instinct was in full fight mode. *Don't think, just do.* She charged at him, shoulder lowered the way her brother taught her, and added the business end of the control rod to her drive.

He gasped when she hit him, but didn't fall back like she expected. He grabbed her around her waist and trapped her against him. "I thought you'd be happier to see me, Sierra. Been looking forward to this since the laundromat."

She struggled, but he had a solid grip on her, his height giving him an additional advantage. He lifted her off her feet.

She jerked her head back and caught his chin.

Rune didn't drop her as she hoped. Instead, he tightened his arms around her chest until she fought to breathe. "That wasn't very nice."

"Here's a thought," the voice said. "Why don't you just ask her?"

"Like that worked with the others." Rune squeezed her tighter. "Where are the files? You took that pet cage and shit. Did you take the files, too?"

He knew she took stuff from the apartment. He must be the one who attacked Cate and killed Tori and Pete.

"So what if I did?" Her lungs started to burn from lack of oxygen. "Even if I knew what the hell you're looking for, I wouldn't tell you." On a whim, she went limp. Dead weight was heavier, right?

His grip loosened. Her feet touched the floor. She sucked in a breath, stabbed the screwdriver into his thigh.

He yelped and released her. She spun to face him. Shot a knee into his gonads. Swung the control rod at his head. Connected. He dropped like a sandbag to the floor, howling.

She turned. Another man in an expensive-looking long wool coat, not as tall but just as broad as Rune, blocked her escape. She dropped the screwdriver, then brandished the control rod with both hands like a broadsword. "Let me go."

"Sorry, we can't do that." The man stepped closer. "Tell us where the files are, and we'll talk about it."

She stole a glance at the rest of the hangar, seeing but not seeing. Planes were parked around the perimeter of the floor with another in the middle, nosed in, tail pointed toward the hangar doors. Not much cover to evade capture until Quinn got there.

"So, you're saying after trashing Tori's apartment and trashing my apartment you still haven't found whatever files you think she stole?" She angled toward the front of the hangar, where she had a clear path to a twin-engine Cessna.

"We know she stole. She showed them to me."

*Stall.* "Oh, *those* files. She told me not to give them to you."

"So you do know where they are." A scowl turned his businessman countenance sinister. "Tell me, and I'll let you go."

*Sure you will.* "Tori told me how much you were going to pay her. I want double."

The man grimaced. "Pay her? Don't play games. Look where it got Tori."

She'd never been good at lying, and she wasn't sure how long she could keep it up. "What was the point of planting that hydraulic pump in my apartment?"

Rune pushed to his feet, still doubled over. Hinckley blocked a door marked with an EXIT sign.

The man stood near the parts room door, hands deep in the pockets of his coat and looking like he should be in the lobby of a New York office building rather than a hangar in Minneapolis. "We thought the cops would like to know you hadn't learned anything from your FAA investigation. In fact, I believe the FAA is suspending your license as we speak."

Something inside told her to run. *Now.* She dashed toward the Cessna.

A deafening crack echoed in the hangar. Something whizzed by her ear. A hole appeared in the smooth skin of the plane in front of her. "Stop, or the next one goes through your head."

If she stopped, she'd be dead anyway. She dove toward the belly of the plane and scrambled to the other side as another shot assaulted her ears. Heavy footsteps followed her. She got to her feet and dodged around the nose of the plane toward the twin-engine King Air in the middle of the hangar.

Rune appeared, blocked her. "Seems we've been here before." He stalked toward her, madness in his eyes. "You can't get away this time." He slid a hunting knife from behind his back. "Remember this? It's just like the one I used before. Nice and sharp."

A door crashed open. "Police! Put your weapon down!" *Quinn.*

She couldn't see him or how many other officers he brought.

Rune lunged, grabbed the back of her shirt. Metal flashed.

Her arm burned.

Adrenaline spiked. She kicked at his knee. He side-stepped, losing his grip on her. She raced past him.

Stopped.

A maze of metal work stands trapped her on one side, a squat Mitsubishi high-winged turboprop on the other, with an engine on a stand blocking her way.

She backed toward the plane, pain engulfing her right arm from shoulder to elbow. She pressed a hand against the agony. Felt the slick wetness.

Blood.

Rune stood in front of her like he had six years ago.

Fear. Shock. She started to sweat.

"Oh, no. You're not taking this away from me."

Sierra didn't dare take her eyes off him. She backed into a mobile work-bench, stumbled as it rolled away. Black washed through her vision. Her throat, thick with fear, locked her voice.

Rune crept forward, closing the distance between them. She moved left toward the plane, fighting to stay on her feet.

She grabbed the Mitsubishi's metal propeller. Rune lunged. She turned, shoved the prop with all the strength she could manage.

The blades spun and struck Rune in the back. His head jerked, chest thrust forward from the blow.

He dropped to his knees. The next propeller blade hit his head. A thud echoed in the hangar when his skull hit the concrete.

# 52

She slid down the fuselage. Slipped into darkness.

Sierra.

Quinn's voice. Her body resisted the command to respond to him.

"The ambulance is on its way." A blurry shadow crossed her field of vision. "Cuff him. Get him out of here. I want someone with him at all times, and that includes in the ambulance."

Dark, flat eyes. The long blade. He hadn't shoved the knife into her this time.

She survived.

"You're going into shock, Sierra." She felt his breath in her ear. Sensed him close, so close.

The world came into focus. His eyes. Like a spring sky captured in twin orbs.

"He cut you pretty bad." Quinn reached to her face, his hand coated in red. Looked away, then back at her. "The ambulance just got here. They're coming."

"Quinn." Her voice sounded a million miles away in her ears.

He bent low. "Don't talk."

"Rune."

"He's got a nasty head wound where the propeller nailed him, possibly a concussion."

"Good. He deserves it."

# 53

Quinn entered the emergency room waiting area, somewhat surprised at the number of patients waiting for their turn. Busy night, he thought. He scanned the room until he saw the dark uniform of the APD officer he'd sent in the ambulance with Sierra. Once he reached them, he thanked the officer and dismissed her with a request for a copy of her report in the morning. Well, later this morning.

He sat in the vacated chair beside Sierra, anxious to hold her, to reassure himself she was okay. *It could have been worse.* If he lost her, it would destroy the part of him she'd awakened, a part that glowed with a vibrancy he never imagined he could feel.

"Quinn." Her voice settled the worry he'd been struggling against since the raid at Castor Aviation. She straightened, sucked in air. "Shit, that hurts."

White bandages wrapped her right arm from shoulder to elbow, where the sling took over the job. They cut her sleeve off, he noted. A small brown paper bag he suspected held extra bandages sat on her lap along with papers that looked like instructions. Her eyes were dull, glazed with fatigue and pain. "You okay?"

"No. The anesthetic is wearing off. I got thirty stitches. My arm hurts like hell, and the drugs are making me loopy." She struggled to stand. Quinn guided her to her feet. She poked at the coat he'd brought with him. "Is that mine? I need to get out of here. These chairs suck."

He helped her don her coat, draped the right side over her shoulder, then led her out into the cold. "I still need to get your statement. We can do that when we get to the house."

She stopped. "I know I shouldn't care as long as he's in jail, but what happened to Rune?"

A surge of anger surfaced at the thought of what the man had done to her. Of what the man could have done to her. "He's at a different hospital. I made sure they didn't bring you to wherever they brought him. I've got him under guard until he's discharged. Then he'll go straight to jail, no chance of bail if I have anything to say about it."

"What about Lowell?"

Quinn couldn't help himself. He brushed her hair from her face, that brilliant white tress glowing under the parking lot lights. He resisted the urge to kiss her. This wasn't the place or the time. "He's in custody, along with Gil Randolph, the snappy dresser. They've all lawyered up, so I don't know how much we'll get out of them. They're involved in Tori's death, but right now the only one I can charge with anything is Thorsson."

❖ ❖ ❖

THE CLIMB INTO THE EXPLORER DREW MUFFLED CURSES from Sierra despite Quinn's help. She spent the moments after he closed the door until he took the driver's seat trying to find a mental space where her arm didn't feel like a blazing torch.

Sierra felt his eyes on her, and knew if she looked at him she would lose the control she had been struggling to maintain ever since the EMTs picked her up off the hangar floor. No, since Quinn reached her after she evaded Rune.

She managed to remain calm through the ambulance ride, through the wait in the emergency room, through each stitch, through the wait for Quinn. That part was the longest, waiting for Quinn to pick her up. She barely managed to remain dry-eyed when he appeared in front of her.

He started the vehicle, then reached to her, took her left hand in his. Squeezed reassurance. His grip distracted her from the throbbing pain in her arm. She squeezed back, grateful for his anchoring effect.

Realization settled through her, a *rightness* that bloomed from her chest to the very tips of her fingers and toes. A flood of things she wanted to say threatened to spill out, emotional things she imagined saying to the person who managed to fill that empty space inside her.

*Like he did.*

This wasn't the time or the place for those conversations. Still, she wanted to say something.

"Next time, don't take so long to find me."

He tightened his grip once more before he let go. "Let's not have a next time."

Sierra avoided looking at him during the entire silent ride to his house. She focused on keeping her emotions in check. Her quiet place started as a Hawaiian beach, but morphed into a green mountain vista by the time they slowed to a stop in his driveway.

Without a word, Quinn shut off the Explorer, then helped her out of the vehicle. He grabbed something from the back seat before he led her through the garage and into the house. He didn't say anything. She didn't know what to say either. Nothing seemed appropriate, and anything she said would trigger an emotional avalanche.

Once inside, he tossed her hat and gloves—that he retrieved from the back seat, she realized—onto the bench in the entry way and helped her out of her coat. While he hung up her coat and his own, she made her way into the kitchen where almost twenty hours ago she made him breakfast. Where they shared their first mind-blowing kiss.

He entered the kitchen, notepad in hand, service weapon still in his shoulder holster, badge clipped to his belt. She recognized his attempt to draw a boundary. He was Detective Moore now. She found a seat at the table before he could do more than breathe a resolute sigh.

"Sierra, I wish ..."

"Let's just get this over with." She knew how it went. She remembered the night's events in more detail that she expected. She took him through her evening, from the arrival at the hangar, to Lowell's insistence on accompanying her to the gate, to the sudden blackout, to waking in the parts room and her escape. Quinn didn't interrupt except with grunts and other non-verbal indications of his opinion of her ordeal, asking more specific questions when she got to the point where she freed herself.

Her retelling felt mechanical, so different from the emotion-ridden testimony from six years ago. Was it shock? Was it because she didn't feel she had to prove the bad guy actually did the things she said he did?

She reached the part where she faced Rune. The sequence replayed in her head. Desperation to find an escape. Fear he would succeed in killing her this time. Panic when Rune came after her with a hunting knife like before.

The silent plea to see Quinn one last time before she died.

She lost the battle. It steamrolled through her, a swelling rush that drowned her in anger, anxiety, worry, regret, guilt, all the emotions she'd been holding back. She couldn't breathe. Her chest couldn't contain the flood; it would blow her apart in its effort to escape.

"Sierra?"

Tears. Her voice nothing but a quiet keening. She crossed her arms to staunch the tidal wave and hold her chest together against the pressure. Huddled into a ball, ignored the agony in her arm. *So much.* Kendrick. The FAA investigation. Dead bodies. Rune returned. Kidnapped. Tied up. Attacked.

*She fought back.*

Strong arms encircled her. Lifted her. Settled her onto something hard. Someone curled around her, whispered reassurances in her ear.

*Quinn.*

She mourned until her breath hitched, her head ached, and her arm burned.

He brushed her hair from her face. "You okay?"

She nodded, wiped her face with her remaining sleeve. "This is getting to be a habit with us, isn't it?"

"Sierra, look at me." He tipped her face up with a finger under her chin. Her eyes met his, and the void left by the escaping emotions filled back up with the comforting warmth of knowing she had him. "I'm here for you. Remember that." He rested his forehead against hers. "I wish I could show you how relieved I am you're going to be okay, but for now, I have to be the cop. Okay?"

"I get it."

He pushed to his feet and helped her back into her chair before he reclaimed his seat. He looked through his pages of notes. "They never said exactly what they were looking for?"

"Files that Tori stole. One of the men said she showed them to him."

"Which one?"

"Guy looked like he should've been in a lawyer's office, not a hangar."

He nodded. "Tori's boss. He's the financial guy for Castor. I'm still not sure how much he knew about Tori's paper. He said she asked him a few questions, but not that she *interviewed* him." He slumped in his chair. "If they hadn't lawyered up, I might be able to get something useful out of them, like whether they know who killed Tori or why."

The dull ache in Sierra's head pulsed in time to the throbbing in her arm. She needed to tell him something else, but damn it, she couldn't think.

*Wait.*

"I know why they killed her."

# 54

Quinn chewed on Sierra's theory while she headed to the bathroom to "take care of business", as she said. Counterfeit parts. He knew aviation involved money, a large portion of which paid for the regulations and oversight of the FAA, which resulted in one of the safest types of transportation in existence. As traumatic as accidents were when they did happen, most people didn't realize how many thousands of flights made it from Point A to Point B without incident every day, all as a result of strict regulations.

Because every aircraft part needed to be certified and inspected, even something as innocuous as an inspection panel screw could cost upwards of a dollar. And if a panel had twenty screws, it could be more than twenty dollars to fasten that panel to an aircraft.

In short, counterfeit parts could make someone a lot of money. Charge the customer for the regulation part, buy a counterfeit part to use instead, and pocket the difference. The problem: if something happened to the aircraft, and the authorities discovered counterfeit parts, the person or business responsible would be shut down, fined, and likely prosecuted. If Tori discovered through her bookkeeping that Castor Aviation was using counterfeit parts, and if she leaked the information to the FAA, the entire company would be subject to an investigation. And since the company had bases in several states, it could add to the quantity and severity of the charges.

It could ruin the entire parent company, not just the remote FBO.

And that was a definite motive for killing Tori.

They needed to find those files. When Tori wouldn't give them up, they killed her and moved on to Peter Manelli. Remembering his conversation with Peter's brother, Quinn felt certain Peter hadn't known where Tori stashed the files, which got him killed as well.

Tori's files were still missing, or they wouldn't have ransacked Tori's apartment, or Sierra's apartment, or abducted Sierra. Anger washed through him. He almost lost her because of an old connection to a woman who thought she could blackmail a company like Castor Aviation.

Not blackmail. Revenge? He remembered what Cate said about Tori finding the truth about what happened and setting the record straight.

He reviewed his notes. Of the three men he'd arrested, only Gil Randolph was part of the "upper echelon" of Castor Aviation Service's Minneapolis base. If anyone knew about the money end of dealing with counterfeit aircraft parts, the financial administrator would. He had been Tori's boss, and according to Sierra, the one to whom Tori showed her files.

Lowell Hinckley had a connection with Rune Thorsson. Quinn had seen them talking the day he went to Castor Aviation in search of Peter Manelli. Hinckley worked for Range Air at the Detroit-Wayne County airport. Castor Aviation had an FBO at DTW. Was Hinckley some sort of go-between? Trying to get in on the action?

Maybe he was using Range Air to move counterfeit parts.

Rune Thorsson had the only rap sheet of the trio, with charges including assault and breaking and entering, courtesy of his unhealthy obsession with Sierra. He had also needed medical care from injuries. Sierra got in a few good shots. Quinn smiled at that and enjoyed a wave of pride.

There had to be more people involved in this. If this really was a counterfeit parts operation, someone besides these three would know about it. What about the parts inspector? The buyer? The mechanic or mechanics who installed the parts?

He tried to fit the pieces together. If Thorsson was, for lack of a better term, the muscle for this operation, how much did he know about the reasons behind his "job"? Better question: how did Thorsson manage to pass the checks required to work in the AOA?

Sierra's voice broke him out of his thought process. "Quinn, can you come here, please?"

He reached the guest bathroom and knocked before he entered. Sierra, sitting on the floor, scooted as far from the door as she could to give him room to squeeze past the door into the bathroom. Rascal stood on her hind legs, muzzle pressed between the bars of her cage like a convict.

Quinn had to smile. "Sorry, Rascal, but ferrets just can't play the pity part very well. Blame your weasel cousins."

Sierra reached toward Quinn. "Help me up."

He pulled her to her feet. Now they were both stuck with a cage in the middle of the floor and not quite enough room to move past each other unless they got a lot closer.

Closer wasn't the idea. He was supposed to be the cop now.

He couldn't wait until he closed this case.

"I know there isn't much room in here, but can you grab her? I'd do it myself, but I'm a bit short-handed."

Quinn chuckled. "Nice one. Why do you need her?" he asked, not enamored with the idea of picking the creature up.

"I think I know where Tori hid her files. We need to check Rascal's harness for a compartment."

Confusion set in. "Why would they be that small? I don't think microfiche would even fit in there."

"Not the files themselves, but a key would fit. Think about it. Who would bother checking a ferret? Anyway, I talked to the officer you sent with me while the doctor sewed up my arm. She had a ferret once. She said harnesses shouldn't be kept on ferrets just like they shouldn't be kept on dogs or cats for long periods of time. What if Tori just put the harness on Rascal whenever she left, so in case something happened, the files would be safe? She knew Cate would babysit the ferret, so there was no danger of the key ending up at an animal shelter."

"Except Rascal would have ended up there if you hadn't agreed to watch her while Cate was in the hospital." If Sierra was right, he would have hard evidence for the motive behind Tori's murder.

They switched spots so Quinn had better access. He handed a treat to Rascal before he lifted the creature out of her cage by the harness. Rascal didn't seem to mind, the treat the more immediate pleasure by far.

He took a close look at the harness. Black straps fit around the ferret's sleek body, offering a secure way to lift the creature without risking her slipping away. It was a typical harness with a strap along the spine, straps fencing the front legs, one girdling the chest below the ribs, and another along the breastbone where the others were fastened. The chest strap was wider and thicker than the rest.

While Rascal was preoccupied with the treat, Sierra worked the clasps loose so they could slip the harness off the slender creature. Quinn set the critter beside the litter box, filled her food and water, then shut the door and followed Sierra back to the kitchen.

She handed him the harness. "See if there's something in the chest strap."

He examined the chest strap. Black fabric was sewn to the back of the strap along with a very narrow strip of tight Velcro on either side. Sierra was right; no one would think to look here, and most people wouldn't try to take the harness off unless they were familiar with ferrets for fear of being bitten or scratched.

He peeled the Velcro apart and slid a key out of the pocket. No grooves along the length of the key. Square cuts formed the edge. A number was stamped on the head.

"What kind of key is that?" Sierra asked.

"Safe deposit box." Once he found out which bank Tori used, he could get a warrant if he could find a judge willing to grant one today. He couldn't hold the Castor execs much longer unless he found more evidence.

*This is it.* He swallowed a shout of triumph. Not until he had the files in hand.

"How do we find out what bank she used? Can we get access to—oh, crap. It's Sunday."

"Super Bowl Sunday."

She groaned. "Even worse. No one's going to want to be interrupted on Game Day." She glanced at the clock in the kitchen. "Especially at four in the morning."

That wouldn't stop him. With the potential to solve this case sooner rather than later, he'd call every judge he knew to get a warrant long before sunrise. "Police work doesn't stop on weekends or Super Bowl Sunday."

"I need to change and take another pain pill, then we can—"

"We?" After the night she had, there was no way he was going to take her anywhere. Her complexion, pale and drawn, made the puffy bruise-colored circles under her eyes even more evident. Fatigue drew thin red lines through the whites of her eyes. Quinn shook his head. "You are going to stay here and rest. You can barely stand."

When her eyes flashed with temper, he knew he'd made a mistake.

"Bullshit. I'm in this, Quinn. They broke into my apartment, planted a counterfeit part, and kidnapped me. Hell, they shot at me." She tried to gesture with her injured arm, winced in pain. "They did this. Rune did this."

"I'm coming with you."

I know, he thought. I wouldn't expect anything less.

# 55

"Sierra, sit down. You're worse than a second grader who needs a bathroom break."

"I can't." She continued to pace the length of his small office. Quinn recognized her struggle against exhaustion in the pallor of her fair skin and the lines at the corners of her eyes.

He held his own fatigue at bay through sheer willpower paired with a churning mind and a cup of break room coffee. "I wish you would have stayed at home. You need to rest," he scolded.

She stopped pacing long enough to glare at him. "I will if you will. I'm not going anywhere until we finish this."

They were close. He had the key to Tori's safe deposit box, where they expected to find whatever Tori had that had gotten her killed. Though he had gotten the name of Tori's bank from a sleepy Cate, woke a judge for the search warrant and a bank manager to let him in, he couldn't do anything until he had the paperwork.

Yvonne knocked on the door jamb before entering his office, yellow memo slip and a warrant ready for the judge in hand. Her brilliant royal blue and orange blouse glowed against her coffee skin. She stopped in front of his desk and pressed the slip to the blotter in front of him.

Sierra, at the board, didn't seem to notice her. Maybe she was sleeping standing up, he thought.

"Look at me, kiddo."

He tipped his head up. "You're in early. And on a Sunday? What's wrong?"

"I switched with that adorable cadet. He's got something special planned for today, and it has nothing to do with the Super Bowl. Besides, it's good to mix things up once in a while." Yvonne tsked and frowned, arms crossed over her chest. "I heard you were out on an all-nighter. How do you expect to put the bad guys away if you're half-asleep?"

"We caught the bad guys." Quinn leaned back in his chair and rubbed his eyes. "Has CSU called in yet?"

She tapped the memo. "Right here. Call them at Castor Aviation." She straightened, gave him another once-over, and then shook a finger at him like the neighborhood grandmother. "If I see you in the office tomorrow, I'm going to send your ass home with the chief's blessing."

Quinn couldn't help but smile. "Yes, ma'am."

"And you, girl."

Sierra twitched as if startled, then turned. The fine red lines in the whites of her eyes had multiplied. Even her white tress seemed dull. "Me?"

Yvonne shook a finger at her. "You, too. What is with you kids these days? Didn't your mommas teach you to get a good night's sleep? You make sure he gets some sleep. Promise me."

Sierra's eyes widened. "Yes, ma'am."

With one more stern look at Quinn, Yvonne left. A stunned silence filled the office for a moment.

Sierra broke it, a grin washing some of the fatigue away. "You better do what she says or I'll tell on you."

Quinn chuckled, the humor energizing. He reached for the phone to call CSU. Before he lifted the receiver, the phone rang.

"This is Andrew Jindahl, FAA. I'm trying to do an inspection at Castor Aviation. Your people are in my way."

"We have an active investigation on the premises. We'll clear the area as soon as we can."

A pause. "You don't have jurisdiction here, Detective."

"I do when it's a crime scene."

Quinn reassured Jindahl, then ended the conversation. An inspection? His usual FAA contact, Frank Iverson, had mentioned on occasion the list of hangars and parts suppliers he inspected regularly, less now that he'd been promoted to a more supervisory position. Quinn called Castor Aviation and asked to speak with Lani Connors, the CSU team lead on site. He hadn't worked with Lani as often as he'd worked with Kevin, but he knew her to be fastidious when it came to processing scenes. Kevin was exacting, but Lani had a reputation for double-checking her team's work, not because she didn't trust them, but because she had an obsessive-compulsive streak she couldn't shake.

"Wanted to let you know I'm sending your primary suspect's fuel truck to our BCA facility," Lani said, her voice quiet. Quinn often thought of a mouse when he spoke to her, but he knew a laser-keen mind lurked behind that meek facade. "We found some trace evidence we need to look at. We have that other truck you were interested in, don't we? The one they found in the river?"

"Yes. I'm waiting for the final forensics report on that. Fuel truck?"

"We found some fibers and what appears to be blood residue. And a pale strand of hair. Did any of your vics have blond hair?"

He glanced at Sierra. "No, but one has a white streak in her brown hair."

"Poliosis," she said. "I'll check if the strand has any melanin."

"Melanin?"

"Pigment. Poliosis is the lack of it. I'll get a report to you by the end of the day."

❖ ❖ ❖

AFTER AN HOUR OF TRYING TO REST in Quinn's worn office chair, Sierra gave up and doodled on his blotter. She knew he had to leave her behind while he went to get the contents of Tori's safe deposit box, but that didn't mean she liked it.

Her right arm throbbed with every heartbeat, a muted pulse that reminded her she had a forced vacation for the foreseeable future. Two to three weeks, according to the doctor who sewed her up. *Dammit.* What the hell was she going to do with herself for two weeks?

*Gawd, I'm going to go nuts.*

She was already going nuts. She could pick up a new book to read from one of the shops in the terminal, but that seemed like a lot more effort than she had energy for right now. She stared at the board where Quinn listed information about the case. In crime novels, they called it a "murder board."

She pushed to her feet and made her way to the board. Quinn had laid out the timeline, his theories on motives, the list of suspects. Her name appeared there, lined out, along with Peter Manelli.

Lowell Hinckley's name, along with Rune Thorsson, Marshall Kline, and Gil Randolph marked the timeline location labeled "FBO".

Why would Lowell be at Castor?

*Lowell.* That's how Rune got her unlisted number. The Range Air supervisors had contact information for all the mechanics. Lowell could have looked hers up on the sly and given it to Rune.

Rustling of a winter parka heralded Quinn's return. Sierra turned. "Success?" she asked.

He waved a thick manila envelope. "If we're right, this holds the key to the entire case." He settled behind his desk as she slid a visitor chair next to him. He pulled a couple pairs of latex gloves from a drawer and handed one to her before he opened the envelope and slid papers onto the blotter, along with a diskette.

She skimmed the pages as Quinn sifted through them. Account numbers, debits, credits—the columns of numbers made little sense. Sierra knew rudimentary accounting, but this was beyond her. She focused instead on the descriptions of the entries. Flight control brackets. Cables. Engine mounts. Fuel pumps. Steering linkage bushings.

"You were right," Quinn said as he handed a stack of papers to her. "It looks like Tori found the ledger they used to track the purchases and sales of the counterfeit parts. The legitimate parts show up on the general ledger with the rest of their accounts."

She studied the pages. "That Queen Air, the one that hit the de-ice truck? I think they used counterfeit parts. Here's a line for steering linkage bushings. I'd have to see the maintenance log for the plane, but I wonder if the bushing was replaced because of a service bulletin. Those don't really wear out."

"Service bulletin?"

"Like a recall for cars. When there are enough reports of issues with a particular part on a plane, the manufacturer will issue a service bulletin for replacement or special inspection of the part."

"Wouldn't the part be inspected once it's installed?"

"Depends. The part is inspected before it's accepted into inventory. Once it's in inventory, it's assumed to be good." Sierra paged through the file, then stopped.

A dull buzzing echoed in her ears. She barely heard Quinn's question.

"You okay?"

# 56

When she didn't respond, Quinn gripped her arm. "Sierra, you okay?" he repeated, concern filling his voice.

His touch quieted the static. Sierra shook her head slowly. She read the sheet again. Her cheeks grew hot. "I knew it. It wasn't pilot error." She shoved the papers toward him. "Tori made copies of the maintenance log and the ledger entries that matched. They put a counterfeit fuel pump on that Cherokee months before Ken bought it." She shuffled through the rest of the stack. "Here. She made notes here. The plane her parents were ferrying up North had seven counterfeit parts on it. One was a pitot heater. Her dad would've checked the heater before he took off."

Sierra shoved the papers at Quinn before she headed to the board. She grabbed a marker with her left hand—she should have practiced being ambidextrous when she was a kid—and added barely-legible scribbles to the timeline. "Before Ken bought the plane, I looked through the maintenance log. Castor Aviation did a lot of the maintenance on it."

She acknowledged him with a glance when he joined her. "You left a message asking where Ken kept his plane. He had a hangar at Flying Cloud. The previous owner had it at MSP. Ken only had the plane for a couple months before he … "

250

This changed everything she knew about the accident. Everything she thought she knew about Tori.

Guilt dragged cold thick fingers through her.

"Quinn, you said Tori's parents died in a plane crash. Do you know where they were going?"

"Cate said they were ferrying a plane from MSP to her grandfather's FBO. It started snowing during the flight."

Sierra added the information. "Snow isn't usually a reason for a crash unless it's a blizzard or the anti-icing equipment fails." She turned toward him. "Why would a forensic accounting student get an internship at an FBO instead of a regular business?"

Quinn picked up a marker and corrected the motive he listed. "Because she wanted to find out what really happened."

Sierra studied the board. She knew some of the parts she found at Castor Aviation were not legit. Tori's files confirmed her suspicions. Certain parts, especially serialized ones, had indelible stamps on them indicating the part was authorized by the FAA, similar to the UL markings on electrical appliances. That, along with telltale indications of quality like precise machining and accurate paperwork, were signs of authentic parts.

Each part was inspected on arrival and yellow-tagged with the part number, serial number, and date of inspection by a mechanic who'd been authorized by the employer to perform the inspections. At least, that was her experience at Range Air. Consumable items like oil filters, fasteners, and light bulbs didn't need the same scrutiny, but those items were still required to be purchased from authorized resellers or the original equipment manufacturer.

Some of the parts she had seen at Castor Aviation were missing the indelible stamp. Some, like the landing gear bracket she'd found, lacked the precision machining she was familiar with. Parts that could be overhauled or were sent to the manufacturer for cyclical inspections, like landing gear cylinders and the fire bottle she used, lacked additional paperwork certifying the part for continued use.

Something else bothered her, but she couldn't quite pinpoint it. She needed to clear the fog out of her brain. She pointed to another note. "What about Lowell here?"

Quinn stood beside her. "I went to Castor Aviation looking for Peter Manelli. I ran into Lowell. He and Thorsson were arguing about something."

Realization swept away some of the cotton in her head. "We know why Tori was shoved into the hell-hole."

"We do?"

Pieces started to come together. "You said when killers pose or place victims like that it's often a message for someone. It was a message for Lowell. The pendant was a message for me."

"Presuming Thorsson killed Tori, the pendant makes sense. But Lowell?"

The more she thought about it, the more certain she felt. "Castor Aviation is regional, but set up like a franchise, where every base has its own management, etcetera. Say the Minneapolis base has a good thing going with the whole counterfeit parts thing. Say Lowell's connected with someone at the Detroit base, and the Minneapolis base is trying to work with or through the Detroit base. What if someone threatened to expose them, like Tori?"

"Lowell?"

"I don't know. Maybe. I don't know anything about him, if he had money troubles, or was having second thoughts, or if he was just the messenger boy. In any case, they knew he worked for Range Air and they knew he was working in MSP this week."

Quinn stared at the board in silence. "We didn't even identify the body until the next day. If it was a message, how would he know it was for him? There's no way to know which airplane he'd be working on ahead of time, is there?"

"No," Sierra said. "It wouldn't matter if he worked on the plane or not. If he knew Tori was causing trouble, and someone found her body, he'd know the message was for him even if the body couldn't be identified right away."

"Maybe. Or what if he was trying to work Range Air into the system, maybe to swap parts—buy counterfeit and swap with the good ones at Range Air."

She shook her head. "All our parts are for either the Dash-8s or the Metros. We don't even have any Fokker parts anymore. Pretty hard to swap a Dash-8 part for a Cessna or Beechcraft. Besides, not only are our QA inspectors nit-picky, but Chuck, our FAA guy, does spot inspections every month. I'm pretty sure he'd find anything that looked wonky."

Something still didn't seem right. "I can't figure out how Rune could've gotten a job with access to the AOA."

*Sonofabitch.*

"Quinn, this is big. There aren't many ways an operation like this could work."

# 57

"We have to bring the FAA in on this." The words sent bile northward.

Quinn returned to his desk. "With counterfeit parts involved, that's a given."

"Have you contacted anyone from their office yet?" she asked.

"No. The agent from the Queen Air incident called to complain about CSU interfering with his inspection. We can have him look at the parts you found."

"I'm not sure that's a good idea." She explained how the parts game worked in aviation, and how the FAA agent assigned to Range Air made periodic inspections. When Chuck Ziegler showed up, every mechanic kept one eye on him and the other on making sure every task was done by the maintenance manual and appropriately signed off. She knew Chuck did spot inspections in the parts room because she'd been there the night he'd ordered a review of all paperwork that had arrived with a pair of Metro propeller assemblies.

Sierra pulled out a piece of notebook paper with dates, times, airplane types, and parts listed. "The mysterious phone calls." She tapped the sheet before paging through a half-dozen copies of log book entries that matched the dates. "Someone called and told her when questionable parts were installed on aircraft. Did the FAA agent assigned to Castor Aviation spot-check the parts? If so, how closely did he look at them? Tori found hard evidence Castor was using counterfeit parts. I think another FAA agent should do an inspection."

Quinn stared at her. She held his gaze, willing him to understand. Wished she wasn't involved.

"Rune's uncle is a deputy chief. Maybe even the chief by now." The thought made her shudder. "If someone did a background check on him, his uncle could have fudged some of the details."

Quinn grimaced. "He's a cop."

"And there's no such thing as a cop who plays a little too close to the line, right?" she said, knowing how close to home she hit.

"He wouldn't be able to expunge the charges that landed Rune in Moose Lake."

She waited for him to put the final piece into place.

His eyes widened. "Holy shit," he breathed. "An agent even went over to Castor Aviation after everything last night." He paused. She imagined the wheels in his head whirring away, fitting and refitting pieces like some complex tangram until his phone rang.

He answered it, the conversation short and clipped on his end. He thanked the caller and hung up. His brow furrowed. "Agent Jindahl is at Castor Aviation. How sure are you about this?"

Her gut twisted like she'd chugged sour milk. "From what Tori found, and what I know about aviation maintenance, I'm ninety percent sure."

"Let me call my contact at the FAA office. Frank's good. I trust him." He pulled a business card from a drawer and lifted the phone receiver. "We can meet him there."

Apprehension tightened her throat. Her own experience with the FAA discouraged her from getting involved in anything having to do with questioning their authority. "Leave me out of any suggestion of why you're asking him to make a special trip in on Super Bowl Sunday. I'm good with being invisible to the FAA."

❖ ❖ ❖

WHEN THEY ARRIVED AT CASTOR AVIATION from the AOA side, Quinn parked beside the APD squad he called in to secure the scene. Before they left the Explorer, Quinn reached to Sierra. "You okay?"

The pain meds were wearing off, leaving her to enjoy the agony of her injury. "Nope. If I take my Vicodin, will I be arrested?"

Quinn shook his head. "I knew I should've made you stay in the office."

She gripped the envelope holding copies of Tori's evidence. "Not a chance.

Tori found something that might have contributed to Ken's accident and the accident that killed her parents. I'm seeing this through."

Inside the hangar and outside the yellow tape cordoning off the parts room, a uniformed APD officer stood arguing with the FAA agent she'd seen the day she looked at the Queen Air's nose gear.

"It's been an hour. When is this detective supposed to show up?" Jindahl turned, eyes widened for a breath. "Oh, there you are. It's about time. I've got things to do. I can't be held here like some prisoner."

Quinn reached out a hand. "I'm sorry. Agent Jindahl, right?"

Jindahl returned the greeting. "Detective, this officer said you wanted to speak with me. I'm not sure how I can help. I came here to do my periodic inspection."

"You crossed the police tape without authorization. I hope you didn't tamper with my crime scene."

Sierra recognized the cop in Quinn's voice, and something more. Anger?

"This is an aircraft parts room." Jindahl rocked on his heels, hands deep in the pockets of his khakis, coat hanging over an arm. "The FAA has jurisdiction."

"As I told you on the phone, it's a crime scene, and it is *my* territory, even if CSU is finished processing the area. Until I release the scene, it's mine."

Jindahl turned up the lumens on his smile. "Well, I'll have to check the regulations on that." He shifted his gaze. "What's she doing here?"

Before Sierra could speak, Quinn reached to her. His eyes warned her to stay quiet. She handed the envelope to him. "She's here as my civilian consultant," Quinn answered. "Why are you here on Super Bowl Sunday to do an inspection?" He swept a hand to indicate a hangar populated only by aircraft. "No one's working today."

"Well," Jindahl chuckled, "I'm not much of a football fan. Hockey's more my style. Besides, I get more done when no one's here." He focused on Sierra. "She looks like she should sit down."

A retort sat heavy on her tongue. Jindahl was an FAA agent; he had the power to kill her career with one signature.

Quinn tucked the envelope under an arm. "I have some questions for you, but first I want to look at the parts room." He glanced at Sierra. "Show me."

Jindahl stepped into his path. "Excuse me. I just inspected the parts room. Everything is in order."

Quinn's voice took on a razor's edge. "Excuse me, Agent. I have a consultant who will confirm your claim."

Now Jindahl stood firm. "I inspect this facility every month. I think I know—"

A bang echoed in the metal hangar as the door slammed shut. The man who entered the hangar carried a soft-sided briefcase and greeted Quinn like a long-lost frat buddy, shaking his hand with gusto. His short black hair curled tight against his scalp, matching his very short beard. Under his open coat, a pale blue button-down shirt accented by a navy tie covered with tiny propellers completed an image straight from a Sears-Roebuck ad.

Quinn introduced Sierra to FAA Principal Agent Frank Iverson, who stared at her for a moment. "I know you. Your brother flew a Piper that crashed in Colorado."

She didn't remember him. "Did you work on that case?"

He shook his head. "I was assigned to FBO inspections at the time. I do remember the case, though. You're one of the few female A&Ps around here."

"Frank, what are you doing here?" Jindahl's demeanor went from cautious to defensive. "I was just telling the detective here I finished my inspection. There's nothing for you to do."

Iverson pursed his lips and ignored his colleague. "Show me what you found," he said to Quinn.

Sierra's gut twisted. If Jindahl was here before CSU finished processing the scene, he knew they worked in the parts room. If he'd been waiting for an hour under the eyes of the APD, it still left time between CSU's exit and the officer's arrival to cover up anything wonky.

They had the evidence Tori found, but would it be enough?

Quinn waved her over. "Sierra saw the parts. She was the one who suggested some might not be approved. According to the evidence we have, she's right."

"Wait." Jindahl held up a hand. "What is this? Frank, I've been doing inspections here for years." To Quinn, "Are you suggesting I'm not doing my job?"

"Mr. Jindahl ..."

"*Agent* Jindahl," he corrected.

Quinn dropped the salutation. "I'm here to do *my* job. Sierra," he said, and motioned her forward. "Show us what you found."

Jindahl's features hardened, but he remained silent. Sierra made her way to the parts room where she'd been held prisoner less than twenty-four hours ago.

Inside, the door to the cage held the spent fire bottle like an oversized tennis ball stuck in a chain-link fence. She swung the door open and led the way to the shelves holding the parts she'd noticed with questionable paperwork. Quinn stayed at her back, with Iverson behind him.

She stopped.

When she was looking for a way out, paperwork in press-sealed plastic bags had been tie-wrapped to the associated parts. Now only the yellow-tagged parts occupied the shelves, no paperwork in sight.

"What the hell?" she breathed. "It was here. All of these parts had paperwork attached." A glance at the cage door showed Jindahl leaning against the door frame, arms crossed, eyes narrowed.

"I file the paperwork when I do my inspections. Everything is in order, just like I said."

Sierra searched for the landing gear bracket she'd noticed with low-quality machining. Its home on the shelf was empty. "It's gone. There was a landing gear bracket in that spot." She scanned the shelves, but couldn't find it. "It was right here."

"I don't know what the fuss is about," Jindahl said. "I told you, I did my inspection."

Once they were back in the main hangar, Agent Andrew Jindahl donned his coat. "If you'll excuse me, I've got a prior engagement."

"No, you don't," Iverson said. "How long have you been assigned to Castor Aviation?"

"Oh, I don't know. Ten years maybe."

"That's a few years too many, don't you think?" Iverson set his briefcase on a wooden workbench. He addressed Quinn and Sierra. "Agents are rotated every couple of years. Fresh eyes are good for finding things. How did you manage to miss the rotation?" he asked Jindahl.

Jindahl shrugged. "Not sure. Must've been an oversight."

Iverson slid a manila folder from his briefcase. "There have been a dozen anonymous reports of questionable parts from Castor Aviation in the past five years." He zeroed in on Jindahl. "You took the complaints."

"Never found any evidence to substantiate the claims. What's going on here, Frank?"

"That's what I'm trying to figure out. Quinn, you said you have some information for me?"

Quinn pulled out the copies of Tori's files. "These are copies. The original copies and a diskette are in Evidence at the APD office." He pointed to the maintenance logs and the corresponding ledger pages. "These are from the planes involved in the deaths of Kendrick Bauer and Mr. and Mrs. Daniel Hjelle."

Sierra's stomach clenched at the mention of Ken's name. She remembered the registered letter on her parents' kitchen table. The conclusion a combination of weather and pilot error had caused the accident.

She knew the truth now.

Iverson sorted through papers in his folder. "Andrew, you signed the final approvals for these investigations." He turned toward his colleague. "I'm putting this facility under quarantine."

Jindahl's face darkened like a storm cloud. "You can't—"

"I can inspect any aviation parts room," Iverson said. "And due to evidence Detective Moore has brought to my attention, I have reason to believe Castor Aviation may be using counterfeit aircraft parts. You, as the assigned inspector, should have spotted any counterfeit parts during your inspections. Bottom line, Andrew," he said, "you're suspended until this investigation is complete."

# 58

Within an hour Iverson found enough discrepant parts at Castor Aviation to launch a full-blown, no-holds-barred investigation from the federal side. Once the Castor Aviation executives learned Jindahl was detained, Tori's incriminating information had been found, and the FAA seized the maintenance logs of as many aircraft the FBO serviced as they could, they were quick to point out Andrew Jindahl as the brain behind the ring, and Rune Thorsson as the hand behind Tori's and Peter Manelli's deaths. With any luck, Rune would be out of her life for a lot longer than five years.

Iverson ordered a review of all Jindahl's paperwork, starting with Jindahl's approval of Rune's AOA access despite the "softened" background check courtesy of Rune's uncle, at Sierra's suggestion. It added a hefty weight to the charges against him. At Sierra's insistence, Iverson agreed to keep Tori's mechanic "confidential informant's" identity out of any paperwork that could come back to haunt him. She knew what it was like to have the FAA breathing down one's neck.

By early afternoon, the Castor Aviation hangar teemed with FAA officials, and Sierra and Quinn had returned to the APD offices. While Quinn interviewed the newly-cooperative Castor personnel and did whatever he needed to do to close the case, Sierra spent the time at the terminal reading a mystery novel. By the time she reached the middle of the book, the sun had long set, and Quinn had finished his reports and was ready to head home. About time, she thought. He was tired but keyed up. She felt the same when she trouble-shot and fixed a problem on an airplane. To have what started as a homicide case turn into a break in a counterfeit aircraft parts scheme? That, she thought, would be far and away better than anything he came across on a daily basis.

It turned out Lowell was not only Rune Thorsson's cousin, but also related to an executive of Castor Aviation's DTW base. According to Quinn, Lowell happily blamed Rune for persuading him to convince the Detroit operation to join the network, adding the promise of a cut of the lucrative business.

Then there was Tori. Guilt fought anger for control. Tori discovered commonalities between Ken's accident and her parents' crash. She searched for and found evidence proving their deaths were not entirely accidental. She wanted justice not only for her parents, but for Ken.

Sierra owed Tori for finding the truth.

Tori didn't force Ken to take off that morning. Tori didn't encourage Ken to buy the plane. Could Sierra stop being angry at her? Could she forgive her? Tori had tried to do the right thing. Doing the right thing had also gotten her killed. Jindahl, eager to share the blame, said Tori had contacted him about finding evidence of counterfeit parts. They arranged a meeting after her shift at Range Air. Jindahl had Rune meet her instead for the purpose of getting the evidence and making sure she kept quiet.

According to Rune, he didn't intend to kill Tori, just rough her up until she handed over the evidence.

Sierra knew first-hand Rune's version of "roughed up".

Since neither of them had eaten most of the day, it didn't take much to convince Quinn to pick up some Chinese take-out. Once home, Quinn went to his bedroom to change, but didn't return to the kitchen.

She headed to his room and discovered him sprawled on his bed, sound asleep, snoring softly. She found an afghan in the linen closet and covered him, adding a gentle kiss to his temple. He stirred, then lay still, breathing regular. A tender heat flowed through her. Even now, less than a week since they'd met, she couldn't imagine a life without him in it. Maybe the belief everyone had someone out there in the world just for them was legit.

❖ ❖ ❖

WHEN QUINN WOKE, he found himself tucked beneath an afghan on his bed, with a vague memory of intending to change clothes. A glance at the red numbers on his bedside clock elicited a groan. He'd slept for almost sixteen hours. The cottony taste in his mouth supported the assessment. He made his way to the master bathroom to take the shower he'd planned earlier, before he fell into a dead sleep.

After a hot wake-up, he checked the guest room. It was empty and missing the patchwork quilt that had covered the bed. Panic flashed through him. He checked the guest bathroom. Rascal yipped in her cage, pacing the small area like a trapped predator. He assured her he would return to let her out once he found Sierra.

His search ended when he reached the living room. Sierra lay in a recliner, patchwork quilt drawn up to her chin, eyes closed. The sight struck him as *right*, her presence something to be expected. After more than a year of bachelorhood, more than a year of focusing on work because it kept his mind occupied, he found a reason to anticipate coming home.

*Sierra.*

Except her stay would come to an end. The situation was intended to be temporary, until he caught the person responsible for killing Tori and breaking into Sierra's apartment. He'd done that with Thorsson's arrest.

With her injury, her nurse practitioner father would be the best person to make sure she followed the doctor's instructions. The prospect of her absence, even though she had only been at the house for a couple days, made him long for more time with her.

He crouched beside the recliner and gently brushed a stray hair from her eyes. She didn't stir. He relished the sense of completeness, the love that settled in every cell of his being. He needed this woman like a castaway needs to return home at any cost.

She stirred, leaned into his hand, then woke. "Quinn," she said, eyes bleary and voice rough. The single word, his name from her lips, sent his pulse into a sprint.

He cupped her cheek, caressing her skin with his thumb. "I'm so glad you're here." He kissed her. She responded, opening herself to him. Desire surged. He deepened the kiss, raked fingers through her fine hair, drew her closer.

She broke the kiss, sucked in air. "Ow."

He pulled away. "Sorry, I forgot. How do you feel?"

She shifted, grimaced in pain. "Like someone ran over me with a 747. I had to sleep here if I wanted any sleep at all." She leaned forward to work her way out of the recliner. Quinn steadied her with a hand under her uninjured arm, lifting just enough to allow her to slide from the recliner to her feet.

He kissed her again, taking full advantage of the opportunity to wrap his arms around her and pull her against him despite the sling. He craved the feel of her body. She pleased him with a moan.

She flinched in pain and broke away. "This isn't going to work until I take more pain meds. I'm sorry, Quinn."

He stroked her hair, then planted a gentle kiss on her lips. "It's okay."

"You're going have to help change my dressing. I was supposed to change it twice by now. I think." Her face reddened. "And a bath. I shouldn't get the bandages wet."

He grinned. "I think I can manage that."

Her stomach growled like a rabid animal. "And food. I put everything away when you crashed."

His own stomach complained. "Let's take care of that first."

❖ ❖ ❖

AFTER THEY QUIETED THEIR RUMBLING BELLIES, Quinn raised his water glass for a toast. "To closing a case that started out with an unknown victim and ended with a big 'thank you' from my buddy at the FAA."

"To putting my stalker behind bars. Again." Sierra met his glass with hers. "I hate déjà vu."

A sense of awkwardness settled in her, nerves tightening. *What now?* The case that brought them together was closed. Her apartment, a disaster area at this point, was no longer a crime scene. She should stay at her parents' house while she needed some extra help with things because of her injury, at least until she got her apartment put back together.

Could she stand to stay in her apartment again? Should she get a different one?

"Sierra," he started, his voice quiet, without the enthusiasm he'd displayed just moments ago, "I know this whole thing's been, well, unconventional to say the least. And I haven't been around—"

"Quinn, you're a cop, you had a homicide case that involved two bodies. It's your job." And you have no obligation to me, she thought as her stomach impersonated a knot of nightcrawlers.

"That's no excuse."

"Are you kidding? It's a legitimate excuse. Besides," and the knot that had been her stomach twisted itself into a leaden lump, "I appreciate you letting me stay."

He combed fingers through his hair and fidgeted like a kid who couldn't decide if he should make a confession or not. He met her eyes, and the lump melted away under his spring blue gaze. "Look … God, this is going to sound … I can't believe … I don't … Shit." He took a deep breath and chuckled nervously. "Okay, here it goes. I want you to stay here. With me."

Her pulse thundered in her ears. Words crumbled like sand castles under a rising tide. She opened her mouth, but nothing came out.

"I know this is sudden, and illogical, and all those other things that say normal people don't move in together after a week without a single date, but I—" He shook his head and rubbed his hands over his face. "I don't expect you to … I mean … I'll understand if you want to do things the usual way. You know, you go back to your apartment, we date like normal people, and after a few months we do this, but … you … I feel like you belong here. It was never like this with anyone else. Ever."

Static filled her ears. Hell, after her ex-boyfriend almost killed her, she kept men at arm's length, never giving them a chance to get to know her. She never felt uncomfortable around Quinn the way she did with anyone else.

"Sierra?" He sounded worried. Scared. Those blue eyes of his weakened her resolve.

*She fought. Survived.* She needed to savor that victory. As much as she wanted—*longed*—to accept his offer, she couldn't. Not yet. "I'm sorry, Quinn, but I need time." The admission hurt worse than her arm. "I still want to date."

His brow furrowed. "What are you saying?"

"I'm saying even if I'm not staying here, you're not off the hook. Like you said, we haven't even gone on a date yet."

He helped her to her feet and wrapped his arms around her. His kiss made her toes curl and her core ache with need.

"So, what are you doing tomorrow?"

# ACKNOWLEDGMENTS

WHEN I THINK OF ALL THOSE WHO HAVE HELPED ME, encouraged me, and tolerated me on this journey, I am amazed at my fortune. From the author who visited my elementary school for a week and complimented my rutabaga story—which unleashed the writing monster, to my seventh-grade English teacher who didn't dock me too many points for submitting seven pages for a two-page story assignment, to the writers at FanStory.com who took the time to critique my work, they were all stepping stones that inspired me along this path.

In 2012, I took a chance and attended a Master Novel Class at Write-By-The-Lake (UW-Madison Continuing Education). There I met a group of talented writers with whom I have bonded. To my Writing Sisters: Barbara Belford, Cheryl Hanson, Blair Hull, Lisa Kusko, Roi Solberg, and later Martha Miles, along with our writing teacher and mentor extraordinaire Christine DeSmet, I cannot begin to express what you mean to me. You have challenged me to become a better writer. Without you, and especially Roi and Cheryl and our video chats, this book would not be what it is. I wouldn't be here without all of you.

I must also thank my agent, the fantabulous Cynthia Zigmund, for seeing the potential of this book and this author. I couldn't ask for a better advocate.

A special thanks to my beta readers: D. Wallace Peach, Bob Hanson, Barb Mahovlich, and Peggy Turnwall. Your feedback and suggestions ensured I didn't make silly mistakes like dumping a body into a frozen lake or complimenting décor.

To the team at Camel Press, thank you for bringing this book to readers. To my editor Jennifer McCord, your suggestions, advice, and experience—and patience—helped guide this story to its full potential.

To my children, I apologize for being huddled away writing for so many nights. I love you both.

Last in the list but first in my heart, I thank my husband for his enduring patience, his encouragement, and for tolerating my plot-addled brain as I have made my way along this path to publication. I don't tell you enough how grateful I am, or how much I love you.

A WRITER SINCE ELEMENTARY SCHOOL, Julie Holmes has had short stories published in small press magazines such as *The Galactic Citizen* and *Fighting Chance*. A graduate of Thief River Falls Technical College's Aviation Maintenance Technology program, she worked as an aircraft mechanic for a commuter airline at Detroit's Wayne County Airport and the Minneapolis-St. Paul International Airport. Beyond aviation, she spent sixteen years in computer technology, and now works as a technical writer for a software company. Julie is a member of the national Sisters in Crime (SinC) writers' organization, and is an active member of the Twin Cities SinC chapter. An empty-nester, she lives with her husband on an 8-acre hobby farm in south-central Minnesota, and spends her non-writing time reading, cultivating garden vegetables, and walking as she ponders her next book.

CPSIA information can be obtained
at www.ICGtesting.com
Printed in the USA
LVHW051531230419
615240LV00003B/542/P